POHAINAKE PARISH

Books by Katie Wainwright

Cuba on My Mind
Secuestro
The Azaleas

POHAINAKE PARISH

KATIE WAINWRIGHT

RED DUST PUBLISHING  WINDERMERE

Pohainake Parish by Katie Wainwright

Printed in the United States of America by Red Dust Publishing

First edition: March 2015

ISBN-13: 9781506163437
ISBN-10: 1506163432

Book layout and cover design by Pattie Steib

This is a work of fiction. Any resemblance to persons living or dead
is purely coincidental.

Dedicated to all of those elected to public office, who aspire to make a difference and soon discover they can't.

ACKNOWLEDGEMENTS:

I am grateful to Pattie Steib for the cover artwork, computer skills, author photograph and life-long friendship; to Joan Davis, Lee Collins, Margaret Hawkins and Carli Chapman for their editing skills and positive suggestions; to Mary Pirosko for both editing and scheduling signings and appearances and for her companionship on the road as we went from one place to another. *Pohainake* was a team effort, and nobody ever had a better team. Thank you.

POHAINAKE PARISH

PROLOGUE:

In 1992 I was elected to serve on the Pohainake Parish Council. This government body met twice a month and dealt with monumental challenges: jail, garbage, roads, bridges, financing, bankruptcy, as well as other issues. The jumble of court orders, indictments, state mandates and federal deadlines that we dealt with, one right after the other, was so confusing that the council members barely understood what damage we were doing. In order to simplify this process and to make it clearer for the reader, I have chosen to relate each problem from its beginning to its end. In several instances this caused a time over-lap. For that, I ask your indulgence.

Hannah Kelly

CHAPTER 1

JAIL

The court address was 500 Camp Street, New Orleans, but our instructions said to use the Poydras Street entrance because it had ample parking. They lied. We couldn't find a slot and had to circle the block three times before we jackknifed into a parking space that would probably get us a ticket. Sonny, Pohainake Parish's CEO and driver, said, "Get out." Red Harper, mumbling and grumbling, cussing and objecting, spilled from the car. Sonny came around to open my door, but I was already standing, armpits damp, heart beating fast and mind in turmoil. What the hell was I doing here? How did I get into this jam? When I ran for the parish council seat, I had no idea I was getting into a rats' nest lined with indictments and court orders. The job was more difficult than PTA president—I knew that— but jails? What the hell did I know about jails? Zero, zilch, nada!

Inside the building Sonny's car keys activated the security alarm walk-through. The guard took Red's Swiss army knife, assuring him he could retrieve it at departure. Security recognized country bumpkins come to the big city and they weren't wrong.

An aide ushered us into a side room for a pre-hearing conference. The other council members were already seated at a long table. Southern gentlemen that they were, the men stood when

I entered the room and then sat again. Beneath the glass top, I saw their feet. Henry Johnson wore black silk socks and narrow patent leather shoes. Peewee Reese (named at birth after the famous baseball player in hopes that the boy would learn to swing a bat and make a fortune) had pennies in his loafer slots. Will Fleming's brown shoes were buffed and shined every morning by the shoe stand owner doing business near the Pohainake courthouse door. Red pulled back a chair, sat and planted his boots heavily, cow manure traces lodged in a leather crease. The parish executive officer said, "I'll be back." I guess Sonny went to take a pee, relieve the pressure. I would've liked to do the same. Instead, I sat and for some unexplainable reason couldn't control my foot. Under the table my black pump swung back and forth, kicking air.

While we waited for the judge to appear, Red Harper went on his familiar rampage.

"That judge can't make us do nothin'. We're councilmen. Excuse me, Miz Hannah, council*woman,* person. We represent the people. We got rights! It ain't legal anyone forcin' Pohainake Parish to build a jail."

Red, a robust dairy farmer, whose lower lip nursed a bulging Skoal wad, had already milked 80 cows, washed up and done a day's work before he got here. He'd traded his denim overalls for khaki pants and a sport coat and stuffed the baseball cap, Pohainake Feed & Seed across its front, into his back pocket.

"I gotta plan that'll work jis' fine," Red said, "All we gotta do is remodel the jail we got upstairs over the council chamber. Insulatin' the walls and damp'nin' the sounds won't cost that much. Buy new sheets and pillowcases. Unplug the toilets. Clean the kitchen some. They's convicts. They don't need to be livin' in no Hilton."

The jail was definitely no Hilton as the five new council members had soon discovered. Filled with newly elected energy and vim, holding the political world by the tail, we had no doubts that we could stop the downward spiral, steer the parish to solvency and efficiency while insisting on honesty and transparency, the way a mother holds a new baby in her arms and dreams her dreams.

Arguing with Red was useless. The dairy farmer refused to look at a problem from more than one side. According to him, everything was black and white, one issue and one solution— his. Castrating a bull was easier than changing Red's mind.

"I'm telling that judge in no uncertain terms where he can stuff it."

"Yeah," Sonny said, coming through the door. "You do that. Judge is on his way."

The judge had jet black hair, oversized black rimmed glasses and a black robe. The Pohainake Parish Council jumped to its collective feet. The judge neither smiled nor greeted us. He threw down a legal pad. Our eyes followed the yellow blur as it slid the length of the glass table, finally stopping before Red, "he can't tell me what to do" Harper.

"Pohainake Parish?" He asked in a deep, resonant voice. We nodded like punished students mute before the principal. "Sign that pad. Put your name, address, work telephone number, and home number."

In devastating silence, Henry Johnson, District 5, the elected council president signed first. In my estimation Henry wasn't the best choice when we voted for president, but since I wasn't eager to be the first dissenting vote, when four hands shot up quickly, mine followed. The hunch persisted that the majority vote for the Harmony Motors salesman had been prearranged. Johnson, mid-forties, Elvis style pompadour and side-burns, had sharp, weasel eyes. His blinding white shirts were starched and perfectly ironed. Gossips whispered that he beat his wife if he found a wrinkle and that he chased women, dandy, cocky like a Bantam rooster strutting the hen yard. Two women came forth during the campaign and revealed that they'd had sex with Mr. Johnson. Rose, his martyr-faced wife, stood by his side while he categorically denied the accusations. People in the know said he had political ambitions, state legislature, maybe even governor one day.

His Honor read each name aloud, looked directly at Henry and pointed. "Henry Johnson? That's you? Harper, where's Harper?" Red lifted a finger. "Hannah Kelly." His eyes met mine. He seemed pleased the council had a woman. He deliberately counted the names on the list then counted council members. "Okay. Everybody's here." Satisfied, he handed his aide the tablet. She glanced at it and left the room.

3

"You're wondering why I did that. I did that so if I have to send the marshal after you, I will know where to find you. Now let's get this hearing over with."

Entering the somber, wood paneled court intimidated me. My only prior courtroom session was for the property settlement, child custody, and my ultimate divorce decree, a devastating time that left a lingering pain and an emotional scar forever associated with courtrooms and lawyers. The bailiff intoned in a bored voice, "All stand, Honorable Joseph Amato presiding." The judge entered through a side door, more daunting than he'd been in the conference room. The black-robed Solomon sat high on his bench. The court reporter's little machine began clicking, taking down every word everyone said, every breath everyone took, every "um" and "er" included.

This situation I'd so blithely gotten myself into now sent chills down my spine. This wasn't a club meeting delegating tasks to volunteers, or Habitat organizing fund raisers and building houses to help the destitute and needy. The decrees issued by this court affected the entire parish's well-being, every single citizen, the living and the yet unborn.

The parish found itself in this predicament, the first of many, because the council was under court order to do something about the jail's horrendous condition. The problem was the bankrupt government had no money to do anything. Every attempt to finance a prison facility met with defeat. A possible $50,000 a day fine for non-compliance loomed threateningly. Council members had to keep a straight face whether fined one dollar or one million dollars. The amount made little difference. We couldn't pay!

When it came to the jail question, the citizens were 75% *agin* and 25% *fer*, the *fer* being the sheriff, the people indebted to him, his deputies and whomever they could coerce, plus the federal mandate backing their position. He brought along a big group who were too intimidated to balk and looked as uncomfortable as if they'd been kidnapped and dragged into the courtroom. The jail coordinator sat on one side of the sheriff and the architect anxious to get paid for the building he'd designed on the other.

Those against could care less where the prisoners rotted. They would've been happy to ship the culprits to Devil's Island, if that dungeon was still available, or as an outstanding citizen said,

"Send 'em convicts to the moon. Ain't that what England did? Shipped them to the jungles of Australia and America, live or die and see what they done? Colonized the places!"

Across the aisle from the sheriff's crowd, the five councilmen, our CEO and our lawyer sat at a table, no big audience to back us. We were as vulnerable as bowling pins about to be struck by a big black ball rolling down the lane coming straight at us; no way would it swerve into the gutter.

In a surprise move, attorney George Gypson, III, representing those for a new jail, called Red Harper to the stand. Our own councilman testifying for the opposition!

Red stated his name, put a hand on the Bible and swore to tell the truth and nothing but the truth.

Gypson stepped near the witness chair, put a foot on the low railing surrounding the judge's bench, leaned forward, his face inches away from Red Harper's nose. "Mr. Harper, what are the conditions of Pohainake Parish roads?" He asked in a friendly, non-confrontational way.

"Impassable."

"Do they need to be repaired?"

"In the worst way."

"Garbage?"

"Piling up everywhere."

"Does Pohainake Parish need a new sanitary land fill?"

"Yes, indeed."

"Why aren't these situations remedied?"

"Ain't got no money."

"Why is that?"

"Parish is bankrupt, that's why."

"Does the parish have money for a new jail?"

"No, sir, need to fix the existin' one with the $3 million the state has already allocated to us. Three million ain't money enough to build a new one."

"The council has selected an architect for this jail?"

"Yeah, them before us gave the job to him sitting over there. He's owed a huge designing fee."

"Does the council have that money?"

"Hell, no, we ain't got a pot to pee in or a window to throw it out of."

The listeners twittered and the judged banged his gavel for quiet.

"The previous council hired a jail coordinator even though the jail project is not yet a reality. Is that correct?"

"Yeah, that's so—hired the sheriff's cousin."

Sheriff Branson, sitting in the audience jumped to his feet. "He's the most qualified man for the job!" he yelled. "Relations have nothing to do with it!"

Again the judge banged his gavel. "Any more outbursts and I'll instruct the bailiff to clear the courtroom."

His mission accomplished, lawyer Gibson had no further questions. "Thank you, Mr. Harper."

The judge said, "You may step down."

Red Harper came and sat next to me, looking straight ahead, red in the face. Nobody spoke to the Judas. By spouting forth in favor of not building a new jail, he had split our tenuous solidarity. The council members had decided we'd stick together. Red was the first serious rift. Many more were to follow.

Next it was our turn to defend the parish's right *not* to perform a federal mandate.

Mel Green, a recent LSU graduate assigned by the DA to provide legal counsel to the parish, had little if any court experience. Our only salvation was the young man's connections. Everyone in his family was a lawyer. His grandfather was a judge, his brother-in-law a Louisiana senator and Mel dated the governor's daughter. An impressive law firm had his back, years of settling and manipulating, bribing and making concessions, backing some political hopefuls and dashing others to pieces. Hopefully the clan would help Mel if we got into some humongous jam he couldn't solve. Mel rose from his chair and glanced nervously around the courtroom.

"He looks like a teenager masquerading in a man's suit," whispered Captain Fleming, sitting next to me.

"Look at the bright side. Whatever he learned is still fresh in his mind."

Mel Green called Wendi Walsh to the stand.

Aware that the new council didn't understand the jail situation, our attorney had served the council clerk a friendly subpoena.

Having been privy to what went before, Wendi had a better grasp of the facts than we did.

Wearing a tight black leather mini and a red V-necked Jersey blouse, Wendi sashayed down the aisle, bracelets jangling and hoop earrings swinging. Her stiletto heels tapped a staccato beat. Fluttering lashes, teased black hair, a fake mole painted above her upper lip, she must've thought the federal hearing on Bourbon rather than Camp Street. When she walked past, her perfume made my nose twitch. Henry Johnson visibly squirmed, Red's face turned purple, and Will Fleming observed her critically, eyes half-closed as if he were standing on deck of his yacht looking through binoculars. She slithered into the witness chair, crossed her legs and flashed the assembly.

"Whaat... ith your pothi-thion with the counthil?" Lawyer Green lisped and stuttered.

"I guess I'm the secretary and whatever else."

"Wha-at doth your job en-enthail?"

"I take minutes, file papers, make coffee and do anything necessary at the moment."

"Are you fa-famili-ar with the jail si-situation?

"I guess so. It's been going on for years."

Hearing Mel Green's sputtered interrogation was pure torture. The judge waited patiently while each agonizing syllable quivered on Mel's tongue before being spit out. In order to help the lawyer along, the Judge said, "Forget the $3 million that the state has designated for this project. We understand that. We are here over the $7 million Pohainake Parish must raise."

Her dress might be wrong, but Wendi had the facts, knew her stuff. She answered every question accurately, her drawl stretching "on" to three syllables, "aw-oh-un". The only nervous sign was her gum. She chewed, chomped and swallowed, chomped and swallowed.

"How di-did the coun-counthil pl-plan to fi-finance their share of the jail cost?" asked Mel Green.

She moved the gum wad from one cheek to the other. "Way-ell, y'all, the council first attempted to levy a prop'ty tax, but the voters defeated that proposal," Wendi answered, batting her eyes at the judge, who looked down and shuffled papers. "Next they tried to sail bonds, but the State Bond Commission refused approval, just as well, nobody would've bought our junk bonds. Then the council decided the only avenue left open was to pay for construction by usin' future gen'ral fund revenues, but a class action lawsuit filed by the opposition stopped that, even though fourteen other parishes have done it this way," she stared pointedly at the lawyer for the pro-jail contingency.

"The gen-general fund gets ith-ith mon-money where?" asked Mel Green.

"Sales tax, property tax, ad valorem taxes. The council planned to earmark $350,000 a year for the next 20 years to retire the bonds."

Judge Amato leaned toward Wendi. "If the council earmarks that money, I presume it will have to cut other services because as I understand there are no excess funds in the Pohainake Parish treasury."

"There's still another way. Housing federal prisoners would bring in the needed revenue."

I glanced askance at the council's CEO. He looked confused. This was new territory for him, too. The council members leaned forward not to miss a word.

Wendi tossed her black hair and through slit eyes directed a knowing gaze at the council, as if to say, *listen up, group*, and learn something.

What was the difference between a federal and a state prisoner? Did a rapist commit a federal or a state offense? Was stealing from the IRS federal, but robbing a local Pak-A-Sak, a state charge? Thoughts like wriggling tadpoles swam across my mind. To the last person, we, the parish leaders, had the identical baffled expression.

Wendi continued. "If the prison houses fed'ral prisoners, the feds pay $40 a day per fed'ral inmate. The state pays $20 a day for state inmates and the parish pays the sheriff $4 a day to house and feed local prisoners. The new prison is designed to hold 220 inmates. If the facility kept 100 fed'ral prisoners that would bring $4,000 a day; plus 100 state inmates would bring in another $2,000 a day; 20 locals, $80. Those numbers would gen'rate 'nough revenue to run the facility *and* retire any bonds issued." She swung her crossed leg. Her shoe sling strap came loose. She reached and slipped it back over her heel.

Judge Amato turned his owl-rimmed eyes toward Wendi. "Whose plan is that?"

Teased black hair and theatrical makeup aside, Wendi totally grasped the situation. She knew some stuff. "Mr. Sellers, the jail coordinator. He discussed it with the gov'nor, the one before this one, and the insurance commissioner, y'know the one that's in—"

The judge deliberately removed his spectacles. "Move on," he said.

"The gov'nor, former one, that is, liked the idea, but a few amendments to present laws had to be made, you understand?"

His Honor's head snapped back. "Of course, I understand. Don't explain procedure to me. What you're proposing is not legal."

Wendi went right on: "Under the present statutes it's forbidden for prison revenues to retire parish bonds, but, Your Honor, it would solve the parish problems if this fund shift could be legally arranged." She looked at the judge to emphasize this solution's practical good sense. "We have to make room somehow. Y'know, one out of five persons in this country will spend time in somebody's jail."

The clock at the back of the room struck twelve. The Judge declared a noon recess.

We reconvened after lunch. The session was short and succinct. The Judge had this to say: "Whether Pohainake Parish remodels an existing prison facility or builds a new one is their decision. My ruling is that the federal court has ordered Pohainake Parish to have an approved correctional facility one way or another and if the council does not comply, it will be held liable and in contempt." The judge banged his gavel. "You have thirty days to appear in this court with a definite, workable plan. This hearing is over. You are dismissed!"

Leaving the courthouse, I said to Captain Fleming, "*Liable and in contempt,* does that mean we can go to jail?"

"If we build it in time, my dear, we may be the first tenants."

CHAPTER 2

Riding back home to Harmony, Red hitched a ride with Henry Johnson, a move that probably saved our lives. Red wanted to kill us. Captain Fleming rode with Sonny and me. We were silent, marooned in our own thoughts.

Jail! Blessed jail! How did I ever get myself into this mess? I had only been on this blasted council ten days! What if we couldn't build a jail? What if the judge truly meant the consequences if we didn't obey the federal mandate? What would happen to my children? How could I so brashly, thoughtlessly, ruin their lives? The jail hearing would be tomorrow's Daily Sun headline. I'd snatch the newspaper from the box and hide it. Maybe my kids wouldn't read that their council woman mother might go to prison. Those little shoulders couldn't support another weight.

My first visit to the jail, fourth floor above the council meeting room, filled my mind. The five council members and Sonny Barth had stepped into the elevator that lurched and rattled to the fourth floor. We entered a vestibule. Pine oil smell stung our eyes. Following Sonny's lead, we halted before a bullet-proof glass enclosure.

A buxom deputy gave us an evil eye. "Yeah?"

"Hi, Lois," Sonny said, "This is the new council. They're touring the jail."

Lois shrugged and returned her attention to the Daily Sun crossword puzzle. "Leave your watches, pens, car keys, wallets, purses, jewelry. Pick them up on the way out."

Everyone complied. My big overstuffed bag wouldn't slide through the opening. Lois opened the door a crack and pulled in the purse.

We followed Sonny into a steaming kitchen. Aluminum pots and pans hung from a ceiling crossbeam and half-hid a black woman with big, fleshy arms stirring a boiling pot. An inmate wearing an orange jumpsuit scrubbed pans. Rubber gloves protected his hands from the scalding water. Big cauldrons bubbled over, hissing and spitting as the contents dripped onto eight gas burners going full blast. *Double, double, toil and trouble, Fire burn and cauldron bubble.*

After two weeks as council CEO, Sonny had the complete courthouse layout in his head. He'd familiarized himself with the convoluted government procedures and already knew the hired help by name. "Hello, Beauty," he addressed the cook. "Where's Nate?"

The cook looked over her shoulder. "He'll be cheer." She bent over, opened the oven door and retrieved a pan of golden cornbread bigger than the flower bed by the courthouse front door.

The oven's flickering blue gas added to the kitchen's unbearable swelter. Through the wavering heat, the jailer appeared like a giant genie released from a bottle, an ex-Marine sporting a shaved head and a dragon tattoo wrapped around his upper arm. "Hey, Sonny, this here the new council done come to check our Hilton, yeah?"

"I leave you to your jailer," Sonny said to us and turned on his heel.

"You'll have to wait here, Miss," Nate said, "can't take women through."

Sonny looked over his shoulder. "You wanna come back down with me?"

Red raised a skeptical eyebrow. "Anybody wanna bet?"

Peewee, District 4, said, "Bettin' agin' my church rules."

Henry, our newly-elected council president, hung back, his face mirroring concern. Women trying to do a man's job always caused trouble. He'd already ventured that sentiment more than once.

"No way am I leaving, Sonny. Did I hear you right, Nate? If the councilmen from District 1, 3, 4, and 5 are going through the jail, so is the District 2 councilwoman. I have to vote on solutions to your jail problem."

"Listen, lady, jis' so you get it straight. It ain't *my* problem," Nate said.

"It's immaterial to me whose problem it is," I snapped.

Night after night, while my kids did their homework I pored over jail mandates, nine plus years of legal mumbo-jumbo, wrangle and extensions. The situation had finally landed in federal court. The feds couldn't force Pohainake Parish to abandon the old upstairs jail, but they turned down every renovation plan submitted, thus backing the council into a corner where the only option left was a new facility. The deadline for compliance, six months away, looked at reasonably, sensibly, didn't make sense. A jail couldn't be built in 180 days left, even though the facility was designed and the site recently purchased, following endless demonstrations and injunctions by neighbors. Nobody wanted convicts in their back yard.

Nate said, "No women allowed, that's right, it's a man jail."

Captain Fleming came to my rescue. "Listen, Nate, either she goes or nobody goes. Give that a second thought, won't you? Should Sonny call Mel Green?"

"Thank you, I can handle this," equal rights pushing chivalry aside.

Nate asked, "Mel Green, who?"

Sonny turned away from the door. "He's the council's new attorney," he said. "Big fellow, you don't want to tangle with him." He touched the jailer's dragon arm. "Hold up a minute, Nate. I'm sure this can be resolved." The two walked a few paces and turned the corner. Sonny returned a few minutes later. "Let's leave this steam room and wait outside."

I planted my heels firmly on the sticky linoleum tile floor. "I'm not leaving."

"Fifteen minutes. Give him time."

"For what?—" These guys weren't pushing me around.

"For to dress the inmates, Hannah," Sonny's voice echoed down the concrete corridors. "If you had to live in Hades without air conditioning, wouldn't you shed your clothes, too?"

We backed into the hallway and waited standing against the wall, waited twenty minutes, maybe more, until Nate reappeared. Looking sullenly in my direction, he motioned us to follow him.

"Okay," Sonny said. "They're yours now, Nate. I got other burning fires to douse."

Nate balked. "Nosiree!" He removed a key from a ring as big as a hubcap. "Something happens here, I need a witness."

We crossed an area where steel tables and benches were bolted to the concrete floor. The smell from the kitchen couldn't overcome the disinfectant.

"Mess hall," Nate said. "First shift be coming soon."

"What do you feed them?" I'd ask so many questions, this man would rue the day he tried to bar my entry.

"Red beans 'n rice Monday. Today's Tuesday? Stew on Tuesday, grits fer breakfast."

We filed through a heavy steel door. It clanged shut behind us. We were trapped in a confined space. I cast a furtive look at my fellow councilmen. They didn't seem the least disturbed. They probably were familiar with jails while my knowledge came straight from movies and television where well-groomed prisoners wearing black and white stripes, serial numbers neatly stamped on back, lived behind gleaming steel bars, eating hot dinners in a noisy cafeteria, planning their escapes while exercising in an enclosed prison yard, nothing, nothing like this place.

Nate turned a key in a second steel door. "Miss, please, center aisle. Don't walk too close to the bars. We are terribly overcrowded."

The door swung open onto a narrow, dark hallway. An acrid odor belched forth, diffused excrement, urine, disinfectant, stale cigarettes, tomato sauce. Vomit rose to my throat. I swallowed hard, choking down bile. Upchucking would be disastrous. The men would deem puking a female weakness and automatically assume me unfit for this work.

We followed Nate single file: Sonny Barth first, then council president Henry Johnson, Red Harper and Peewee Reese. Captain

Will Fleming, 5th District councilman, walked behind me. His hand brushed my shoulder and I jumped two feet.

"Sorry."

Nate pointed to a filthy pen holding ten derelict-looking men. "Drunk tank—"

We'd ridden the elevator up, yet the feeling persisted that we were in a basement dungeon. Cement and steel, hard and impenetrable, trapped the inmates in gray haze. A single light streak came through a barred window. Half the bare bulbs imbedded in the plaster ceiling were burned out.

"Any reason," I asked, "why the light bulbs aren't replaced?"

Nate had answers. "Maintenance people have t'get here, drag a ladder tall 'nough to reach the ceilin', unscrew the bulbs, wires in every direction, big job and a good chance to get 'lectrocuted. Jail ain't toppin' their list."

Two-man cells lined both sides of the corridor. A look into a cubicle and my breath caught. The cell, the size of my walk-in closet had two bunk beds, bare striped ticking mattresses, a combination steel toilet and washbasin bolted to the floor.

"Them things is leaking." Peewee Reese came straight to the point. From day one, at the initial political forum Peewee Reese never beat around the bush. The other candidates cataloged the good they'd do, the improvements they'd make, shared lofty expectations and fine credentials, mentioned stellar background and experiences and their absolute true blue intentions to enhance Pohainake Parish's quality of life. Not much difference existed between one speech and another. Then Reese, a truck farmer who drove a yellow school bus, the last speaker, could add nothing, so he dispensed the blather and candidly introduced himself, introduced his wife Precious who worked for Sheriff Branson, and went over his family tree, voice tentative, not sure what to say. "My great-great-grandfather was a slave and a *nigger*," he started, stopped, reconsidered then plunged ahead, "My grandfather, a dirt farmer and a *man of color;* my old man, a construction worker and a *black.* And here I am a candidate for councilman, an *African-American.* Who says things ain't getting better?" For a moment, a dead silence enveloped the room, disbelief at such raw honesty when everyone expected platitudes. Then, Mount Zion Baptist's preacher clapped his hands and cried, "Hear! Hear! The truth shall make you free, brother!" A thunderous applause followed; an approving black and white wave. Peewee Reese and I became pals that day, embraced our commonality, minority black and minority woman pitted against that overwhelming majority, white males.

Nate, leading our jail tour, a typical obnoxious white male, frowned in Reese's direction and said, "Toilets leak, they leak. Ain't nothing to be done. You want them replaced? You find the money. You know how much them damn things cost? I bet you have no idea. None of you do. You don't know nuttin'.."

He talked to Peewee as if the farmer/bus driver were an inferior being. I wanted to slap the jailer's insolent face. Later that night I checked the internet for the toilet/washbasin unit especially constructed without removable parts that could be made into a weapon and unfortunately the jailer was right. The price was staggering. We council members truly knew 'nothin'.

The prisoners' laundry, underwear, socks and grimy tee shirts draped the bunks. Those who had made themselves at home had pictures of children, wives or girlfriends taped to the walls.

The inmates, now supposedly dressed, wore everything from orange jump suits with cut-off sleeves, to pajama pants and loin cloths. All were black except two white boys and a mean-looking old man. Nate must've warned them not to raise a ruckus. The unnatural quiet enveloped the cells, as if the convicts had been over-Valium-ed. The heavy, artificial silence was completely at odds with the hyperactivity, the banging, singing and yelling that the council heard during their first meeting.

Gingerly proceeding between cell rows, walking pigeon-toed, I wondered which man we heard preaching, which one sang. They all cursed.

The mean-looking old man stuck his arms through the bars. "Hiya, Nate, gimme a cigarette."

"You behave, Cornpone."

"How old is that man?" Henry Johnson asked.

"I dunno, been here since before I got here."

My God! A lifetime spent restricted to forty square feet, no sunshine, no privacy, no music nor love.

"Who'd he kill?" asked Henry Johnson, morbidly interested.

"His wife," replied Nate. "She wouldn't drink with him. Ain't that right, Cornpone?"

"Yeah, that's right. Hee...hee...hee..." His sinister laugh raised goose bumps on my arms.

"One day Cornpone goes to a bar, sets a paper bag on the counter, buys two beers, pops both open. 'Now, you'll drink with me, bitch,' he said, and pulled his wife's head from the bag." Nate laughed. He'd told the story a thousand times. Repeated often enough everything lost its punch, the extraordinary wore off and became common place. "Ain't that the way it went, Cornpone?"

"So dey say—"

We moved past the evil old man. The caged men's eyes followed us, silent, sullen. Their doomed gaze settled between my shoulder blades, heavy upon my back.

"Four to a cell and how many cells did you say?"

Before Nate could answer, an inmate, both arms dangling between the bars, said, "Howya doin,' Miz Hannah?"

Instinctively, I jerked aside, breath a knot in my throat. The face, the Afro, the insolent black eyes looked vaguely familiar, as if I'd known him in the past, when he was younger, before he became a hardened man.

Nate said, "Shut your trap!"

"Remember me? Ben Two?"

I drew my arms close to my body, raised my shoulders until they touched my ears, sucked in my stomach and held my breath, as if this would make me smaller, less conspicuous and invisible. Who was this man?

The man's eyes narrowed. His gaze caught mine, an ogling, disrespectful stare. He ran his tongue slowly over his lips, a suggestive, insolent gesture.

Will Fleming said, "Next time, wear pants."

"Excuse me?"

"I said—"

"I heard what you said."

Nate informed the council. "A new jail would certainly be nice. We have 26 cells here, 13 each side, 52 bunks, federal max. Over yonder, you'll see four who are handcuffed to the bars, livin' in the aisle. That murderer arrested last week, we got him in isolation in the broom closet, awaiting extradition."

It didn't take a genius to do that math. There were nearly three times as many men incarcerated as the law allowed.

Nate growled authority as we turned the corner of the L-shaped corridor, "Comin' through, comin' through!"

I'm not sure where the Billy club came from, but suddenly Nate clutched the weapon. The men squatting in the aisles, the ones with no room at the inn, pressed against the iron bars to make space for us to walk through. Chains around their ankles shackled their life.

"What are most in here for?" Henry asked.

Nate looked over his shoulder, counting us, making sure everybody still followed and no one had disappeared into a black hole. "Dope, robbery, spouse abuse, since we got that woman judge she's jailin' 'em for non-support—a pain in the ass, we ain't got room. Every now and then we'll see a genuine first-degree murderer, but that ain't often. Most killin' is either lovers' quarrels or kinfolk. Shootin' or knifin' the people you love is second degree."

The tour completed, I fled to my car, drove two blocks and pulled over behind a ramshackle nightclub of dicey reputation called the Moon Rise. The car door barely open, I upchucked in the parking lot.

CHAPTER 3

In the back seat of Sonny's car, I closed my eyes, lids pulled shut like a theater curtain after the last act when all is done, the drama over and there's nothing more to give, a bow and a curtsy the only gestures remaining and that wasn't taking place anywhere in this landscape.

Sonny looked over his shoulder and said to me, "You have to tell her."

The question cut through my mental muck. "What?"

"Better if a woman tells her."

"Tell her what?" I struggled to focus, rise to the surface and understand what he was talking about.

Sonny said, "If I tell her, she'll think I've been ogling her."

"Wendi?—you talking Wendi?—"

He snickered. I clamped my lips into a tight line. While I was worried sick about this whole mess, he was stuck on Wendi. Men! All cut from the same cloth.

***

Next morning, having weathered a frightful night, tossing and turning and dreaming about dirty little cubicles, clanging doors and judge's gavels, I explained to my kids not to believe everything they heard or read. Things were fine.

"Sure, Mom," Bobby said. "Seen my baseball cap? We've got a game tonight."

"Can I spend the night at Jenny's?" asked Suzy.

"I'll be here tonight and so will Gramma. Why don't you ask Jenny to spend the night here and we'll all go to Bobby's game?" a familiar activity, harmless, safe, a touchstone, an anchor to reality, to what truly mattered.

"Jenny has a new workout video we're watching. We're going to lose ten pounds."

"That's silly. You're not fat. Jenny's not fat."

"She's chubby, Mom."

"Tell Jenny to bring the video. I'll call her mother."

Normal, everyday life abated my panic, calmed my fears and brought serenity to my soul.

***

When I stepped into Wendi's cubicle, she was painting her fingernails.

"Chewed all the polish," she explained. "I was so nervous."

"You didn't look nervous."

"Oh, but I was. Thank goodness Henry bought me a drink. After that ordeal, I needed it bad." She blew on her fingers. "There's no way in hell this parish can find money for a new jail." She rolled her chair and hit a filing cabinet. "Shit. There's no room to turn 'round in here."

A computer and accompanying gadgets cluttered her desk. Under it were stacked black binders labeled by year. Strewn among staplers, mugs overflowing pens and pencils, file holders and in-out boxes were lipsticks, nail polish, creams, eye shadow, combs and hairbrushes. Add a shampoo bowl and Wendi could've moonlighted as a hairdresser.

"You did a good job in court yesterday."

"Hmm," naturally suspicious—

"Your services are vital to his council."

"Hmm—"

"Nobody knows as much as you do. You have an awesome grasp on what's taking place here."

"I hear you."

19

"How old are you?"

"Twenty six—"

"And you've been here?—"

"Eight years."

I did the math. "Since you were eighteen years old?"

"That's right. My uncle hired me. I'm one of those *nepotists.*"

"Well, you're an exception," meaning every word.

She glanced at me then, her questioning eyes wondering what the bottom line was. "Did I do something wrong? I'm not getting fired, am I?"

"Of course not!" She looked relieved. "But I do have to talk to you about something."

She grew instantly defensive. "Listen, Henry bought me a drink, that's all. I swear it. Nothing else happened."

"I'm not worried about Henry. It's…it's…" stumbling to find gentle words that didn't sound harsh, as if I were talking to my Suzy, who bristled at the least hint of criticism. "The outfit you wore yesterday is fine for cocktail hour, but not for a visit to federal court."

Wendi laughed aloud and tugged at her skirt. "The judge seemed to like it."

"They all liked it, but it wasn't the place. We'll be going back there, and you're instrumental to our cause and you know…y'know, maybe you could dress in a more business-like manner… less make-up?" Wendi looked as if she were going to cry. "We can't lose you, Wendi. We need you. You know more than all five council members put together."

She didn't answer. Her lips tightened as if she were holding back a sob.

"You okay?"

"Okay," she mumbled.

"I believe you have great potential."

I reported to Sonny and Will that I'd given Wendi my best talk and had no idea how she'd dress at the next session, but regardless, even if she arrived naked, we had to take her. Under the teased hairdo, inside her little head, she had all the answers.

Wendi, Sonny and I, the architect with his vested interest, and the jail coordinator, worked late nights formulating a workable solution. Though the situation was vital to Sheriff Branson, he remained aloof, uninvolved in the proceedings. He was due a jail and he would get a jail. How that took place didn't concern him.

Whether the council approved or not, the sheriff's cousin was the jail coordinator. His contract would take court action to break. His relation to the sheriff aside, Snapper was extremely knowledgeable and intelligent, determined to get the job done. He crisscrossed the state visiting prisons and talking to correctional facility coordinators, phoned his findings to Wendi who typed them in a coherent fashion and forwarded the numbers to Sonny. We were in a time crunch. Sonny took the numbers and pounded away at the calculator as if it were a lifeline. Never had I seen a man be so happy grappling with figures. At times, I'd peek into his bailiwick and he'd have long strips of white tape hung around his neck, clutched in his hands, tucked into his belt, overflowing from his pockets. He was in numbers heaven.

A month later we were back at the federal courthouse presenting His Honor the Combination Plan, part federal prisoners, part general fund and part revenue bonds. The press labeled it the Big Combo and the name stuck.

Wendi wore a long black skirt and a high-necked, long-sleeved white blouse, and sensible black shoes. She'd pulled her hair into a bun and had no makeup except pale pink lipstick. The crowning touch was rimless eyeglasses.

Sonny laughed. "She looks like a Jehovah's Witness."

Appearances aside, she explained the "Big Combo," to Judge Amato, in an intelligent, coherent way, answering every question he had, overcoming his skepticism.

"I do believe," Captain Fleming, 5th District, chuckled as we drove home, "the girl over-corrected."

"Whatever," I said. "Give credit where credit is due. The Judge approved the plan."

CHAPTER 4

Three days later, fresh from our time-extension triumph at the federal court, I climbed the courthouse steps, opened the door and saw prisoners in orange jump suits shackled to the wide stairway leading to the second floor. The convicts leaning against the railing looked sullen, mean. Depending on their attitudes, people entering the clerk of court's office or waiting to go upstairs to the district courts gave the men a wary glance and a wide berth and grumbled, laughed or snickered.

An orange-clad prisoner sat on the steps, blocking traffic.

"Excuse me!" I said.

The man gave me a sullen look and inched aside. His ankles were shackled to the railing. "Sure, Miz Hannah—"

Same voice! Same man who'd called my name when the council toured the jail. My heart went into triple beat. "Who are you?"

"Don't ya remember me? Ben Two? Harmony High's best tackle? You always comin' to the school house tryin' to make the place better. I seen you last week. Whatcha doin' now, improvin' the world?"

Ignoring him, I took the stairs two at a time and burst into Sonny's office. "What's with those prisoners shackled downstairs?"

He shrugged, "Sheriff Branson's idea of public relations."

"Well, it's not funny. He's got to move them back upstairs to the jail."

"That's his point. The jail is more than full and the sheriff doesn't want us to forget it. Federal max is 52. Sheriff Branson keeps at least a dozen floating before he calls the judge with a count."

"What count?"

"Judge Amato doesn't trust us. He's demanding a daily 5 p.m. tally on how many prisoners Pohainake Parish has locked up. Over 52 and the marshal will come after you. Believe me! Sheriff Branson is saving the council's hide."

"By keeping prisoners afloat, what do you mean *afloat*?"

"Not *afloat*, floating. There's a difference. Before Nate takes the count, he puts the excess in sheriff's vans and a deputy rides them to Greenhouse Parish jail. They eat supper there and then return. Technically, they aren't behind bars in our jail at the time the count is called in."

"Deceitful! Circumventing court orders!—"

"Watch it, Hannah. Walls have ears."

"I don't care how full the jail is! What happens if an inmate downstairs reaches and grabs somebody?" specifically thinking of Ben Two, terrified of Ben Two whose sinister eyes promised damage.

"You've been watching too much TV."

I hadn't watched TV in months. Not since I got elected to this crummy job that kept me working all night and worrying all day. "Go tell him to move the men."

"Not me, Hannah. I'm not crossing the sheriff. It's not in my job description."

He wouldn't confront the sheriff! My disappointment, the agony I suffered when I compromised my integrity, my self-respect to get Sonny Barth this position, *traded my vote for his job*, was nothing compared to the indignation I now felt. I was a ticking bomb ready to explode and Sonny sensed it.

"Calm down, Hannah. Take a deep breath. Cross the sheriff and there goes your protection. You'll be arrested for any little thing."

Sheriff Craig Branson had power and might and he knew it. The law man wanted a new jail, demanded a new jail, was backed by state and federal mandates, and still he had no jail, only the vague promise at some future date. Law-enforcement was his bailiwick. Financing wasn't his concern. He'd made that perfectly clear.

The funding procedure, long and tedious, took forever. Our state representative filed an amendment allowing bonds to be repaid from prison income. The house would vote on the measure when that august body convened in the fall, and if the bill passed, send it to the senate for those fellows to tear apart. If it survived that destruction, then the senate would forward the final outcome to the bond commission and lastly, to the governor for his signature. While this process moved at a snail's pace, we waited, holding our collective breaths as the judge's clock ticked its relentless ultimatum.

I had been elected council treasurer, a position I had lobbied for and the others were glad for me to have, since the parish was bankrupt. In my naïve estimation, if the parish's tangled finances were solved, everything else would fall into place. I knew more about budgeting and pinching pennies than my fellow councilmen. At this initial juncture, I had no idea this thankless job was as dangerous as crossing a mine field. Could the treasurer get those prisoners moved? Probably not. Henry Johnson, the council president should do it.

Wendi appeared as she always did at crunch time, red tank top and skin-tight jeans, and stood at Sonny's side. He said, "Wendi, get Henry on the phone, please."

She dialed Henry's number from memory and handed me the receiver.

"Listen, Henry, you have to come right away. We have a crisis."

"Another one?—"

"Yes. A big one—"

A slight pause—"You talking 'bout the prisoners in the lobby?"

"You know?"

"Yeah, Sheriff told me 'bout it. He said it's a way to bring home to the general public that there's no more room. He's not going to arrest anybody else until he's got some place to put them."

"You can't let him shackle prisoners in the courthouse lobby!"

"Who's gonna stop the sheriff? He can do anything he wants."

"Not in this courthouse!" I slammed the phone, ready to whip somebody.

That caught Sonny's attention. "Where are you going?"

"To find the son of a bitch—"

"Careful, Hannah—"

"What can he do to me? I'm elected. He can't fire me."

"You have children."

That stopped me cold. "What do you mean?"

"Teenage kids get into things."

My heart dropped to my stomach and twisted my guts. "What things? What are you talking about?"

"Sheriff gets mad at you and he sends deputies to raid the high school lockers. They find a joint and bust the kid. Or he has a deputy make a pass through the mall parking lot and nab a teenager drinking a beer, or stops one sliding through a stop sign. It's not only your boy doing it, they're all doing it. It's harmless. It's part of growing up, unless they get arrested. Know what I mean?"

My legs turned to rubber and I collapsed in the nearest chair. Bobby didn't do that, did he? Two months into this job and I'd lost touch. I had no idea what my own son was doing, and my daughter? Could she be smoking dope, too? Oh, God, oh, God.

The urge to flee that courthouse and race home, embrace my children and smother them with hugs overwhelmed me. I wanted to shuck this horrible job and become a normal mother again, one who went to basketball games and baked cookies for the PTA. I pined for my old life where the word *jail* seldom if ever entered conversation.

I'd taken an oath. Duty weighed heavy. Rising slowly, like an old woman, feet as heavy as sand bags, I shuffled from the room, down the stairs and across the lobby where the shackled prisoners sprawled everywhere.

Sheriff Branson had three receptionists. I dragged past them, pointedly ignoring their looks and questions, and barged into the big man's headquarters.

He shuffled papers and avoided my eyes. "Hello, Hannah."

"You have to move them." Straight to the point, no beating round the bush.

"Sure," he said amiably. "Where do you want me to put them?"

"Upstairs."

"There's no room."

"Bullshit."

"My, my, Hannah—"

"Don't you Hannah me! You don't run this courthouse. The council runs this courthouse. The safety of everyone here is our responsibility. Suppose those cons hurt somebody?"

"Suppose they do?"

"My God, Craig!—"

"Listen, Hannah. My campaign promised a new jail. This is my fifth year here, six months into my *second* term, Hannah, and still no jail. You tell me. What should I do?"

"I have no idea. We're all jammed into corners where we don't know what to do. But your solution is unacceptable." I slapped my hands on his desk. "Get a deputy to unshackle those men and send them back upstairs."

Our argument went no further. It stopped right then, right there. A sudden boom sounding as if a transformer blew made the lights flicker, dim, brighten and go out. The computers made funny, whirring sounds. The phones quit ringing mid-tone. The building shuddered and went dark. Sheriff Branson leapt to his feet. "What the hell?"

And then we were both running, stumbling over chairs and desks, ramming into furniture, skirting secretaries and receptionists stunned motionless.

Taking the stairs two at a time, I reached the council chambers. The big back-up generators had kicked in automatically and the building hummed anew.

Henry Johnson, pale as a ghost, and Sonny were in the hallway.

"What happened?" I asked. The shutdown lasted a minute, maybe two, time enough to scare everyone who worked or lived in the building.

Henry squeezed his head with both hands. "You called— prisoners in the lobby. Sonny called—light bill, Power & Light threatenin' to cut the power for sure this month. Everybody callin', complainin', wantin' somethin'—can drive a body nuts—I told Sonny 'tell 'em to go ahead, cut the damn power.' I never expected they would. They'd never done it before."

The sheriff stood behind me, breathing fire. He shook a finger at Henry, a rather ridiculous gesture for a problem this huge. "You told the power company to cut the lights?"

Downstairs, bedlam reigned. The law clerks plying their trade were re-booting the computers. Deputies surrounded the shackled prisoners and blocked the hallways, guns drawn. Receptionists and secretaries gathered in little knots, unsure whether to go back to work or not. Upstairs, the prisoners rattled their cages, beating the iron bars and pounding the floor. The jail cook tumbled down the stairs, hurting her back. "I'm a-calling Mr. Gyp. I'm a-suing. Oh, my back! My back! I'm a-suing fer sure!"

I confronted Sheriff Branson. "We're getting you a new jail, but you need to cooperate. You have stashed reserves. My suggestion is you pay this month's light bill and every month thereafter."

His eyes sparked lightning. Nobody talked to him this way. Nobody dared question his finances. "I'm not paying the light bill for this fuckin', inefficient council!"

Henry Johnson, upset and anxious, his rash act responsible for the black-out, took personal offense. Screwing his face into a big scowl, he balled his fists and stepped forward, shuffling his feet, doing a little boxing one-two. "You lyin', stealin' bastard. If it weren't for you and your family—"

"Sheriff," I stepped between the two men, presuming neither would hit a woman, not really sure. "The press will be here in another ten minutes. You can save the day and be the parish hero. Think headlines. I'm sure you can use good press."

Craig wasn't stupid. He grasped the concept—his glory at our expense. What could be finer? "I'll pay this month's light bill."

Eyes narrowed, I measured his stance, his determination, calculated how far he could be pushed and stuck to my guns, "Every month."

"Can't do that, Hannah, I'll pay 'til the end of the year."

Six months. That bought some time. "Okay." Could the council treasurer make financial deals? "Through December—that's okay, Henry?"

Before Henry could throw a monkey wrench into this off-the-cuff bookkeeping, a local TV reporter bounded upstairs, his mike thrust forward. "Okay! Okay! Let me have the real story!"

Anxious to cover the courthouse's power failure, to headline another inept episode in the sorry council's life, he missed the really big scoop.

A prisoner shackled in the lobby escaped.

CHAPTER 5

The electricity crisis, deafening generator racket, yelling coming from the darkened cells, the jailer didn't realize a convict was missing until the five o'clock count. By then, the man had a two-hour head start.

"Which way did he go?" the sheriff asked Nate.

"He never came back from downstairs."

"And you didn't miss him? Goddamit! Who?—"

"Ben Two."

"Where's Nelson?"

Nate raised his arms, the snake encircling his forearm slithering across his bicep, tongue flickering. He waved a hand. He had no idea.

The sheriff huffed down the back steps. "Get on the radio!" he bellowed to his bewildered staff. "Get every deputy we have here right now. Have them search this parish from end to end. He can't have gone far. He may still be hiding in the building."

Comforting thought!

Captain Fleming heard the commotion and raced upstairs, taking the steps two at a time as I had. "What's up now?"

Wendi made a face. "You don't wanna know," she said.

Seldom did a crisis such as this happen in Pohainake Parish. All deputies responded: paid, volunteer, and honorary. Harmony police deemed it their duty to join the sheriff's search. Off-duty cops came to help. Adrenalin pumping, a fully armed regiment launched forth to comb the area surrounding the courthouse. In addition to the standard issue hardware encircling their waists, the men had headlights, flashlights, bullhorns and two-way radios, guns and extra ammo, canteens and thermos bottles.

Henry Johnson didn't miss an opportunity. "You comin'?" he asked Will.

"Naw, there's plenty enough guys looking. I'm hangin' here with the girls."

Relief flooded me. I wouldn't have to wait alone. Pretending I wasn't terrified was difficult when the sole prisoner who knew me ran loose.

The recently arrived court-appointed administrator, commonly referred to as the CAAd emerged from his make-shift cubicle. The state attorney general sent the CPA to supervise the parish finances since no Louisiana state subdivision had the preposterous right to declare bankruptcy, and that was how the former council had intended to settle the debts. The CAAd's job was to oversee bookkeeping and he never became involved with courthouse hijinks, but now, dressed in his usual conservative gray suit and maroon tie, he surfaced from his cubicle. "You own half a dog," he said, an amused smirk twisting his face.

Henry, Will, Sonny and I simultaneously, "What?"

The CAAd removed his horn-rimmed glasses, withdrew a white handkerchief from his pocket and deliberately polished the lenses. "Council paid for half a blood hound. Greenville Parish owns the other half."

Captain Fleming laughed, "Which half is ours, the tail end?" already punching the Greenhouse sheriff's number.

The K-9 dog arrived in the Greenville Parish sheriff's car, and so did another dozen deputies who didn't want to miss the hunt.

I called home. "Mom, keep the kids in tonight and do me a favor? Lock all the doors."

Mom didn't ask questions. She caught the drift.

Will took his leave. "I'll be in the building if you need me."

All night long the men crisscrossed the woods around Harmony. The sheriff divided them into squads and assigned each to a quadrant. One group took apart the courthouse. They stalked hallways, whipped into every room, looked into closets, bathrooms and under desks. Sirens blaring, the fire truck came, extended a long ladder onto the courthouse roof. Ten years ago another inmate escaped and spent two days crouching up there before vaulting to the flagpole. He missed. Courthouse lore said it took days to clean the mess.

Betty, the council bookkeeper, and I waited in the council chamber. At 10 p.m. we had not left the building, anticipating the capture.

A deputy slinked into the room, gun drawn.

Betty looked over her shoulder, "For God's sake, Nelson. Put that damn thing up before you kill somebody."

At midnight, Captain Fleming entered the council chamber. "Let's everybody go home," he said, "and not waste our rationed electricity. Deputies just radioed in. He's nowhere to be found, probably made it north to Mississippi by now. The manhunt's suspended until morning. Can I give you a ride?"

"My car is in the lot," Betty said.

"Mine, too. I'm fine, thanks." Not really. Thinking Ben Two could jump from behind a tree and grab me, made my knees weak.

"I'll walk you to your cars, then."

The night was black, no stars pricking the darkness, no moonbeam lighting a path. Street lamps cast yellow circles on the dark pavement. Happy to be escorted, Betty and I walked with Captain Fleming. We came to Betty's Chevrolet first. Will opened the door, checked the front and back seats. "Pop the trunk," he said, and looked in there, too.

When we reached my new Cadillac, symbol of my marital emancipation, I clicked the door open. Sonny poked his head inside, and motioned for me to get in.

"You're not going to check my trunk?" I asked.

"Nah, you're okay. Nobody would dare come near this red Caddy."

"Why not?—"

He laughed, "Because you're the treasurer. You hold the purse strings. Mess with you and there goes their money."

"Who said?"

"That's the word on the street. Everybody wants to stay on the treasurer's good side."

"Believe me. I do intend to find where all the parish money has disappeared to."

"Good for you."

I astonished myself. When had I developed this toughness? When I signed the divorce papers? When I left my comfortable home and became a public figure? When I donned armor for the weekly visitation battle with my ex, Joe? Rather than something concrete and specific, was it the underlying fear pulling at me like an undertow, that I would lose my children for some unexpected, unexplained reason? That because of my constant absence from home something terrible would happen to them? Or was this hardening a gradual happening, the difficult decisions I daily made eroding the feminine me?

I didn't realize I'd rested my head on the steering wheel until I felt Will's hand on my shoulder.

"I'm driving home right behind you. I'll see you safely to your driveway."

CHAPTER 6

Once I had slept like the proverbial baby. These nights sleep eluded me. Shadows crossed my mind, whirled over me, settled heavily on my chest and released me when daylight crept into the bedroom. I tossed and turned, twisted the covers, padded into the kitchen and brewed tea, dug around for a sleeping pill then reconsidered. What if the house caught fire and I was out cold? Mom's gravelly voice filled the void, loud and clear, "Pick up the pieces...pick up the pieces... keep on keeping on."

My life hadn't been the same since Joe left. A friendly divorce, what an oxymoron! Nothing amicable existed when splitting up a lifetime, particularly one started on the fairy tale premise, impossible dream, until death do us part. Dividing the children, weekdays for me, Saturdays and Sundays for him, was like cutting them in half, King Solomon's wisdom aside, neither of us willing to forego our share. The savage arrangement wrung both our hearts and we shed torrential tears, briefly considering the idea of living under the same roof together but apart in order to spare our seed the trauma. But then, where would we put the girlfriend? Would the cheerleader the professor had fallen for be comfortable in the guest room? Would I cede my half of the king's bed to the new princess?

Our marriage dissolution split our friends, something that never occurred to me, but it happened that way, the academics forsaking me for Joe and the new wife, our old friends remaining loyal.

Though our mutual friends tried, most found neutrality impossible. They could hardly invite Joe, his princess and the ex to the same dinner party much less sit us at the same table, a rift as deep as the San Andreas Fault between the happy couple and the former wife. The selection they made, Joe or Hannah, sealed our fates. Before long I discovered welcome mats favored couples over divorcees. Divorcee! The word crushed my soul and fractured my social life. It was so different from *wife*, one syllable, soft and sweet, flowing easily from the tongue.

In my turbulent sleep, I reached for my old life, puttering around the kitchen, cooking, setting the table. A strong wind blew the blue-checkered kitchen tablecloth, tore it and whirled it away. Behind it went the yellow roses. I followed them until they mingled with the stars, leaving the two white legal sheets. Take them, too! Take them away! I saw the signature, Joseph Robert Kelly, Sr., familiar left-handed slant, shredded the menacing words into a hundred little white pieces and flung them into space. They dissipated like snowflakes.

The Magnolia Street house and its mortgage was mine. The court ordered Joe to pay alimony and child support, but who knew. I handled the cash, paid the phone company so AT&T wouldn't cut communication, juggled car notes and tuitions, floated on extended credit and lame excuses in lean times when a medical emergency crashed our finances. Paying bills was never Joe's priority, but okay, he did his part, going to work every day, bringing home the paycheck. The papers stayed glued to my bedside table for a week, hoping circumstances would change, a miracle would happen, terrified to sign and be cast into new, unexplored territory filled with pitfalls and dangers. What to do?

My pillow! Wet? Why was it wet? How would I survive? How would the children survive? That sound, was it weeping or a broken heart splintering? Mom, go away! Let me wallow in my pain! Please don't tell me to *praise the Lord and pass the ammunition.*

A job...a job...a job, what in the world could I do? After we married and before Bobby came along, I worked as a teller in Pohainake Bank, counted currency all day and hoarded pennies at night, initially not knowing the first thing about debits, credits and balancing cash, but quick to learn, seemed light years ago, working to build a bridge to the moon, a pathway through the stars, crashing now, the falling debris clogging my thoughts every moment. Could new life be forged from broken and dishonored fragments?

"Whatcha doin', Mom?—" Suzy streaked into my dream straight from basketball practice, wearing blue gym shorts and a No. 13 Jersey, hanging onto a comet.

My 13-year old daughter, hair the color of yellow jonquils and eyes purple-blue like Louisiana irises, a bud ready to open, her life petals ready to unfold, deserved better than this. Her parents had failed her and she must suffer the consequences.

"Looking for a job, listing my limited skills. Do you think PTA president counts?"

"Depends—" She stepped away, disappeared.

Where was she? I couldn't find her. I had to find her.

"What's for supper? It's cold in here."

"Where are you? We're having yesterday's leftovers. How does organizer for fund raisers and bazaars sound? Would that carry any weight?"

"Can we go eat? It's Friday." Her voice came from the refrigerator depth, a vague accusation in the tone, altered schedule, slightly veiled resentment.

Work over, school over, weekend coming, time to celebrate. The Friday evening family pizza was a ritual. My daughter wanted life to remain the same; her mother wanted to break the old pattern, find something new, "Oh, alright, but not Pizza Hut. Let's try Chinese." Could we afford to keep eating out? Our finances were in disarray, unpaid lawyers and checks not yet in the mail.

"Ugh." Suzy came down from the ceiling and took the pen from my hand, studied the classified and circled a couple. "There are two things you can definitely do," she informed me with the clarity of a child whose mind is not numbed by pain or warped by discord. "You can answer the telephone at some business or drive a taxicab like you did carpool."

"Better a secretary or bank teller than a cab driver. Ah, here," I tapped an ad. "Percival Insurance is looking for a receptionist."

"Go for it. You can do receptionist" She perched on the bedstead like a magical fairy and turned serious eyes on me. "They'll want to know your previous employment."

Nineteen years a housewife, God, did that sound dreary. What pride in being a wife and mother, giving home and children undivided attention, baking cakes and dropping the professor's suits at the cleaners so he'd look spiffy when he stood before his literature class! See where that got me. "How come you know so much, Suzy-Q?"

The look she gave me was as clear as a summer day, no dark clouds muddling her thinking. "I signed up for a job at the snowball stand this summer. It's on the application."

"Suzy!" she hadn't asked or consulted me.

"I want my own money."

"Suzy!—"

"We're probably going to be poor."

"No, we're not, honey. Come here." I needed to hold her, hug her and reassure her. "We're going to be fine. You're not to worry. We'll be okay. Did you tell your dad you got a summer job?"

"No. Why should I? He doesn't live here anymore."

"You know what? Forget Chinese. We'll go get pizza. Where is Bobby?"

She melted away. I awakened, startled, my arms wrapped around my chest.

CHAPTER 7

I left my bed, tiptoed into Suzy's room, then Bobby's. Both were sound asleep, sprawled across their mattresses, legs flung one way, arms another.

Antsy, wide awake, I slipped into jeans and a tee and drove downtown to Murt's Diner. Any news hit there first. The café opened at 4:30 a.m. for blue-collar commuters. At noon, secretaries, bank tellers and store clerks crowded into booths. The ladies that lunched, the young go-getters who played tennis, the blue-hairs who played bridge gathered in the dining room to the rear. Beyond the red and white checkered table cloths, Murt reserved a private room for luncheons, dinner parties and Mr. Percival.

The comforting smells, donuts, fresh dripped coffee, hot biscuits and bacon emanating from the diner were a touchstone, an olfactory affirmation that life went on, regardless.

The counter stools were taken. I dropped into a booth. Skillets sizzled, egg scrambling, omelets, yolks over-easy, pancakes and waffles ready, the short order cook yelling over his shoulder, "Forty-two! Ready!—" The men bolted quick breakfasts and bantered, main topic the escaped prisoner. They had twenty minutes before they caught their rides, forty miles to the nearest oil refineries and chemical plants near the Mississippi River, longer if they worked in New Orleans or Baton Rouge and traffic jammed.

Two spry waitresses moved to and fro behind the counter, refilling cups. One waved the pot in my direction.

"To go," I said. Why had I come here? Was I going in circles like Dixie chasing her tail?

A steel hat said to the yellow hard hat sitting next to him. "Man, if I didn't have this Chevron job, I'd be lookin' for that sucker myself."

Ben Two still loose.

Murt stood behind the cash register. "Couldn't sleep, huh? Don't worry. Sheriff'll nab him." She punched the keys, money coming in from daylight until 10 p.m.

"Let me know if you hear anything."

"Call ya, right on."

Morning came. My kitchen TV ran mute, not to awaken the children. Sheriff Branson's face flashed across the screen. I upped the volume. This escape was big time news. New Orleans WNO-TV came to cover it. Baton Rouge WRM-TV sent Stephanie Tringle to interview the sheriff, that jackass! If he hadn't handcuffed those prisoners to the lobby stair rail, we wouldn't be in this predicament.

Stephanie, an alien from California, assigned by the TV station to cover Pohainake Parish, a sunshine girl, all smiles and good intentions, was cut from the same cloth as the bimbo who stole my Joe. I met her at the first candidate's forum. She moderated the session, a radiant, smiling young woman holding a clipboard, wearing a two-piece blue suit that hung flat and straight like a dress on a coat hanger. "Hi, everybody!" she said, "I'm Stephanie Tringle from WRM-TV and I'll be the moderator tonight!" Such assurance! Such confidence!

Now Stephanie held the mike to Sheriff Branson's face and looked appropriately concerned. "Sheriff, do you expect to capture the escapee soon?"

"We'll apprehend him before long." The sheriff sounded confident, as he should be. Two hundred men were beating the bushes looking for the escapee.

"How did he escape?" Stephanie asked.

"We're not sure," replied the sheriff. "We had a little confusion and he came up missing at the count."

"Are you referring to the lights being turned off? What do you think of that?"

"You'll have to talk to Sonny Barth, the parish executive officer."

"Was the escapee a man shackled to the courthouse steps?"

Sheriff Branson walked away and answered no more questions.

After the sheriff disappeared from the screen, the reporter explained to the viewers that the man subject to the wide spread manhunt was Ben Two Placent, age 20, former Tin Pan Alley resident, serving time for holding up a Pak-A-Sak. His heist was $20. This was his third arrest, prior ones drug use and sale. His father was Big Ben and he had an older brother Ben One, and a younger, Ben Three. Authorities considered Ben Two extremely dangerous. The screen flashed the felon's full-face mug shot.

"I know him!" Bobby entered the kitchen, eyes glazed, hair disheveled, peach fuzzy cheeks, sleep-walking.

Bobby knew this man who sold dope! Who stood on street corners and enticed youngsters to smoke pot! Become addicts! Users! Regular customers! Who had a gun! Who held up corner groceries! "How do you know him?" I asked feigning outward calm.

"He mowed our yard once or twice one summer, remember? He came in and sat on the back porch and had his feet on the table drinking a coke when Dad came home and threw a fit."

"I remember that," said Suzy, "a real scum-bag."

Relief rose in my heart like an upward wind draft. I remembered, too! Joe had been outraged when he returned home unexpectedly to find the tired, sweaty young boy resting a few minutes. The boy had come around looking for work when Joe was away. Joe went away regularly, teachers' conventions, university exchanges, long lapses when my heart sank, the grass grew and the gap widened.

"Anyone looking for work is hardly a scum-bag." Mom, wrapped in a red Chinese print silk kimono, entered the kitchen. "He may have been down on his luck, but at least he was trying."

"Dad said he was casing our house," Bobby said.

"Sometimes your dad over-reacts," Mom said, and again my heart surged. She was on my side for once! "At least he's not a rapist or a murderer." Mom's cheerful assessment did little to lift my gloom. She reached the coffee pot and poured herself a cup.

"I think I'll keep the kids home from school today," I said.

"That's silly. It makes no sense and adds fuel to the fire. You'll make them unnecessarily nervous. If that goon shows up here, the kids will be a lot safer in their classroom." Mom, retired army nurse, was always practical and level-headed.

After the morning broadcast, everybody knew the situation. Television reporters advised citizens to lock their doors, bolt their entries, secure screens and latch windows. Children were told to come straight home after school and not dally. At the crossroad groceries, owners placed loaded guns under their cash registers and waited.

A distant whirring drew our attention. It came closer, closer. A loud clack-clack filled the room. Suzy, first to the living room window, cried, "A helicopter! Two!" she yelled above the din.

Bobby shoved his sister aside for a better look. I stepped between them. Mom stood behind me, hands on hips.

"Wow! Look at that!" Bobby cried, "Right over the tree tops! Where'd they come from?"

"State police, maybe?"

Dixie went crazy, a miniature cannon ball hurling herself at the door, her shrill bark hurtful to the ears.

"Stop it! Stop it, Dixie!"

The magnolia tree leaves trembled as the choppers flew over our roof top. The overhead clatter rattled the dishes and shifted the pictures on the living room wall. We ran from the front room to the kitchen window over the sink, bumping heads and elbowing each other to catch another glimpse.

The helicopters hovered above the field behind the house where young people gathered to practice baseball. Summers, players trampled the grass from one rock base to the other, leaving a diamond shaped trail. In the fall, goldenrod bloomed at the field's edges. Grass turned a dusty tan.

"They're not even moving!" Bobby cried.

"Gosh! Are they going to land? Look how low they are!" cried Suzy.

"I'm going outside!"

"No, you're not." I placed a restraining hand on his shoulder.

"Let me go! Everybody is there!"

The houses had emptied. Our neighbors left their kitchens and parlors and spilled onto the sidewalk. To our left Mr. Hiller, clad in striped pajamas, ran into the street for a better look, his two sons at his heels, one in Jockey shorts and the other barefooted. To our right Mrs. Jennings appeared, wearing pink chenille, fluffy slippers and hair wrapped in curlers. Across the street, Mrs. Walsh pushed Mr. Walsh's wheelchair down their front door access ramp, so he wouldn't miss the action, everybody jumping, chattering, gesturing and speculating.

"I'm not letting you go! You're not going out there!"

Bobby shoved my arm away and gave me the injured look only a tethered teenager can manage.

The ground TV news crews raced after State Police patrol cars speeding on Pohainake Parish roads, red lights flashing. Deputies tailed in gun-metal Chevys. City cops drove black Crown Victorias. Nobody could find Ben Two.

I walked Bobby and Suzy to the sidewalk. Both objected strongly to being confined to a classroom with all this excitement taking place. I remained firm. Much to their embarrassment, I kissed them both before they boarded the yellow school bus. "Have a good day. Don't talk to strangers. Come straight home after school, y'hear me?" Faces plastered to the windows, their staring classmates smirked.

The afternoon dragged forever, each minute a lifetime, everyone bright-eyed, alert, danger lurking in every corner, troubled night and turbulent day. That afternoon the kids rode the bus home from school, as they'd been told. Bobby locked himself in his bedroom.

"Leave him there," Mom said. "Best place for him. He's probably masturbating."

"Mother!—"

"That's what teenage boys do."

"Not—"

"Not, Bobby? He looks pretty normal to me. Face it, honey. It is what it is."

I wanted to snap back, 'Thanks for little favors,' but bit my tongue. I needed my mother and couldn't hold this council job without her. While I worked long hours at night, my son could be kissing and groping a girl. He might get her pregnant! Joe would kill me! He wouldn't have to. I'd kill myself.

By six o'clock that day, possibilities and conjectures ran high, and if official information was scarce, people repeated rumors as if they were gospel, until fiction melted into fact and the truth was nowhere to be found.

Fearing that Joe hearing the commotion might appear at my doorsteps increased my anxiety level. He'd give me that riveting, disapproving look that filled me with mother guilt. Plus, I had the new concern, thanks to mother—Bobby's emerging sexuality. I busied myself fixing supper: frozen lasagna in the microwave, a tossed salad; biscuits in the oven. An extraordinary comfort existed in plunging into a familiar chore, the customary moves soothing anxiety, holding panic at bay.

The phone rang an unwelcome interruption. Maybe I wouldn't answer the damn thing.

Impossible with teenage kids! Suzy grabbed the phone as if it were a lifeline. "It's for you, Mom. Somebody says he has information."

"Just hang up," and on second thought, "What information?"

"They didn't say."

"Watch the biscuits, will you?" putting the receiver to my ear. "Yes?" cold, impersonal, daring the person at the other end to unload another problem onto my sphere. I didn't care if their canal overflowed, their road was impassable, or their nephew needed a job. "What *is* it?"

"Ben Two is in your back shed."

The words hit me like a sledge hammer, knocked my breath away. It took me a few seconds to regroup. "How do you know that? Who are you?"

My panicked voice brought Mom to her feet. My face must've gone white because in a second she was by my side.

"A concerned tax payer!—" Clunk! Line dead—

Two hundred men searching for this escaped prisoner, cop cars, helicopters, sniff dog and an anonymous caller tells me he's in my back yard, my very own back yard, in my tool shed crammed full, old rakes and shovels, woodworking tools, half-empty paint cans, nail kegs, broken lawn chairs, all the junk Joe left behind, plus our lawnmower, edger, blower.

"What is it?" asked Mom.

I forced a casual shrug. "It's nothing. Somebody's idea of a sick joke," dialing the sheriff's private number, the one to be used only in dire emergencies, fingers trembling. My world moved in slow motion as I waited for Craig Branson to answer the line. Suzie, looking for her essay folder, let the biscuits burn. Smoke drifted from the oven. The acrid smell filled the kitchen. Bobby scraped back his chair and took a step toward the back door.

"You stay right here," Mom said, "until your mother gets off that phone."

"Come on, Gramma!"

Gramma locked the door and pulled down the kitchen shade.

"Sheriff, Hannah Kelly," I talked in a whisper. I didn't want to upset the kids or Mom. "Someone just called—"

"Who?—" Sheriff Branson sounded skeptical.

"I don't know. He didn't say."

"Another wild goose chase?—we've combed every road in the parish. The man's in Mississippi. We've alerted the Walthall County deputies."

"Listen to me, Craig." I would beg if need be, grovel if necessary. My children's safety eclipsed all dignity. "The caller said Ben Two was in my shed! What do you suggest I do?"

"Okay! Okay! I'll send a deputy!" angry, frustrated, impatient.

"Please hurry," replacing the receiver. "Kids, stay in the kitchen. Don't leave the house."

"And where are you going?" Bobby asked.

"I'll be right back."

The pistol had been on the top closet shelf for years. I was barely a teenager when Mom showed me how to load and fire a gun, but right now in my nervous state, I wasn't sure if I remembered how. What I did know was that if that escapee came near my children, I'd find a way to kill him.

I returned, gingerly holding the gun by the handle.

"For Heaven's sake," Mom said. "Give me that thing. I can shoot it."

"You can? Are you sure?"

"After 20 years in the Army? You bet I can. Where are the bullets?"

"Bullets?—"

"Ammunition, Hannah. Gun is no good without bullets."

"I'll go look."

"Tell me."

"They're on the top shelf of Dad's closet," Bobby said.

"Bobby!"

"We know Dad has a gun," Suzy said. "He forgot to take it with him."

"Maybe he left it on purpose," Mom said. "Give me that gun. You guys stay right where you are. Don't move. I'll get the bullets." Walking through the living room, she called back, "You have a flashlight somewhere?"

Five minutes, ten minutes, fifteen and she didn't return.

I wrung my hands. "Where in the world could she be? Where did she go?"

Suzy tapped on the kitchen window, excitement turning her voice shrill. "There she is! There she is!" We pressed against the glass.

Mom had tucked her jeans into old army boots. She tromped toward the shed with military precision, her angular back ram-rod straight, her shoulders two feet across, a combat nurse, indomitable spirit, the flashlight in her left hand, the gun in her right held firmly, pointing ahead. Had she ever killed anybody? When she nursed wounded soldiers did she ever shoot the enemy?

How courageous she was! What a coward I! She stalked the back yard at her own risk, her own peril, while I cowered in the kitchen, hugging my children, afraid for their safety, afraid of their father, afraid of life.

"Mom, let me go! You're choking me!" Bobby cried. "There comes Gramma! Mom! Mom! Look! Look!"

Suzy cried, "Dad's here!"

I ran to the front room, jerked the door open and stood on the steps, ready to explain, to make excuses, to assure him the children were safe. Joe parked his truck, got out and stood mute, his mouth hanging open. He pointed to our back yard, the plot we had so lovingly turned from weeds and wilderness to flowering petunia and rose beds, every brick in the patio a labor of love; the birdhouses he collected strung from a dozen different tree limbs. Fury snagged his tongue. "Look! Look! Look!" The dagger look he sent in my direction spun me round.

My knees turned rubbery. My head exploded as if a judge had hit it with a child custody gavel.

Mom walked behind a man wearing an orange jumpsuit, gun pointed at his back.

CHAPTER 8

Bobby and Suzy didn't want to go with their father and miss the excitement. Short-tempered and abrupt, he pushed his children into the pickup, kicking Dixie away. "They're not coming back for a month!"

"Mama!—" Suzy cried.

"Don't do that, Joe."

"God's sake— you've got a convict in the back yard! A crazy mother with a gun! This house isn't safe anymore!"

"Bring them back Sunday afternoon."

"Over my dead body—"

"The court order says—"

"I don't care what the court says. I'll have a new order on Monday."

"Mama!—" Suzy's anguish broke my heart.

"Mama," Bobby said, his young face set, eyes ablaze. "Don't worry. We'll be back. I promise." His voice for the past months had been like a slinky wire toy, coiling, spiraling, flipping uncontrollably, shrill rise and husky descent, defiance beneath each note, rebellion the main chord. Now his words were deep and resonant, contained as though he'd left the sweet symphony of youth and entered the discordant adult world.

The Daily Sun headline the next morning read, *Manhunt Ends in Councilwoman's Shed*. The New Orleans States Item, not as kind, *Councilwoman Harbors Criminal*.

Any normal person would think the sheriff would be happy to have the escapee apprehended. Not so. A sixty-five year old woman stole his thunder. No big finale, no showdown, no AP wire picture op. The let-down infuriated him.

Sonny later confided that Sheriff Branson stormed in at midnight, kicked walls, hurled ashtrays and smashed chairs. Sonny catalogued the destruction. The council owned the sheriff's furniture.

Sheriff Branson snarled, "*No big deal*," and banged his desk. "That's what the old woman said on the ten-o'clock news, '*No big deal! When I opened the shed door a crack, the man was crouching in a corner. When he saw the gun, he rubbed his eyes and said, 'Oh, ***!' and came out peaceably, both hands over his head.*' The sheriff swiped his desktop clean. Calendars, files, pen and pencil holders hit the floor. "I will not be humiliated this way! I'll make sure that bastard Ben Two spends his entire miserable life in jail." The dragon breathed fire, red in the face, neck tendons swollen like ropes. "Is there anything I can do to shut up that old woman?"

Sonny replied, "I'm the executive officer, not your lawyer."

***

The weekend was a nightmare; every minute a lifetime spent wondering whether or not Joe would return the children.

Mom did her best to calm my frazzled nerves. "They'll be back. Believe me, that young wife won't stand teenagers for any length of time."

Breakfast, black coffee, and pace the kitchen, skip lunch and pace the living room, supper time and pace the driveway, suffocating, my heart pounding in my chest, sun going down, night time coming soon.

"I'm calling the police."

"Won't do any good," Mom said.

"He's kidnapped them!"

"He's their father."

"Don't take his side! I'm their mother! I'm calling Sam Blanchard." The judge could do something, surely he could. I stopped pacing the sidewalk and ran back to the house.

Last night, I'd called Barbara, Sam's wife and my best friend, my pain beyond endurance, a need to talk, to spill my angst. Couldn't talk to Mom, didn't want to. She was much too calm, too detached and way too *reasonable.*

Barbara and I were college roommates and stayed close over the years. She graduated. I quit after my junior year to marry Joe, the English Lit professor. Our children were the same age and until Sam was elected judge and they bought the big house near the golf course, we lived in the same block. After the divorce, Barbara was the rock I clung to when I felt as if I was swirling downstream to imminent disaster, though sometimes, I had to admit, my dear friend's cheerful smile, happy glow, shining auburn hair and lively hazel eyes didn't uplift me, only sank me lower. When sad and depressed, sunshine aggravated more than helped. Beneath the rouge and the powder, I felt wasted and worn by grief, *used,* ugly, rejection etched into every furrowed line, a leap away from 40, the dividing line, the chasm between youth and old age, the point of no return. True friend, Barbara never abandoned me.

"I'm calling Sam!"

Mom gave me her best army nurse look. "Turn around."

The kids jumped from their dad's truck and ran past me, throwing a hasty "Hi, Mom!" over their shoulder. They vanished into the house, a joyful Dixie barking at their heels. They purposely avoided the skirmish, circumvented the battle, two innocent pawns torn between one parent and the other. What would our mounting hatred do to their psyches?

"Joe, listen. We promised not to—"

He didn't answer; his face sullen, hard.

"We can't do this to them. We need to get along for their sake." As much as I disliked his Jezebel, her intolerance of the children worked to my benefit.

Joe got in his truck, slammed the door. His withering look shriveled my good intentions. I begged for bread and he handed me stone. He peeled rubber backing down the driveway, looked in the side view mirror and saw me standing there, stranded in my pain, bursting with anger and frustration. I raised the third finger, right hand and gave him the universal 'up yours' —juvenile, I know, but somehow satisfying.

Behind every munificent gesture came consequences. Ben Two's capture was no different. The same as giving birth, the placenta had to be expelled, the aftermath handled. After the high, the excitement, the press and crush of neighbors and well-wishers, life slid to a new low. "Did Mrs. Belle Johnson (Hannah's mother) have a license to carry a gun?" "Did Hannah?" "Why had Ben Two picked the Kelly shed to hide?" "Did he know the family?" "Was he once their yard man?" When the Daily Sun reporter cornered Bobby and Suzy in the school yard, I called the paper and threatened to sue. My children were off limits. Joe refused to talk to the Daily Sun reporter. At least we both agreed on something. I heard he slammed the door in the woman's face which made her more relentless, delving into every rumor and sordid detail— my divorce, Mom's divorces and every army base where Mom was stationed, her duty tours. What did that have to do with anything? We were news, where the reporters had no news, so the Daily Sun milked the incident like a dairy farmer stripping the last drop of milk from a cow's udder.

Mom handled the situation a lot better than I did. "People," she said, "are just people. They love to gossip. It doesn't mean a thing."

"They're ruining our reputation! Smearing our good name! Insinuating that Ben Two"—Gossip never died. It sprouted like crabgrass and spread and spread until it ruined a perfect lawn. "Y'know what this is doing to the children?—"

"Lighten up, will you? This tempest isn't bothering Bobby and Suzy. It's consuming you. What are you afraid of? Make a list! Write it down! Get the problem out of your head and into the open where you can grapple with it."

"Sure, Mom, it's that simple."

"Yes, Hannah, dear, it's that simple."

In my bedroom, the door locked, the blinds drawn, my mind a turmoil, unable to concentrate, no coherent thoughts, jumping from one crazy notion to another, trying as I had a thousand times before to determine when the split started, why it happened, how dumb I was not to notice it, but yes, I did notice and ignored it, thinking it would go away and it didn't.

Joe walked away and I ran for the council impulsively, without a plan, without support, driven by revenge, hell-bent to show the bastard I didn't need him, when every bone in my body ached for his return. My life became afternoon teas, back yard barbecues, door-to-door knocking. The contributions to my campaign weren't so much because the donors had faith in me, but because they had a beef against my opponent, Bubba Egger. Helpful friends held a fund-raiser. We pooled the proceeds, bought a few yard signs, ran six radio spots—television was not an option— and two quarter-page ads in the Daily Sun. At the last minute, Mr. Percival sent bumper stickers and handbills. Saturday before election he had his secretaries man a phone bank.

Before I realized what I had gotten myself into, the first public forum loomed large. "Just don't give a dumb, boring speech that'll put everybody to sleep," Bobby said.

Boring, the image stuck to me like an ominous shadow. I had to shake it. "What do you suggest?"

My son looked at me critically. "Dye your hair. Wear a mini-skirt!"

"Bobby!"

"He's right, Mom. Matronly doesn't cut it," Suzie concurred.

"I am the respectable mother of two teenagers!"

"And we know what grooves. Listen to us. You'll get elected."

The dreaded evening arrived. A fretful crowd filled the Harmony Town Hall, every seat occupied. People streamed into the building and finding no place to sit, leaned against the wall or milled about. The faces came into focus: Barbara and Sam, Harmony's mayor, Mr. Zachary, the hardware store owner, Mr. Percival and his cadre, my neighbors, chamber of commerce members, university professors. Conversation drifted to the raised platform where we hopefuls sat, the sound rising like bees buzzing, ready to sting. I had no idea what people said, the roar in my ears affected my hearing. My heart fluttered like wash hung on a line to dry on a breezy day.

Where were my children? I cast quick, searching glances. Not against the wall, not on the front row, but, oh, hell. There was Joe, head ducked a little to one side, hand clutching his forehead, doing his best to show a good face under the circumstances. Where was his princess? I spotted Barbara and she waved and gave me two thumbs up. Judge Sam stood a few feet away, shaking hands with anyone within reach.

Where were Suzy and Bobby? I needed my children, much more than they needed me. They were my shield, my armor, my reason for being. They gave me courage to fight, to continue, color my hair, raise my hemline and tackle the world. Without them I was vulnerable, exposed. Where were those brats?

The District 2 incumbent seeking re-election, Bubba Egger, spoke first. He rose and crossed to the podium, looking uncomfortable in a tweedy coat, brown slacks and work boots. Seeing Bubba sans his customary blue jeans and plaid shirt, someone in the audience whistled appreciatively. Bubba didn't waste time or mince words. His big hands grasped the podium, the fingers tightly curled around the edges as if he were clutching a cow's udder. He came right to the point. "We gonna be havin' to pave roads, fix potholes, rebuild bridges near fallin' down. We gotta build a new jail, place is overflowing convicts right now, murderers and rapists and drug addicts. Then there's the garbage problem, stinky mess if I ever smelled one. This is too crucial a time for experimentin.' I've been here, servin, you for three terms. Vote for who you know will get results. This is," his eyes turned in my direction, "a man's job."

His words stabbed my soul. Who better than me knew my place was in the home, cooking and washing and running car pools, my old life, my fractured old life, a bleeding wound. My turn at the podium! My eyes searched the audience for Suzy and Bobby? Where were they? There they were! Joe now stood beside them, the new bride nowhere in sight.

"Ladies and gentlemen, it's my pleasure—" After that my mind went blank. I remembered effectively trapping my butterfly hands, placing them on the podium, holding them tightly, consciously straightening my backbone, lifting my chin. No one wanted a slouch for a councilwoman.

"Ladies and gentlemen—" I'd already said that. "Take a look at these candidates." I waved my hand in the direction behind me. "All men—" I threw back my shoulders and found my voice. "Several have been on this council for years. Today we are facing the problems they created. Pohainake Parish's most successful governing body was back in the 80's when Janice Light served on the council. Initially, she wasn't elected. She was asked to step in and finish her husband's term, a convenient and expedient request.

He had six months left on his term when he suffered a fatal heart attack and to hold an election for such a short term was not feasible. But Mrs. Light fooled them. Next election she ran for her husband's seat and she won. There hasn't been a woman on the council since then. I'm asking you to elect me. The men have had their chance, a long and destructive tenure. It's time to let what they call the *weaker sex* show what we can do." Suddenly, the feminist words rang in my ears and I bit my tongue. The wrong thing! This was male territory! They'd crucify me! Polite applause, like light rain pattering a rooftop came and I returned, drenched in sweat, to my seat.

An agonizing question and answer period followed. Finally, the forum ended. I moved quickly away, looking for Bobby and Suzy, wanting their input, their candid assessment. They'd tell me if I bombed. Swirling this way and that, passing through, working the room, inching toward the exit, I was acutely aware that Captain Fleming was doing the same, knowing without looking where he stood, hearing his easy laugh, the low, rumbling voice, Stephanie Tringle at his side.

A hand on my elbow startled me and I whirled around. Will Fleming's arm was draped around Stephanie. "Come have a drink with us aboard my boat," he said.

Street gossip had it that women—models, TV personalities, socialites from other places, Dallas and New York—constantly partied on Will Fleming's boat. The tales washed ashore, fodder for the grist mill. My heart and soul were too bruised to enjoy frivolities, my existence too tenuous to jeopardize. "Thanks. I've another commitment."

Deep down, I didn't think I'd get elected—shoestring budget, no endorsements, zero experience. Working diligently, subconsciously waiting for the inevitable end, no one was more surprised than I was when in November I was elected by a narrow margin, six votes. Bubba Egger was stunned. In his mind, he owned the seat. Victory brought a significant rush, a high and also confusion and self-doubt as if I'd been cast into orbit by a force beyond my control and was whirling through space.

What did I know about governing? Same question Joe asked the first day he came to retrieve the kids for his weekend.

He approached the house, a jauntier step than I recalled, brown hair disheveled and shirt wrinkled as if he'd just rolled out of bed. Conflicting emotions stirred my heart, as my former husband, my life's amputation drew near. Welcome him civilly? Give him the cold shoulder? He didn't contribute a single red cent to my campaign, a disappointment; somehow I expected my children's father to be bigger than that. It was his idea that though we were no longer married, that didn't mean we couldn't still be friends. Easy for him, he wasn't the injured party. He had wrecked our life and now he expected a conciliatory pat, *that's okay, sweetie, I didn't mean any harm,* to be a cure-all. Joe sensed my reluctance, my hesitancy to accept the intolerable terms, and threw in the clincher: *for the children's sake.* Manipulate me for their sake. For Bobby and Suzy I would walk through fire. The jerk knew that.

Getting the kids packed for that first weekend with their dad was a struggle. They didn't want to go and I didn't want them to leave. Bobby and Suzy resented Joe's new wife, and though I encouraged them to be nice, I was secretly glad.

"She giggles a lot," Suzy said, "and she's always kissing Dad, utterly gross, Mom."

Past Joe standing at the door loomed the interminable weekend ahead. The house without the kids' laughter and bickering was wrapped in silence, loneliness seeping through the window cracks and air conditioning vents. Mom tried to get me to join her old lady bridge club, go to the movies, walk through the mall, but I wasn't interested. Weekends such as this, my blue funk was deeper than Atlantis.

Let Joe in or let him stand there? This was no longer his house, but it had been his home, however in no way was he to feel free to walk in any time he pleased. He looked puzzled, unsure. The professor, who thought he could read me like one of his text books, was now unable to pinpoint anything specific. "You changed your hair."

I started to retort, "You changed my life," but thought better of it. What for? What was done was done. Our joint past no longer existed. The future was all I had. "Yes. Someone told me blondes had more fun."

He took the remark personally, turned and walked to his pickup, changed his mind and returned. "Congratulations," he said through clenched teeth.

"Thank you."

"Bubba is requesting a recount."

"That's his privilege."

"He's been there 12 years."

"That's the problem."

"And you're the solution?"

"I can't be any worse."

"They say that Mr. Percival—" he looked over his shoulder. The kids came through the door dragging backpacks and roller blades, tugging Dixie's leash.

How could Joe possibly give any credence to the Percival rumor? After 19 years together, shouldn't he know me better? Had he ever known me at all? "For God's sake, Mr. Percival is 70 years old." If Bubba Egger couldn't lift himself, he'd drag me down.

"Can we bring Dixie?" asked Bobby.

Joe hesitated. "Elizabeth doesn't like dogs." Bobby's face fell. "Okay, okay. Bring her. We'll work it out." The dog rubbed against Joe's legs and he reached down and patted Dixie between her floppy ears. "Miss you, too, mutt."

Dixie shook her head as if to say, *don't touch me, you traitor,* echoing my exact sentiments. Children, dog and ex-husband bounded down the sidewalk, blue jeans and tennis shoes, white tees, *Vote for Hannah District 2* stamped across the back and Dixie darting everywhere, entangling the leash, energy in motion. I raised my arm and waved goodbye. Suzy turned and threw me a kiss…threw me a kiss…threw me a kiss.

On a torn composition notebook paper, I did what Mom had suggested a while back. I wrote down my fears:

That Joe will take away my kids.

Take the kids.

Take the kids.

Nothing else truly mattered.

CHAPTER 9

During the next few days, I seriously considered submitting my resignation to the council. I was endangering my children's welfare. In another week it would be summer, school over, Bobby and Suzy home, wandering to Murt's for a hamburger, to the park for Lord knew what. Even a simple outing such as going to a movie became a threat. Bobby could be groping a girl in the darkness. Hadn't Mom said that? And Suzy, were boys ogling her long legs and budding breasts? What kind of a mother was I? Neglectful! Egotistical! My teenagers needed their mother at home! What was I thinking? My world was upside down. And whose fault was that? Not mine! Joe's! It was all Joe's fault.

Mom challenged my decision. "Johnsons are not quitters." She lit a cigarette, blew a smoke ring, narrowed her eyes and looked through its center, far, far away. She didn't see me. She saw my father, her young husband, her first, tender love, zigzagging through a mine field, leading his unit somewhere in Korea. She held the telegram, fingers trembling. *'We regret to inform you.'* The news came on my second birthday. The war had been over a year, and my dad was driving to the troop transport moored at the dock, happy-go-lucky, carefree, going home to his wife and baby girl he'd never seen. "The irony of life!—" Mom would say, "Made it through the war and got killed in a car crash." I never knew my daddy. Mom kept his framed picture on her dresser. He had a big smile and a cap at a jaunty angle. "Your father was a fighter." She draped an arm over my shoulder and gave me a little squeeze. "I know what's troubling you, honey. Nothing's going to happen to the kids as long as I'm here. That's why I'm here. So go in peace and do your job. The people elected you and you owe them respect. Walking out on those who put their confidence in you, well, you're not a shirker."

Shirker or not, I felt like wilted celery, limp and flaccid, all the starch gone from my being.

Mom did her best to stop my sliding self-esteem. "I mean it, honey. I'm here for the kids and whether you know it or not, Mr. Percival is covering your back."

"Mr. Percival! How do you know that?"

"We talk on the phone."

"He calls *you*?"

"He may be mega-rich but he's a lonely old man and I'm a good nurse. I recommended he stop eating those fatty foods and walk a mile a day. It would do wonders for his health."

"Mom, you're too much." I hugged her. Oh, what comfort those strong arms around me! What consolation her reassurance! What security knowing she loved and cared for me and my children, *no matter what*. I was five years old, hanging to her coattail, safe and protected as we crossed a busy street. "Did you know I applied for work at his office?"

"So I've been told."

"After Joe left I had to find work someplace. The council seat wasn't as much as a blip in my mind. The possibility had never occurred to me. The insurance company advertised for a receptionist and I thought, surely, that's not so difficult. I can do that job."

My army nurse mother was all iron and guts. Nothing daunted her. I didn't tell her how much courage it took to do something as simple as interviewing for a job. I had to convince myself it wasn't like marching to war or a deadly cancer diagnosis, or going to jail for murder, though that last could've been a possibility, had I known deep in my heart which one to kill. Mom wasn't much on details. She wanted the bottom line. I withheld how bummed I was, how nervous, how I had to force myself to phone for an interview. Mr. Percival's secretary informed me Mr. Percival was somewhere in the Caribbean and wouldn't return for two weeks. In my situation, two weeks was a lifetime. I pursued other avenues. Harmony Bank and Trust had no openings. Suzy and I toiled for hours over the one-page resume I left there. As the days went by, I slid down the employment scale, left offices and banks and worked sales: D. H. Holmes, cosmetics, no, dress department, no, Sears appliances, no. Maybe start my own business, get a license and sell real estate, couldn't do that, it would take weeks, months and my bank account was hitting bottom. A gift shop, how to stock it? Another day mustering courage, making rounds, waiting hands folded, leaving the resume— nothing, nothing—in the afternoon, a martini, sometimes two. Some mornings the challenge was too much to face and I didn't leave the house. Scanning the help wanted ads daily proved futile, no new jobs, only the same old ones.

Tuesday, the phone rang. Mr. Percival had returned. A female voice I assumed belonged to a secretary, reminded me my appointment was for 10 a.m. Wednesday.

Revlon and Maybelline covered my pain. Fresh tears oiled rusty skills. Five minutes, ten minutes, fifteen, sitting in the hardback chair in the reception room, time stretched to eternity. The girl behind the glass partition multi-tasked, eating a McMuffin, slurping a coke, answering the phone and saying to me in a breath, "He'll seeya in a few minutes."

Charles Percival, known to everyone as Mr. Percy owned the insurance agency, bank, gas station, stationery store, multitude investments and a race horse, too. He was the only man in Harmony who owned a Rolls Royce, a chauffeur, a colonial mansion, a golden retriever and no wife. She'd been erased from the picture years ago. Mornings, Mr. Percy stopped by his enterprises. At noon, he gathered his presidents and vice-presidents and they walked to Murt's Diner on Main Street, Mr. Percival in the lead, followed by Mr. Songe, Mr. Agee and Mr. Gendre. Jesus and the three wise men, people called them behind their backs. Lesser minions followed a few steps to the rear. The procession stopped when Mr. Percy stopped and started when he started. Nodding and shaking hands right and left, they filed into the diner's back room, bloody marys waiting. The old men's standing order was pork chops or fried chicken, collard or mustard greens, bread pudding soaked in rum sauce, cholesterol off the charts and diet didn't matter. The younger ones ate pasta.

When I entered his upstairs room, Mr. Percival was hunched over a toy train set, tracks nailed on a 4-foot by 12-foot plywood sheet. Seconds became minutes before he extended a big fat finger, tripped a switch, slowed down the caravan and swiveled toward me. Facing me he resembled a bloated bull frog, enormous head, huge sloping shoulders, tummy like a pregnant woman's, nose spread over a face that melted into double chins. Behind horn-rimmed glasses, the bulging eyes were quick, sharp, the thick eyebrows snow-white. When he spoke his thick lips stretched from ear to ear. "Do you like trains?"

"Not particularly."

"Uniforms holding up?—"

Last year I came to his office asking for a donation for Harmony High School Band uniforms. He wrote a check for the whole lot. He remembered. I suppose you don't get this high up in life with a faulty memory.

"Yes. The uniforms are fine, thank you. I'm applying for the receptionist job you advertised."

"How are the kids?"

"Fine, thank you."

"So, you and Joe split and you need a job."

My wreckage concerned nobody but myself and I resented anyone picking over the debris as if it were flotsam. "That's my business." The words spurted like an unexpected burp and instantly I wished I could swallow them, take them back, but they were out there, between me and my employment.

Mr. Percival grimaced. The motion lifted his cheeks and pulled apart his lips. His small yellow teeth were crooked and uneven. "Well, it becomes my business when you apply for work here. Is this a temporary thing, an interlude until you get your bearings?"

"That would be nice, wouldn't it? Unfortunately, as far as I can see, work will be a permanent way for me."

"In that case, you're hired."

His quick decision stunned me. "May I ask what my duties are?"

He rolled back his chair. On the figure eight track two black locomotives nearly collided. A warning whistle blew, a switch tripped, the crossing arm descended and the train veered onto a side track. A box car tipped sideways and Mr. Percy gently straightened it. He didn't bother to look in my direction. "Talk to Claire. She'll show you the ropes."

"I got the receptionist job," I told mom, bent over the dishwasher, loading it. "He gave it to me, no resumes, no qualifications, nothing." I had anticipated an overwhelming sense of accomplishment, the first step in a new single, un-joined life. Instead, depression swamped me. I had just abandoned my castle, crossed the moat and became hired help. "But I didn't take it." That was the end result, all she wanted to hear.

Mom's backside toward me, she swung her arms back and forth flinging dishes into the dishwasher. "Good for you," she said not turning her head, or giving me an approving or disapproving look. "Johnsons never made good hired help."

CHAPTER 10

Crazy things happened in the summer and the Fourth of July canoe race was among them. WHHO radio and the Daily Sun newspaper, both looking for advertising revenue in summer doldrums, hatched the idea to have public officials paddle down the Pohainake River for a heart benefit. If the council drowned in this ridiculous enterprise, the incident would make awesome copy.

The media went overboard promoting the event. New Orleans and Baton Rouge heard about the race. City folks eager to spend a day "in the country" kept the council phone lines ringing, asking the dates, times and whether or not they could canoe, too.

The council hardly managed to get any work done, Ned Morales or some other aggravating soul always sticking a mike in our faces, wanting to know the particulars, the odds, the river depth (we should know?) and the generic, most aggravating question: 'How do you feel about this?' After months of relentless bad news, interest in the light-hearted diversion rose like yeast overnight, a little dab of enthusiasm ballooning into a regular frenzy.

The race was a tacit proclamation that the parish was normal. *See us play? We can play. Run, Dick, run.* Citizens having good, clean fun, raising money for a good cause, the council persons weren't all thieves. We weren't always embattled.

From Kaplan south to Cloy's Marina the entire parish became obsessed. Everywhere people talked. The canoe race was the main conversation topic. The men discussed it in feed stores, over coffee at Murt's, at the barber shop. The Half Moon Bar was taking bets, making book. At Hoaxley, a board with squares, a council person's name in each space, hung over the bar. Customers paid $2 and picked a winner. In the grocery aisle, friends and acquaintances bumped into me, made *tsk, tsk* sounds and commiserated. A frail woman couldn't beat those big, strong men. At the Methodist Women's Circle, my lack of stamina and endurance cut into Bible study time.

Having never set foot in a canoe, but sick and tired of hearing everyone dump on me, *can't...can't... can't*, I deliberately changed my tactics, bluffing my way, assuring anyone who bothered to listen, that if they were smart, they should bet on the dark horse, the District 2 councilwoman.

My first inclination was to ask Will Fleming to share my canoe. He captained a ship, had a yacht. Certainly, he knew how to paddle. Thinking it over, I scuttled the plan. A favor granted was a favor owed. Instead I went to Pohainake Landing to ask my good friend Maggie Deep to give me a few quick paddling lessons. She lived in a cottage perched high on the river bank and owned two skiffs, a bass boat and a magnificent party barge. She could make boats move in the right direction.

Maggie's daughter came to the door.

"Hi —where's your mother? I need her to teach me how to paddle a canoe."

"Oh, sorry, Miss Hannah. Mom's in the swamp. It's that time." Summer, mushroom season, Margaret disappeared into the swamp to harvest chanterelles. She packaged and sold the wild mushrooms to restaurants in New Orleans. "She may not be back for a month."

Scratch Maggie. I couldn't wait that long.

At supper that evening, eating cheesy noodles and a quick salad, I bemoaned my fate. Bobby stuffed his mouth, late for baseball practice, paying little attention to his complaining mama. Suzy and her girlfriends trolled the mall. Mom left to play poker, no idea where she found this group, most elderly ladies played bingo at the Catholic Hall.

"Mom," Bobby said, "Have you noticed? We have no canoe."

"Surely the organizers will supply a canoe."

"No. Everybody has to have their own."

Oh, shit. Not aloud for my son to hear, though certainly thinking it. "How do you know that?"

"Mr. Fleming told me."

"Will Fleming! Have you been talking to him? I don't want you anywhere near that man. He's a womanizer, a bad influence!"

"He's cool. Do you know he lives on a boat? He said we could visit if it was okay with you."

"Well, it's not okay with me. Not another word! Where did you talk to Will Fleming?"

"At school, he teaches Thursdays."

That took me aback. "Teaches what?"

"Motorcycle safety—"

Will had a motorcycle, a red Honda something-or-other. Occasionally, he rode the machine to the council meetings. He'd asked me once to take a spin, an invitation pointedly ignored.

I made a fist and beat my head. "Don't even dream motorcycle!" Every teen-age boy wanted a motorcycle. Was Will encouraging Bobby? He'd better stay away from my boy! Enough problems already; no need for a new one.

Bobby scraped back his chair and stomped away. He did that a lot lately. When Bobby was born, I'd cradled the universe in my arms, and unfortunately, the relationship was foundering. A sixteen-year-old boy needed two interactive parents, a mother to elicit his soft and gentle side, a father to read him the riot act and keep him straight. How comforting it would've been to talk to Joe about the acne on our son's face or the Playboy under the bed, or the girls who called at all hours, day or night, not to mention the sullen attitude, the constant rebellion, rejecting his mother one minute, bear-hugging her the next. Were all boys the same? Joe would've known. He was a boy once. We could've raised our children together, if it hadn't been—*Stop! Don't go there.*

I opened the door and yelled after Bobby. "Do you want to canoe with me? Suzy is going!"

He didn't even look over his shoulder.

***

Pohainake Parish wasn't a tourist destination, and there were few canoe rental places. At Sports World canoes cost $800 or more, not in my budget.

No canoe, no paddle and people lining the river bank ready to throw tomatoes and rotten cucumbers at the parish treasurer, the woman who held the purse strings so tightly, everyone was suffering. Did I really need this? Was there a way to skip this trip? What would happen if I put my foot down and said no, absolutely not? Would such a cop-out be tolerated? Would the media crucify me? This parish had humongous problems. Why lather this canoe thing into an Enquirer blast?

One, two, three days, Saturday! The clock kept ticking. Open Space Camp Ground had rental canoes.

My luck! Oh, my lousy luck! Arrived at the camp ground early Friday morning. Indians overran the place. Not India Indians, but the Apache kind sporting magnificent feather headdresses, beaded outfits, moccasins. Men circled a grassy field, hopping on one foot, stomping the other, raising little dust clouds, drumming a war dance. Colors flashed red, blue, green and silver. Beads glinted in the sun light. Other Indians squatted, passing a peace pipe, a funny smell filling the air, but what did I know. It might be an Indian substance.

Booths surrounded the perimeter. The sign hung on each post designated the tribe: Houma, Cherokee, Chappapeela, Tchefuncte, Pohainake, etc. The women manning the booths sold hand-woven reed baskets and wool blankets, beaded blouses, tooled leather accessories, feather ornaments, wood carvings. A wrinkled old man fashioned bows.

"Osage wood," he said.

His helper inserted steel tips in arrow shafts. They looked lethal. A fierce warrior constructed tomahawks. He whipped a leather thong around a razor sharp triangular stone and lashed it to a handle. That might be a good weapon to have under my chair at the council, an impressive counterpart to the gavel Henry Johnson wielded so well.

"Welcome to our powwow!" a young princess cried. "Are you a photographer? Do you want to take my picture?"

"Sorry, honey. I'm not a photographer. I'm here to rent a canoe." Pounding drums drowned my voice. "Do you know where Mrs. Space is?"

"She left for the day."

"Mr. Space?"

"Gone with her—"

My luck! My lousy, rotten luck! "Do you know where they keep the canoes?"

"Over there, next to the river, see those racks?"

Nothing left but to steal the canoe, a heinous act that would have ample repercussions: *Council Woman Steals Canoe! Hannah Kelly Charged with Theft!* Still, what else to do?

Stealing a canoe, actually lifting it from the rack and packing it away, wasn't that simple. Anyhow, these canoes looked extremely iffy, patched bottoms, sides scratched and gouged. Originally the canoes must've been silver-colored, but now they were river-scum green. Some paddles were metal and others wood. What was the difference?

Did I have the strength to hoist and lash something that awkward and heavy onto my car? Would the canoe balance on top? For sure I couldn't tow it because the car didn't have a trailer hitch.

My luck! My lousy rotten luck! At that moment, this behemoth Indian emerged from the woods zipping his fly. His headdress resembled a mama turkey's ruffled wings. Red, white and black war paint striped his face. He wielded a tomahawk.

"Hi, Miz Hannah—"

"Hi, Rambo," I recognized the Clearwater fire chief by his huge size, almost seven feet tall, and his tremendous paunch trapped by red suspenders. A fuzzy gray beard covered his lower face and hit his chest. He had one keen blue eye and a black patch covering the other. He looked like a pirate. When his dairy operation floundered he turned his fields into commando war territory. People came from New Orleans and Baton Rouge and sometimes as far away as California and paid good money to hide in bunkers and artificial mounds, crawl through brush and wade across ponds to shoot each other with paint pellets.

Rambo and I were old acquaintances. At the initial fire board meeting, Rambo led the rabid argument over fire ownership rumbling like Thor and pointing an accusing finger at the parish fire chief. The white-headed old man smiled and nodded. Younger fellows wanted him gone, but he'd been there so long, he'd known every sheriff since the depression and nobody dared touch him. "Pine Hill took our fire. It was well across the river—hooey! Pine Hill knows fires on the east side belong to us."

Captain Fleming leaned close. "What's he talking about?"

Obviously, Fleming hadn't done his homework. He knew zilch about the process or the parish. His good looks, charming manner and his rich Uncle Percy swept him into office while I worked day and night and barely squeaked in. Who said life was fair?

The parish's unincorporated, rural areas were divided into five fire districts manned by volunteers who elected their own "chief." Each headquarter had a tin shed that housed a fire truck and a non-stop poker game. The paperwork stated the Clearwater station was in my district.

"Council pays the volunteer stations $100 per fire. If somebody else horns in, they have to split the fee."

The data sheet said the parish extinguished 69 fires the previous month; $6,900 went to the volunteer fire stations. The math was simple.

"Two fires a day?" Captain Fleming laughed under his breath as if the whole business was a colossal joke.

The argument concerning the proprietary interest in the fire raged. Clearwater firemen battled Pine Hill firemen, everybody jumping and yelling an opinion and a say so, Captain Joyce nodding, smiling and saying nothing.

Finally, Red, having been duly elected fire board president, had enough and banged the gavel. "Fire east side of the Pohainake River, fire belongs to Clearwater—$100 to Clearwater. Captain Joyce, you make sure Pine Hill don't cross that river."

"Eh?"

Red raised his voice a decibel. "The river, Jimmy!—don't let Pine Hill cross the river."

Now Rambo stood squarely before me, a bemused look on his pirate face. "Whatcha doin' here, Miz Hannah?" he asked, "You Injun, too?"

"No. Are you?"

"One-sixteenth Cherokee—got to preserve that smidgen to get in on the fed'ral settlement. You gotta problem?"

"You know that canoe race Saturday?"

"Oh yeah!—"

"I need a canoe."

"You ain't got a canoe?"

"No."

"Well," he said as drums rolled in the background. "You ain't got no problem. I'll take care of that for you. I'll have a canoe for you at the Landing. Nine o'clock is it?"

"Would you do that?"

"For my favorite councilwoman?—absolutely!—"

That remark unnerved me. I was nobody's favorite councilwoman.

"Counting on you, then—nine o'clock, sharp—"

He went one way and I went the other, and then it occurred to me to turn and yell, "Rambo! Rambo! Paddles! I need paddles, too!"

***

All night sleep evaded me. Would Rambo show up? What type canoe? What if he didn't come? I didn't count sheep. I counted paddle strokes. That ploy made me bolt upright. At 3 a.m. I shuffled into the kitchen and made hot tea and toast to warm my stomach and settle my nerves.

Next morning I sat on the toilet and practiced paddling: bent my elbows, made a fist with each hand as if holding oars, extended my arms, then drew them back to my chest and repeated, left, right, left. The stroke seemed simple enough. After all, this wasn't brain surgery. No life or death matter, here. Whatever happened—happened.

Friday before Canoe Saturday, Will Fleming called before breakfast. "You got everything under control?"

"Yep—"

"Got a canoe, paddles, bottled water?"

"Everything, thank you," If the other councilmen paddled their own canoes, so would I.

"Good luck, then. See you at the landing tomorrow."

"See you there."

Four hundred people gathered at Sunny Landing. Suzy and I had trouble making our way through the crowd. The people pointed and laughed and called my name.

I approached the river bank, a false swagger in my step. The CAAd stood there wearing a blue seersucker suit, white shirt and Panama hat.

"Hi, Ken, didn't expect you here!"

He settled his horn-rimmed spectacles on his nose and lifted an elaborate clock. "I'm the official time keeper at this end," he said. "Another AG representative is at the finish line."

"You're kidding me."

"No. This race is big all over Louisiana, most innovative fund raiser. The AG wants to make sure the income all goes to Heart." He gave me his funny, lopsided grin. "Hurry—Ten minutes! Race starts!" He sounded as excited as everybody else.

Most canoes were already in the river, lining the bank, ready to go. The sheriff had wired colorful banners on his canoe, tip to stern. The flag flapping in the wind said "CRAIG BRANSON Sheriff Pohainake Parish." The clerk of court had lightning streaks painted across the bow. The marshal flew the skull and bones. Will Fleming didn't bother with flags or banners. He had Stephanie Tringle in a yellow polka dot bikini. The bobbing canoes were sleek metal jobs, slim like bullets, aerodynamic construction, built to fly on water.

Suzy and I walked the river bank looking for mine and spotted Rambo. He waved, standing ankle deep in soggy river sand, holding the tether to a canoe. One look at Swamp Queen and my knees went weak.

"Made it myself," Rambo said. "She's a beaut."

Swamp Queen was really a hollowed tree trunk, an upward flair at both ends, much bigger and bulkier than the other vessels. The word sleek didn't in any way fit this floating tub. Her rough sides were probably hewn with a chisel and hand-held plane. She had a plank board seat across each end, and one in the middle. Two paddles rested at the bottom in an inch or so of water.

"It doesn't leak, does it?" trying my best not to hyperventilate.

"Took care of it, gum tarred the bottom yest'day. She's fit as a fiddle. Threw in that life jacket," he pointed to a ragged orange vest, "See that?"

"Okay. Sit where?"

His eyes bugged. "Why, in the middle Miz Hannah," and looking baffled, added, "you paddle first one side and then the other. You best shuck them shoes."

Shed the sandals, roll pants to the knees and step into the water. The bottom was muddy and squishy. "C'mon, Suzy, give me a hand. You're coming with me."

Suzy laughed. "Oh, Mom— oh, Mom— oh Mom—you want me to sit in *that?*"

Must I drown us both? She was too young for a watery grave.

"Hey, Mom!—" Bobby slid down the bank, a nice surprise. "Jay and I are coming!"

"Thank God," Suzy said. "I'm skipping, Mom. I cede my place to Bobby and Jay."

The boys waded into the water. "We're paddling for you."

Bobby's change of heart was greatly appreciated, but— "That's not legal."

"Yes, it is. Mr. Fleming said to show you this." He waved a paper, a paragraph highlighted: 'Each public official must have his/her own canoe.' It doesn't say you have to paddle your own," already shoving the Swamp Queen mid-stream. "Jump in, Mom."

Hoisting my rump over the side was not a pretty sight.

"Sit in the middle." Bobby took the front seat. The canoe lurched from side to side. "Sit still, Mom. Don't move." Jay tumbled onto the rear plank, nearly overturning us. Water sloshed in and swirled on the bottom. "Give Jay the back paddle."

Mr. Percival, the race grand marshal, fired the starting shot. The canoes sailed forth, six at a time, three minute intervals between starts. This staggering order avoided a massive river traffic jam. The normal drift time between Sunny Landing Bridge, the starting point, and the finish line at Open Space Camp Grounds was two hours, but this being a race, the officials figured speed would enter the equation, and probably ninety minutes would suffice. At the starting point CAAd recorded each canoe's departure, hour, minute and second. The other AG rep noted the arrival time at the finish line. The canoe traveling the distance in the shortest time would be declared the winner.

First pistol shot and the sheriff and his deputies launched; second, clerk of court and his entourage; third shot, the council! Our turn! Canoes were more or less lined across the river, bank to bank. Bobby put his paddle in the water and pulled. The Swamp Queen didn't move. Jay tried the maneuver in the rear and we made a half-circle and almost rammed Henry Johnson's canoe. Wendi, wearing skimpy white shorts and a wet tee waved her arms over her head. "Don't hit us! Don't hit us!"

A quick thought darted across my mind, but I had no time to dwell on it. Wendi in Henry's canoe! Where was Henry's wife?

Our start was bumpy, very bumpy.

"Both to the right!—" Bobby yelled over my head at Jay. "Now left, right!—"

The awkward, unwieldy Swamp Queen moved forward, not at lightning speed, but at least in the right direction, downriver.

I had imagined floating down a serene, placid waterway. Not so. The Pohainake River had currents and cross currents, eddies and sand bars. The stream made big, sweeping curves, the water deep. Other places the current forced us into the shallows and twice the boys jumped out and pushed the Swamp Queen back into deep water. Frequently, fallen trees blocked forward passage, okay because we saw the trunks and branches and avoided them or the boys miraculously found a narrow opening. The unseen snags were the problem. They ripped across the Swamp Queen's hull. We wondered aloud if the old tub would hold together.

Between Sunny Landing and Open Space Camp Ground there were six bridges. People lined the overhead spans. They looked down and yelled and laughed and hollered. I heard the familiar "Hoo-ey!" Rambo leaned over the railing.

"Got my two cents on you, Miz Hannah!—crack that whip! Make them boys paddle harder!"

The river widened. The current became more uniform. Sitting between two strapping young boys, I felt like Cleopatra being barged down the Nile, and finally relaxed and began enjoying the ride. The muscle shirt Bobby wore bared his arms. His wide shoulders tapered to a slim waist and the bare thighs looked like strong pillars. Under a baseball cap, black hair curled around his ears. I overcame the urge to reach and smooth a strand into place.

Jay hollered, "Okay, Bobby, let her rip!"

I once saw a truly obese woman enter a dance competition. In her living room, she was a bungling elephant. On the dance floor she moved as if she were Tinker Bell. Her feet barely touched the floor. She became weightless. That's what happened to this canoe. The boys found their rhythm, and suddenly we were skimming over the water. Both paddles went down at the same time, up simultaneously, a water spray, a forward surge and repeat.

People ran alongside the river bank, jumping over downed trees, sinking in the muddy sand, yelling encouragement. The last bridge we went under was a blur. Spectators standing on the north side roared. We slid from under and glided past. The south side spectators hooted and yelled.

We caught up to the others. A stunned Henry Johnson turned his head quickly, a jerky, unexpected move that tipped his canoe. Wendi shrieked as she hit the water.

From somewhere behind me came Suzy's voice. "Go, Mom, Go!"

I turned to look. What was Suzy doing in Will Fleming's canoe? In a halter top! Where was her shirt? Stephanie in her polka dot bikini posed like a poster girl next to my daughter. My agitation had no outlet, no time to object or scold. We were overtaking the marshal's skull and crossbones canoe, leaving it behind.

"Let's get the sheriff!" Jay yelled. He was really into this. "Let's get the son of a bitch!"

"Okay! Okay!" Bobby hollered. "Hold on, Mom. We're going to get the son of a bitch."

Motherly instinct told me to stop the language, fuss at the boys for using profanity. Instead, my lips clamped shut. I was into it, too. I wanted to triumphantly streak past the big man who controlled the parish, that bastard.

The boys paddled with superhuman strength, every muscle vibrating like a rope pulled taut. In, pull, repeat, in, pull, repeat, the Swamp Queen caught the sheriff's canoe. We were side by side.

"Hi! Sheriff!—" Sheriff Branson ignored my gay wave. "Douse him!"

My son roared approval. "We'll get him!" He slapped the water with his paddle and drenched the astonished sheriff as the Swamp Queen scuttled past him.

Meanness had its own reward. It felt *soooo* good.

***

Afterward, we endured the inquiry, but Will Fleming was right. The rules didn't say the public servant had to paddle his or her own canoe. Guilt reared its ugly head and was quickly squelched. It wasn't my fault the contest rules weren't specific.

The trophy with a big gold heart was mine. The pedestal engraving read: Hannah Kelly, Winner, First Annual Heart Race. Five thousand dollars went to the Heart Association. That's a sizable sum in our poor woods. The Heart people were happy. I was happy. Bobby was happy.

Suzy was happy. Rambo was happy. He cashed in on his bet money and Mom did, too. She'd run along the river bank, waving encouragement and yelling, "That's my daughter! That's my daughter!"

CHAPTER 11

GARBAGE

Saturday, Joe arrived to retrieve the kids. He pulled to the curb and honked the horn. He saw my new red Cadillac with a cream-colored top parked on the driveway, left his truck and asked, "You got company?"

My initial reaction was to say none of your business. "The Chevrolet died." He'd graciously left me the old clunker and took his brand new Ford Camino.

"Died? That good car! How did it die?" A querulous note spiked his voice, the rising crescendo a familiar scale I no longer had to suffer.

"A natural death, probably—the valves needed replacement and the motor a four-way bypass."

His lips clamped into a thin, tight line. "Did you check the oil?" He mistook my stoic silence for guilt and glared at the Cadillac's wire wheel covers, silver crest on the grill, chrome trim. "And you bought *this?*"

The liberation symbol was a buy of tremendous magnitude. Reflecting now, the impulsive act sprung from profound pain, a parched heart aching for relief. Women did it all the time. They went on buying sprees and returned home laden with goods they didn't want or need, something new, something untouched, something unblemished, no history attached to it, no memories clinging like cobwebs. The draw was so strong, so vital to the psyche that merchants preyed on the feeling.

Since Joe left, I'd had the Chevy at the GM dealership three times because it wouldn't start, or abruptly came to a dead stop. The first time was January, council installation day, blustery and cold, damp seeping to every bone. The wind blew, rain poured, temperature dipped to 38 degrees, a gray, bleak day, a desolate beginning to my tenure.

Mom had arrived from Ft. Lauderdale for the occasion.

"You brought a jacket, Mom?"

"I don't own a jacket anymore. The sun always shines in Florida."

My black wool coat was too small and tight.

"Don't worry. I'm waterproof. Hand me that umbrella."

We piled into the Chevrolet, Mom in the front passenger seat, Bobby and Suzy in back, headed to my new public life. I wore a tailored navy suit, a white carnation corsage pinned on the lapel, a gift from my children. The starter ground several times. *Oh no, oh no, what if this is it? What if it the motor conks out right here, right now and I can't make it to the*—my high heel pump slipped off the accelerator. The old Chevy didn't deal well with near-freezing temperatures.

"Pull the hood latch." Mom opened the car door.

"You'll get soaked! What can you do?"

"Person doesn't spent twenty years in the army without learning a thing or two. Put it in neutral."

Mom fiddled with something under the hood. The motor coughed once, then again, choked, turned over and caught.

"You need a new carburetor." Lightning and thunder underscored her diagnosis.

"How much?—never mind! I can't worry about it now." If the car fell apart, it fell apart. I'd tackle that later. Backing slowly down the driveway, my immediate, heart-attack inducing panic subsided, leaving my stomach knotted, a familiar, fearful twist. Next to me, Mom, henna-orange hair dripping water, tucked her cold hands under her armpits. She looked like a wet chicken with folded wings. The windshield wipers worked. Thank God for little favors.

The car was a constant pain in the ass. Three days ago when I dropped the Chevy at the dealership *again* for repairs, an overeager salesman nabbed me as I crossed the showroom and before fully understanding what had taken place, I'd traded the paid for family sedan for a car note.

"Yes, I bought this," I informed Joe now, "and I didn't consult Consumer Guide or shop for competitive prices, either." Like Eve impulsively picking the red apple from the tree, I committed this folly in less than an hour.

"Have you lost your mind?"

"Not really. I believe I've gained confidence. You want a closer look?" I opened the car door and let him peek at the plush leather seats, the sleek dashboard and the leather-wrapped steering wheel. The interior had that delicious new car smell. The beige upholstery, the sleek console, the styling struck him mute. His totally baffled look gave me unexpected pleasure. For 20 years we had lived under the same roof, shared a bed. He had molded and shaped me and I no longer fitted his norm.

"Did your mother buy this car?"

"I should say not. I bought this car myself."

"I think I'm paying too much alimony."

"Not enough," I retorted, "for the life style my children—"

"*Our* children—"

"Okay, *our* children and I plan to pursue."

He had his princess. I had my car. He looked old and tired, maybe more sex than he could muster. In his forties he was half the man he was at twenty. I should know.

"This is reckless. How are you going to pay for this Cadillac?"

I cut him short. "That's for me to know and you not to worry about." I didn't have to listen to his carping anymore. Though still heartsick, I felt younger, rejuvenated and capable of managing my own life without dependence on anyone else. The fortitude the divorce ordeal required awakened a hidden inner strength. A hard core emerged, a steel blade that cut down the sweet violet, the pale magnolia. A poignant sadness existed in the death of innocence and trust. "And don't be taking the kids to the mall and buying them everything they want. Bring them back early Sunday afternoon. Don't be late. They have homework."

Joe had a hard time accepting his former wife as a councilwoman. Previously, when I tried to discuss political events, he furrowed his brow and said, "Honey, that's current events. I teach literature," and buried his nose in a book.

"Yes, but isn't the best literature a reflection of place and time?"

I attributed his disinterest in Louisiana's plight to classroom fatigue. Who wanted to teach students all day and come home to debate political issues with the wife? Following the city and parish council meetings, their arguments and inept fumbling had been my escape from the kitchen, my entertainment. The ordinances and decrees passed by those august bodies had a profound effect on our everyday life. Often, analyzing their reasoning, their logic, I wondered how those councilmen could be so ignorant, and promptly found myself named to another committee: recycling, park improvements, litter control.

As far as Joe was concerned, whenever I expressed a thought other than a new cornbread recipe, I crossed an invisible barrier built over the years one frown at a time, a slammed door, a prolonged silence, nothing big, nothing earth-shaking, little termites quietly eating down the house, unseen, unfelt, unnoticed until the roof caved in.

We were having this discussion standing on the driveway, me leaning against the Caddy, Joe with a spread-eagle stance and hands on his hips, ready to pounce. At that moment Suzy opened the door and yelled, "Mom! Gramma is on the phone!" probably stopping us from a full-fledged argument. "She said to tell you she's back in Florida safe and sound and she wants Bobby and me to go visit her Easter break. She says she'll take us to Disney World! Can we?"

"We'll talk later," I called over my shoulder.

"Am I not being consulted about this?" Joe asked, belligerent.

"Absolutely, if they go, you'll probably pay for the trip." Turning that screw gave me unbounded pleasure.

Suzy yelled again, "Mom, phone!"

"Who is it?"

"Mr. Percival!"

Joe's eyebrows hit his receding hairline. "Why is he calling you?"

I snickered. "Maybe the old man wants my opinion on something." I hollered at Suzy. "Tell Mr. Percival I'll call him right back!"

"He wants to know if Gramma is still here! I told him she left yesterday."

The third time the phone rang, Suzy said, "For crying out loud! It's Captain Fleming! I'm trying to get my stuff together! Coming, Dad!"

"Excuse me," I said, walking toward the door, getting a second high knowing Joe stood on the sidewalk, a mute witness to my busy life. I had not fallen apart. I had gathered the pieces he shattered and moved on. What a secret pleasure to kick his monumental ego!

When I picked up the phone, Will Fleming came right to the point. "It's rough going to that garbage dump. Would you ride with me?"

I greatly appreciated the offer. "Thanks, but Joe is here for the kids and I'd delay you. Sometimes this takes a while." Juggling kids between two houses, Gramma gone and Joe adamant, could be a nightmare.

"I can wait."

"Please. Do go on. Sometimes it's complicated," and messy.

Joe didn't want the kids to bring Dixie. He said Dixie pooped in the house and upset Elizabeth. Dixie rarely did that. She must be uncomfortable, insecure in the new surroundings, looking for her corner on the couch, her doggie bowl, yelping and chasing her tail when excited. Already late for the dump tour, I said through clenched lips, "We mustn't upset Elizabeth." If Dixie were a Pekingese or a French Poodle instead of a rescued short-hair, mix breed, white mutt with a black patch over his left eye, the Princess would've loved poor Dixie.

Joe and I had vowed that if we couldn't be friends, we would at least be civil to one another around the children. Civility in theory didn't always function in actuality.

Bobby balked. "If I can't take Dixie, I'm not going."

Suzy hung back sulking, holding a squirming Dixie tight against her chest. Our hurting innocents clung to the little talisman they toted from one house to the other, the umbilical cord between their two lives.

"Well, you are coming and Dixie is staying so get in the truck." The old, commanding voice, king of the universe, bow and obey. That phase I didn't miss.

The dog stayed home, tucked his tail between his legs and crawled under the house. The kids went, faces ugly and resentful, a look Joe would erase by taking them to the mall, letting them buy anything they wanted, treating them to a movie and pizza afterward, returning our progeny to me in a spoiled, indulged state that took three days to overcome and then it was Saturday again.

I waved goodbye with a heavy hand and a heavier heart. "Behave yourselves. Have a good time and be nice to Elizabeth."

CHAPTER 12

A new car, before hamburger wrappers and spilled coffee, smelled of good leather and a fresh life. I backed my apple red Cadillac onto the street. Magnolia trees lined the sidewalks. The lawns were cut and neatly edged. Flower beds bloomed in riotous colors.

Almost ten o'clock and the breakfast crowd had left Murt's Diner, the lull before plate lunch time. The few sidewalk strollers gawked at my passing Cadillac, a befuddled look, not sure if that was Hannah Kelly or not, looked like Hannah, but that wasn't her car. Past the theater, furniture store, Dollar Store, shoe shop, dress shop, red light. A block further and over the railroad tracks, except this car didn't clatter and shudder as the old Chevy did. Finally through town, speeding north on Highway 51, a red streak, silent as a whisper, total liberation, the speedometer—oops! 90!

The episode with the dog, the unhappy kids and the unyielding father filled my mind, more intimidating and frustrating than garbage. For the children's sake, I refrained from accusations and petty arguments, but now as pine trees, mobile homes, green fields whizzed by, my inner turmoil and resentment seethed. Full orations blossomed in my mind, everything I should've said and didn't. Joe had to decide, either the children or the princess, but he couldn't have both. The system was too destructive for them, for me.

The state highway, two flat, straight lanes, dirty white stripe down the center had drainage ditches either side. The pavement rose slowly, imperceptibly, until the cypress trees and fan-shaped palmettos reflected in the side view mirror gave way to the pine trees that grew in higher land, big thickets, dense and dark, the pungent pine scent dissipating the swamp odor. The air turned clear and crisp, the fragrant needles sterilizing impurities. Truck farms paralleled the highway. Long rows of tomatoes and bell peppers lined the fields. Here and there a farmer, wearing a big straw hat, rode a tractor tilling and shaping the earth into brown mounds for strawberry plants, the parish's main crop. Past verdant, level pastures encased by post and wire fencing where Charolais, Herefords and Black Angus chewed cud beneath shady oak clumps or near cool ponds. Past crossroads where a single yellow caution light blinked. To the west, traffic whipped by on the four-lane interstate, legal speed 70 miles per hour, but everybody driving faster. To the east, the railroad tracks, New Orleans to Chicago. Beyond the tracks, behind the pine thickets the Pohainake River flowed. How beautiful our parish! Green land against blue sky, bright and shimmering like a soap bubble!

On my way to a dump! What did I know about garbage? You dragged the metal can to the curb, city workers jumped from a big truck, grabbed the can, dumped the contents and that was that. Outside the Harmony city limits, the parish had "dump stations" where yellow metal containers were placed for the rural citizens' convenience. The Department of Environmental Quality had informed the council the dump station system was helter-skelter, hit and miss, and totally unacceptable. Without prior basis, without initial knowledge to draw on and build upon, my mind couldn't grasp the situation.

Inside the car, the air conditioning created a cool cocoon that insulated me from the blistering August heat. My thoughts deep in garbage, I exited west on La. 36 looking for Booty Road, found it, a two-lane parish disaster of interconnected pot holes, a boggy marsh on either side, a few straggling pine trees, then open space. The noon sun turned strewn tin cans into bright spots, hit broken bottles, sparkling glass resembling diamonds. Paper caught in tree branches hung limp. Bedsprings, rotting furniture, rusted car parts, life's discarded debris littered the roadside.

Booty Road tapered to a dusty washboard littered with garbage that flew off dump trucks. In an improvement effort, the parish had dumped loose gravel on the rutty surface. My new car zigzagged, left, right, right, left avoiding pits. Ping! A loose rock hit the windshield. Damn! An asterisk in the new glass! Paying for repairs atop the ghastly monthly note would be disastrous. What if I got a flat? Turn around? Go back? No place was wide enough for a U-turn so I drove slowly, ever so slowly. Trucks ahead! My fellow councilmen were stopped at the red-lettered sign, "Danger Bridge Out," cab doors flung open. Every road in the parish had posted signs that said "Bad Road," or "Bridge Out," the general interpretation being that if a driver saw those signs and chose to proceed, the consequences were not the council's fault. The drivers had been duly warned and in case of harm, the person had no basis for a lawsuit. I pulled over and stopped.

Red Harper and Henry Johnson stood and looked over the rickety railing, studying the river below the bridge. Peewee Reese scratched his head while Sonny Barth and Captain Fleming leaned casually against a truck fender and smoked cigarettes. Red waved his arms over his head, a signal that spurred activity. The men climbed into their trucks. They were going across! Teeth gritted, I started the engine. If they were going, I was going.

Oh, my God! They weren't driving across the bridge! They were going into the river!

Red's truck inched into the stream. Water reached the fenders and sprayed a silver arc. Sonny Barth, driving the second truck nosed down the bank. I placed a hand over my eyes and prepared to drown, saw myself floating down river, not in a nice little canoe, but in a water-logged Coupe De Ville casket.

What would happen to Bobby and Suzy? They couldn't live with Joe and the princess. *Mother! I needed my mama.* She'd look after my children. *I didn't have a will!* Why hadn't I done that?

A relentless tapping on the driver's window caught my attention.

"Leave your car here and come across in my pickup," Will Fleming said. "It's safer."

Abandon my brand new Cadillac? I momentarily hesitated— *relieved to be helped across, mortified not to be able to tackle the problem alone—* evaluating the alternatives. "Thank you, appreciate that."

Captain Fleming had an industrial strength F-150 Super Crew 4x4 Ford truck, monstrous wheels, a deadly winch in front, and a rear trailer hitch. My army mother would love this truck. It forded the river like a Sherman tank. "If you had a truck like this, you could drive across. It's the Caddy that won't make it." He leaned over and yanked the seat belt. "Brand new truck and the seat belt jams." The truck angled up the river bank and we were back on the road.

Truck windows up, AC going full blast, we couldn't smell the dump. What we did see was a black shroud, an ominous, moving cloud. Ugly black birds extended their wings as they drifted in lazy circles, casting a moving shadow.

"Buzzards," Will said, "after carrion."

"Good grief!"

"Best disposal system the parish has."

"The owner, what's his name, Standish? He has the garbage disposal contract. He's supposed to bury this stuff."

"Have you run into anybody yet that does what they're supposed to do?"

"Not really. We have to find new funding, another cash pipeline into our coffers."

Captain Fleming gave me a resigned look. "You're preaching to the choir. Sonny has been saying that since day one."

"A new tax?—"

He laughed outright. "Get real. The only way the people will vote for a new tax is if a "no" vote on the ballot means "yes."

"What?"

"A "not" vote for example: 'Pohainake Parish will *not* be entitled to levy a tax for prison construction.' You wrap that in enough gobbly-gook and all the voter sees is 'tax' and votes no instead of 'yes'."

"That's dishonest, to confuse the voters that way."

"My thoughts, exactly, but Sonny says that in order to obtain the desired results words have to be manipulated."

Such deceptions! Such warping of truths! The voters who elected us didn't trust us, and we, elected by the voters, didn't trust them. Did all governing bodies reach this sad state?

We arrived at the dump. Oh, the dump! It's impossible to describe this Rocky Mountain Ridge, not just a peak or two, but a chain of elevations reaching the sky. The yellow bulldozer pushing garbage looked like a Tonka toy. A putrid rot and decay smell rose in steamy clouds and hung over the site like a low pressure system. The garbage mountain range was alive. Sliding, slipping, burrowing, crawling insects, droning horse flies and stinging hornets covered the trash.

"Do you really want to tackle this?"

Maggots, rotten carcasses, roaming dogs and vermin, ugh! I lifted my legs from the floorboard and hugged them close to my chest, so this sickening mess wouldn't touch my body. "Yes, I'm going."

"Here," he reached over and undid the recalcitrant seat belt buckle, "if it doesn't offend your feminist beliefs—"

"Why do you say that?"

"You're so endlessly independent."

"I have to be or you fellows would run all over me."

"A steamroller couldn't flatten you," he replied.

"You hurt my feelings."

"Didn't mean to—"

"I wasn't always this way, you know."

His eyes were very green and understanding. "I know."

"How could you?" He didn't know my struggles, the burden of facing life alone, raising teenagers, running a slap-dash household, never enough time, never enough money. I was spread in so many directions I'd lost my central core.

"You don't have to hold it all in, y'know."

His eyes met mine and again the feeling came over me that he looked past my outward appearance straight into my heart, knowing my strengths, my weaknesses. What a relief it would be to unburden my woes! To share my worries, my grief! "I'm okay."

The men ahead left their pickup cabs and walked toward the valley where the dozer cranked back and forth.

Captain Fleming looked at my sling-back red pumps. "Whatever you say, then, but do watch your step."

My heels sank into the mush and I wanted badly to clutch his arm, but held back. These guys had to understand that I was tough enough to do anything they could do, except cross a river in my brand new car. That was a little much. Carefully following in Will's footsteps, placing my high heeled shoe exactly where he planted his leather boot, exploring no new territory, we walked fifty feet into the dump site. Mr. Standish spotted us. He shut down the big machine and dismounted.

My ankles itched. I looked down. "Gracious!" White worms crawled all over my red pumps.

Captain Fleming slapped at his trousers, "Maggots!"

"Maggots!—" I jumped away. He caught me in his arms.

The others had forged ahead and were talking to Mr. Standish.

Captain Fleming held me close against his chest. "Put me down!"

"What if I don't?"

"Put me down!"

He swung me easily to the ground. "When you get home, wash your feet in kerosene."

"Kerosene?—I don't keep kerosene in my medicine cabinet."

"And you'd better buy yourself a good pair of Bayou Reeboks."

I did a crazy dance, shaking my feet. "Tennis shoes?—Boots? What are you talking about?"

"You don't know what a Bayou Reebok is?"

"No! No! Never heard of it!—"

"You'd better find out fast."

The entire council wriggled and writhed, slapping our legs and scratching our armpits, doing an impromptu Hawaiian hula dance same as the doll people placed on a car's dashboard. We made a semi-circle around Mr. Standish who stood by his bulldozer. A white pit bull with pink-rimmed eyes stayed in the cab, keeping watch.

My insides were tied in knots. I'd probably contract some rare, incurable disease carried by maggots. Mr. Standish's sly smile catapulted me over the edge. "Mr. Standish!" Hearing my agitated voice, the buzzards swooped away, whirring and flapping their wings. I realized I'd screamed. I didn't want to scream. I didn't want to get hysterical, so I said again, my voice lowered, calmer, "Mr. Standish."

"Yeah, honey?"

I looked to the others, hoping they'd address the existing problem. They were too involved in slapping and scratching.

"This," waving my hand in every direction, "is not what the parish contracted for. The parish contracts for this trash to be buried."

"It's getting buried."

"At the rate you're going," I pointed to a mountain, "it'll take a thousand years."

"You dig a hole and the parish pays you for the dirt you excavate then returns it to you to cover the garbage," Captain Fleming said.

"That's so, savin' the parish alota money, not loadin' and unloadin' the dirt."

Captain Fleming informed Mr. Standish. "The AG says that's double-dipping and he's after all double-dippers."

"Yeah? So what—? He don't scare me!"

The council had no Plan B and Mr. Standish was well aware that if he closed his dump there was nowhere else to take the garbage. He said in a more conciliatory tone, "We're digging another pit over yonder then we'll get behind the biggest trash hill and push it down into the hole."

Henry Johnson snickered as if the situation were a funny joke. "DEQ is on our butts."

"Yeah—yeah, yeah—been so for years. Y'all are a new council so don't waste time worryin'. DEQ ain't got no funds. They do nothin' 'cept send memos they can't follow up."

"You gotta cooperate, Stan, conciliate," Henry Johnson said in his whiny twang. "We got this Ken White, court-appointed administrator, breathing down our necks. He's double-checking everything we do, turning every stone. Our ass is in a crack. You gotta do better."

Mr. White, a CPA sent by the attorney general, came to make sure the parish solved its financial problems. Wearing a conservative gray suit and maroon tie, he seemed a proper bookkeeper, staid and dependable. He observed much and said little. For two months the CAAd was quiet and unobtrusive, spending his time sitting behind his assigned desk, chewing his pipe stem and staring into space. Or else, he stood against the wall, quietly watching folks coming and going. Like an alligator sunning on a log, he made everybody nervous without moving a muscle or opening his mouth.

"Listen, Standish," Captain Fleming said, "There's no way the council will continue to pay the current price for substandard garbage collection."

"Substandard, my ass, this here the best you got. You don't pay, I'll let the stuff rot wherever it's dumped, and the stink will reach from here to Mars."

"You have to revise your numbers."

"I ain't revisin' shit."

"Your equipment isn't adequate," Captain Fleming said.

"The other council ain't had no trouble with my trucks. You want fancy garbage trucks? You buy 'em. I'll run 'em."

Henry Johnson objected to outsourcing our garbage to a New Orleans or Baton Rouge corporation. "We have an obligation to our people here. We'll manage. We can get new trucks."

I wondered where he got his information. We had zero funds for new garbage trucks.

"Top of the line, yeah," Mr. Standish said. "I'm waitin'."

Captain Fleming dropped the heavy anvil. "The AG has mandated the council put garbage collection for public bids next month."

Robert Standish laughed as if this was the biggest joke he'd ever heard. "And where do you propose to dump the garbage? In my dump? On my land? I don't think so. What you gonna do with all that fuckin' shit? Send it to the moon?"

Mr. Standish, legs apart, huge beer belly restrained by red suspenders, arms crossed over his chest, stood ready to battle the council, the parish, DEQ and the Feds if those fellows wanted to join the fray. He removed the cigar clenched between his front teeth and spit. The glob landed near my left foot. He was much more certain of his position than we were of ours.

The maggots were to my knees. We were all itching and scratching.

"I got an iron-clad, solid, unbreakable contract," he said.

"That's the problem," Red Harper explained, "Attorney General says that contract ain't legal."

"It fuckin' is legal. My lawyer, George Gypson, says it is, already done asked him. Jis' you follow me inside and I'll show ya." He snapped his fingers toward the cab where his dog slept on the front seat. "Git here, Pluto."

The council crowded into the metal shed and we stood shoulder to shoulder, shuffling our feet to the maggot's dancing. A dingy coffee maker sat on a wooden table next to brown-streaked mugs surrounded by scattered Splenda and Cremora packets and a Jack Daniels bottle, half-empty. Papers spilled from every drawer of a desk shoved into a corner. The pit bull at Mr. Standish's heels jumped into a basket under the desk and wriggled on a dirty blanket until he was comfortable. Mr. Standish opened the metal cabinet standing against the wall and thumbed through files.

"Mr. Standish," I said. "I'm the council treasurer. I sign all payment checks."

"Good for you, darlin'," he replied not turning his head.

"I'm not signing another check until this garbage is properly buried."

That dart didn't hit the mark, either. He continued pawing through the files. "Sure thing, honey, you go right ahead. First check don't come I quit emptyin' the dump bins."

"You do that and I," my eyes swept over the slack-jawed men, "I mean—we—will have Sheriff Branson lock you in his jail."

Robert Standish whirled about, faced us and laughed. "Are you threatenin' me, Little Bit?" He looked at the others and winked. "Goin' to lock me up in a jail ain't got no room and you can't build a new one?" He had that right.

Henry Johnson pulled on his crotch and Red Harper rolled his eyes and slapped his neck. Peewee slid through the door and walked away, not wanting part in any confrontation.

"The parish owns a 16th section," I said, "six hundred forty acres near Kaplan. We can establish a landfill there."

The dump owner wasn't at all intimidated. He knew the parish finances. "Feisty little woman y'all got here—cute red shoes. Ain't nobody ever before come tell me what to do in my own place wearin' cute red shoes, and threatenin' me, too!"

"You either bury this stuff or I swear—"

"She swears! How about that? The little lady swears! Swear what, Miss?"

"You will be number one on the attorney general's investigation list."

Nothing fazed Mr. Standish. "Bring him on!" he said. "Bring him on! Ah! Here it is!" He drew a legal-sized folder labeled 'Garbage Contract' and set it on his desk. Next to the folder he placed a black pistol. "Do what you have to," he said. "And I'll do what I gotta do."

CHAPTER 13

The council hired loggers to cut the pines in Section 16, 640 acres acquired years ago from the school board in a land deal nobody seemed sure about. The going rate for pine timber was $1,000 an acre, so $640,000 was a good start toward constructing a sanitary landfill if we could manage to keep the income dedicated to the project. A sum that large was the same as a big, rotting carcass when it came to attracting vultures. The scavengers were bound to circle, swoop and pick the bones to pieces. Nevertheless, the council proceeded as if we could actually do this, though in reality we knew we couldn't. The plans called for an access road, fencing, a secure gate, a weigh scale, and a metal building for the sanitation director. Pohainake Parish already had 30 applications for the as yet non-existent job.

One Friday I said to Wendi, "I'm going to ride to the 16th Section and see what progress those loggers are making."

"This kinda weather," afternoon thunder, summer showers, "they're probably not working. Anyway, it's Friday."

"What about Friday?"

She looked at me in that funny way she had, as if she were talking to a Greenwood Sanitarium escapee. "Loggers drink Fridays— get a leg up on the weekend."

That information gave me even more cause. If the loggers were slouching on the job someone had to prod them. They weren't entitled to three-day weekends. "You want to ride with me?"

Again, she gave me that cross-eyed look. "Not on your life. Y'all don't pay me enough for that. Let me find you a map. That'll help you some."

She drew a red line: north, Interstate 55, exit at Kaplan, then east La. 10 almost to the parish line, then a red squiggle north Westmoreland Road, then back west, north, east, north.

"This is almost in Mississippi."

"You got it."

"It'll take hours for the garbage trucks to get there, dump, and come back."

She shrugged. "Too late to think logical, Hannah—y'all should've figured that out earlier."

My God! How could we be so collectively obtuse? Why didn't we show some common sense? The council had been so elated over owning the timbered land, selling the trees to finance the dump, (such a brilliant ploy in our estimation, real genius) that the location never came into play.

I pressed my fingertips against my temples. Stupidity was a humbling experience.

Wendi put her arms around me and gave me a sympathetic squeeze. "Don't shoulder the whole load. There are four others here." To be unanimously obtuse was no consolation. "Anyhow," she continued in her logical way. "It's the garbage company's problem. They'll compute how much gas it'll take and figure how to make the screaming citizens foot the bill. Don't sweat it."

Young, astute and sharp, she deserved to go a lot further in life than secretary to ignorant fools.

I followed Wendi's map down a gravel road that became a muddy dirt track. The loggers had set down wooden pallets. If the pallets supported the heavy logging trucks, my Cadillac could certainly make it.

The pine trees shot a hundred feet in the air, the sun barely filtering through the branches. The tree cutters had started at the furthest point and worked their way forward. As the Cadillac bumped and dipped over the pallets, my car must've looked to the unseen loggers like a red beetle crawling through the forest.

The pallets' ending began my dilemma. The car couldn't go forward another inch. To turn around, the front wheels would drop off the wooden boards. Trees on either side had giant trunks to maneuver round. Dark shadows splashed the ground. It looked soft, marshy.

Couldn't turn around, couldn't go forward. The only option left was backing up. Inhaling a big breath for courage, the car in reverse, gently pushing the accelerator, watching the speedometer read five, six, eight miles, slowly, carefully, feeling the tire bump over each pallet, hands gripping the steering wheel, eyes glued to the rear view mirror, a big bird, huge, not a vulture, I had learned to recognize them, flew by and gave a tremendous squawk. The steering wheel jerked. The tires sank into the mud.

I honked the horn. If the loggers were anywhere near, they'd hear and come to my rescue. A deep, ominous silence was the only response. What if they'd already left for their Friday drinking spree and no one was there to rescue me? Cold chills ran down my spine.

The way my luck ran these days, I didn't get a break. It began to drizzle. A few drops hit the windshield, then a deluge the wipers wouldn't handle. Huddled in my car, mired in the middle of 640 acres, I'd die and it would be at least Monday before anyone found my decomposed body.

Blow the horn! Blow the horn! I literally sat on the horn, blaring without letup. Somebody had to appear. Honk! Honk! Honk! SOS! Come! Come!

Visibility dwindled to zero. Could I walk to the gravel road? How far away was it? Men hunted foxes and coyotes and sometime bears. What if I ran into one? Honk! Honk!

Dark and quiet, wet, lost, alone, cowering and panicky, I had no rescue plan in mind. Somebody had to appear. Somebody must.

I opened the window. Rain whipped my face, "Help, help!" A loud rumble swallowed my pitiful yelp. The noise grew louder and louder like a tornado approaching. "HELP!" oh God. Oh God, "HELP! *Please!*"

Barreling through the woods, making a racket to rival a supersonic jet, came a logging truck, a big rig, tires as huge as those on army trucks built to crush the enemy. A derrick-like structure with a grappling hook dominated the flatbed. Two men perched on it, two rode in the cab, all so mud-encrusted I couldn't tell whether their faces were black or white, young or old, friend or foe, and didn't care. It only mattered that somebody had come to my rescue.

The driver jumped from the cab. He had a beard down to his chest. Two disbelieving, walnut-sized eyes peered from his mud-smeared face, "Lady?" He spit tobacco juice into the rain and tossed a Dixie beer can.

I stuck my head out the window before this character, real or a figment of my distorted mind, vanished. Rain splashed my face and ran in rivulets down my neck. "I'm stuck."

"I kin see that, but what the hell ya doin' here?"

"Please help me!" never too proud to grovel if the occasion warranted it. "I'm Hannah Kelly."

His eyes sparkled, an insane gleam, "Councilwoman—?"

"Yes."

The news gave him a big kick. He hollered to his cohorts. "Hey, man! Here's the councilwoman come to check on us!"

The other three clambered down, wet and muddy, rain streaming down their bearded chins. They guzzled beer and stared at me as if I were a butterfly pinned to a specimen board.

"Oh, no, no, please. Didn't come to check on you, just wanted to see where the landfill was. I never—"

They laughed big gurgling sounds that belched from their stomachs and echoed through the trees.

"Please."

"Get her boys!"

My heart melted. *"Deliverance"* scenes filled my head. I braced myself. Fight the loggers or submit? Which would be less painful? What would the headlines say? What spin would the relentless media put on my untimely death? If I were lucky enough to die! Facing the consequences would be worse than death.

A tremendous jolt derailed my thinking. Two fellows raised the Cadillac's front end and tilted it upward.

They were going to make it look like an accident! Like my car turned over! *Oh, God, please help me, God. I'll do anything. Just name it. Donate more to the church, contribute to all charities and say novenas. So what if I'm not Catholic?*

The third man clambered back onto the flatbed and lowered a grappling hook, "We gotcha, lady!" In seconds, he and his buddy attached the car's front bumper to the grappling hook and slid under the chassis, dragging chains and banging wrenches. "Jes put it in neutral and don't tech de brakes," the burly driver instructed.

"Don't even tech de steerin' wheel. We gonna make a circle, head outta here. Ain't gonna be easy. Don't mess us up." Set to go, my car hanging mid-air, the driver cranked his truck. The motor whined, coughed, spit, and died.

"Fuckin' bastard!" he tried a second time. "Shit!" Nerves strung like a cheap guitar, tears filled my eyes. The third try and the motor turned over. The gears stripped and whined. The truck shook like a rumbling freight train.

The two men in the cab grinned and pulled beer can tabs. The two riding the flatbed hooted, "Hoo-ey!" and drank their beers. A whiplash jolt and the Cadillac lurched forward.

By the time we traversed the wooden pallets, the men had downed a six-pack each, pitching beer cans right and left. The driver knew his job, driving in a slow and torturous way, making sure the big truck wheel stayed on the pallets. The grappled Cadillac bumped and bounced along with me frozen behind the wheel, too afraid to touch anything, staring traumatized through the arc the windshield wipers periodically cleared.

When the logging truck reached the gravel road, the driver stuck his mud-smeared hand through his window and waved approval. The two on the flatbed hoo-hooeyed again and did a crazy little jig. Friday, beer drinking time!

Hands shaking, shoulders hunched to my ears, heart racing and pounding in my throat, I waved at the men, fingers splayed in supplication. They must've taken that as a sign of rejoicing, because they all gave me thumbs up.

"It's okay now! I can take it from here!"

They grinned, waved Dixies and sped onward, dragging my Caddy. We hit Westmoreland Road. The Cadillac speedometer read 50, then 60. The car swayed to the right, to the left, making big sweeping swerves, one lane to the other.

Had I just escaped death in the forest to become a highway statistic? I honked the car horn, one long, endless blare. "Turn me loose! Turn me loose!"

The men in the cab waved more beer cans. The ones in the back pitched the empties into the air, caught them on the way down, crushed the cans and sent them banging against the Cadillac hardtop, "Hoo-ey! Hoo-ey!—"

The La. 10 stop sign loomed ahead. Would these idiots stop? Or would they barrel right through the sign into the highway traffic? I grabbed the door handle, ready to jump out break a leg or arm, but I saw no other way. The logging truck slammed to a stop, skidded to one side, barely missing a little red sports car that came to a stop. The door flew open, a man leapt out, running toward us. He banged a violent fist on the logging truck's battered hood and shot back to my car hooked onto the derrick.

Will Fleming reached up and pulled open the Cadillac door. "Jump down!" He grabbed my arm and yanked, "Right now!"

CHAPTER 14

Labor Day weekend, the entire council except Peewee Reese, District 5 council member, flew to the Bahamas. Peewee wouldn't abandon his school bus route though his wife, Precious, did her best to convince him to get a substitute for Friday, just one day. He obsessed over what would happen if they didn't get back by Tuesday. What if we got stranded down there for days? Peewee had every excuse not to board an airplane. We left him. The three-day weekend special, $650 including air fare New Orleans to Nassau came from Sonny Barth's wife, Charlene, who owned a travel agency. She made the arrangements.

Was this trip proper or not? Would writing a check to Barth Travel be considered a nepotistic act? Would the trip be misconstrued, public officials jetting to sun in the Caribbean? Sure it would! If the entire council abdicated to the Bahamas, what would happen if the parish had a crisis?

How tiring it was to examine every little move, to not be able to take a step without thinking how the public would perceive the action. Weary business this loss of freedom, being shackled to real or imagined propriety. How enticing my old life seemed, a life where one could joke without hurting somebody's feelings, laugh without seeming callous, talk simple English and not double-speak.

Then there was the on-going problem with Joe. Instead of mellowing, every passing day he grew meaner. As my confidence and self-assurance deepened, as my parish-wide influence grew and my horizons expanded, his world shrank, the university, old hat, his princess, not so new anymore, and his children, reluctant weekend visitors.

The longing to spend quality time with my children, away from the telephone, the endless council hours and my mother's good intentioned meddling overwhelmed me. I yearned to have my youngsters to myself, insulated from the crazy world we lived in. In this coupled world my children protected me from the disjointed status that divorce created. My children at my side, I was never the odd woman, the third wheel. I wasn't vulnerable. I had purpose, status. I was their mother.

Joe wasn't sympathetic. "Weekends are mine." Enveloped in his own selfish little world, he refused to understand.

"You can have them three extra days during their Christmas vacation." We haggled as if we were trading baseball cards. I'll give you a Mickey Mantle for two Catfish Hunters.

"Can't do that, we're going skiing—"

"Were you planning to take the kids and not tell me?"

"We're not taking them."

"Oh!" thinking that over. "I suppose Elizabeth doesn't want—"

"You leave Elizabeth out of this."

"Excuse me!"

"You can't take them out of the country."

"For God's sake, it's just three days! It's not as if we're going to disappear forever."

"No."

A court order could stop our little vacation. If I defied the child custody arrangement, I might be arrested upon my return. Jail no longer terrified me. The threat hung over my head so often nowadays, confinement had lost its menace. If Joe wouldn't give his permission, I'd forge ahead, ask for forgiveness later and pay the consequences.

"Mom, can Jenny come with us?" Suzy asked.

"Jenny Kennison?"

"Yeah, she's my best friend. I don't want to be at the beach all by myself and just grownups. Y'all will talk business the entire time. I need a pal."

I mulled over the request: Cork Kennison's daughter? What would the consequences be? As council treasurer I'd recently tangled with the marshal over his budget and expenses. "Her dad probably wouldn't let her go."

"He said yes. She's already asked him. Her daddy said he'd buy Jenny's airplane ticket."

This particular aspect of politics amazed me. Pros in the political game held no long term grudges. One day Cork chewed on me and spit the pieces, the next he allowed his daughter to vacation with me, as if life was compartmentalized, *this is this* and *that is that* and the two events were unrelated and didn't mix. The winner often hired the loser even though the opponent had spent months slinging mud, as if the vitriol and hatred was simply a part of the process and once done, differences ended. Amateurs kept the little black book, listed the slights and offenses, never forgot and never forgave. Pros rose above that niggling aspect.

"If it's okay with her mom and dad, she can come."

Bobby, Suzy, Jenny Kennison and I flew to Nassau. Mom went back to Ft. Lauderdale to check on her condo and visit with old friends.

Warm sand, blue sky, balmy wind, stretched on a lounge chair, hiding behind a book and oversized sunglasses, watching the kids surfing, our first trip outside the country. Formerly, our family trips were budget camping vacations.

Bobby stood on his board and crested a wave. His leg muscles bulged and he balanced himself, arms extended. At 16, he was a man, strong, the school football quarterback in the fall, the basketball center in the spring, baseball in the summer. Since the divorce Bobby kept a ball in his hand, dribbling, dunking, passing, pitching as if the constant motion was necessary to fill the gap in his fractured life. Suzy's board shot into the air and dumped her. Jenny treaded water. She was afraid to surf.

Soaking the rays, feeling warm all over, not talking to anybody, not having to think, simply being, how wonderful, a dream world, Wyndham Resort with pools, waterfalls and bars, an exotic landscape, palms and coconut trees, tropical flowers, gazebos and thatched-roof cabanas.

The biggest attraction was the Crystal Palace Casino. Slots, video machines and fast-paced game tables attracted the high rollers and arm pullers. The crystal chandeliers were as big as Egyptian pyramids, a thousand crystal drops in concentric circles, circle inside a circle, whirling down to one little final teardrop. Last night the noise, the music, the noisy, drunk laughter was overwhelming. Roulette, red or black, who knew? Nobody explained. The process was too fast, too hectic. The dealers slapped down blackjack cards quickly and precisely. Players called, "Hit me," or "Stay," or gave a subtle hand signal. Charlene Barth giggled loudly and with a long, red fingernail tapped a card.

"Please keep your hands off the table, ma'am," said the dealer.

"I didn't touch the table!" Charlene Barth had too much to drink.

The dealer politely repeated his warning. "Please keep your hands off the table."

Charlene flipped her auburn hair and deliberately slapped the green velvet surface. The other players stared, disgusted. The game stopped. Before a second breath could be drawn, security appeared. Sonny Barth's wife didn't go quietly.

I fed nickels into a machine and squealed delightedly when three apples appeared in a row and a jangling silver stream fell through the slot. Before long my jackpot vanished. The slots constant ting-a-ling, the sweeping strobe lights, the cigarette smoke were too much for me. I wasn't ready to climb this rung, but had fun peeking into that world, knowing it existed.

The white sand beach was much more alluring. I shared space with a few mothers watching their toddlers, and teenagers barred from the casino.

Will Fleming dropped into the lounge chair next to mine. "Hi."

"Hi yourself— where's Stephanie?" He'd taken a lot of kidding concerning his Barbie.

Earlier, Henry Johnson had asked Will. "Where do you find these fillies?"

"Easy, Henry, buy a boat and they come to you." Will replied.

The jealous men needled the captain. Instead of beautiful, exciting companions, they had their wives along.

Unexpectedly, I, too, experienced a jealous tinge followed by an unsettling disappointment. Somehow, I had imagined this trip would be *our* vacation. Hadn't he said a while back we should take a break from the council business?

He dribbled sand on my bare thigh. "How's it going?"

"Quit that," brushing off the sand more vigorously than necessary.

"Stephanie's gone to the casino. The kids?—"

"Loving it," I pointed to the ocean. "They're swimming."

"They're great kids." He looked at me quickly as if concerned that complimenting my children would somehow upset me.

"Thank you. I think so, too."

His sailor eyes slowly scanned the ocean, observing the rolling waves, the horizon rim, the terns soaring, dipping. His gaze caught my children, bobbing in the water, "Your protection."

"What do you mean?" He had the uncanny way of knowing me through to the bones as no one else ever had, not even Joe.

"We all use something or somebody to insulate us from real life."

"My life couldn't be more real."

"Nothing missing?—"

I shifted away, curled my legs under and gave him a cold shoulder. Sure, something was missing. Both Will and my mother knew it. The desire to be physically and emotionally linked to another human gnawed like unsatisfied hunger. "My life is perfect, how's yours?"

"Perfect, my blonde keeps me out of trouble."

"You mean she keeps you in trouble."

"No, out of trouble—are you feeling better?"

"Much. Thanks. That council seems a hundred light years away."

He dribbled sand through his fingers. "It can get to you, all right. You have to learn, Hannah. In politics "no" doesn't exist. You say yes, *but* and qualify *but*. You form a committee, you put it on the agenda, you shepherd it along until sometime, from somewhere, some solution materializes."

"You mean talk out of both sides of your mouth."

"That's a crude way to put it."

"I can't do that."

"You need to learn. You're too valuable not to be re-elected."

"Heaven forbid. I'm not running for re-election."

"Everybody says that and in the end they have a change of heart and run again."

"Why is that?"

"Because you get caught up in the work and there's so much left to do. Before you know it, the term is over and you need more time."

"These two years are stretching from here to eternity, as far as I'm concerned. The longest two years of my life. Are you running again?"

"Probably not, it's been quite an experience, but the whole thing has a surreal quality."

Will was my much-needed ally on the council. "Whatever made you run for council in the first place?" I'd been dying to ask that question since day one. "New people never do that."

"I've been here three years."

A giggle escaped me. He needed an education. "I've been here twenty, since I married Joe, and I'm still not one of them."

"What does it take?"

"Blood line to General Robert E. Lee, for starters, and the ability to connect to all the aunts, uncles and relatives hanging on the family tree; and if an ancestor fought in the Civil War, so much the better."

"Which side?"

I looked at him in mock horror. "Must you ask? You'll never make it."

"To tell you the truth, Uncle Percival goaded me into it. He said there was a good chance that I'd settle down and hit gold on the council. I bet him I wouldn't."

"Gold?—what are you talking about? There's no gold! There's no money! Only problems and headaches! How in the world did you ever get elected?"

"Befriended the shrimp people, helped seed their oyster beds and gutted catfish for Mooney over at his restaurant. Any of that will get a person elected."

"It will not."

"I'll confess, then. I engineered a contract for the shrimp fishermen to sell their catch in Chicago. Shrimp brings four times as much there. The men were grateful. They gave jambalaya dinners and fish fries and invited their friends. I'm sure you know that routine."

Campaigning had been so easy for him! No schedule to rearrange, no meals skipped, no side job to make ends meet. His vote stomping was more lark than challenge. "Well, I want to forget the whole business for three entire days. Is that possible?"

"Doubt it," he replied companionably.

The book resting on my chest, I closed my eyes and basked in the sun's warmth. Will did likewise. After a while his hand reached over and clasped mine and we had a link, a wordless connection, a right feeling. When I opened my eyes again, my kids had disappeared, and Stephanie was running lightly over the sand toward us. The youthful bikini-clad girl, legs long and slender, wafer thin, surrounded by the vaulted blue sky, white foaming waves and swaying coconut trees, formed a perfect picture postcard.

I retrieved my hand. "Your girlfriend is gorgeous," bit my tongue and swallowed, "so young."

"I like gorgeous women."

Stephanie kicked sand on Will, her pretty face a pout. "Did we come all the way to the Bahamas so you could sit and talk jails and dumps and Pohainake Parish with Miz Hannah?" Without meaning to, she aged me a generation. "If you don't quit, I'm going to pack up and go home."

She was cute, vibrant, brimming with youth and life. She had a bright smile, and white, pearly teeth. "We both think alike. Take him away, Stephanie."

She reached for Will's hand still warm from mine, and pulled him to his feet. "Come, Sweetie." She rubbed his bare thigh with her bare foot, blinked her lashes and gave him a promising look. "We have lots better things to do than this."

***

In the evening, torches lit the hotel patio, the flames flaring into the starlit night. A marimba band played. Drummers wearing shirts with ruffled sleeves beat bongos while thrusting forth one hip and then the other. Two barefoot natives, stripped to the waist, their bodies sweaty, gleaming, held a limbo stick across one side to the other.

Suzy jerked her way under the stick, hopping forward with little motions, a red hibiscus tucked in her flowing hair, bending back from the waist until her head almost touched the ground. I thought she'd break in two.

"Now, that's a beautiful girl." Will Fleming took the stool next to mine.

"Yes, she is." My eyes followed Suzy as she bent and gyrated. She had long, tanned legs and a slim build. A few more years and she'd be gone. Bobby would be gone.

A tremendous nostalgia overwhelmed me, a desire to freeze time, a longing for my old life: PTA, baking cookies, vacuuming rugs and driving carpool, a peaceful, uneventful existence, a safe haven compared to my present situation. How radically my life had changed since the divorce! One crisis after another! Naturally, Joe and I had problems, what couple didn't? How naïve I was to think the situation a bump on the marital road, something we'd get over and laugh about in our old age!

Captain Fleming ordered a Margarita on the rocks. "For you?—"

"Frozen—"

When the drinks came, Will asked, "How long have you been divorced?"

"Two years and four months."

"And how many days?—" I detected the same impatient tinge in his voice I often heard in Mom's. Let it go! Move on!

"I have my children, my wonderful children. They give me purpose."

"Nothing wrong with having purpose—"

I thought of Mom. Sending for her to come and help me had given her renewed purpose, a new lease on life. "What's your purpose, Will?"

"My purpose is," he narrowed his eyes, "to seduce you."

"Oh, my, my!—"

He took a long swallow of his drink, "Whenever you're ready."

My glass was empty and Will had it refilled. The margarita made me light-headed. Was this my third or fourth? I swallowed a hiccup. "I have purpose. You know what my purpose is? My purpose is to pave every road! Pour black tar over the whole wide world and fill every pothole!" The captain observed me closely. His eyelashes were pale gold and very thick. "No trash anywhere!

One little Milky Way wrapper thrown from a car, hundred dollar fine! Jail, maybe. Wouldn't that be just dandy?"

"Those goals are commendable, but they are for other people." He stared at the ice cubes in his glass as if they were tarot cards. "What is your goal for you?"

Suzy made it under the limbo stick. The onlookers clapped. She joined us giggling and laughing as only a fourteen-year-old can. I was spared an answer.

"Hi, Captain Fleming, are you buying my mom a drink?"

"No," he replied. "We have a tab going. We're charging it to the parish council."

"That's not even funny," I protested. "First thing you know somebody will repeat that and we'll have to crawfish our way out."

He patted my hand. "Relax. Suzy won't tell."

"Where's Jenny?" I asked.

"Somewhere, I dunno. She went with Bobby."

That registered. Bobby had lately taken to long hours in the bathroom, shaving and slapping cologne on his cheeks. He spent every spare minute sleeping and one day last week when Gramma was tidying his room, she found a *Hustler* under his bed.

"His hormones are raging," Gramma announced. "You need to give him The Talk."

That thought had also entered my mind, but I hadn't found the right opportunity to broach the subject. What did you say to a boy? Hey, you can get girls pregnant now and they are wicked and will lead you on, so keep your dick in your pants so you won't get in terrible trouble? Or should I use political double-speak as Will Fleming recommended? Cloud the issue with condoms, The Pill, masturbation, AIDS and HIV? Did they have a sex class at school? I should inquire and make him take it. To let the school instruct my boy on such a vital subject didn't seem right. Had Joe talked to Bobby?

My imagination jumped hurdles. "Go find your brother." Suzy meandered along the veranda, skirting the dancing couples. With a sigh, I confessed to Will, "I have to sit down and have a serious talk with Bobby. He's discovered girls."

Will laughed. "Most boys do."

Another sigh escaped me. "It's not easy."

"Sure it is. Go for a ride with him or dunk a few basketballs. Don't make it a big deal." Will's voice was deep and comforting. My head grew lighter and lighter. Eyes green as the sea, chin cleft, reach and touch, no, no, NO! His hand rested on the bar, mine next to his, my fingers, his fingers, ten fingers. His were strong and thick, nails cut blunt and fine blonde hair; mine, long and slender, the flesh soft, the nails manicured and colored dark pink. His slow and moving fingertips trailed across the space between us and came to rest on mine. My head found comfort in the shoulder pressing against me. The closeness, the intimacy!—I turned away. Was this maudlin condition brought on by my loneliness, my broken heart? Too many margaritas, yes, okay, only one more—

"Here." Will Fleming reached for a cocktail napkin. "Blow your nose. There come Suzy and Jenny."

"We can't find Bobby," Suzy said.

My heart jumped into my throat. Had he drowned? Gotten lost? Been kidnapped by a native? Had he sneaked into the casino and been nabbed by security? These things happened.

"Don't panic," Will said. "Keep drinking. I'll go find him."

Not much later, Will returned, Bobby in tow. My son's face was flushed red and he wouldn't look me in the eye. He stared over my head and I just *knew,* the way a mother knows, intuition, built-in radar, that sixth sense one has when it comes to one's children.

"Where have you been?" I asked.

"Around—"

"Around where?—" My head was spinning.

"He's okay, Hannah," Will said. "Let it ride. You kids go to your rooms and stay there."

Suzy saluted him, "Aye, aye, Captain!"

As they walked away, the two girls flanked Bobby as if protecting him.

"Where was he?" I asked Will.

"You don't want to know."

"Yes I do. He's my son and I need to know."

"Well." Will drained his glass, put it down and looked away for a second. Then he said thoughtfully, "You know that talk you planned to have with Bobby?"

"Yes?"

"It's too late."

"You found him with a girl?"

"Better than with a boy, for sure, but it wasn't just any girl." His wry laugh made me angry. I saw no humor in the situation.

"Every boy needs to have an older woman in his life. Somebody experienced who will introduce him to the art of mating with finesse and gentleness. Young kids, y'know, just grope, grasp and gasp, not a very rewarding experience."

"For crying out loud!—" Red bombs were bursting in my brain, giving me kaleidoscopic vision, bits and pieces of color dancing before my eyes—"*Who*?"

"I can assure you from personal experience she was the very best."

I grabbed him by his shirt collar, "For God's sake, who?" Who'd led my boy to this low point in his life? Seduced and induced him, a minor, a child, not yet 18, not old enough to smoke or be drafted! My baby boy! I'd kill her. Will's sardonic laugh infuriated me. I lost control, went berserk, not aware that I'd raised my hand until I heard the whack, "Who, dammit, who?"

"Stephanie," he said, rubbing his cheek, "My very own Stephanie."

***

Days when the council didn't have a regular or an emergency meeting, I declined all invitations, stayed home, cooked supper and attempted to interest my children in family quality time. They were not receptive. Suzy preferred her friends. Ever since the Bahamas trip Bobby had been withdrawn, the only answers to my questions sullen grunts and monosyllables. When he came home after school, he stayed in the back yard, throwing a football or went directly to his room and locked the door.

We had not spoken about his indiscretion since the original shouting match, and the deed hung over our heads like Marie Antoinette's guillotine. The two times I attempted to have The Talk with him, he pursed his lips and turned his back.

"He hasn't been his old self since the Bahamas," Gramma said. "What's the matter with him?"

"I don't know."

"What happened down there?"

I wasn't going to tell her my son lost his virginity to a woman I thought too young for Will Fleming and too old for Bobby. I was a bad mother and must live with the consequences, but didn't intend to share my guilt. At night, tossing, worried sick, wondering if Joe knew, did Bobby confide in his father? Would our son talk to *him* and not *me?* Me who fed and clothed him, struggled to keep him safe, lived through his everyday highs and lows, his teenage moods and rebellion? My one consolation was the thought that Joe didn't know. If he had known, he'd be knocking down my door, yelling obscenities, threatening to take the kids away, screaming court order. My salvation was that his princess didn't want to be bothered with my children. For that I loved the woman I hated.

For the hundredth time I asked myself why had I run for a council seat? Was it to escape the *boring* label? Was it to prove something, I knew not what? Was it anger at Joe for abandoning me? Was it one martini too many? Was it the day I bolted from Murt's Café, leaving Barbara with a half-eaten meal, and wandered aimlessly through the mall, killing another hour until the kids got home from school, wondering what I was going to do with my life, what was to become of me, trying jeans two sizes too small, loitering at Books A Million and finally buying a book, *Dress for Success*. By 5 p.m., I'd wandered home, fixed a Martini, then a second one, took the drinks into the den and collapsed into the wing-chair (Joe took *his* recliner), watching the news, the Louisiana attorney general on a rampage. Upper body resting half way across the desk, he raised his head at an angle and gnashed his teeth. "Today I have appointed an administrator to oversee the Pohainake Parish government, his tenure concurrent to that of a newly elected council. I cannot emphasize enough how important it is for honest citizens—*me*— to express concern—*me*—be watchdogs—*me*— run for the council—*me? Too much gin, Hannah Han, too much gin—* The blonde, 5 o'clock news anchor with the sleeveless dress and perfect arm muscles, loomed on the screen to interpret what the AG had said in plain English. Her saccharine smile ignited an all-engulfing rage that swept through me like a red hot blaze, burning my stomach and sending boiling acid into my throat. From the molten heat fueled by drink emerged an impossible thought. *Why not, why the hell not? I'm not going to live in a rut. I'm me. I'm free. I'm intelligent. I can lose weight. I can do anything that girl can do. I can do better than any man on that council.* No one was going to bury me alive—not my ex-husband nor his princess, not the richest man in town, nor my friends, not even my children. My tense fingers trembled when I dialed Mr. Percival's office.

My mother's voice dragged me back to the present. "Listen! Are you listening to me? Bobby will get over whatever it is," Gramma said. "Boys that age need a male figure in their lives."

"Great. I'll order one from Sears and Roebuck."

"It's you I'm worried about. It wouldn't hurt you to start looking. Go party. Have some fun. Work, work, work all the time is making you dull."

"Please!" *Dull!* Did everybody classify me as *dull?*

"Date somebody, anybody."

"Thanks a lot."

Maybe Gramma had a point. Maybe I should start circulating, dating someone who wouldn't mind two teenagers hanging on, become the type woman who painted herself like Cleopatra and frequented bars, the mirrors reflecting her desperation. Courting took time, a luxury I didn't have. I recalled my friend Barbara's rationalization when explaining why after Sam's frequent escapades, she never left him. 'The nerve!' she said. 'One hussy sat in my living room and told me she loved my husband! What did I say? Honey, I know the feeling. I do, too!' Barbara's theory was simple and direct: 'Finding a man,' she said, 'is akin to buying new shoes. Go to the store, eye the merchandise, select a pair, try them for size, either buy them or not. If you do take the shoes, it may take a lifetime to break them in right." In my exhausted state, finding a new mate took more energy than I could muster.

Mom persisted. "Go out with that nice Captain Fleming."

Will Fleming came close to melting my frozen heart, and try as I might, the icy numbness that had made life bearable would not solidify again. Let down my guard and what happened? His bimbo seduced my son! I hated Will Fleming! Despised the man!

"I'm managing just fine, Mama."

"Sure," she replied. "That's why you cry yourself to sleep every night. You'll have a breakdown if you don't lighten up. Your children deserve better."

Mama had done it again. Skewered things around until the blame, the guilt settled squarely on me. My mother was good at that.

CHAPTER 15

Our Southern fall didn't have the dramatic Northern color changes, but nevertheless, the season invigorated us. The relentless heat abated, the humidity lifted, and we felt as if we were floating in thin air. After Labor Day, everyone put away sandals and white shoes and found a sweater or two.

Pohainake Parish hosted the annual October parish fair. School closed for three days. Friday night was beauty pageant night. The occasion resembled a mini Miss America contest. Pohainake Parish Queen and Princesses were selected. The Prettiest Baby title was awarded. Mothers trained and preened their toddlers as if they were registered poodles entering an AKC competition. The girls in Suzy's freshman class entered the Princess competition. Suzy didn't want to be left out. At 14, she wanted to do whatever everybody else was doing.

"You're the most beautiful girl I know," I said, kissing her forehead. "Go for queen."

"I can't, Mom. You have to be 18. And I need a sponsor for princess. Can you sponsor me?"

"I wish, but that's not possible. I'm on the council."

"God, I'm so sick of that council! Everybody talks! Everything we do!"

"Oh, Sweetie—"

"You like it, Mom. You like the attention and being important. I hate it! I hate it!" and she stormed from the kitchen, leaving me frustrated and confused.

Next afternoon, she asked, "Can Habitat sponsor me?" A logical request, so innocently presented.

"They do houses, not beauty pageants," a non-profit organization. "Your dad, have you asked him?"

"Hold my breath, the university is sponsoring Dean Miller's daughter."

Four days before the deadline, "Gramma said she'd ask Mr. Percival."

"You talked to Gramma about this?"

"I see her more than I see you, Mom." Spread the guilt like peanut butter on bread, smooth and even from edge to edge, then the clincher, the noose around the neck, feel bad of all feel bads. "I guess I'll be the only one not in the pageant."

"Oh, Sweetie, don't say that. I'll find you a sponsor."

"Sure, in three days?"

Another day passed, and no sponsor. The businesses, enterprises and civic clubs had their own obligations. The girls at school yakked about the dress they planned to wear, the first high heels, the trip to the beauty parlor. Suzy grew quieter, more and more withdrawn, the girl at a ball waiting to be asked when her classmates were already dancing.

I debated calling Joe. Could he help his daughter? Did he have any connections? Did he know how upset Suzy was? My hand reached for the phone a dozen times, lifted the receiver and put it down. Suzy was at his place this weekend. Certainly, she told her dad. He knew. Did he care?

Thursday night Gramma played poker. She came in the kitchen door, nearly eleven, too late for a senior citizen to be roaming the planet. I sat at the table nursing a cup of tea, restless, unable to sleep, my daughter in pain, my mother gadding about, my son not talking to me, life one huge colossal mess. Mama's cheery demeanor rubbed me the wrong way. She was happy, beaming. "How much did you win?" I asked.

"I took them to the cleaners, but better still, I have a sponsor for Suzy."

"Not Mr. Percy."

"No, a Florida yacht company, remember? I live there. It came to me like a lightning bolt. What's $100 to them? Chicken feed! I called and they were delighted to do it for me."

My heart surged and I restrained the inclination to wake Suzy. This good news could be a Gramma pipe dream having no foundation in fact. "What yacht company?"

"International Yacht Design and Sales, you can check if you want."

"You sure?—" My mind jumped to Will Fleming's boat, the drawings tacked on the wall, the blue print rolls in the cubby holes. "How did—?"

She gave me her top sergeant nurse look, the one that made a soldier turn over and expose his butt for the hypodermic. "Never mind how I did it. I did it. This is your daughter's happiness we're concerned about."

The activity that followed Gramma's coup should go on record. Suzy and Jenny spent the afternoon before fair day applying lemon and hydrogen peroxide to highlight their hair.

"That concoction will make your hair fall out," Gramma warned. "You'll look like bald eagles."

All night long the girls talked and giggled in Suzy's room, happy teenagers, not a care in the world.

In twenty-four hours we managed to transform Suzy from a gawky freshman to a Hollywood star. Blonde hair conditioned to a shine, cascading to her shoulders. Lips red and blush highlights, pale lavender eye shadow; mascara emphasizing long, sweeping eyelashes. Wearing a flowing emerald gown, her first strapless top, she looked royal, a true princess.

She won a place in the Queen's Court. Overcome with pride and excitement, I jumped from my front row seat, bounded to the stage steps and gave her a big, embarrassing hug. The photo taken by the Daily Sun reporter appeared in the local papers. The cut line read: *"Councilwoman's Daughter A Princess."*

At breakfast the next morning, Suzy asked, "You think I won because of you?"

"No, Sweetie. You won because you were the most beautiful girl there."

"Then why does the newspaper have to say 'councilwoman's daughter?' "

How could I explain? It made no sense to me, either. She was a person in her own right, a young girl competing with other girls on an equal footing. Why did the press always have to muddle everything?

Gramma laughed and said, "Listen, Suzy. Your mother is now a public figure. Deal with it. Suck that teat for all its worth."

"Gramma!—" Suzy and I both cried at once.

Suddenly, the whole ridiculous situation made Suzy and me laugh and Gramma, too, and we waltzed around the kitchen. Suzy grabbed a plate with scrambled eggs remnants and flung it in the air. It hit the floor and broke to pieces. Gramma yanked the table cloth and dishes crashed. My daughter leapt on the table and waved the fork she held in her hand as if it were a scepter. Gramma and I bowed to her as we second-lined around the upturned chairs.

"What in the world?" Bobby stood at the kitchen door, surveying the damage.

"I'm a princess," Suzy said, "and these lowly ones are my subjects."

"Come dance with us," I invited.

He gave us a sullen look and left the room.

"Reality check," Gramma said. "Am I going to be the one to clean up this mess?"

***

Next morning Suzy entered the kitchen dressed in the new tailored navy blue suit and black high heel pumps. She looked so grown up! I offered my good pearls, but she turned them down. "They're dated, Mom," she said, snapping the catch on funky glass beads. "These are in." Somewhere Gramma found a perky navy and white cloche. Susie immediately donned the hat. "Perfect, Gramma! Perfect!" I felt a jealous twinge. My pearls had been rejected.

A 10 a.m. parade started the Saturday festivities. Bands from every school assembled at Harmony Square, noisily tooting their instruments. Sparkling dance teams strutted in place. Civic associations decorated flatbed trucks with fall motifs, pumpkins, crepe paper flowers and fleur-de-lis reflecting our French heritage.

The governor arrived to lead the grand march. The Parish Queen, riding a silver Mustang convertible, looked resplendent in her rhinestone tiara and blue sash.

A Baton Rouge Mercedes-Benz dealership had offered the fair committee Mercedes convertibles, an act that generated great controversy. Why go to another city for cars when we had local dealers who supported the fair as well as other parish projects? The Mercedes Benz people didn't vote in our parish while Ford Harmony Motors where Henry Johnson worked had 20 people who did. And GM?—were we going to ignore them? No way! To keep the balance and the peace, the fair committee obtained a car from each local auto dealer. Such great energy expended on nit-picky arguments left diminished stamina to tackle bigger issues.

Each princess rode in a convertible, her name and her sponsor's name on the car door. Tiara in place, holding a rose spray, their smiles as wide as the Grand Canyon, waving their royal wave, they perched on the car trunks, feet dangling over the back seat.

Suzy and I rode in Will's Corvette. "It's okay," he said, his crooked smile in place. "I ordered it through the Harmony dealership."

The Parade committee saw no logic in my request for another car assignment. They were short on convertibles and Will Fleming was willing to lend his to the cause. My daughter was riding and my fellow councilman was driving, what was the problem? I couldn't properly explain the problem.

Sitting next to Will for two slow, torturous miles, one end of Harmony's Main Street to the other would've once been fun. We would've laughed and made sardonic comments about the people in the crowd. Amid the noise and gaiety, we would've discussed strategy for overcoming the next big hurdle. We would've been friends, but no more.

The Corvette followed the Harmony High School Band. The kids played a loud, off-key Sousa march, the heat and effort staining their red uniforms. Twirlers threw batons high and with a quick wrist twist caught them. The dance teams swayed and strutted, lifted their boots and shook red and white pompoms.

"Hey! Will! Over here! Will! Throw me something, Mister!" a big-breasted girl wearing a skimpy halter top and short shorts yelled the Mardi Gras mantra. She approached the Corvette. "Will! Will! Over here! Throw me something, Mister!"

He leaned and handed her a trinket. She squealed and kissed his cheek. The crowd loved it. Other young girls surged toward the Corvette. Suzy knew them all. The girls hooted and howled. "Lucky you!—" "Wanna trade places?" "Don't ya love him?"

I felt as if I were my daughter's bodyguard, suspicious and alert, protecting her from the evil that Will Fleming brought into our family.

Suzy beamed and waved. She tapped Will's shoulder. "Wow, man! You're a cool dude!"

"My, but we're popular," I hurled a plastic cup stamped Pohainake Parish Fair into the crowd. The real politicians flung engraved key chains. "Whatever happened to your Stephanie?" *Jezebel who ruined my son!* "She couldn't make it?"

He gave me a contained look as if he were laughing inside and didn't want his merriment showing. "You know," he replied as he handed another admiring cutie glittering, second-hand Mardi Gras beads. "I think my Barbie found her Ken."

"You must be heartbroken."

"Oh, for sure, can't you tell?"

Barricades restrained the jumping, ebullient crowd. A young boy wearing a Harmony High School football jacket called, "Hey! Suzy! Suzy! Over here!"

An overwhelming angst engulfed me. If I dealt so poorly with Bobby's problem what would happen when Suzy discovered boys? She could get pregnant! She could be ruined! Joe would take her away from me! My baby! My little girl! My beautiful little girl, growing up!

As if he had read my thoughts, Will reached and squeezed my hand. I pulled away. "Suzy is a beautiful girl. Before long she'll have boys swarming all around her. You've got to deal with it."

"Shut up."

"And if you hold her too tight—"

"Exactly what I need," I snapped, "Advice from a derelict bachelor."

"You are a wonderful mother. You have great kids. Just remember, you've made a nest, not a cage."

Before a proper, scorching retort escaped me, (what business was it of his?) the parade came to a standstill, half the bands and floats east of the railroad tracks, the other half west. Amtrak's City of New Orleans zipped through town going to Chicago. Train passengers looked through the windows and waved.

The parade resumed and school children slipped past, red, blue, green shirts, ribbons and satin bows. A dog escaped his leash, running alongside. A daddy hoisted a kid onto his shoulders for a better view. Mothers hung onto toddlers.

"Look, Mom!" Suzy cried. "There's Gramma!"

Gramma and her friends, one in a wheelchair, another in a walker, and suddenly my focus changed, and I thanked God that Gramma hadn't reached that stage yet, that she could still load the dishwasher and wash my clothes. Where would I be without her? In an insane asylum, probably—I determined to be nicer, kinder to my mother. After all, she could bail and go back to Florida, and then I'd really be in a jam. And she was the one who found the sponsor, bless her heart.

The cranky one in the wheelchair yelled what was on her mind, the way old people do. "Politicians!—no-good politicians ruining our parade—Nobody wants to see you! Shoo! Shoo! Get on by!"

I agreed. Never in my worst nightmare did I dream that a councilwoman would be so constantly in the public eye. In my naïve way I thought, the council meets twice a month, how much time could that entail? Then I'd go home to my normal life. What was my normal life? I no longer remembered.

***

Flags and streamers decorated the Pohainake Fair Grounds. Every civic organization had a fund-raising booth. Kiwanis sold pies, Lions collected eye glasses for the blind, PTA advertised chicken barbecue plates. Besides the talent contests, there were pie-eating, jambalaya cooking, beauty pageants, racing competitions, sack-hobbled relays, apple-bobbing and a dunking booth.

Magnum Carnival Inc. arrived a day early to place the Ferris wheel, roller coaster and merry-go-rounds in place. Excitement mounted as the kids watched the big trucks loaded with bright-colored equipment rolling through town headed for the fair grounds. In addition to the rides, the Magnum workers manned dart and ring tossing booths and a distorted mirror maze. The same fat lady came every year, as did a contortionist and a midget who swung a heavy maul. He drove the tent pegs into the hard ground.

Every politician, elected or aspiring, was present. Where else could one gather a crowd as big as this to stump for votes?

Will and I had the official duty of judging the livestock in the Cow Palace, an open shelter. Since our political onset, we'd been paired and the arrangement was hard to shake.

"I don't know a thing about cows," I said, tight-lipped, as we picked our way between brown patties.

The stalls held heifers, foals, horses, chickens and rabbits and the rarer species, emus, alpacas, and llamas. The place smelled of hay and dung. The young owners anxiously waited for the judges, stroking their animal, combing a hairy coat, shining a hoof, braiding a tail.

"There's nothing to worry about," Will assured me. "The university Ag department is doing the actual judging. We'll hand the winner the blue ribbon and a certificate and let the press take a picture."

We flanked the winners, Will Fleming left, me right, a great and complicated tension between two council members barely speaking to each other. We smiled for the camera.

***

Everything paled in comparison to Saturday afternoon's event, the Dunking Booth. The man running the dunk helped me to climb the tall ladder.

"Don't worry, Miz Hannah. The vat is 10 feet deep. If you fall it's perfectly safe. Somebody has to hit that gong," he pointed to a big brass plate, "and that doesn't happen often."

When a dunker threw a hard rubber ball and struck the plate, a mechanism triggered, tipped the narrow plank seat and toppled the dunkee into the water below. I followed Sheriff Branson. He'd been walloped twice. From this perch high above the vat, the water below looked murky and roiled. Ugh! I hoped the sheriff hadn't peed in it.

The booth had a long line waiting to pay $10 and receive three baseballs. The first ten minutes seemed interminable. I flinched every time a person threw a ball, but when nobody hit, I relaxed and enjoyed the view from the top: people milling, Ferris wheel slowly turning, cars parking in the nearby field, entire families arriving, unfolding strollers for toddlers, picnic baskets and soft drink coolers, no beer or hard liquor allowed, everywhere perpetual motion, people meandering booth to booth, children running freely while adults chatted and visited. Twenty minutes more and I'd be down from here, another ridiculous mission accomplished.

Looking down again, scanning the crowd, I couldn't believe my eyes. Bobby, clutching three balls, stood in line. A cheering crowd egged him on. His face was set and his eyes had a determined look, as if his hour had come and he could now get even for all that stood between us.

The only way my son would miss was on purpose.

Mentally, I measured the vat below. I must fall feet first, keep my arms close to my sides and hit the water dead center.

I tried to catch Bobby's eye and engage him in mental telepathy. *"I am your mother. Don't you dare,"* but he wouldn't return my look, preferring to stare somewhere above my head.

He missed the first throw. I gasped, relieved. He wasn't going to dunk me! Or was he purposely extending my agony?

A man yelled, "Best baseball pitcher in the Harmony High League and you can't hit that mark?"

A woman hollered, real hate in her voice. "Get your mother! Hit that woman!" I looked for the person belonging to the voice, but couldn't find her.

Bobby pitched the second ball. Another miss!

"Here, give me that ball! I'll show you." An old man tried to pry the last ball from Bobby's hand.

A scuffle ensued. The old man was no match for Bobby who shoved him away. We now had a situation that wouldn't be solved unless the best baseball pitcher in the league hit the mark.

I gritted my teeth, no point in us both suffering. "Go ahead!" I yelled. "Hit the mark! Hit the mark! You can do it!"

Bobby gave me a long, hard look, an eye-to-eye packed with sullen resentment, teenage rebellion, and manhood crowding in.

He rubbed the third ball between his two hands, raised his arms above his head, touched left ankle to right knee, brought the ball to his chest, drew back and hurled.

CHAPTER 16

Thanksgiving week, Dr. Moore removed the sling. I'd been cradling my left arm close to my body while the dislocated shoulder mended. Catapulted from the plank seat above the water vat, I cringed, halfway turned and dunked at an angle that smashed my shoulder against the metal side. Bobby was apologetic. "I'm so sorry, Mom, *so sorry!*"

"It's okay." The gulf between us widened.

Since Joe and the princess were going skiing during Christmas vacation, we had swapped holidays. He had the kids for Thanksgiving. Mom flew to Fort Lauderdale for the week. The house was big and lonely. I rattled through the empty rooms, empty nest! A catch phrase coined by a pop psychiatrist. How often those words with little thought and less hope were bandied about!

The kitchen cleaned, the beds made, the rugs vacuumed, what else to do? The weather was chilly. We might have a frost. The fern baskets on the patio could turn brown and die. I moved them into the shed where not so long ago Ben Two had crouched in fear; plucked stray weeds sprouting in the rose bed; tamped dirt into a hole a mole burrowed and packed the earth solid—death to all destroyers of fertile lawns. Ten o'clock, just ten? The whole day loomed long as a year before me.

I'd turned down several invitations to dinner. Thanksgiving was a time for family, for sharing with relatives and loved ones, the blessings of food and camaraderie. I wouldn't be the odd woman invited because I was alone on this day, without husband, without children who today were happily eating at Murt's Café or Jake's Restaurant. Bobby and Suzy tattled. Their stepmom didn't cook! *Stepmom!* Was she gaining their favor, taking them away from me?

A thought unexpectedly entered my mind. What was Will Fleming doing this family day? Did he spend Thanksgiving alone or visiting Uncle Percy and the old men? Or did he have beautiful girls aboard his *Serenity* drinking wine and feeding him grapes, Nero fiddling while Rome burned?

I was angry at Will, but I missed his friendship, missed the way we discussed serious issues and brainless trivia, missed sharing the little daily triumphs, the ones he helped me achieve, seconding the motion, silent rock in the background. I resented, despised and hated this loyal friend while pining for our old relationship. Nothing made any sense.

More than anything, I yearned for my family, the ideal home, mom, pop, children, banging doors and yapping dogs, the *"Father Knows Best"* sitcom life. The silent, lonely house overwhelmed.

A good run, a fast dash around the park would clear my head, lift my heart and erase this blue funk mood. I changed into jogging shorts and running shoes, circled the Harmony Park jogging trail twice and couldn't relax, growing more tense worrying about the jail that wasn't built, the land fill not constructed, the court date on Monday to explain to the judge why nothing, absolutely nothing, was happening. His Honor might put us all in jail. He'd said in no uncertain terms, come back with a plan or suffer the consequences.

Thinking of Gramma raising my two kids because their idiotic, dumb mother was behind bars in a four by six cell, or worse yet, Joe taking them and the princess becoming their *mom* instead of their *stepmom,* drove me crazy. I ran and sniffed, then bawled and ran, three, four, five laps on the winding trail, tears streaming and nose running. I don't know how long this maudlin spree lasted. I was digging for a tissue when across the street at the National Guard Armory army trucks, tanks, bulldozers, and varied heavy equipment rumbled into the terminal. Men wearing camouflage swarmed.

Thanksgiving Day and these fellows weren't with their families eating turkey and cranberry sauce. These weekend soldiers, trained to defend our country, regardless of holiday, family or career, were at work, doing their job.

So much equipment! The council spent untold hours figuring how to buy or lease machines to do the landfill work. I didn't know the difference between a Bobcat and a bulldozer, but we needed both and could afford neither, and here were all these shiny, new machines rumbling into the armory, brownish-green monsters beep...beep...beeping as the drivers backed them into place. I was drawn to those machines like a nail to a magnet. Running across the street, I raced through the gate, ignoring the No Visitors sign. A soldier in full-fledged battle gear stopped me. He pulled off a gas mask and took a deep breath. "Can I help you?"

"I need to see the person in charge."

"Captain Hennessy?"

"Yes. That's him."

He looked suspicious, but led me into headquarters, a squat brick building. A dozen men walked in, wearing helmets and gas masks. I seriously wondered if this was a good idea, but too late now. The captain entered the room. He scanned me quickly, visor cap to jogging shoes, raised an eyebrow and extended his hand. "Captain Hennessy."

"Hello." No point beating around the bush. "Captain Hennessy," I blurted, not thinking too clearly, not wanting logic to disrupt irrational thought. "I'm with the parish council. The council has a problem and the National Guard can help us."

He looked skeptical but replied politely, "Let's step into my office."

I took the chair across the desk. Rifles and submachine guns leaned against the walls. Two hand grenades in a wooden box labeled "Out Basket" sat atop his desk. Scattered boxes warned: "DANGER EXPLOSIVES."

"The parish is under a court order to build a sanitary land fill." Captain Hennessy frowned, no doubt wondering how this concerned the National Guard. "We have a deadline December 31st and won't be finished by then because we haven't the equipment or manpower." I didn't share the fact that the council stood a good chance of going to jail since Captain Hennessy didn't know us from Adam, so what did he care if we spent our remaining life behind bars.

Suddenly, Captain Hennessy caught the drift. "And you think the parish can use the National Guard equipment?"

"Yes! Yes! That's it!"

He stood. We were done here. "I'm afraid not."

"One little bulldozer?—you have so many! You wouldn't miss it."

"You understand we're not allowed to do that."

It seemed such a good idea!—a stroke of genius, "Why not?"

"The equipment is for defense in case of war or for rescue in the event of a natural disaster."

In my mind, the landfill qualified on both counts. Was Captain Hennessy the decision-maker, the dominant party, the one who had the ultimate authority? "Captain, all those men, where did they come from?—"

"New Orleans. We're staging a mock war. They're the invaders."

Jesus. They were playing games while garbage buried our parish.

"Is there a general I can talk to?"

He frowned mightily and his upper lip twitched. "Well, our units are under General Zeldom in Algiers, across the Mississippi River."

"Could I talk to him?"

"With the *general*?—"

You'd thought I'd asked to talk to God Himself. "Yes sir, the general. Does he have a phone number?"

Captain Hennessy laughed aloud. "Sure," he said. "Talk to the general. I'll dial him for you." Amazing thing, he did reach General Zeldom. "There's a—" his hand covered the receiver, "what did you say your name was?"

"Hannah Kelly."

"General, there's a Hannah Kelly here in Harmony wants to speak with you." He handed me the phone.

Maybe the general was God, because holding the phone, I became tremendously intimidated, stunned by my own audacity, by that terrible habit of following an impulse, barreling forward without a second thought, consequences aside.

"Hello, General. I'm with the Pohainake Parish Council and we need equipment to build a sanitary land fill and you have all these machines sitting idle here in the armory, and I wondered if we could borrow a couple."

He cut me short. "Not possible," he said, "Can't be done. Good day," Clunk, line dead in my hand.

Captain Hennessy looked smug. "I told you."

"Thank you, anyway. We are desperate. It was worth a try."

***

Sometimes I got on a roll, wanting to see a thing finished, barreling ahead without rhyme or reason, knowing that there should be a solution, that somewhere, somehow, there must be somebody who can help, who can provide answers and not endless carping, negativism and denial. Maybe Mr. Percival could help. He knew everyone, contributed to most causes, and politicians, judges and important people constantly knocked at his door.

Several cars and a motorcycle were parked in Mr. Percy's circular driveway, giving me instant cold feet. What was I doing here Thanksgiving Day? He had company. Guests sat at his table. He carved turkey. Was I crazy? *Throw the car in reverse, back away, bad timing and a real bad plan.*

A hand on the door handle stopped me. Mr. Percy's driver and body guard, said, "I'll park it for you, Miss."

"No, listen—"

He held the door open. The housekeeper appeared on the steps. Trapped by the help! "They're in the den," she said, motioning for me to follow. "I'll let Mr. Percy know you're here."

Standing in the foyer, the curving stairway to the second floor, the oriental carpet runner, the Chinese vase with an immense fresh flower arrangement sitting on a circular table, I saw my reflection in the ornate floor-to–ceiling wall mirror, not just a glance at my face, but full scale view, cotton running shorts and a tee shirt! Bare legged! Bare armed! What was I thinking? Had I lost my mind? Gone crazy? Off came sunglasses and baseball cap. The attempt to smooth my hair was not successful.

I heard footsteps. "Listen," I said over my shoulder. "This wasn't a good idea. I'll see Mr. Percy tomorrow."

"He won't be here tomorrow. He's leaving for a week," Will Fleming answered.

His voice surprised me. I pivoted to face him. "Oh, good, glad you're here. This was a mistake."

"Absolutely not—they're old men killing the day and they'll be happy for the interruption."

"I'm not dressed, I—" suddenly self-conscious.

"Come on, what does that matter?" and then, intuitive as always, asked, "something the matter?"

"Well, I thought I found a solution to the landfill problem, but it didn't work and I thought maybe Mr. Percival—"

"Good timing, the old guys are in the den having a drink."

Mr. Percival, Mr. Songe, Mr. Agee and Mr. Gendre, the elderly gentlemen who quietly kept the parish from falling apart, rose from big leather chairs. The room smelled as if it hadn't been aired in a long time, musty like old money. Bookcases lined the paneled walls, a pool table nearby.

"Please forgive me for barging in," apologetic, at a loss.

"Best intrusion we've had all day," Mr. Percival said, tapping his cigar ashes into an ashtray. "What will you have to drink? Will, fix her a drink."

Not a Margarita. Margaritas got me in trouble in the Bahamas and at this moment I needed to gather my wits. "Wine will be fine."

"Red or white?—"

"Doesn't matter," The only thing that did matter was that I get the hell out of Dodge. "How are you?"

"It's hell to get old, Hannah," Mr. Percy said. "The mind holds, but the body falls apart. How's your mother? How are you?"

I plunged. "Disappointed again, had the neatest solution to the landfill problem, but it was another dead end."

"What was that?"

The white-haired men leaned closer. Mr. Agee wheezed when he breathed, Mr. Songe smelled of good bourbon and prime tobacco. Couldn't tell which one for sure used Old Spice after shave. Will at the bar opening a wine bottle had his back towards us.

I spilled the whole National Guard episode, General Zeldom's instant refusal, my noble intentions and my dashed hopes, the bulldozers and heavy equipment sitting idle, the platoons playing war, the unfairness of life, the constant struggle and the overwhelming weariness. While I whined (well, what else would one call it?) Mr. Percival and his cohorts listened and Will handed me a glass and I gulped wine as if it were a liquid elixir for the unsolvable troubles.

"Ben Zeldom? Went to LSU with his dad, wasn't he a fullback or was it halfback?" asked Mr. Agee.

My bitching and complaining were vents to get the anvil off my chest. Mr. Percival was a good ear, cheaper than a psychiatrist and much more knowledgeable. I never dreamed they knew the army general.

"Can't recall," replied Mr. Percy. "I didn't make the team."

Hard to think these wrinkled, bent-over old men were once vigorous, young bucks. "The general didn't tell me his first name," I said, "but he was rude and abrupt. He hung up on me."

The old men chuckled. "We could give Ben's boy a call," Mr. Agee said. "Wouldn't hurt, might help."

"Would you do that, really?"

"Only if you stayed for Thanksgiving dinner," Mr. Percy extended the invitation.

"Thanks, but I'm not dressed, I couldn't really."

"Yes, she can," Will Fleming said.

So I did. Dinner was a pleasing affair: turkey, dressing, salad, sweet potatoes, green beans, spinach, platter after steaming platter coming through the door, followed by pecan pie, pound cake and baked Alaska, amid stimulating conversation, jokes and laughs, the help dancing through the swinging kitchen door, balancing trays, smiling big, glad to have a fresh face in the stuffy old house.

Time passed quickly. When I left, the sun had set. Captain Fleming followed me to my car. "They'll take care of it," he said.

"You think so?"

"I'd bet on it. You were magnificent."

"I was a disaster," a crash waiting to happen, a hurricane about to hit, a mine ready to explode.

"Sometimes," he said helping me into the car, "it takes a force to makes things happen."

***

Overnight, the National Guard unit erected a tent city on their premises. I looked with great jealousy at the equipment: jeeps, trucks, motor graders, cranes, dump trucks, excavators, forklifts and backhoes scrubbed clean and parked in neat rows. I drove by every day, counting machines and lusting over that equipment the way I once drooled over a spectacular pair of high-heeled shoes. Priorities change.

Soldiers in full battle gear overran the parish. They squatted on street curbs, hid behind pine trees, dug trenches and built bunkers in fields, sped around corners and assaulted each other. Red Cross ambulances roamed our streets, rescuing casualties hit by florescent spray paint bullets. The army invaded Rambo's field, artificial hills, bunkers and water barriers already in place. "Made to order"— Rambo boasted. "Ain't charging 'em nothin', them boys larnin' to defend our country! This is America!"

After two weeks, the mock war ended. Greatly disappointed, I watched the National Guard pack their gear. When the phone rang, the last person in the world I expected to hear was Captain Hennessy. "Okay, take me to this 16th Section."

"You're helping us?"

"Looks that way, somebody tapped the general."

Mr. Percival! He'd saved us again!

The entire council accompanied Captain Hennessy to north Pohainake Parish, to the 16th Section we planned to transform into a sanitary landfill. Our engineer unrolled the blue prints and showed Captain Hennessy the plan.

Engineer Phelps wasn't an optimist. He embraced low expectations, his theory being that if one didn't anticipate much, one wouldn't be greatly disappointed. Since the onset, he'd had few hopes for the sanitary landfill, while I envisioned 640 rolling acres, the garbage buried as soon as dumped, grass growing over it like a green velvet carpet, the place looking like a park.

Captain Hennessy studied the plan carefully then said, "Did you say December 31st?

Henry Johnson nodded vigorously. "That's right."

"Five weeks?"

We were hopeful. The Guard had all that equipment, all those men. "Yes! Yes! " we chorused.

He deliberately rolled the plans. "You people gotta be kidding," he said. "This will take a year."

CHAPTER 17

No, we didn't finish the landfill in six weeks. Captain Hennessy was right. The job would take a year. We did what politicians do, finagled an extension, doctored our evidence and presented the data to Sam Blanchard, our district judge, who bent the federal judge's ear and His Honor Joe Amato gave us three months, then three months more and then the axe. Don't come back again.

True to his word Robert Standish, who collected the parish garbage, didn't voluntarily step aside. His contract, legal or not legal, had been signed by the former council.

"This is endless," I said to the CAAd as we sat in his cramped cubicle going over lawsuits, injunctions, pleadings, court orders and appeals. "Ah! Here's the one we've been waiting for—Robert Standish. He's hired Gypson & Gypson to sue the council." The lawsuit would entail days and days frittered away, lawyer's sessions, hearings, trials, verdicts guaranteed to be contested, and appeals to higher courts. "He will tie us up in court for the next twenty years."

I didn't read the lawsuit. Deciphering whereas and therefore, the double-speak and gobbledygook took a Philadelphia lawyer. Mel Green didn't know Philadelphia, but he understood the syntax and that was his job.

"Relax," CAAd replied in his droll, dry way. "This won't go to court."

"You think Standish is bluffing?"

"No. He thinks he has a legitimate case, but I'm going to talk to him this afternoon."

The council was drinking coffee in the back room during a break in the session called exclusively to deal with garbage. The CAAd had gone to the dump site by himself, and we didn't know exactly what took place. Disjointed bits and pieces of the event drifted into council knowledge.

According to Peewee Reese's version (which no doubt he got from his wife Precious who worked for the sheriff) Ken, the CAAd, arrived at the dump and entered Standish's shack. "Standish kicked the pit bull, y'know de one, white wid dem pink eyes, and said 'Sic him!' The dog sprung from under the desk, growlin' and snarlin', jumped six feet, goin' for the throat. Mr. Ken grabbed the dog round the neck, 90 pounds that mutt weighs, if he weighs an ounce, and when he was through squeezin', the mutt's tongue turned purple and hung down a foot, and dem pink eyes popped clear out of de sockets. Fer sure, Mr. Ken don't look that strong, but when he let go, the dog fell wid a thud, whimperin' and in great pain. He dragged on his belly back to his owner. Mr. Ken's wipin' his lapels and straightenin' his sleeves. They're all messed up and y'all know how finicky he is about his clothes, white shirt, tie and a coat every day in all dis heat. 'I could've killed it,' yessir, that's what he told ole man Standish, 'but that's not what I came to do.'

Standish opened a water tap, soaked a towel and squatted under the desk. He tried to wrap the wet rag round the dog, but the pit bull growled and bared its teeth, Standish coaxin' him all along, 'Come here! Here, Pluto! Pluto!—' He draped a towel over the dog's back, leavin' its tail and snout visible. 'I'm gonna take Pluto to the vet,' Standish raged, 'and I'm sendin' the council the bill. If my dog dies, I'm addin' criminal charges and pain and suffering, too.' Standish breathin' fire, he so mad— 'That's your privilege,' says Mr. Ken. Standish asked, 'What else you think you come to do beside kill my dog?' and Mr. Ken replied, 'I'm here to void the garbage contract.' Dat's right. Dat's what the CAAd said." Peewee knew every little detail and had no qualms sharing information. We were glued to every word he uttered.

"What else did Ken White say to Robert Standish?" Henry Johnson asked.

"That he's goin' to jail for grand larceny," replied Peewee. "Standish laughed in his face."

"Cocky bastard," commented Will Fleming.

"Wasn't cocky when Mr. Ken got through wid him," Peewee said. "Standish met his match."

A mild-mannered mouse conquering a trampling elephant, "And then what?"

"Mr. Ken pulled out his FBI badge."

I knew it! My gut feeling had been right the whole time! The FBI was above the council, the sheriff, the judges. Why, they were the ones who put the insurance commissioner and the registrar of voters behind bars. My CNN image of men wearing gray suits guarding presidents, investigating mafiosos and inserting phone plugs in their ears and talking into their wrists was drastically altered. The FBI men and women were ordinary people doing extraordinary jobs. Ken White was a CPA! "So he's really one of them!" I blurted. Where did that leave us, between a rock and a hard place?

"Mr. Ken gave Robert a choice to either back out of garbage gracefully or—"

We leaned forward not to miss a word. Never in my previous life had I had such a frenzied interest in garbage.

"Or what?" asked Henry.

Peewee's next words fell like a dropped anvil, made my heart beat faster. "He handed Robert Standish a warrant for his arrest."

Henry Johnson didn't believe a word Peewee said. "You're full of shit."

Peewee ignored the remark. "Sheriff Craig Branson signed the arrest warrant himself."

"I'm never going to believe *that!*" Henry Johnson's face turned red. "Sheriff wouldn't do no such thing. Why, Robert Standish is Craig's biggest supporter. He has that huge barbecue every year, invites 600 people and raises all that campaign cash. They're partners in a deer camp. No way would Craig arrest Robert."

Red contributed his two cents. "Reckon CAAd showed Craig Branson the big badge, too. Everybody's out to save their own skin."

The buzzer rang for the council to reconvene. Will Fleming moved that the council draw specifications for garbage collection bids. Red seconded and it passed over Henry's strenuous objection.

"This—" the council president banged the gavel and said, "ain't never gonna happen."

***

A few days later, Wendi handed me the specifications for a Mercedes-Benz garbage truck. The specs rivaled those of a space rocket. Henry Johnson aligned Red Harper and Peewee Reese to vote with him and since no company in the entire South had Mercedes-Benz garbage trucks, he dropped that notion and moved we buy two ISM 305V Cummins engine 305hp, diesel fuel, automatic, Hendrickson suspension, 244 wheelbase; tri-axle, 46,000 lb. rear axle weight; 18,000 lb. front axle weight, all Greek to me, but it didn't matter. He had three votes and Will and I couldn't stop the process. The council would buy the trucks and lease them to Robert Standish, who'd been charged, released on bond and stuck to his guns. He had a valid contract and he would prove it in court.

"The trucks are not the main problem," I said. "The unsanitary dump site is."

"He's working on that," Henry smiled triumphantly. Dump in his territory, he'd run it any way he wanted.

The CAAd sat quietly at the table. Blank-faced, he scratched a few notes on a pad before him.

To finance the garbage trucks the council passed an ordinance that each household must pay $4.50 a month for garbage collection. The citizens revolted. They were okay stuffing their garbage bags into car trunks or truck beds and toting the sacks to the yellow mini-dumps. What happened after that didn't concern them. They could care less whether maggots ate it, or the parish threw it into the Pohainake River, or dug a pit and buried the stuff. The very idea! Paying to have their garbage hauled away! What new graft was this? Whose pockets was this new revenue lining? The citizens had never paid for garbage collection! They would never pay! Nobody could make them pay!

A few days later, sitting in Sonny Barth's office, I asked Sonny, "What happens if people refuse to pay?"

"Tack it on their tax bill."

"Is that legal?" Voice raspy, throat aching, probably some lethal virus picked up at Mr. Standish's dump.

"Pass an ordinance."

Snap your fingers just like that—nothing to it. Make a motion, get a second and carry it by majority vote. Voila! A new law on the books! If people only knew!

"We have to have more money."

"Hannah, you're a broken record, my dear. You know the old saying, can't squeeze blood—"

"Yeah, yeah, we're turnip."

Later that afternoon, I entered Wendi's cubicle. "We've got a citizens' uprising on our hands."

"No doubt—a Mercedes-Benz garbage truck— the ridiculous elevated to the sublime!"

"Where does this go?"

"Give it here. Court orders are filed in the top drawer. Garbage goes right behind Fuckup."

"*Fuckup?—*" I pulled open the drawer and sure enough, the fattest, biggest file there had an orange tab labeled "*Fuckup.*"

Wendi shrugged, "Frivolous lawsuits and threatening court orders that aren't going anywhere."

"Why not a folder labeled *"frivolous"* instead?"

"Probably I was pissed when I filed that day. It takes patience to deal with you people. You're so goddam inefficient."

"Thanks a lot."

"I can't get fired for telling the truth, can I?" She stood and smoothed a postage-sized mini skirt. For a few days after the federal court visit, she'd worn demure skirts and blouses, but soon abandoned the charade. "It's not me," she confessed. "I feel like a maw-maw in those outfits."

"What happens if the council can't meet the garbage deadline?"

"Oh, I'll move the court order from G-Garbage to F-Fuckup and I'll come see you on visiting day."

The ominous threat again! The nightmares about that little enclosed cell! "Anybody ever really gone to jail?—"

She looked at me funny. "Where do you think the insurance commissioner and the registrar of voters are, Disneyland?" She giggled, a long, trilling tinkling laughter, and then without reason or just cause, or perhaps we did have cause, we were both belly-laughing and guffawing until our sides hurt, punch drunk, the whole governing business one great comedic farce.

CHAPTER 18

The day after Thanksgiving Harmony city workers strung white lights across Main Street. Red bows fastened green wreaths to telephone poles. Salvation Army ladies wearing blue uniforms and sturdy black shoes stood in the Wal-Mart parking lot, ringing bells and begging donations. Folks filled with Christian goodwill and abundant cheer clinked coins into the red buckets. Store windows trimmed in tinsel and crammed with toys, electronic gadgets, holiday dresses and Santa Clauses, added cotton tufts or white foam peanuts used for packaging to create the illusion of snow, Southern ingenuity.

Kids pressed their noses to the glass, pining for a Barbie or a train set. When a shop door opened, "Silent Night," "Oh, Little Town of Bethlehem," or "We Three Kings of Orient Are," filled the air then abruptly stopped when the door closed, so that the familiar carols burst upon the sidewalks in uneven sound waves. Shoppers strolled Main Street, hailing one another, stopping to chat, to open a bag and brag on a perfect something they'd found for somebody special.

The Christmas parade the first week in December featured decorated floats, high school marching bands and Santa sitting high on a sleigh and throwing candy.

The only thing the Kelly household had managed to do so far was hang last year's wreath on the front door. Gramma had extended her Fort Lauderdale stay to attend a 75-year old friend's wedding.

"There's always hope," she said when she called. "Love springs eternal. I'll be back next week."

The kids were antsy. Christmas around the corner and we had no decorations, no gifts, no Santa Claus.

Garbage obsessed me. I drove to the 16th Section every day, goading the men to work harder, faster, faster, longer hours, the deadline three weeks away. What would happen when the judge discovered the landfill wasn't complete?

I stopped by the armory one day and talked to Captain Hennessy. We were on good terms now. We visited almost every day, me begging and him refusing. "We need more equipment, more men," I moaned, "or we're not getting it done."

He laughed. He was a gentle, sympathetic soul, easy to get along with once you knew him. His rough, tough demeanor was a façade, a steel armor suit he donned for protection like the knights of old. "I told you in the beginning, this project could never be done by the end of the year, but don't sweat it. I'll send a whole platoon bearing cookies to Angola."

"I'm not going there," I retorted. The sprawling, 1700 acre prison north of Baton Rouge bounded by the Mississippi River and the swamp was for men only. No inmate had ever escaped. They got mired in the swamp and blood hounds retrieved them. "I'm going to St. Gabriel, the woman's prison."

Captain Hennessy reached for the ringing phone. "Hello?" He listened attentively. Okay, I gotcha. She's right here. I'll tell her." He replaced the receiver. "That's Zawesky calling from the landfill. You have a new wrinkle."

My hands flew to either side of my head and squeezed my brain as if were in a vise. "I can't take any new wrinkles. I have enough old ones."

"This one may not be so bad. It could help you."

My eyelids fluttered. Seldom did the council have any good news. "What are you talking about?"

"They're digging the pits and hit gravel."

The import of the discovery went over my head. "So?"

"*So*? Did you say *so*? My dear, finding gravel is like finding gold. Gravel mixed with cement makes concrete. You can sell the stuff by the yard."

My heart palpitated, my excitement monumental. "You really think we can do that? Is there a lot of money in it?"

"Tons—"

"Oh, my God, then we've really got to get after it! I'm dead serious now, Captain Hennessy. You've been so kind, such a big help, I know you won't leave us in a lurch. We need more equipment."

"You have every spare piece of machinery we have. In case of disaster, we'd have to retrieve all *our* gear from *your* 16th Section."

"Can I call the general?"

"He's going to say *'no deal'* and then he'll chew my ass. You can't call the general."

"Is there anything—?"

He shook his head, a resigned motion. "You're something else, you know, a piece of work."

"But there must be something—"

"Okay. Okay. You can't have any more equipment. You can't have any more men, but you can work the ones you have longer, work 'em nights, run a twenty-four hour shift. That's the best I can do. That's *all* I *will* do. Don't come back asking for anything else." He was as challenged as I was. This formidable project was a bigger hurdle than any mock war he had ever presided over.

"Thank you, thank you, thank you—"

Captain Hennessy looked the other way while the council borrowed every generator in his army. Will Fleming's friend who worked for the Power & Light Company hotwired lights and beacons. Men and equipment toiled through the night, backhoes digging dirt, bulldozers pushing dirt, dump trucks dumping dirt, motor graders smoothing dirt, the whole operation a big dirt mess.

At night the beacons lit the woods. The machines' droning and humming disturbed the rural quiet. The monsters dug dirt and unearthed gravel. We sold the pebbles by the yard to ready-mix concrete companies.

The landfill was in Red Harper's district. The guardsmen liked Red, the burly dairy farmer who could sling as much dirt as

135

anybody else. Wearing no shirt under his denim overalls, Red wielded his shovel, pulled his weight. Rambo worked by Red's side. The two men lived frustrated because they couldn't run the heavy equipment. Though either could drive any and all heavy equipment, the National Guard's ironclad rule was that their men must run their machines and if Captain Hennessy caught any Tom, Dick, Harry, Rambo or Red on army equipment, the whole regiment would be pulled off the job.

Henry Johnson's starched white shirt and well-creased pants were conspicuous as he walked around the landfill, holding a shovel, pretending. He contributed nothing, but as council president he couldn't risk being absent. The guardsmen walked around Henry as if he were a totem pole.

The increased activities caught Robert Standish's attention and he arrived one afternoon for a firsthand look. He laughed in Henry's and Red's faces. "This'll never be done by the end of the year. Y'all be crawlin' back on your hands and knees beggin' me to pick up garbage."

Henry was ambivalent. He wasn't crossing Standish. One never knew when one might need the man again.

Red had no qualms. "You're probably right," he said, "But we're giving it one helluva try."

***

After toiling at the garbage site for five months, Captain Hennessy dropped a bombshell. The National Guard was leaving in ten days. They were needed in Florida after a hurricane. The council quadrupled our efforts, gave a shovel to every spare man available and sent them to the landfill. We printed invitations for the official ribbon cutting a month hence, a bold, pie-in-the-sky move.

In Sonny Barth's office, the usual confusion reigned. I moved old newspapers, computer data sheets, two red ties flung across a chair back and sat. Betty, the bookkeeper, bent over Sonny's desk. She and Sonny were checking long columns.

"Quit with the numbers," I said. "They're never going to add up. Talk landfill to me."

"Thank God for gravel and the National Guard," Betty said. "The landfill is the only project not in the red."

"Instead of cutting a blue ribbon," I suggested to Sonny, "for the opening, let's string together tin cans. Let them glitter in the wind, a silver garland."

"Let next year's council worry. Ribbon-cutting won't happen on this shift."

"Why would you say such a thing? Look how far we've come!"

"This far is not all the way, Hannah. There's still a long road ahead."

"But the bulk is done," came my obstinate reply. He had to acknowledge how much we'd accomplished. "We have two weeks left on the extension. We can finish the grading and the fence and the other stuff by then." Sonny looked doubtful. "So what's the problem?"

"The problem is, the National Guard leaves and you people start fussing and arguing and tearing everything apart and the whole business comes undone."

"We won't do that."

He looked at me disparagingly. "Speak for yourself. You're one vote."

Betty looked away from her computer. "The problem is next year is an election year. Who knows who'll be on the council next term? Voters are fickle. Hopefully, we won't have five new people to contend with."

The heavy truth dampened my enthusiasm. I wasn't a fool. I was debating whether or not to run for a second term, knowing a monumental battle loomed ahead. Bubba Egger, former councilman, had already announced he was running. Thieving bastard! The voters would never return him to my District 2 seat— would they?

I put aside my own anxieties. "We need to do something nice for Captain Hennessy and General Zeldom. If it hadn't been for them, we never could've done this."

"You're doing the nicest thing you can for them," Sonny replied. "You're letting them return to their own business. They're retreating tomorrow at daybreak."

We slumped in chairs, triumphs and defeats both equally as exhausting. The door opened and Will Fleming filled the frame, calm and cheerful as usual, a wide smile showing the crooked eye tooth. "Anybody wanna ride to the sanitary landfill not to be referred to any longer as the garbage dump?"

"No way," Sonny replied, "I've had all the garbage I can take."

I raised a tired hand. "Me."

We went in Will's pickup. "Why all those boxes in back?" White foam boxes and drink coolers were piled in the truck bed.

"Catfish dinners and beer for the guys—"

"They'll love it."

What pride! What a monumental accomplishment! We left the main highway, drove the newly paved Wendell Road and onto the secondary Fulder Lane, fresh gravel spread evenly over the surface. Where the wood pallets once began, the boards had been removed and gravel spread. The trail ran like a winding grosgrain ribbon all the way to the 10-foot-high hurricane fence topped with angled steel bars and barbed wire. As we crossed the electric beam, the gate opened. Fifty yards into the landfill, to the right stood a metal building, small but practical. Will honked the truck horn and the newly hired sanitation engineer, related to no one, poked his head through the window. He beamed a smile and pointed to the big crate standing nearby. The new weigh scales! Once installed the trucks would drive over them and a computer would register tonnage. High tech! High tech!

"Hiya," Will Fleming greeted the engineer. "Call the men. We've brought lunch."

We surveyed the landscape. Over 300 acres had been cleared for Phase One. The pine trees were gone, the trunks sold and hauled away. The land, brown and smooth, rolled in all directions as far as the eye could see, the pits aligned in concentric circles.

The National Guard swarmed over the sight, loading gear, dismantling temporary sheds, hauling away Port-A-Cans. I was so proud of them! They'd been helping us for five months. They were efficient, jovial, hard-working and had a command system that didn't break down. Leaning against the pickup, we waited for the men.

"At least you're dressed more sensibly today," Will said. I wore jeans and white rubber boots, the famous Bayou Reeboks. "I remember that first day at Robert Standish's old place, those ridiculous red heels and your ankles were covered with maggots."

"Yuck! Don't remind me. That was awful."

He looked at me through narrowed, laughing eyes. "You were trying so hard to be brave and equal."

"Listen, if I hadn't conquered that first hurdle I would've never gained your respect, anybody's respect."

"You jumped right into my arms."

"Yeah," I made a face at him. "I have my flaws."

The men drove their equipment up from the pits, across the leveled land, headed toward the gate, a lifesaving fleet, dull green machines in the distance coming nearer, growing larger and larger; advancing toward us, a formidable moving barrier. When they reached the shed, the drivers killed the motors, pushed open heavy doors and emerged from bulldozers, tractors, forklifts, excavators, backhoes, cranes, bobcats, dump trucks and motor graders, slipping, sliding, crawling down from cat seats and high buckets.

A war action must take place thus, advance or retreat. Tanks and trucks pushing forward or going backward, mud-streaked, sweaty men hanging from cabs and looking through turrets, the great machines rumbling, groaning as they moved, enormous wheels turning, treads catching and spitting mud, tramping boots marching relentlessly, the camouflage caps and steel helmets dirt-spattered. This army was leaving, retreating not in defeat, but in absolute triumph. This landfill was their victory as much as ours.

"We done it, Miz Hannah! We done it!"

"Yes indeed! Yes indeed!" I wanted to hug their smelly, sweaty bodies, kiss their faces tanned brown and shake their hands. These men were heroes, my heroes. They had rescued our parish.

"Thank you," gratefully handing each tired man a boxed catfish dinner. Will reached into the ice chest and gave them each two cold Millers. "We can't thank you enough. We couldn't have done it without you."

Pohainake Parish hadn't paid National Guard a red cent. Not a penny for oil, gas, maintenance or equipment repairs. A catfish dinner and a beer seemed so inadequate a reward!

Will let down the truck tailgate and we sat, eating catfish, potato salad and coleslaw comfortable and at ease with each other and with the guards. "Actually," he said, "this is better than those banquets we've attended, don't you think?"

"Absolutely—this is—this is—" I couldn't find words to express the joy, the fulfillment I felt.

***

A few weeks later, the council had the Sanitary Landfill grand opening. The governor waved big scissors and cut the tin can ribbon made by local Boy Scout Troop #52. The bigwigs from state government in Baton Rouge showed, everybody angling for credit—election year coming up. No politician aspiring or already elected missed an opportunity.

The press arrived in full force. The Daily Sun plastered the council's picture across the front page. WHHO's Ned Morales poked the mike in our faces and we gave him the expected twaddle: team effort, everybody working together, no one person could do it alone. We owed the National Guard a great debt blah, blah, blah. We didn't mention the arguments, court orders, fines and setbacks. We forgot maggots, vultures, bloated cows, dead horses, rotting dogs, bleached skeletons and blue bottlenose flies. The foul smells that made one vomit were history. The deed was done. It took what it took to accomplish. Everything else was a memory. The baby had arrived. The labor pains were forgotten.

WRMTV's Stephanie Tringle strutted onto the landfill followed by a full crew and her new husband. She wanted her young man to meet Will Fleming. She avoided me as if I were Bubonic plague.

Captain Hennessy came, with him a tall, erect, gray-haired stranger wearing a khaki uniform, medals and bars decorating the shirt. Mr. Percy made a big to-do over the soldier's appearance. He waved in my direction. "Hannah, come meet General Zeldom."

The general here! He knew! He let this happen! What a day! A great, great day!

Riding home with Will after the ribbon cutting, we stopped a few minutes near the steel skeleton rising into the blue sky, the new Pohainake Parish prison, construction at last under way, after more than a year of lawsuits and counter-lawsuits, trips to the legislature, judges conferences, and Lord knows what all. Finally, the combination plan, partly housing federal prisoners, state inmates and locals, using general funds and revenue bonds, the "Big Combo" the press labeled it, was approved and the project moved forward. We had Wendi to thank for that financing arrangement. Cement trucks backed into the site, their big bellies turning, spewing concrete made from our own gravel. Plumbers and electricians crouched or reached high, laying thin conduit lines. Carpenters, tools hanging from their belts, balanced on scaffolding. Girders, beams, columns and iron bars protruded vertically, horizontally, a symmetry I didn't understand but recognized as progress, 220 cells, electronic locks, day rooms, library and modern kitchen, a humane facility.

The voters must be happy. The landfill was a fact, the jail a reality, the federal mandates satisfied. The roads were getting paved, not as quickly as the council promised, but fast enough. Our world was returning to normal, to order. Compared to the first two years, the second term would be a snap. The hard stuff was behind us, from this day forth, nothing but easy sailing.

"You've done a good job." Will sounded more sad than joyful.

"*We* did a good job."

CHAPTER 19

ROADS AND DRAINAGE

Henry Johnson, Will Fleming, Sonny Barth and I put on our Sunday best and drove to New Orleans to the brokerage firm, Hancock & Jones, whose specialty was public issue bonds. Their office was in the Shell Building, an intimidating 51-story tower. Riding the elevator to the top floor popped my country ears.

We wandered down the long corridor like aliens landed on a strange planet, marching forward, determined to conquer, checking one brass plaque after another, until we found Hancock & Jones. Henry Johnson, unsure as to whether or not to open the heavy mahogany door, pushed lightly against it and it gave so easily he fell headlong into the room, the rest of us tumbling in behind him. We entered a world of pale gray walls, gray carpet, gray couches and glass-topped tables. Real potted plants sat everywhere, not a single drooping leaf. At a distance we could see through the plate glass window, the Mississippi River curling around the city, its waters a highway for tugboats pushing barges, freighters from afar, oil tankers, ocean liners, ships coming from someplace, going somewhere, steaming with purpose.

A voice said, "May I help you?" and we collectively jumped.

Henry cleared his throat. "We're from Pohainake Parish. We have an appointment to see Mr. Jones."

The woman smiled. She was made up like a runway model, hair page boy style. She wore a black suit, a diamond (rhinestone?) pin on the coat lapel. "Mr. Jones is expecting you. One moment, please." She whispered over the intercom, pushed a button, heavy panels slid open and we entered Mr. Jones's inner sanctum.

He sat behind a massive desk, the American flag to his right, and the blue Louisiana flag with the pelican crest to his left. He had thinning gray hair, faded blue eyes, a weak chin and wore a gray-striped seersucker double-breasted suit and vest, a gold pin holding the solid blue tie in place. He adjusted rimless glasses, raised his chin, looked down his nose and pursed his lips. He motioned for us to sit, waited, and then said, "About Pohainake Parish—the bankrupt one—? Hardly! We can't ask anybody to buy bonds guaranteed by Pohainake. You're a breath away from default, one hellacious mess. A real hell of a mess and we're stuck in it."

Our mission didn't take long. We weren't tossed out on our collective butts, but pretty close. We returned home whipped, totally defeated. I was mixing a stiff drink when Mom returned from playing cards.

"Charlie called earlier. He wants to see you."

Not ready to tackle any problem a constituent had, big or little, up to my gullet with politics, I asked, "Charlie, who? Tell him I'm not here."

"Okay." She dialed. The phone rang twice before someone answered in a sing-song receptionist voice. "Is Mr. Percival in?" Mom asked.

I jumped across the room and snatched the receiver from Mom's hands. "*Charlie?*"

"That's his name, isn't it?"

***

Next morning in Mr. Percival's upstairs office, watching him play with his Lionel train, my eyes following the locomotive pulling box cars, the crossing arms coming down, the short and long whistle blasts, I sat there waiting, wondering how my mother, who'd had three husbands and was looking for a fourth, had become Mr. Percy's great friend and confidante in the short three months she'd been in Harmony. Most people lived in this town for years, knew who Mr. Percival was, saw him walking to Murt's Diner, saw his Rolls Royce, but nobody I knew ever got chummy enough with Mr. Percival to call him *Charlie.*

Mr. Percival placed a paper clip on the track. "Watch this." His hand hovered over the black locomotive, wheels clacking and steam rising, 3025 written beneath the miniature window that framed the engineer wearing a striped cap. The locomotive pulled flat-beds and coal bins, boxcars and tankers. The long line crossed under a steel bridge, disappeared, chugged past an elaborate depot, crisscrossing the figure-eight tracks. The locomotive's front wheels rolled over the paper clip and derailed. Behind it, the cars toppled.

Absorbed as he was in playing with his trains, I sat impatient, wondering why he had summoned me to come here, if he'd forgotten I was there, or was this appointment another huge mistake.

He observed the upturned locomotive, the wheels spinning in the air, the cars at a crazy angle behind it. "Any little snag," he said, "and the whole thing derails." He retrieved the engineer's cap that had fallen away and replaced it on the miniature engineer's head. Suddenly, he turned the locomotive upright. All the cars came back on track "You see this boxcar?" he tapped a little red boxcar loaded with black coal. "It's important, necessary, but not strong enough to pull the line and neither are any of the rest of these." He touched each train, a loving tap. "The locomotive is the only one that has power enough. Every train has to have a locomotive or else the whole lot languishes on the tracks, can't move."

"You really do carry on about your trains!" I grabbed my chance and wedged a question. "You wanted to see me?" Unable to stop myself, I blurted, "We can't sell road bonds. We can't fix a single road." There went another campaign promise. *I will fix your road! My road! All roads!* Oh, yeah. The parish's predicament didn't need to be explained to Mr. Percy. My face told the story. Yesterday's trip had been a total disaster, a crushing experience, a shameful embarrassment.

Mr. Percy kept his eye on the locomotive. "Mr. Jones wasn't cooperative."

"You know?" *Of course, he knew. He knew everything.*

"Played poker with Will last night—"

Will Fleming came home and blabbed about our disgraceful encounter! *Mom played poker last night!* No, it couldn't be...never mind...the thought made no sense.

"It's hopeless," and making a feeble attempt at flippancy, I concluded, "We're permanently derailed." *Derailed!* The word flashed in my mind, a yellow caution light. *Derailed!*

Mr. Percy smiled approvingly and didn't stop playing with his trains. The black locomotive was speeding, wheels clacking and whistle blowing, pulling the other cars, crossroad signals flashing, barrier arms flipping down, flipping up. "I've dealt with Hancock and Jones before. Let me make a phone call. It might help, then again, it might not."

***

The council never knew what Mr. Percival said to Mr. Jones, but as I've mentioned before, Mr. Percival was super rich and influential, and had no wife or children to inherit his money. He gave anonymously to many charities, quietly funded college tuitions, kept the city recreation department afloat, donated the baseball field and established the Percival Children's Hospital in memory of his one child who died shortly after birth. Though he never acknowledged his donations, whenever much-needed money surfaced, the people knew it came from Mr. Percival. But bonds? Roads? We were into millions.

Perhaps his cronies helped. Gossip at Murt's had it the Messrs. Songe, Agee and Genre spent two days closeted in Mr. Percival's inner sanctum. Mr. Songe arrived swinging on his crutches. He came by himself the first time. Next trip, he brought his younger, second wife, Marisue. She lugged his briefcase, stayed a few minutes, then left.

Mr. Agee came wearing his black wrap-around glasses, a constant fixture since his cataract operation. The Harmony Homestead president was reported to be tighter than Scrooge. To get a loan from his bank, a customer had to get down on his knees, grovel effectively and present proof he was a good risk. Mr. Agee's suffering wife continued to teach piano so she'd have spending money.

Mr. Genre as open-handed as Mr. Agee was close-fisted, loved everybody and wanted to hug the world. He and his wife, an elegant New Orleans aristocrat, had no children. They held fabulous dinner parties every Friday night where they served exotic food imported from Antoine's and Commander's Palace, and expensive French wines. They rode the train to New Orleans every Friday and returned Monday morning. The couple walked hand-in-hand from the station, stopped at Murt's Diner for breakfast, then on to their brokerage firm. At Christmas Mr. Genre showered gifts on everyone within his reach. Lately, his stomach was bloated as big as a watermelon, but he refused to see a doctor. "I'm pregnant," he told the diner patrons. "I'll deliver a nine-pounder any day now."

After a few days closeted with Mr. Percival, they came downstairs, stepped outside and limped, shuffled and staggered around the block.

"We think better in fresh air," Mr. Agee said.

The last few days the old men must've walked ten miles. Murt's customers saw the four stooped-shouldered bodies inching past the plate glass window. Silently, with stumbling steps and clouded eyes, the old men walked. Then one day, they walked no more.

Soon afterward, Mr. Jones phoned the courthouse and informed Sonny Barth he had reconsidered the road bond issue and perhaps his firm could offer limited help. Sonny relayed the information. I yelped gleefully, jumped into my Cadillac, drove across town and barged into Mr. Percival's upstairs office, inner sanctum no one entered unless invited.

"Mr. Percy!" How grateful I was! How indebted. "Thank you. Thank you. Thank you."

He ignored my gratitude and said in his raspy voice, "Go find that lawyer of yours, the stuttering one, Mel Green, and tell him to get busy fixing the legal tangle that goes with issuing bonds."

Impulsively, overwhelmed by his goodness, without thinking consequence, I reached over the desk and planted a big kiss on his cheek. He stiffened and drew back, raised bushy eyebrows and held his breath. His fingers reached for the intercom button connected to the secretary-receptionist.

"Get in here, quick!" he said. "This woman is attacking me!"

CHAPTER 20

Throughout the South, villages with a single street light have one truly impressive building, the courthouse. Pohainake's, a four-story building, Corinthian columns and green shutters, faced Harmony Square. Rain dripped from the Spanish moss hanging from the hundred-year-old oaks. Water puddles mirrored the French Quarter-style street lights. Government buildings surrounded the perimeter: school board, board of health, food stamp, social security, Veterans administration, and other less destructive offices, shimmered wet. Wind gusts swayed the gold-engraved wooden shingles hanging from former residential houses converted into law firms.

Certain hubris existed in driving into a parking lot and seeing a sign: RESERVED FOR HANNAH KELLY COUNCIL. Fighting the wind-blown umbrella and the driving rain, splashing through puddles and running into the building, I shook my head like a shaggy dog.

A sheriff's deputy held open the door. The vestibule had high ceilings and a curved stairway to the third floor. Wet-haired people jammed into the elevator. They wiped their faces on their sleeves and stomped their feet, shedding rain drops. The door opened, second floor, home to the sheriff and tax collector (one and the same) and the law enforcement agencies. No one moved. The doors slid closed, opened again, third floor, domicile to three district courts, judges' chambers and lounges. The east wing of this floor housed the council meeting room and two cramped offices.

After I was elected, the council swearing-in ceremony had taken place in a crowded District Court A. Guests, clerks, courthouse personnel, other elected officials crammed into the room, sat where they could, or stood against walls. Mr. Percival, Mr. Songe, Mr. Agee and Mr. Gendre were present, solid touchstones in this shaky beginning. Honorable Sam Blanchard, presiding judge, flanked by the stars and stripes, right, and a Louisiana flag, left, wore a black robe and looked impressive. The wives held the Bible for Henry Johnson, Red Harper and Peewee Reese. Stephanie Tringle did the honors for Will Fleming. Bobby and Suzy held my Bible.

Afterwards, we had punch and cookies in the hallway, foregoing the usual lavish luncheon because the parish was bankrupt and having a big shindig would send the wrong message, give the people a wrong impression. Reporters interviewed us and photographers asked us to stand here, there, turn toward the center, smile.

I recalled my practical mother saying, "This installation will go on a while. I'll drive Bobby and Suzy home and you catch a ride." Hugs, kisses and well-wishes and away then went. They walked through the arched doors, my six-foot-tall mother flanked by her two grandchildren, Bobby as tall as she was. I had the feeling my family was slipping away from me, circumstances altered, our existence never to be the same. When I placed my hand on the Bible, my life took a turn, a change of direction, I knew not what. I knew not what.

That was then, a year ago. Today, when I entered the packed council chamber, the word had spread that road bonds were being issued and sold. The council room overflowed with citizens wanting their road patched or their bridge reopened. They jammed every bench, stood outside in the hallway and lined the stairway from the third floor to the main landing. *"Bad Road"* signs were posted on every impassible road and *"Bridge Out"* signs were nailed on spans that barricaded people from their homes. Anticipating this day, the council sent the parish engineer to check every road and catalog its degree of disrepair.

The parish had plenty road workers. At the very first meeting Peewee, Red and Henry submitted names they'd promised to hire, time for payback and score settling. I refused to vote for unqualified relatives. The prior council had employed mostly kinfolk who did little or no work but who surfaced Fridays to retrieve their paychecks. My main campaign promise was to stop waste and nepotism. With that in mind, I had coerced Sonny Barth, Percival Industries recently retired controller, to apply for the executive officer job, had twisted his arm without mercy, followed him around the golf course, ignoring his argument that he was no longer in the rat race and wasn't planning on working for a bankrupt parish. The former council EO upon learning the AG was sending an investigator, had resigned, crossed the state line and barricaded himself in his Mississippi hunting camp. The only councilman who had nobody in mind to employ was Will Fleming. As far as this line item was concerned, he was out at sea. Ken White, the CAAd, looked blank. He had no idea who was kin to whom.

Several rounds later, the hiring votes were tied, two to two, Will Fleming and I voting no hiring relatives, and Red and Peewee voting yes, and Henry Johnson, the council president, abstaining and refusing to break the ties, as if suddenly he was far above this common fray.

The ACLU Trench Coat jumped to his feet. "According to Robert's Rules of Order," he had a raspy, thin voice as though a major disease affected his larynx, "Henry has to break the tie."

Henry got stiff-necked. "I ain't breakin' nuttin'."

Lawyer Green dispatched Wendi for the Rules. She returned empty-handed, said there was no Robert's Rules of Order that she could find, but she would go buy the book in the morning if the council appropriated the money for the purchase, or maybe the judges had one in their chambers they'd be willing to lend.

Will Fleming had a hard time restraining a chuckle. "This is a merry chase," he said under his breath.

The council turned the whole hiring operation into a farce. Two hours later nothing was settled. During the break, Will Fleming and I ducked into the coffee room. Surviving this hassle required caffeine. "This isn't going anywhere," I said.

"That's right."

"I'm not going to vote to hire their nephews and their friends."

"I hear you."

"You're not voting for them, either."

"I'm voting "no" so you won't be on the poop deck all by yourself. What's more important, a qualified executive officer, or a ditch digger?"

That was a no-brainer, "The EO, of course."

"Then when we go back, vote for their ditch diggers and road superintendents and they'll vote for Sonny Barth."

His advice left me speechless. For six weeks at forums, coffees, barbecues I had pronounced in a loud, self-righteous voice: no more hiring relatives! Only qualified individuals for the jobs! "I can't do that!"—backtracking before newspaper reporters, before hostile people listening to every word uttered, watching every move made. "It's against my principles! Against all I stand for! I promised to eliminate nepotism. I can't reverse my stand."

"In politics it's not called reversal. Picking between the least of two evils is called compromise. No one gets his or her way 100%. You give in to the lesser evils to accomplish the greater good. Weigh a common laborer against a qualified executive officer and let's go back there and move this show along, okay? We haven't even gotten to the important things yet."

Compromised integrity, friendly divorce, what oxymoron! In the end, I capitulated, tumbled from the lofty heights of inspired rhetoric to black pit reality. To get Sonny hired, I succumbed to peers' pressure, a flaw, a weakness that worried me constantly. Theoretically, deciding between right or wrong was a matter of morality and good judgment, a straight and narrow path. In actuality, curves and angles intersected, black and white turned gray, there was evil in all good, and positives in every negative.

Captain Fleming offered congratulations. "You did great. You'll learn horse traders make the best politicians."

The prisoners on the fourth floor became increasingly noisy, relentlessly stomping on their cell floor (our ceiling). Plaster dust rained upon us. A preaching felon began sermonizing, driving the other inmates crazy. "Shut up, you fuckin' sonofabitch! Shut up! Shut up!"

Attorney Mel Green pointed his finger at the newly elected council president, "For Heav-heav-en's sake-sake! Call a recess-cess Mr. John-john-son!"

Henry Johnson did so, and Mel Green motioned a deputy. "Go-go up-up-stairs and tell-tell the jail-jail-er to con-contain that god-god-damn rack-racket."

***

The road meeting droned on interminably, everybody touting their road's horrendous condition and demanding the council fix it first. Just when we thought we had conquered that problem, a Mrs. Brown had the floor. The doctor's wife had recently moved to Harmony from California, purchased 200 wooded acres abutting the Pohainake River and wanted to construct an artists' retreat, a place where painters, sculptors and musicians could purchase a small house featuring a north-light studio and create in peace and in harmony. She requested a variance to put meandering cinder roads, 16 feet wide that wouldn't disturb the property's natural beauty.

"My architect," she summoned a man to join her at the podium, "Kevin Vinyard from Tulane University and my landscaper," she beckoned for a second suit to join her, "Mr. Gary Martin of New York, have assisted me in the planning. Mr. Martin is a descendant of the New York's Central Park designer."

No need to explain how little weight that carried with this audience. As far as our people were concerned Central Park was as far away as Mars and about as accessible to the common man. Before the council and our suffering constituents stood this middle-aged dilettante playing with land, entertaining herself drawing plans and cutting lots, while people who had to abandon their cars when they came to a pothole so big it was not maneuverable, who had to walk their children to the school bus because the bus couldn't come to them, who met the postman halfway down the road to get their mail, listened in utter disbelief.

Mrs. Brown, bespangled in her flat gold chain and diamond earrings, was refined, well-spoken, endorsed by qualified henchmen. President Henry Johnson didn't know exactly how to sweep her off the podium, even though she was wasting our collective time. If she'd been an average working person, Johnson would've jumped down her throat in a New York second and told her to go fly a kite. Instead, he asked, "Whose district is this land in?"

Give Mrs. Brown credit. She'd done her homework. "Mr. Peewee Reese."

"Mr. Reese explained the road regulations to you?"

Peewee looked down at his clenched hands. He could deal with the yelling, screaming, bouncing children on the bus, but he had no notion what to say to Mrs. Brown.

Mrs. Brown said, "We've been unable to reach Mr. Reese. He's a very busy man."

School bus route ran twice a day, farming his fields between trips. Peewee turned pleading eyes in my direction. Would the treasurer talk to Mrs. Brown? Explain we had regulations that must be followed and no money to implement anything?

"Mrs. Brown," I said, looking at Peewee, tacitly reminding him that he owed me big time, "the parish has regulations for subdivisions. The roads must be 20 feet wide with a 10-foot drainage ditch on either side. The total width is 40 feet. The parish is not accepting dirt roads, cinder roads or gravel roads. The roads must be paved."

"Oh," she replied in a sweet, injured little voice. "That would never do. It would ruin the land, defeat the purpose. My landscape designer says two eight-foot lanes are ample. Cars could pass each other."

Sure, until all the lots were sold and vehicles began backing down driveways and piling into each other. And water swamped the road. The bumper to bumper traffic jam would become one more problem for the already overwhelmed council.

"Those are the rules. The developer must maintain the road for one year before dedicating them to the public," I stated clearly and firmly. We didn't have another minute to waste on this.

Mrs. Brown looked me in the eye and for a second we stared coldly at each other. "If the council could see the property first hand you'd understand. To scar it with concrete, oh, dear! What a horror! No! Never! Could I invite you," she waved a hand in our general direction, "to come and take a look? Mr. Reese, could you come?"

Peewee mumbled, "Sure."

"When you come," she said, her hand fluttering to her heart. "I will prepare a little luncheon. Say, next Thursday?"

To pacify her we quickly agreed. She returned triumphantly to her seat, gathered her Gucci bag and her entourage. Her assured stride as she exited the room left no doubt that her subdivision would have narrow, wandering lanes, not regulation streets.

Next, we proceeded to the truly big headache: bridges.

In 1945, after World War II, farmers gave permission for the parish to cut canals through their fields to drain the land, on the condition that bridges were built so they could get their cows and their tractors from one field to the other, a win-win proposition. The parish wouldn't go under water every time the rivers overflowed, and the farmers would have drained fields for their livestock and crops. Fifty years later, the farmers had sold their cows and their fields became residential subdivisions connected by rickety bridges that were falling apart. The developers said that bridges belonged to the parish. The parish, in a confused and defensive move, claimed the bridges belonged to the farmers. The original farmers were long dead and really didn't care. The living developers refused to take ownership of decrepit bridges. The liability was too great.

"There are 942 bridges," Our engineer said. He had counted them.

"If...if... you f-fix the f-first one," warned the attorney, "You'll have n-nine hun-hundred f-forty one m-more to re-repair."

A commotion outside stopped the bridge argument. A television crew toting camera and lights noisily entered the council chamber. Behind them came Stephanie Tringle. She hadn't been here since the canoe race.

"What's up?" I asked, turning to Will Fleming. "Why is she here?"

He nodded toward the front row where a woman sat doing her best to restrain three mentally challenged children. They'd been making gurgling noises during the meeting, toppling from their seats. "Steph is here about the bridges."

Stephanie batted her eyelids and smiled at Will. A beautiful girl, she had the council's full attention. Electricity zapped through the men. I shot Henry a charged look. Did he know what this was all about?

He nodded, scribbled a note and passed it to me. *"The woman with the kids—I thought she'd get tired and go home but now I've got to let her talk."*

Will Fleming whispered, "Get ready. She lives in your district."

My dumb luck, "Who is she?"

"I dunno, but the scuttlebutt is she's got it in for you."

"You knew this and didn't warn me?" The cad!

The woman was on her feet, addressing the council, TV cameras grinding.

"State your name for the record, please," The council clerk said.

"Maryjane Perkins."

"Two words or one?—"

"One: Maryjane."

"Address?—"

"One Perkins Lane."

"How many houses on your lane?—"

I appreciated Betty's effort. She was trying to give me a break, extract as much information from Maryjane as possible before the woman attacked.

"Only mine—"

"One house on the other side of one bridge, correct?—"

"Yes'm."

Henry Johnson took over. "And what's the problem?" he asked as if we didn't already know.

"My children have seizures," she said, "and this woman," she pointed in my direction, "refuses to fix my bridge. The only way the ambulance can get to my house is to cross that bridge. If my children die," she shook her finger at me and gave me a rabid, mad-dog glare, "you are responsible."

Anger and frustration distorted the woman's face. The upturned faces sitting in the audience mirrored disbelief. The spectators muttered their collective wrath. Those poor children! That poor mother! Their rage rose like steam through cracked earth.

As if on cue, the children fell to the floor and howled. The camera man swung his equipment about, filmed the scene and beamed it to the world.

My breath caught. A shallow cough escaped my throat. The room circled, the special needs children floating on the ceiling, diving beneath pews, the walls a crazy tilted angle, the prisoners above banging for forgiveness, plaster dust falling on my cheeks.

Henry Johnson pounded his gavel, called a recess. Will Fleming pulled me into the hallway, dragged me through the people jungle, steered me into the coffee closet and slammed the door.

"Don't want you to get lynched," he said, reaching for the coffee pot. "For being such a nice gal, you sure make enemies in a hurry." He handed me a mug. My hands shook violently. Coffee slopped over the sides.

"Why me?—you have bridges in your district. Henry's got bridges. Why is it always me?"

"Because you're the easiest target—"

"What do you mean?"

"A woman, a newcomer, a greenhorn, somebody people think they can topple, the easiest inroad."

"Jesus! Why did I ever get myself into this mess?" putting the mug down and burying my face in my hands. Causing the future death of the bridge woman's children! How did I ever stoop this low? All my initial good intentions dashed! Me, the one who blithely promised to save the parish! Now, see this! An angry mob was ready to lynch me. Resign? Throw in the towel? Was it legal for an elected official to quit when the going got rough, the seat too hot? Better to wait and be impeached? Or maybe killed? What about my own children? What would happen to them?

"Why? Why? Why?"

Will placed his hand on my shoulder. The warm touch was reassuring. "Because you're good at it," he said. "You're methodical. You're persistent. Without you, we wouldn't have a budget. We wouldn't have road bonds. The guys would never put that much study and diligence into this. They'd delegate it all to Wendi or Betty and we'd be in one helluva mess. You can't see it right now, but we're making great progress."

His deep, rumbling voice had a calming effect. "You think so?"

"I know so." He offered his handkerchief. "Wipe your face." I twisted the white cloth into a knot. "Here, let me." He plucked the handkerchief from my fingers and dabbed my cheeks. "You okay now?"

I nodded, shaky and unsure.

"Let's go back and give 'em hell, hang tough." He held me by both elbows as if he were at the helm of a ship. "District 1 will back up District 2."

"Okay."

"What we all need is a break. End of summer is here. Maybe we should go somewhere for a weekend. Get away for a few days."

Something in my mind clicked. Had Will Fleming asked me for a date? Or was the "we" the generic, political "we" elected officials used to spread blame?

CHAPTER 21

The wheels of government ground slowly and crushed plenty stuff along the way. Instead of "next Thursday," as Peewee Reese promised Mrs. Brown, several months passed before the council visited her proposed 200-acre subdivision. The woman persisted, relentless in her insistence that the governing body view first-hand her proposed 16-foot wide scenic, cinder roads.

Mrs. Brown was as annoying as a fly buzzing around one's head. The office staff recognized Mrs. Brown's voice on the phone and ducked her calls. We already knew we were going to say no to her road proposal, but we went for two reasons: to get her off our case and more importantly, to support Peewee, who had no idea how to stop Mrs. Brown. She was in his district and the big resounding *NO* had to come from him.

Peewee, a meek, hard-working man was elected because he drove a school bus for twenty years, stopped at every driveway morning and afternoon. The mamas and papas breathed a relieved sigh when the kids clambered onto Peewee's bus, entrusted to a dependable, reliable driver. Traveling the roads twice each day, dodging potholes, Peewee sincerely believed that once elected to the council, he'd be in position to patch roads and fix problems.

Nine months into our term, all the council had managed to do was make a written list of the roads and rate them by disrepair. We'd found many, many secondary roads that had no name and passed an ordinance that each road must be named. What seemed to be a simple problem became a complex situation. Every citizen demanded the lane be named after his or her grandpa who originally donated the strip, or after the landmark hickory tree, or after the nickname by which the road was known.

"You sure you want to keep Beer Can Alley?" Henry Johnson asked. "This is your chance to change it."

No takers, same thing with Bloody Mary Road, Big Dirt Road and Little Dirt Road, etc. etc. At every meeting, people living on the road arrived to argue road names. The harangues raged for hours devouring the council's precious time.

"Can you imagine having #5 Beer Can Alley engraved on stationery?" I muttered.

Captain Fleming's droll, whispered reply came. "They have no stationery."

"I'm talking to myself." My interaction with Will came to a complete halt after the Bahamas debacle. Sitting stiffly in my assigned chair, I ignored his suggestions, rejected his help, refused to look in his direction.

So far the council hadn't been able to get one single road repaired, and here we were, waiting to tour Mrs. Brown's pipe dream, pretending there was a possibility that the parish could take ownership and maintenance of more substandard roads. We didn't have enough problems that we should be looking for more.

Mrs. Brown, her architect and her landscaper took us on a two-hour tour, prime land, century-old live oaks, Pohainake River frontage, rolling green fields crossed by narrow lanes she'd already named after great writers and artists: Hemingway, Picasso, Mozart, and so forth.

Five council members wasted time looking over Mrs. Brown's pipe dream, while the school kids walked a half mile down a no-name road to catch the bus because the bridge had collapsed and the bus couldn't go across. Go figure.

"The old Stevens place." Peewee said, recognizing Mrs. Brown's land immediately. "Ran a dairy here until his chillens growed up and left home and he couldn't get no help, had a little frame house over yonder."

"It's still there," Mrs. Brown said. She spoke through clamped teeth. "I use it as my office. That's where we're having lunch."

The group straggled along, darting from shade to shade, temperature a scorching 90-degrees and air so humid breathing overtaxed the lungs.

"We're not cutting a single tree," Mrs. Brown commented.

"So," Henry Johnson waved a hand, a crooked, swimming motion, "all the roads will snake around?"

"Exactly, preserve the land's natural beauty." A wreck waiting to happen—

"Is that possible, Peewee?" Henry asked, attempting to extract the upcoming "no" from the district's councilman and terminate this outing. What was the point cluttering the works when we all knew Camelot was never going to happen in Pohainake Parish?

Peewee looked away and ignored the question. There wasn't any point wasting time explaining anything to Mrs. Brown. She wasn't listening. Her ears were waxed up with her own ideas.

Will Fleming said, "The land is beautiful and I'm sure your plans for subdividing it are excellent. Why don't you send the package to the council and we'll have the building permit people go over it?"

We trailed Mrs. Brown into the farmhouse turned office, trooping through the door into a room where the window air conditioner fluttered chintz curtains. White wicker furniture looked cool and inviting.

"How long will that process take?" she asked.

I bit my tongue. Forever wasn't a good answer.

Will said, "I'm sure Permits will get to it as quickly as they can, then forward their findings to Mr. Reese. Does the subdivision have a name?"

Mrs. Brown raised an offended eyebrow. "We don't refer to our project as a subdivision. Our objective is to make it a cultural experience, a way of life. We've named it Camelot, after King Arthur's legendary castle. The homeowners association will be called the Round Table."

Peewee looked purposely blank, as if he'd checked out. Red looked at me and made a face. How much time did this woman have to sit around and dream up this stuff?

The men scattered and leaned against the wall, avoiding the dainty chairs and Queen Anne couch, the fragile end tables and fringed lamps. They warily eyed the pink and blue flowered cloth that reached the floor, set with china, silver, crystal, and pink and blue hydrangeas centerpieces flanked by pink and blue candles. A stuffed artichoke sat on each plate.

Mrs. Brown motioned toward the chairs, "If you please."

The men let me go first, gentlemen to the very end. Red and Henry Johnson took clumsy, awkward steps toward the table, Peewee following, Will Fleming a few paces behind. The fragile chairs scraped the pine floor as the men pulled and tipped them back, holding their elbows close to their sides.

I deliberately unfolded the big pink napkin next to my plate and draped my lap. A flurry of shaking napkins followed.

Globe artichokes with deeply lobed leaves silvery green in color, spread and stuffed, the stem end cut flat, so that the choke sat upright on the plate. By the way the men stared and frowned, one would've thought the artichoke kin to the tarantula. No one wanted to be the first to touch.

Will Fleming reached at the same time I did. Our fingers accidentally touched and I drew my hand away. I could forgive many things, but what his girlfriend did to my son was not among them. Will pulled off a stuffed leaf, brought it to his mouth, scraped the bread and Parmesan cheese filling with his teeth and set the clean leaf down. I pulled a leaf, ate the stuffing and returned the leaf to the plate. Henry Johnson didn't eat his leaf. Peewee Reese didn't touch his artichoke.

"So when can I expect an answer, Mr. Reese?" Mrs. Brown asked when we reached the demitasse coffee stage. "The lots must be ready for sale by next summer. We've already wasted so much time we'll be into winter. The rains will delay us forever."

Peewee looked blank, as if Mrs. Brown was speaking Swahili, a tongue he didn't understand.

Fleming covered for Peewee. "That brings us to another question, drainage. Have your engineers designed the drainage?"

No houses were built yet, but when constructed they'd block the natural drainage paths. The whole place would go under water, cars floating in carports, residents wading knee-deep, hysterical calls for help.

"Yes! Yes!" Mrs. Brown held her temples. "Everything has been done. We simply need the council's approval stamp. We were told that was routine procedure," she said through clenched jaws.

"Get those plans to us," Will Fleming said. "We'll run them through the mill, right, Peewee?"

Peewee's calloused farmer's hand crushed the demitasse cup. We heard the crack when it split in two, "Oh, sorry! Sorry." He set both pieces down carefully. The diminutive saucer overflowed coffee.

"No problem," Mrs. Brown said, dabbing at the tablecloth. "I have more. What about the approval?"

Peewee Reese looked Mrs. Brown straight in the eye and said. "Ain't no way, Mrs. Brown. No way whatsoever."

CHAPTER 22

Earlier when I was ready to call it a day, Will Fleming stopped by the Habitat office. "Come," he said, "get a new perspective on your district."

"Thank you. I have all the perspective I need."

"C'mon. You'll love this. There's a break in the weather. The sun is shining for a change."

Late September, peak hurricane season had every council member on constant alert. The TV weather people were in their mettle, exaggerating for attention, spouting Doppler radar information while pointing to the blur in the Gulf of Mexico, our next possible hurricane. Even when we were lucky enough to skip a big, named storm, we experienced extended rain bouts. For two weeks now, rain had poured, two to four inches every day. Our marshy, clay ground became saturated and couldn't absorb any more water. The rivers rose. The canals filled. Though still upset over the consequences of the Bahama trip, I had to work with Will, a reluctant team. I needed his backing and support to get my motions passed by the council. No way could one person do it alone.

Curiosity got me and I followed Will to his Corvette. "Where are we going?"

"You'll see," he replied.

We drove through Harmony and went east. We turned in at Airport Drive. My hand flew to my forehead. "Don't tell me the airport runways are flooded." The airport was in my district.

"The runways are fine," he said as he parked the car. "Get out."

The authority in Will's voice was a relief. To do as told without debating the issue, without presenting proposals or counter proposals, not having to think twice before uttering a word that might or might not be misinterpreted, lifted a huge weight from my being. Alone with Will, the need to be a steel magnolia faded, and I felt light-hearted again.

"Now, get in."

Before I knew exactly what was happening, Will was buckling me into the Piper Cub passenger seat. "You're gonna love it."

"I'm scared stiff."

"Scared? A woman who can tackle good old boys?" he gave me a mischievous grin, "and give them a run for their money?"

"I wish!"

Fleming filled the pilot's seat. His head nearly touched the cockpit roof. As he reached to turn the ignition, I felt the movement of his big shoulders and muscular arms. He moved his right leg and his thigh brushed against mine.

He grinned sheepishly. "Sorry. It's a little cramped here."

"What's all that?" I pointed to the dashboard's buttons and dials.

"Control panel."

"You have a parachute?"

"Would you know how to use one?"

I shook my head negative.

The plane taxied slowly, past small, tethered aircraft and onto the runway.

Will turned his head and looked directly at me, not over my shoulder or past my ear as so many people did lately, but looked *at me*. "No need for a parachute. You can jump at any time." He assessed my fear index, leaned closer, his face six inches away from mine. He had a good face, an outdoor man's face, sun burnt leathery, deep cleft in his chin, the nose classic, not spread flat or hooked Roman, but straight and well-shaped. Under bushy blonde eyebrows, the green eyes had an emerald sparkle, except that I'd never been that close to an emerald.

He slipped on sunglasses. "You're okay with this?"

The Piper Cub reached the point where the north-south and east-west runways intersected. The plane stopped. My opportunity to say no, one little word and we would never leave the ground. I said nothing and my tacit consent charged the silence that followed.

"Close the window. That latch there." He did likewise on his side.

Will gunned the engine and the plane vibrated with greater and greater force while he checked gauges and instrument panel knobs and buttons. The roar drowned the words he spoke into a slim mouthpiece connected to ear phones. When it seemed as if the fuselage would break to pieces, Will released the brakes, the plane quit shuddering and we taxied down the runway. My hands reached to brace myself. The No Hand Hold sign on the panel stopped me. I didn't want to grab something that would flip us over. I clasped my hands, fingers twined in a death grip, my breath a sharp intake. The wheels left the ground and we were up, up, up, leaving below metal buildings and the orange windsock. I didn't even know we were soaring heavenward until I saw treetops through the windshield.

"If the noise is too much for you, you can wear these." He reached behind the seat for black ear muffs.

My hands clung to the ear muffs, but I didn't put them on. "Do you think the airport should expand the runways?" I asked over the motor's drone. Airport expansion was a tabled argument the council had not had time to tackle. How could we worry about runways for airplanes when cars couldn't safely travel our roads?

Will shook his head.

"No?"

"No council business." He removed his earphones. "Relax. Take in the scenery."

The view took my breath away. Silver lines snaked through dark green forests and sunlit fields. The heavens were in constant movement, clouds racing and dancing across the sky. The surprising color changes, baby blue, bright blue, navy, fleecy white clouds over yonder coming closer, closer, looking heavy, turning gray.

Fleming pointed ahead. "Rain," his finger made concentric circles. "We're going around it." A rainbow momentarily arched across the sky. He banked the Piper Cub, the world tilted, and I hung on for dear life.

Flying! What freedom! How liberating! Transported to another dimension! Soaring like a bird! Everything below shrank, the houses, rivers, highways, problems. Nothing could touch me here.

We veered around a rain-laden storm cloud and headed west into the setting sun. The orange and pink rays radiated outward, a color changing kaleidoscope.

I began to relax and enjoy the view. "It's beautiful!"

A whole new panorama unfolded below me. The world looked lush: dark green swamps, chartreuse and yellow pastures, long, coiling rivers. We flew over lakes reflecting glory, setting sun. This undeveloped beauty touched my heart. This was as God intended nature to be, before man clogged the works.

Fleming said, "Shackman Pass." Lakes Pontchartrain and Maurepas flowed into one another beneath the great arched bridge spanning the Pass.

"Already?—how fast are we going?"

"A hundred—"

"A 100 miles an hour?—" Unless I looked down and saw the landscape slipping past, the sensation was that we were gliding, floating, barely moving. I was weightless, riding a cloud.

"My boat, over there—"

The boats anchored in the marina looked like bathtub toys. The wind-ruffled waters resembled corrugated wash boards, the choppy waves all angled one way. Speeding boats left white wakes, foaming streaks.

We flew over the swampy expanse separating Pohainake and New Orleans. In many places the scummy surface cut into squares, rectangles, circles and triangles resembled an intricate green quilt. The canal networks dredged in the '20s and '30s to harvest the cypress were clearly visible. The logging companies had cut all the great, noble trees, laid down railroad tracks and sent the trunks upriver to waiting sawmills. The naked swamp remained home to alligators and water lilies. Pohainake Parish rose from the wetlands like a phoenix from its ashes.

"My area," Fleming chuckled, "Forty square miles of water and Pinewood."

The plane banked east. The horizon tilted, the swamp rose, the sky shifted.

"We're following the Pohainake River from the mouth north."

The river, brown and roiling, made big swooping curves through the dark, spongy swamp. Cypress and willow thickets lined the banks as if the loggers had purposely left a green buffer zone so no one would see the devastation behind the wooded strip. Weekend camps were the size of Monopoly real estate. The railroad stretching from New Orleans north to Chicago was a big scar with cross stitches.

Will pointed. "Your district—"

Harmony! The church spirals and steeples! He circled Harmony High's football field.

"Your house—"

"Where?—"

"Over there, look down, left, Elm Street, see the cul-de-sac?"

I strained to take a look. We were already past my house and into Peewee's area, pastures, fields and truck farms. In Henry Johnson's district the sun glinted on the chicken sheds' metal roofs, long buildings housing broilers, layers, pullets. Further north in Red Johnson's district, the farmers were releasing cows from the milk barns. At first the cows looked the size of mice, but as the Piper Cub swooped in closer, they grew larger, red Herefords and tan Jerseys. The airplane noise disrupted their peace and they lumbered across the green fields.

"The land is really flat, isn't it?"

"Flat as a pancake," Fleming replied. Past Red's district, he pointed, "the new landfill."

This afternoon flight took place before the garbage disposal dump was completed, when it still looked like a war zone, as if an enemy had bombarded the area. Downed trees were scattered like matchsticks, limbs and branches everywhere, a brown mess. Where the debris had been stacked and set on fire, lazy smoke drifted heavenward. Driving into the site by car, the forest closed in and overwhelmed. From this height one comprehended how man conquered nature, but right now, by the evidence below we weren't conquering nature fast enough.

"It'll never be done!"

Will nodded.

The whole landfill debacle appeared to be a huge mess. I remembered the day I drove into the woods, got the Cadillac stuck and the loggers towed the car to the highway. Will had rescued me that day. He'd barked at the loggers, yelled at them to unhook my car, pulled me from the Cadillac, made sure I was okay then followed me back to Harmony. At my house, Will opened the car door and left me standing on the driveway. The Corvette tires squealed as he peeled off without acknowledging my thanks, without saying goodbye.

I leaned closer so Will could hear. My thigh touched his and I consciously left it there, "Why did you come looking for me that day at the garbage dump? I was never so glad to see anyone in my whole entire life!"

He grinned and the crinkles around his eyes deepened, "Friday!"

"You were so mad!"

"Never tackle loggers on Friday. When Wendi told me," the unfinished sentence filled the air between us. He turned towards me. His gaze struck an unexpected response. Quickly, I looked away.

The cloud banks drifted past, changing shapes, a dream world, a long, bearded man, a wooly lamb, an angel's feathered wings. We flew into a cumulus mass, the soft whiteness swallowing the plane. Unable to see ahead or behind, up or down, lost in this air pillow, my hands fluttered, looking for a place to hold onto. Will's fingers enfolded mine. "It's okay."

My breath caught, unsure of the outcome, flying too high, too fast. As quickly as we entered the enveloping cloud, we emerged into blue sky.

Still holding my hand, Will pointed to the brown stream below. "There's the Pohainake again. We're following it home," going back to business, re-entering safe territory.

"Will it flood its banks?"

He didn't answer. He probably didn't hear me. The cockpit was noisy. I turned to repeat the question and saw that his head was bent to one side and he was staring down intently. He looked worried.

Suddenly, with unpredictable insight I knew why we were flying. He was checking the river, canals and drainage ditches. After all, even if by default, he was Drainage Board president.

At our very first meeting Henry asked, "Who wants to be Drainage Board president?"

Drainage was a broader subject than I could fathom at that ghastly hour. What did drainage entail? "I'm treasurer. That'll take up all my time."

Peewee Reese said, "I drives a school bus." That exempted him from any extra-curricular duties.

"I'll have my hands full with the Fire Board," Red said.

That left Will Fleming. "Sure, I'll do it," he said genially, and after being duly elected, he called to order the same five exhausted council members. Midnight, and we became the Drainage Board.

"It's my belief," Will Fleming's gaze swept the table, "that this body has done enough damage for one night." He banged the gavel, eager to wrap the session. "Do I hear a motion to adjourn?"

***

Below the plane wings, the canals looked full to the brim.

"Hog Wallow Canal," Fleming tapped his window, "over there."

The water was topping the bank. "Can it hold much more?"

"Not much. If it doesn't quit raining, it'll flood. Hog Wallow drains half the parish."

The sprawling houses, built on manmade hills to satisfy the 100-year FEMA flood map requirement, were scattered through the woods. The blue rectangles were swimming pools.

I took a closer look at the swollen Pohainake River. The muddy water roiling towards the lake flapped against the clay banks. "Looks pretty close—"

"Another foot—"

When it rained, the parish drainage canals filled with water. The runoff poured from the northern hills to the swamps in the south, the lowest point, and from there into the lake. In order for the land to properly drain, the southern canals had to be cleaned and widened first. If the northern section was done first, when the rushing water reached the clogged southern ditches, it would spill over the sides and inundate the surrounding territory. That situation was the crux of many arguments. Why was all the work being done around Harmony and Pinewood? Because the south had a bigger tax base? Because city people were more important than the rural folks? Why was the slower-growing north end not as important? Why were Henry Johnson and Red Harper's districts always the step-children? Thank God Will Fleming was drainage chairman. The problems and squabbles were his to handle.

Time zipped past. We'd been flying forty minutes, traveled 51 miles south to north, from the lake to the Mississippi State line and winged back and forth over the 18-mile width of the parish. The sun was setting, a golden moon rising, a magical spectacle.

Flying was the only way to see this incredible over-all view of the towns, farms, houses, industrial plants and baseball fields. This 790-square-mile parish was our territory to govern. Could the council successfully manage our troth? Could we keep the forests and the lakes and the farms and the towns united and not let politics rend our kingdom asunder?

We landed, taxied to the parking apron and Will tethered the plane. Over coffee at a nearby diner, I said,"It sort of reduces you, scales everything down to size. Makes one think of that great line in the Bible, *when I consider the work of thy fingers, the moon and the stars, which thou ordained, what is man that thou are mindful of him?"*

"Psalm 8," replied Will, "Verse 4."

"I didn't know you were a Bible scholar."

"I'm not. I'm a seaman. We revere the moon and the stars. When all else fails, they are a constant heavenly guide. The sun invariably rises in the east, sets in the west. The North Star points north and the Southern Cross, south. A sailor can find his way across the vast ocean if he knows his stars."

"How long were you at sea?"

Captain Fleming seldom talked about himself. With a flip answer or a deep frown he managed to deflect any inquiry that invaded his personal space. He wasn't a raconteur as most Southern men were, babbling hunting, fishing and barroom tales that grew bigger and more exaggerated with each telling.

"All my life, seems like, joined the Navy at 18, four-year hitch, then the Merchant Marines."

"How do you manage to keep your personal life private?"

Reporters never left me alone. Every insignificant aspect of my life was examined and commented upon. My children were fair game, as was my mother. My background had been sifted through a fine tooth comb. The public knew my every move, a suffocating, stifling development.

"I'm not good copy like you," Will said.

"What?"

"Sure you are. You lose your temper, battle the sheriff, win canoe races, harbor criminals and kiss Ken White in the parking lot."

"I did not. That gesture was totally misrepresented. I wanted to sue the Daily Sun, but Judge Blanchard said forget it, that would only exacerbate the problem and Mel Green said that wasn't a council lawsuit and I'd have to foot the bill and it was pointless to fight a newspaper that bought ink by the barrel."

"And you think accepting a compliment compromises your womanhood in some ridiculous way."

"That's not so," I protested, knowing it to be the truth. Compliments made me uncomfortable, made me feel undeserving, felt untrue.

Curiosity was too strong to resist. I needed to know about this man who sat next to me meeting after meeting, backing my positions, seconding the motions, pulling me aside to give me a steer in the right direction. "Do you mind if I ask you a personal question?"

"Depends," the reply wasn't a clear yes or no, but a politician's hedge, a maybe or perhaps.

"Never mind—"

"Go ahead, don't be shy."

Shy? Whatever made him think *shy*? S*hy* was my housewife past. The present Hannah was bold and self-assured. All Will Fleming could say was *'none of your business.'* Lots worse had been shouted at me the past few months. "Have you ever been married?"

A long, uncomfortable silence followed. He looked away, long and far away then said, reluctantly, as if his lips had difficulty forming the words. "I was, once."

Treading on forbidden territory, opening a locked safe, the contents sealed to avoid the pain. How well I knew. "You're divorced, then?"

One hard and painful lesson I'd learned was that rumors, gossip and innuendos (the captain was a playboy, a womanizer, a gambler, rich, had Arab friends, someone had seen a turbaned man board his boat) were not always true. They were seeds carelessly scattered to the four winds to fall where they may, sprout like weeds and kill green lawns.

Again the long pause, this was none of my business. I knew that.

"No. My wife and two-year-old daughter were coming home from a birthday party. A drunk driver crossed into their lane."

The silence was heavy.

"I'm so sorry."

"That was a long time ago. I went to sea then, stayed away 20 years."

So he had grieved for loved ones, had known loss and loneliness.

"I was fishing about, thinking what else to do, when Uncle Percy called, hadn't seen him in years, and didn't know a thing about Louisiana except there were two big, beautiful lakes near New Orleans, remembered coming here once when I was a boy." The jaunty, debonair attitude returned. The mask had momentarily slipped but was now in place. "My mother was Uncle Percy's only sister."

"All those beautiful women aboard your boat, miracle one hasn't snagged you."

"The women I sleep with are beautiful, young and sexy." His eyes twinkled. "The woman I marry has to be special."

"Well, if beautiful, young and sexy isn't special what is?"

"Someone like you—"

That caught me by surprise.

"Independent, smart, not a clinging vine—a woman who wants to be with me, not because of what I can provide, but because she simply can't exist without me. She would be my other self, my better half. We couldn't be whole without each other."

"Your mirror image?—"

"Absolutely not, a soul mate, completely opposite—opposites attract. That's why you and I are drawn to each other."

"Be serious!"

"I am serious." His hand reached for mine.

I let him play with my fingers. He held each one and stroked it, then enveloped my hand. "You're a colleague, a fine one and that's all."

The best way to fight the feeling was to bring it into the open and kill it with words. I shunned men, any man who could be born and could die, who could wound me so deeply I could never recover. The only way to survive was to be left alone, untouched, not to expose myself to pain. What was love but a heartache? I recoiled from the world and took refuge in my children, my work and public service. I could hide in the nothingness of a busy life.

"You know how to hurt a guy, but that's okay." He reached, tweaked my ear and predicted. "One day when the time is right, you'll come around. The invitation is always open."

Drawing quickly away, I replied, "Don't hold your breath." I gave him my best honeysuckle smile, the Southern kind that kills with sweetness like giving a diabetic sugar instead of insulin.

CHAPTER 23

The electric transformer blew with a sonic boom that rattled the windows. One single, intense explosion! The hall nightlight went dark, the refrigerator quit humming and the air conditioning compressor stopped whining.

The racket jolted me awake. Lightning lit the bedroom and rolling thunder shook the bed. The air sizzled as a nearby bolt struck a tree trunk and burned its way to the ground.

The phone rang. Who in the world would be calling at this hour, in the middle of this hellacious storm? I groped in the dark for the receiver. The male voice at the other end asked, "Where the sand bags? We need sand bags!"

"What?"

"Is this the council lady?"

Rubbing my eyes wide awake now—"yes, this is Hannah."

"We gotta have sand bags. River 'bout to flow over, coming up fast."

"Okay," without thinking, without giving the matter judicious thought. "I'll be right there."

Sand bags were crammed into a metal warehouse behind the Drainage Board office. The place was a depository for broken equipment, forgotten shovels, rope coils and rusty boxes. There was even an old abandoned truck.

Groping for the flashlight by my bed, looking for a Christmas candle stashed in the nightstand, knowing matches were in there somewhere, I pulled on jeans and a tee shirt.

Eerie blue-yellow streaks zigzagged across the windows, crashed and disappeared into the pine woods surrounding the house. Another shrill ring came through the thunder clap. What was this, Grand Central Station?

"Yes?"

"Sonny Barth, here, Hannah, we've got a crisis."

"I already heard. I'm on my way."

"The sand for your district is piled south side of the building. I've got workers filling burlap sacks."

"Okay."

The phone rang a third time, "Will Fleming, Hannah."

"I'm coming, dammit! I'm getting there as fast as I can."

"Okay. If you need me to—"

"I can manage, thank you."

Thunder, lightning, phone ringing and my banging into table and chairs awakened Bobby. He stumbled into the kitchen naked except for Jockey shorts. He rubbed his bare chest and squinted at me through sleep-filled eyes. "Get that flashlight out of my face, Mom. What's happening? Where are you going?"

"To sandbag the world—" The Christmas candle I'd set on the table flickered. "The river is flooding its banks."

He yawned, crossed over to the sink, ducked his head under the faucet and drank water. "I'm going with you, Mom. Trust me. You can't lift a sand bag."

"Now, listen—"

But he didn't. He returned to his room and dressed. Suzy, barefoot, in baby doll pajamas trailed him to the kitchen. "Wait for me. I'm going, too."

The candle's flickering flame cast jumping shadows around the room. "Suzy, you stay here with Gramma."

"Nobody needs to stay with me." Gramma shuffled into the kitchen in furry slippers, red hair wrapped around pink rollers, holding a battery-powered lamp that lit the whole kitchen. "Let's make some hot tea."

"No electricity," I said.

"I can rub two sticks together."

"Where did you get that lamp?"

"I live in Florida, remember? Hurricanes hit us every year. I live prepared. This little wind and rain is nothing."

The raging storm seemed a big deal to me.

"We'll go in my truck," Bobby said. "Your Cadillac will drown."

Bobby turned 16 last month. His dad bought a new SUV and gave Bobby the keys to his old Ford Camino, unabashedly courting Bobby's' favor. Nothing could've pleased my son more. Sure, Bobby was taking driver's education, but he wasn't old enough, responsible enough to get a license. The gift was to spite me—*see how much better you'd be living with me, Bobby? Now you can drive whenever you want, not just weekends. We'll take a little road trip, you and me.*

The choking feeling immediately after the divorce returned, a dangerous rage, the urge to kill, a knife in the back, a cup of hemlock, tampering with the brakes, revenge resurrected. I refused to let Bobby behind the wheel. I had monumental battles with Joe and Bobby, two against one, three, really, Suzy on their side, too. When Gramma put in her two cents, I capitulated, "Alright! Alright!—" Together, they were too much for me to fight.

"Mom, have you seen my raincoat?" Suzy wore shorts and rubber boots.

"You're not going."

One more urgent phone call put an end to our argument. Bobby, Suzy and I piled into Bobby's truck.

The night was black, not a streetlight, house light, or neon sign working anywhere. By the truck headlights, we could see the downed electrical and telephone wires. Power company trucks, lights revolving and flashing, lined the street. Caught in the glowing spotlights, the men's hard hats looked like yellow halos, radios crackling as they talked back and forth to each other.

The Drainage Board generators ran full blast, whirring and rumbling, adding to the night's din and confusion. Leaving the kids in the truck, forbidding them to follow me (if something happened to them, Joe would be hauling me into court, neglectful, unfit mother) fearful thoughts tumbling through my mind, walking briskly through the main building and into the rear yard. Through rain and shadows, a platoon wielding shovels filled sand bags.

Will spotted me and hollered. "That's your sand, Hannah! Over there!"

Disregarding my specific instructions, Suzy and Bobby stood behind me, dripping water. They'd get pneumonia and die. They'd disobeyed me, paid no attention to my admonitions. *I'd kill 'em!* "Be careful," I said.

Will Fleming was soaked through to the bone, water rivulets running down his yellow slicker, hair plastered across his forehead. Within seconds the kids and I, too, were soaked. My uncertainty rooted me to the spot. Where to go? What to do? What the hell did I know about flood control?

Last week's casual conversation when Will and I went flying made its way into my brain.

What was it Will said? Hog Wallow canal drained half the parish.

Big, dark shadows, my men, waited, water streaming from their hats and ponchos. The nearest one asked, "Where to go, Miz Hannah? You wanna bag the river?"

A plan entered my head, fully detailed, ready for implementation. "Forget the river. Hog Wallow. Take care of it first."

Will stopped bagging and waved. He saw Bobby and Suzy standing, dripping water and waiting like two wet chickens. He hollered, "Over there, Bobby. Help bag." And to Suzy, "There's coffee inside, Suze. Help there. Tell somebody to show you how to work the radio."

Rain and wind stung my face as I stumbled toward my sand dune, head and shoulders thrust forward, pushing against the gale. The wind whined, long and sibilant then cut off, a stifled, angry bark, buffeting anything not anchored. The whirling dervish had a movie set feeling, exploding bombs, psychedelic bursts and crashing planes.

The rear yard was dark as Africa, except where the spotlights hit. Rushing water quickly washed away fresh footprints. I slipped as the mud slid away from under my feet. A big hand steadied me, "Careful, Miz Hannah." Rambo's yellow hood dripped like rain from a house eave.

Road crews passed bags from one man to another. They worked with chain gang precision, steps synchronized in order not to stumble and fall. The last man heaved the bag onto a flatbed truck. When loaded, the truck pulled away going to the designated canal and another truck rumbled into place.

Every Clearwater fireman was there, led by the one-eyed, bodacious Rambo, one-sixteenth Cherokee, who could fill four bags to anyone else's one. He looked over his shoulder and flashed white teeth in my direction. "I gotcha covered," he said, "Going to Hog Wallow Canal. Be plumb truthful, I'd jist as soon see, what the hell they call it now? Country Club Estates?—go under. Yes, indeed. I'd get a kick watchin' them dudes float outta them little mansions."

"C'mon, Rambo, you don't mean that." Rain pelted my face. I wiped my upper lip and spit.

"Getting a lil' bit of water in yer house," carped another bagger, "is like a woman getting' a lil' bit pregnant, ruined either way!"

Rising water swept away flimsy houses, brought down disputed bridges, flooded farmers' fields and drowned their crops, inundated streets and stalled cars creating traffic jams. Returning our world to normal took months and months, sometime years.

Their councilwoman, their leader, couldn't stand there idle. Bobby was right. I couldn't lift a hundred pound sack. So I did the next best thing, joined the crew holding the burlap bags open, while others shoveled sand into the gap. Once the sack was filled, a twisted wire sealed the opening. Sand spilt everywhere.

In my previous life, this huge storm would've scared me to death. Now, every minute burst with purpose and there was no room for fear. Open, fill, close, stack, load; open, fill, close, stack, load, over and over again until daylight lightened the sky and the darkness slowly melted away. My feet were wet, clothes soaked, arms aching and teeth chattering.

Long, weary hours later, the driving rain stopped, the buffeting wind ceased, the falling drizzle the only gray reminder of nature's power.

Will Fleming appeared behind me and threw a towel over my shoulders. "Tell your men they can stop now," he said. "We've got enough sand bags. All the main canals have been bagged."

Arms raised high, hands waving back and forth, "Hey! Hey, guys! You can quit now! We're done!"

The men didn't need much encouragement. They threw down their shovels.

"Thank you," to each man who filed past me. "Thank you very much." And to Rambo, "You're a very special man. Thank you."

"You're a good guy yourself, Miz Hannah. We're buddies now, canoeing, sandbagging, what next, councilwoman?"

"Hopefully, nothing!" a friendly slap on his shoulder brought a big grin to his face.

Will laughed. "You passed the Rambo test. You're in. "Here, let me." Too tired to argue, I steadied myself against Will as he knelt down and pulled off my white, rubber shrimpers' boots, the Bayou Reeboks I'd bought so many months ago. He tipped them and poured water. "Dry your hair. You'll catch pneumonia and die, then the council will have to spend money we don't have holding a special election to replace you."

My welfare didn't concern me. "Where are my kids?" That something would happen to them drove me to the scary place where imagination overcame reason and the accident or broken body, or abduction filled my mind.

"They're okay. They're coming. We're all going for breakfast."

"There's no electricity."

"My boat has a generator."

"Listen, thanks, but I have to check on Gramma. We left her alone."

A wet, bedraggled Bobby overheard me. "Mom, I'm going to get Gramma. She's coming with us. You and Suzy ride with Mr. Will."

"C'mon, Mom," Suzy begged. "We want to see the boat."

My kids had been so fabulous it didn't seem fair to cross them.

CHAPTER 24

The drawbridge spanning Shackman Pass where Lake Pontchartrain and Lake Maurepas met was the dividing line between Pohainake and St. Luke parishes. Will had moved his boat across the pass from Manroot's Marina in St. Luke to Cloy's Marina in Pohainake because the law said a councilman must reside within the parish and within his district. Will Fleming's opponent, who lost the race, wasted money and time trying to prove living aboard a boat didn't fulfill the residency requirement. What settled the argument was that the U. S. Post office delivered mail daily to the boat, so therefore…

Bobby and Gramma walked to the pier. Bobby had changed clothes and they were both dry as toast, Will, Suzy and I looked like drowned rats.

The gleaming white bulk loomed big as an ocean-going cruise ship. Will Fleming boarded *Serenity,* his step smooth and easy, extended a hand and steadied us as we jumped the gap between pier and boat. "Dry clothes in the locker four steps down and right through there," he pointed to a narrow hallway, "First stateroom to the left."

Suzy and I walked through a room that had a credenza, cabinets, wet bar, ice maker, entertainment center, television, stereo system, burnished wall paneling and navy blue carpeting. The windows had mini-blinds and tan curtains, all the comforts of home.

"Wow!" Suzy said. "This is ritzy."

Two more steps down and we were in a U-shaped galley that had an L-shaped dinette built into one corner.

"Refrigerator, electric stove, oven, microwave, dishwasher, jeez, Mom, this kitchen is ten times better than ours."

Against one wall in the stateroom, opposite a double closet, were upper and lower bunks, the spreads a royal blue. Suzy opened a closet door, "Hey, Mom! I found the washer-dryer!" She pulled open another door. White tee shirts were stacked next to folded sweat pants "This will do for me." Suzy grabbed an over-sized tee shirt. "Here, Mom, take these." She handed me a gray sweatshirt and sweat pants and disappeared into the bathroom. When she flushed the toilet, she shrieked, "It almost sucked me down! Did you hear it?"

I hadn't heard, busy poking around the next room, an office-den. Above the computer sitting on the built-in desk, pinned on a cork board were boat architectural drawings. A closer look revealed neat specifications beneath each drawing, length, beam, draw; wood type, the numbers written in neat writing I recognized as Will's. Blue print rolls were tucked into cubby-holes. Books about boats, the sea and technical volumes packed the shelves.

A visible corner of a Scotch plaid bedspread drew me into the next room, king-sized bed dead center! A mirrored wall! Lamps, two dressers, bedside tables, Curious, I checked the titles by the bed: *The Satanic Verses*, Salman Rushdie; *The Russia House*, John le Carré, *Clear and Present Danger,* John Clancy. Guy books. A Bible bound in black leather. So he was a theology scholar, or maybe he read it for guidance and forgiveness of sins. Or perhaps a Bible made the women he brought into this bedroom feel more comfortable, safer. A framed Fleming coat of arms hung on one wall, beside it an oversized water color painting of *Serenity*. No family pictures.

Everything was spotless. The brass handles polished, the carpet vacuumed all in one direction. In the small, adjacent bathroom no scum on the soap dish, the toothpaste tube squeezed from the bottom and rolled. Was this man compulsive? His boat was a hundred times cleaner than my house, made me want to go home and start scrubbing.

My feet were cold. I opened a dresser drawer, and sure enough, socks and underwear were in neat piles. I boldly helped myself to crew socks. I towel-dried my hair and pinched my cheeks to give them a little color. The mirror reflected a pale, tired face and black circles under the eyes.

"Find everything you need?"

I jumped two feet, as if caught in a forbidden act. "Yes! Yes! I borrowed socks."

He had changed into dry shorts and was barefoot. Maybe that's why I didn't hear him come in. Or maybe aboard his floating home, he walked on soft paws like a cat.

"Keep your feet warm. That's good. Feel better now?"

"Actually, I'm all in."

"Rough night, you want to take a nap?" He flung a careless hand towards the bed.

"No! Oh, no! No! I'm fine, thank you."

I followed him into the galley. Like everything else, it was neat and efficient. Will opened the refrigerator, handed me an egg carton and reached into the cupboard for a bowl.

"Scrambled for everybody okay or an omelet? Your call, Hannah—"

While I whipped eggs, he nuked bacon, made toast and dripped coffee. The reviving aroma of Community with Chicory filled the air.

Suzy busied herself distributing paper plates and plastic cups. Bobby unfolded canvas chairs. Gramma stood on the deck, surveying the other boats. "Oh, look at that one! My, oh my! Just you look at that! Makes me think I'm back in Florida."

The wistful note in her voice touched my heart. She had uprooted her routine, left her friends and restructured her life to come help me. "Do you miss your own place, Mom?"

"Sometimes—"

"You can go back, y'know, anytime."

"And leave my grandchildren? No way!—I stay in touch."

In our past life, Saturday morning Joe made pancakes, and we'd all klutz around the kitchen doing our thing while he flipped flapjacks in the air, short order cook style. Those Saturday breakfasts brought us together and bound us so we could weather any storm ahead. We didn't have to conduct a Spanish Inquisition to torture the truth from our offspring. In the kitchen's warm, loving atmosphere, Bobby and Suzy shared their news, predicted the next football game score, or informed us that the new color for spring was Confederate mauve. Then, one day, without prior notice that camaraderie was gone, destroyed, past.

That feeling of family came over me now, and suddenly catching Will's eye, I saw something deep and disturbing in their green depths. He looked away quickly and said, "Bacon coming up!" and I followed, "Eggs ready!"

When we were putting breakfast on the table, our hands touched. I felt a tug, a response that came from my heart and my heart was an ice block. Any spring thawing was certain to cause big problems.

CHAPTER 25

The public bonds had been sold and the council had $5 million in the bank to patch roads and bridges. My guess was that Mr. Percival made the arrangements.

In order to save money and move faster, our engineer suggested a three course asphalt treatment be used on the less traveled secondary roads, and the traditional soil, cement and asphalt overlay on the high-traffic thoroughfares. I had no idea what he was talking about, what this meant, but the others understood, or pretended they did, and the motion to approve the engineer's suggestion passed unanimously. Work on roads and bridges started after Thanksgiving. Not the best time because the rain caused delays, but the council wanted the people to see that the effort was being made. We dispatched the few ragged machines we owned to start the paving and repairs. We hired anyone willing to work and gave them a shovel. The really big jobs we had to advertise for public bids, but the process took three months and the council wanted action before then. Road gangs roaming about, shovels in hands, appeased the Indians and saved our scalps.

"Look alive," Henry Johnson told the crews. "Your permanent employment depends on those roads getting fixed. The parish is counting on you."

Explanations weren't necessary. "Bad road," and "bridge out," they understood.

One afternoon, driving the roads, checking progress, I came upon a worker lying under a dump truck, a dangerous situation. He looked dead. What if a driver started the truck and ran over him? Then we'd really have an ugly situation.

"Come here!" I cried, motioning to the nearest man, "what's the matter with him?"

The laborer leaned against his shovel. "Looken like he's asleep."

"Asleep on the job?—"

"Yes'm."

"Wake him up."

"Oh, no, I ain't wakin' that dude."

"Why not— I'm telling you to."

"It ain't my place."

"I'll do it, then. Dammit!" grabbing the man's boot and yanking.

"Don't do that, Miz. Jeb's a mean drunk."

The tugging on his boot roused the man.

"Huh? Huh?" He scratched his crotch vigorously then rubbed his eyes.

The other laborers drew near, watching, leaning on their shovels. A repugnant smell rose from the hot tar barrels.

"Get up! You're fired." My voice carried, "Sleeping on the job."

The man crawled from under the dump truck and staggered to his feet. The little runt was dust covered and tar streaked. He had mean, squirrely eyes. "I ain't sleepin'."

"Then what do you call it?"

"I passed out, high blood pressure. I need med'cal attention."

The others laughed. One said, "He passed out all right," and pointed to the evidence, an empty gin bottle behind a big truck tire.

"Drinking! You're fired! This minute! Right now! Leave your tools, go by the council and collect your pay."

He turned angrily and tipped the hot tar barrel. Before I could jump aside, thick, black goo spattered my left leg, a singeing, charring streak mid-calf to the ankle. It burned like hell.

***

Only Mel Green and I sat in the council chamber. The room looked vast. The council lawyer reviewed my defense for the hearing scheduled for January 15th.

"Did... you take a...a pic-pic-ture of him asleep?" Mel asked.

"No, I don't carry a camera around with me."

"Then...then...you'd bet-better start. What proof do...do... you have that he did-didn't have high blood press-pressure?"

"None, the others said he drank. There was an empty gin bottle."

"Was it his gin bottle or some...somebody else's?"

"His, right behind the truck tire—"

"Do you...you have proof that was his gin bot...bottle, not just a bottle accidentally thrown there by some other per...person?"

"Come, now, Mel."

"Did...did you see him drin-drinking?"

"No, he was already drunk and sleeping when I got there." I repeated myself, "The others all said he was drunk."

"And do you, in...in your dreams, think his fell-fellow workers are go-going to come forward and test-testify against him? Read these reg-reg-regulations." Mel handed me three typewritten pages.

Okay, now I know. In private business it's okay to fire somebody for ineptness or drunkenness, but not in public employment. Three warnings, a hearing with concrete evidence, a probationary period, and blah, blah, blah.

"We'll try to bluff our...our...way through it," Mel said, "but...but there's not much hope. He's hired the ACLU Ed-Edgar Evans."

"The guy in the trench coat who comes to every meeting?—"

"That's him. He'll pro-pro-probably get him men-mental an-anguish; dis-discrimination."

"Discrimination?—what are you talking about? I fired him because he was drunk, not because he was black!"

"Weren't you, a white wo-woman, on a lone-lonely road, afraid of this black man when he stood and came toward you?"

"That's ridiculous!"

"That's what Lawyer Evans is go-going to say. You acted pre-precipi-tously, in fear, without cause."

Governing was so complicated. Even terminating a drunk became a federal case. Was this a good way to run a railroad?

I showed him my bandaged leg. "Maybe, then, I'm missing a good opportunity to counter-sue for bodily harm."

CHAPTER 26

FINANCING

One Friday, I ran into a frazzled Betty, the council secretary who also doubled as bookkeeper. She stopped me in the hallway. Her furrowed brow and urgent expression warned me something was wrong. "I've been looking for you everywhere. You're the new treasurer. I need you to sign these checks." She thrust into my hands a three-to-a-page bound checkbook. "Ordinance says each check must be signed by the council president and the treasurer."

Henry Johnson had already scrawled his name. I rifled through the checkbook. He'd signed at least 100 checks. "But they're blank!"

"Of course they're blank. We haven't written them yet."

"I don't sign blank checks. Write the date, the name, the amount and attach a bill or voucher and then I'll sign them."

Betty's frustrated look clearly implied she had neither the time nor patience to educate another greenhorn. "That's not the way we do it."

"It's the way we do it now." I was trained by the PTA ladies, honest souls who accounted for every cent the parents contributed. Lose a dollar and there was no peace until the last penny was found.

"Today is Friday! Pay day! " Betty's tone rose. "The crews will be coming this afternoon for their paychecks."

"You have payroll vouchers, time clocks and pay schedules?"

"Well, *yeah.*"

"Then attach a payroll sheet to the checks."

The request made her mad as hell. Fury twisted her tongue and she spit venom. "Listen, here, you're the new kid on the block. We've been doing things this way long before you got here. Now, these checks gotta be signed."

"I'm not intentionally making more work for you, Betty, really, I'm not, but as treasurer, I need to know who gets paid what around here. You understand? It's nothing personal."

"What about the others, the grocery, drugstore and restaurant bills?"

"Same thing—attach the bill to the check."

The way she clamped her lips and clomped back into her cubicle left no doubt she wasn't going to climb this mountain.

At Habitat, the second job I was lucky enough to land because of my first job, *it's not what you know, it's who you know*, the board was planning a big fund-raiser, the committee meeting at 2 p.m. When I opened the door, Janice, the volunteer who answered the phone, was totally flustered. "Grab that phone. That Mr. Johnson is on the line, won't hang up, chewed my ass, and he's waiting to eat you alive."

Henry blubbered like a madman. "What are you thinking? For the love of Christ! Nobody's getting paid! Everybody's gonna quit! We'll have a goddam riot on our hands. Jesus! What is the matter with you? Don't we have enough shit to deal with already? Do you have to stir the pot some more?"

Henry wasn't intimidating me. "You signed blank checks with the court-appointed administrator looking over our shoulders? I'll bring you cookies to the fourth floor."

He slammed the phone. My ears popped.

***

The unsolvable council problems, plus my own acute insecurity kept me awake at night. My bed was a lonely place, no tangled legs, no warm lips soft against my neck, no shoulder for a pillow, no careless hand flung across my breast, two bodies one, a nest, a nest. I heard the two o'clock freight's lonesome wail, the wheels clack...clacking on the ribbon tracks, rain drumming a tattoo on the roof, tears dripping from the eaves, myrtle bushes scraping the wall sounded the way nails did raking across a blackboard, Oh my, oh my. Sunrise came and brought dark circles under my eyes.

Bobby and Suzy didn't notice. They'd retreated into their secret space, hurt puppies crawling under the house to lick their wounds. When the kids didn't get their way, or couldn't go somewhere because money was short, they blamed me. Something I did or didn't do made their dad leave the house. He never would've gone otherwise. They were too young to understand. Even I didn't understand.

Arguments, verbal abuse, physical violence, there were none, only the chill. I felt it often, that dismal cold of a fire that's turned to ashes. A long breath, a little breeze and embers lit again, wasn't that so? A phase, a mid-life crisis, women talked about the way their men checked for bald spots, complained about beer bellies and problems at work. Not Joe. His hair remained thick, graying over the ears, receding a bit from the forehead. He was fit, trim, ran four miles a day, played duplicate bridge every Thursday night, or did he?

Joe had been discreet, keeping his liaison with the princess secret, though I should've known, should've suspected the long night hours at the university, seminars and papers to grade, lying to me straight-faced, too tired for this, too busy for that. Everyone knew about the affair, and other indiscretions, too. Kind friends brought me up to date. Should I thank them?

The bomb destroyed me because it was so unexpected, *boredom*. The well-ordered life routine, wife and children, dinner on time, friends over for drinks. Couples craved what we had. They told us so—pleasant, compatible, peaceful, words to that effect. We lived life to perfection, gossamer silver web, a spider's tangle, *boredom*.

My life-long friend, Barbara, did her best to assure me it was a mid-life crisis, all men had them. Nobody could maintain an edge forever. Every marriage got boring at some point. "Ride it out." She spoke from experience. "Just don't quit eating and become an anorexic scarecrow, or stuff your face and turn into a hippo."

And when I couldn't overcome the blue funk I was buried in, she advised at lunch one day, "C'mon, Hannah! You're an intelligent woman. You're not the first this has happened to. Men leave with their secretaries all the time. Get over it, honey! Stop brooding!" The waitress hovered, listening to the details, her pen poised over the little green tablet. Barbara ordered shrimp salad.

"The same," I said, not looking at the menu, not caring what I ate. "You think that's what I've been doing? Brooding? Mother hen, brooding?—" She was right. I wanted to slap her.

"It'll get better. Time is a great healer."

Such platitudes! She should be a Hallmark greeting card versifier. "I'm sure that works for death, but divorce is different."

"Why do you say that?" Barbara stabbed a shrimp, plunked it in her mouth and worked her jaws, enjoying the taste, no notion whatsoever of how pain affected appetite.

"Death is something one has no control over. Divorce, there are 1,000 questions, 1,000 ifs, maybe I should've done this, maybe I should've done that."

Barbara deliberately put down her fork. "Hannah, this split wasn't your fault. Buck up. Think of your kids."

"I do! I do! They're suffering because of their parents' mistakes. Heaven forbid they ever make the same ones! I should've listened to Mom. She begged me to finish college before I married Joe. And my step-father—remember him?—he had that walrus mustache that tickled and he never thought twice before speaking his mind. He looked at me and said, 'Stupid move, Hanny Han,' that's what he called me, Hanny Han. I didn't listen. Nobody ever listens to their parents."

***

Not only were the parish's finances in complete disarray, so were my own. The council seat, supposedly part time, two Monday evenings a month paid enough to cover the house mortgage and a little extra. Along with the check came restrictions that didn't apply to me, as I didn't intend to sell the parish any merchandise, bid on building contracts or offer extended or in-kind service. The second job at Habitat for Humanity had flexible hours and supplemented this income. My duties were to organize fund raisers, schedule work crews and buy materials and supplies. Doing for pay what I did free for the PTA for so many years suited me fine. My teenagers sifted coins through their fingers as if it were loose sand. Joe's child support check barely paid the kids' expenses. The check had already been late two months in a row, and who knew? Joe was terrible at finances, and the princess wife probably cared less whether we got the check on time or not. Oh, lord. Oh, lord.

CHAPTER 27

Late one afternoon, Ken White, the court-appointed administrator, the CAAd, crooked a finger in my direction. "Mrs. Kelly, you are the treasurer, right? Follow me, please."

I trailed him into his lair, a cubby hole furnished with a worn leather couch and a second-hand metal desk Wendi had scrounged from the judges' chambers. "Sit for a minute, please. We have a few things to talk over."

He motioned toward the coffee pot behind him. I shook my head. What thievery had he uncovered? Ready to justify, apologize, rationalize, fall to my knees and swear on a Baptist Bible I hadn't signed one single blank check.

CAAd poured himself a cup and drank it black. "I need to make my position clear," he said. "I'm not here investigating ethics or nepotism or whether or not the council follows Roberts Rules of Order. My sole purpose is to discover where and how the money disappeared, and identify any wrong-doing. If the evidence shows that illegally spent public funds bankrupted this parish, then the responsible parties will be prosecuted to the full extent of the law." The mild man with the soft voice carried a big stick. Whenever he swung the club, people better duck.

"Uh huh," I mumbled. Why did I ever run for treasurer? Why? Why? Was insanity my best defense?

"I'm here solely to straighten the parish's finances and make certain that the council adopts a manageable budget using accepted accounting practices. I'm a CPA, but I guess you knew that already."

"FBI CPA?—"

"I don't know who started that rumor, but don't squelch it. It's convenient. The last council let bills slide for four years. There is a debt accumulation that indeed, were this a private corporation, would lead nowhere but to bankruptcy. But the state attorney general has decreed that Pohainake Parish can't do that. So you and I will start where we can." Two strides and he crossed the room. "This is where they keep the bills." He opened a closet door. My eyes popped.

At Habitat, we had a storage room lined with filing cabinets where we kept our correspondence, accounts payable, receivables, and important documents. All the papers were placed neatly in manila folders, labeled and stowed, a place for everything and everything in its place. Neatness simplified life.

Not so here. Cardboard containers were piled floor to ceiling, boxes stacked upon boxes, lids discarded, contents spilled, papers everywhere as though someone looking for a document had hastily rifled through the stacks.

Ken White didn't chuckle. This wasn't a laughing matter. "Welcome to the bookkeeping system."

"Oh, my God!—" Where would one start, with a match? A month behind balancing my checkbook made me nervous. Four years, and this outfit hadn't reconciled anything.

"I've studied the situation. The only thing to do is to drag this stuff out and sort it by date, supplier and job." He noted my dismayed expression. "You have a better suggestion?"

Relief made me giddy. The CAAd's summon didn't lead to prison, my children remained in my primary custody. Life was good. "When do we start?"

"Might as well dig in right now—"

"It's five o'clock." Bobby played baseball at 7 p.m. "How long do you think it will take?"

"Four, five weeks, if we stick to it and don't give up, work at night, can't do this during the day, can't have everybody poking their head in, contributing two cents' worth, can't have that."

Such a rigorous schedule required I reorganize my world. "Let me make a phone call."

Bobby was disappointed and I was, too. The season's opener and I wouldn't be there to see my son throw the first pitch. "I'm sure your dad is going. Give him a call."

"Yeah, okay!"

"C'mon, Bobby, you know he's very proud of you."

To make this split function, both working parents had to pull their share. My employment now took priority over my children, a crushing blow. Bobby and Suzy were my jewels, my reason for living. Convincing Bobby that my missing one baseball game wouldn't crash our world didn't work. A dark cloud covered my universe, miserable darkness, mother guilt.

Ken White and I began sorting bills when the courthouse emptied at 5 p.m. Most nights it was nearly midnight when Ken locked his office door and walked me to my lone car parked in the lot. He had instructed Betty, the secretary-bookkeeper, and Wendi, the council clerk, "Nobody enters this room. Is that clear?"

Henry Johnson, denied access, took umbrage. "I'm the council president."

"And you'll be the first to receive the report," CAAd assured him.

"Why is Hannah—?"

CAAd cut him short. "She's your elected treasurer."

Henry developed a great animosity toward me, conveniently forgetting that he and the others had happily voted me treasurer so that when the budget didn't balance I'd go down with the ship while they remained afloat. At this juncture, he was secretly jealous that treasurer was more important than president. The truth be told, had I known treasurer would be this much work, I would've lobbied for another job.

Yet, there was no denying the adrenalin surge brought by each discovery, by deciphering a problematic money trail, by having an expert present who could solve the riddles.

Nightly my admiration for Ken White grew. He was methodical, systematic, never raised his voice or became angry. I yawned, stretched, propped my eyelids open. He never tired. The closest to disarray he came was the night when he assembled a particularly demoralizing group of bills, a puzzle we'd been trying to decipher for days, loosened his tie and said, "Aha!"

Some nights he ordered pizza and when it was delivered, he said in his droll, dry way. "I expect we shouldn't charge this to the parish."

"Why not?—" making a face. "Everybody else did."

The second week when the five until midnight pattern developed into an on-going situation, I called Florida and un-retired my mother. Leaving two teenagers alone every night wasn't a good move. If Joe found out, he'd give me grief, try to alter the custody arrangement and take the kids. That I would do something foolish and lose my kids was my constant panic. Joe's princess barely tolerated Bobby and Suzy, but Joe missed his children and would welcome any opportunity to gain full custody.

In Pohainake Parish there were no secrets. Before long street gossip had it that Ken White and the District 2 councilwoman were having an affair—sex every night behind closed doors in the big courthouse, vacant except for the noisy prisoners upstairs.

I called Barbara. "Have you heard the ridiculous rumor going round?"

"Uh huh—"

"It's absolutely not true."

"Don't acknowledge it. Don't deny it. That only adds fuel to the fire."

"What if my children—"

"Listen, Hannah. I'm a judge's wife, lived with politics all my life. Get used to slander. Pay no attention. Take care of business as if those idiots didn't exist."

Easy advice, hard to follow; my natural instinct was to fight back. Once the caring public made me aware the CAAd was not an asexual methodical bookkeeper, but a man capable of sex, my perception altered and the situation changed. The friendly banter ceased. Our interchanges became more formal.

We struggled along night after night, frustration and exhaustion, guilt about abandoning the children, fear of repercussions from Joe. My heart was a concrete block.

"I can help," Betty, council bookkeeper, said late one afternoon when she saw that CAAd and I were seriously sorting and labeling and would not be deterred.

"Overtime," I replied. "The parish can't pay."

She gave me an injured look. "I'm a citizen, too."

"Then dig in."

She was quicker than CAAd or me because she knew the invoices: green ones belonged to Robert Standish, lined notebook paper to the grocery stores, blue block print to the drugstore, and so forth. Sorting through Alcore Drug Store bills, Ken White chuckled and asked Betty. "How much Valium can inmates take? Do they keep the prisoners tranquilized day and night?"

Later, when he understood the open-handed charging of grocery bills, he became tight-lipped. "Who authorizes these purchases?"

Betty shrugged. "I dunno. If I had to guess, I'd say probably the road crew chiefs."

The road crews ate lunch at the nearest crossroad grocery store. The bills were for bread, baloney, cheese, cold drinks, potato chips, Tide soap and toilet paper.

Betty defended the charges. "The crews have always charged their lunches. It's considered a job perk. They're minimum wage guys barely making it."

"*Tampax?—*" Ken's eyebrows shot above his horned rim glasses.

Another night, "The utilities haven't been paid in over a year," CAAd said, "How do you keep the lights on?"

"Power & Light and Ma Bell threaten to cut off our service every month, did it one time, but so far the sheriff sends them something every month and they've left us alone."

"And if he doesn't?"

She shrugged. "I guess the council better have a boxcar load of candles available."

CAAd discovered the council purchased concrete by the ton, but the roads went unpaved. "Can you shed any light on that?"

Betty said, "I dunno," but by the tone, she did know and wasn't saying.

Another time he asked Betty what the marshal's duties were.

"He serves subpoenas, summonses and such. He has one deputy."

"Does he shoot anybody?"

"Not that I know —"

"Then why does he buy enough bullets for an army?" Sifting through a green bill pile stamped paid, he wondered, "This garbage dump seems to be the only bill that gets paid regularly."

"Mr. Standish has to be paid or he won't empty the dump stations and he locks out the garbage trucks and there's nowhere else to dump."

CAAd put the green bills aside. "These bear closer scrutiny," he said. "I'll look more closely at them later."

As we got deeper into our bill sorting, CAAd questioned Betty more and more. The night he cataloged the sheriff's expenditures, she left early.

Next morning as I climbed the courthouse steps, Betty stopped me. "I can't do that anymore, Hannah." She looked haggard.

"What's the matter?"

"I'm tired."

"I can understand that."

"Sorting bills was okay, that's easy for me to do, but not the questions. They make me uncomfortable like I'm ratting on the former council and they're the ones who hired me. The sheriff already got wind of this and it may cost me my job. Hannah," her eyes implored. "I'm a single parent. I need this job. It puts food on my table, y'know?"

How well did I know. This job was exacting a high toll from me, too, much more than I had bargained for.

CAAd and I struggled without Betty until we had bills stacked all over the floor, a brick holding down each pile.

"I'll label them." He retrieved a black Marks-A-Lot and wrote: payroll, jail, dump, hospital, marshal, sheriff, judges.

Two months later, at a regularly scheduled council meeting, Ken White handed Henry Johnson 100 single-spaced typewritten pages. "Here is the preliminary report," he said. "You have the first edition."

Wendi placed copies before each council person. We silently flipped through the pages, an apprehensive pall falling over the assembly. The CAAd had pinpointed questionable practices, weak procedures and unauthorized expenses highlighted in red. The pages appeared to drip blood.

The prisoners above banged their floor (our ceiling), the plaster dust sifting down while the preaching inmate sermonized. We could hear his main message: "Everyone is a sinner! Everyone is a *fornicator*! Everyone is goin' t'hell!

The council didn't much worry about going to hell. Our biggest worry was going to jail.

CHAPTER 28

My mother, a former army nurse, had had three husbands and was looking for a fourth. Widowed shortly after I was born, she shed the next two spouses. For her, divorce held no stigma. She viewed it as escaping a gilded cage where she could no longer sing. She and her exes remained friends. They called her when they couldn't conquer a cold or an unidentifiable pain and the nurse went to their rescue. When Eddie, (the second one) was diagnosed with terminal cancer, she moved herself and her nursing skills back into his house and helped his current wife nurse him.

She wasted neither time nor energy placing blame. "Sometimes," she told me, "you can rub against each other until the rough edges wear smooth and you can fit into the same life. Sometimes, you can't." She was six feet tall and had henna red hair. Age had not diminished her intimidating, authoritative air. If anything, the passing years had intensified these traits. "So suck it up or I'll be treating you for an ulcer."

We'd had this conversation after an altercation with Bobby who overnight had become rebellious and resentful, an emotional upheaval I blamed on the divorce.

"All teenage boys get to that point," Mom said. "They want to cut the apron strings and don't know how, so they yank instead of gently untying. Wait until he gets a driver's license. He won't talk to you at all, then. Mark my words that will happen, divorce or no divorce."

"If he had a father—"

She stopped me cold. "Bobby has a father, a good father. What you don't have is a husband. Don't confuse the two. Don't transfer that bitterness to your children."

"Why do you always take his side?"

She encircled me in her comforting arms. "I'm on my grandchildren's side. Who is right? What is wrong? Who knows? Shit happens and one has to deal with it and move on." She gave me a reassuring squeeze. "You're going to be fine. Now, hurry along. You can't be late for that meeting."

***

The meeting was a solemn one. My fellow councilmen greeted me in a reserved manner, quickly getting to the business at hand. The sole item for discussion was the CAAd's report, signed, witnessed and certified.

"Copies," Betty raised the thick volume high over her head, "have been delivered to the governor and the attorney general this very day"

Henry Johnson uttered the thought in everyone's mind. "The old council should be here. They should be the ones reading this. They got the parish into this mess. We're the ones working to solve it." He gave Ken White a significant glare. "Why should we be held responsible?"

"Because you're the ones in charge now," Ken White said. "Be assured, that if any wrong doing is established, that person will be prosecuted. And if the practices aren't corrected, well then—" CAAd let the words hang and the council seated in the swivel chairs surrounding the big table, shifted in their seats.

My heart was in my throat. Add this incriminating report to my big worry, that I'd be the one reserving weekends for my children's visits. The disgrace my children would have to face! How their fellow students would taunt them! Your mother thought she was so smart! Thought she would fix everything. Ha. Ha. Now, see? Where is she? Are you visiting her this weekend? Taking her a cake with a file in it?

"We might as well get started," Henry Johnson said, "Hannah, you're the treasurer."

For the first time he sounded genuinely elated that he was not the keeper of the till, that I had that thankless job.

The knot constricting my throat was as big as an orange. My voice was barely audible. "I yield to Mr. White, the court-appointed administrator. We thank you for a job well done. If you'd be kind enough to go through this report, we'd appreciate it."

Ken White adjusted his horn-rimmed glasses. "My pleasure," he said, "if the council will turn to page one." The report ran well over 100 single-spaced typewritten pages. The enumerated malfunctions and malfeasances, acts and events that the council thought standard practice, took for granted, such as the sheriff holding barbecues (he had the big barbecue rig) at charity events and private parties, the government paying the tab. Deputies taking the police cars home and using them for their own purposes after working hours, gas a perk; the marshal sending a wreath every night to the funeral home for the deceased (whomever) at tax payers' expense. Most deemed these everyday occurrences good PR, not illegal. Ken White read for over an hour before we took a coffee break then returned and resumed. By midnight we knew without doubt we were more than in trouble. We were in deep shit.

Henry Johnson broke the prolonged and uncomfortable silence that followed the report. "What do you propose we do?"

Ken replied, "First, you have to build a jail and a sanitary land fill. Those are federal mandates and there's no way you can get around them, no matter how many citizens file injunctions or hold demonstrations. You have to take that stand and no waffling allowed. Secondly, you have to formulate a budget, have each department, sheriff, marshal, clerk of court, justices of the peace, public defenders, judicial branch, and so forth, submit their numbers, then allocate those funds and nothing more. This council can't run the parish without pre-established budget guidelines. You can't dole money every time somebody asks. Thirdly, you have to stop the waste and the graft and the stealing." He stopped for emphasis and everybody sat upright. This was the part that could get one into court. "And there's plenty of that going on," he continued. "I'm not going to sit here enumerating every unlawful act instance by instance, item by item, you can read that yourself, but it has to stop. Starting with the sheriff down to the ditch digger," his deliberate gaze swept the table. "Stop it. Shut it down, right now!"

One summer Joe, the children and I went to Carlsbad Caverns. We descended through narrow labyrinths into a black hole. The chilling darkness, wet walls and slippery rocks, the bats' flapping wings echoing through the murkiness, frightened me. I lost direction, didn't know up from down, east from west. Agitated, I searched for a light, an opening, a way out, and then I felt Joe's hand slip reassuringly into mine. No such security existed here.

The council, collectively smothered by the heavy consequences and individually swamped by our own dire thoughts, went mute. The silence deepened until we could hear the void stretching from the chamber to the not yet built prison.

We flipped through the pages. The prisoners above banged our ceiling. The plaster dust sifted down. The preaching inmate was sermonizing, usual premise. Everybody was going to hell.

Red Harper recovered first. "Yeah, sure, tell Sheriff Branson what to do! He's the law."

CAAd replied. "I understand it's a monumental problem, but frankly, gentlemen and Mrs. Kelly, what I see here are nothing but big problems and you have to deal with them."

A named hurricane had less force than the report the CAAd handed us. The incriminating evidence made newspaper headlines, the local five o'clock news, as well as Baton Rouge and New Orleans television stations, the aftermath a constant, rumbling thunder.

***

For several weeks after that meeting, the council sessions were unusually quiet and subdued. Business was transacted swiftly. "I make a motion," followed instantly by a second, no discussion and a quick vote. Whenever I introduced the CAAd report, Red moved we table it, Peewee Reese seconded, and the vote was two for tabling, two (Will and me) for not, and Henry Johnson broke the tie in favor. Something was not right, but I had no idea what. They were leaving me out of the loop, and the sad thing was I didn't even know where the loop was.

One morning before the evening council meeting, Betty beckoned me into her cubicle. I'd arrived early to retrieve the agenda, so at least I would know what was scheduled for a vote. Usually, the press knew before I did.

"Come," she said, leading me into the women's restroom and locking the door behind us. I didn't know why that surprised me, since by now precious little shocked me.

"I think you should know," Betty began and my heart sank.

This job had a stress level off the charts. Responsibility for the parish's welfare was equivalent to walking through a mined field carrying a hundred pound sack on one's back. Consequences were dire. We could be ruined for life, good name tarnished, reputation trashed. Was I insane? Whatever possessed me?

"What?" I whispered as I looked over my shoulder to make certain no one entered the wash room.

"Swear you will never tell you heard this from me."

"I swear. Cross my heart and hope to die."

"Okay." She cut her eyes toward the door, turned both basin faucets full blast and flushed the toilet. "The reason all the motions are being made and passing bam—bam—bam!—without any discussion," her whispered words were low and dramatic, "is because the men are meeting at Hoaxley's Tavern at five o'clock and deciding everything beforehand. It's all cut and dried when they get here."

I couldn't believe what she was saying, but it made good sense. The council didn't want to argue before a hostile audience, before a press who pinpointed the most ridiculous, the most sensational, inconsequential item, inflated the facts beyond normal proportion and plastered the news across the front page. The code was to transact our business quickly, smoothly, and give the impression we were unanimous in our endeavors, united in our efforts.

"Thanks." Problem defined; solution pending. "Okay. Thanks."

Hoaxley's had a terrible reputation. Cue-stick fights were notorious. Habitual drunks hung at the bar. Women, unless they were for sale, didn't go there.

I angle parked, staring at the building through the car windshield. Budweiser and Miller neon signs lit the dark, grime-streaked windows. A big crack ran down the plate glass. Next to the entrance, cigarette butts stuck in sand filled a concrete container. The canopy over the door was askew, as if a high wind had twisted one end and nobody ever bothered to fix it. I took a deep breath, tugged my skirt, checked my hair on the visor mirror and opened the car door.

Going from sunlight into the interior darkness blinded me. Stale liquor and old cigarette smells stung my eyes. It took a few seconds for my vision to adjust. In one corner a juke box glowed. The shadowy outline of wooden tables and chairs filled the room. Behind a long bar to the left, mirrors reflected the dim light. Two seedy-looking derelicts wrapped their legs around stools. I knocked on the counter to catch the bartender's attention. He was watching a ball game on TV.

"I'm looking for Henry Johnson."

The bartender's head snapped around. He recognized me. My picture was in the paper more often than I wanted. "Miz Hannah?"

"Hannah Kelly, yes, and who are you?"

"Ben Hoaxley."

"I'm pleased to meet you, Mr. Hoaxley." He had a weak handshake and a confused look. "Where is Henry?"

He glanced over his shoulder. "I'm not sure you can go back there."

"I *can* go back there, Mr. Hoaxley. This is a public bar and that's a public pool room, right? Are you telling me women aren't allowed?"

"Oh, no, no, I'm not saying that. Women are always welcome." He was wiping a hole in the bar surface.

"Good. So what's the problem?"

"They don't wanna be disturbed. They have this kinda private meetin' goin' on."

"I know that. The pre-council meeting, I'm a member, y'know, District 2."

"Let me get Henry. You just let me go get Henry."

I followed Mr. Hoaxley through the door into the pool room. When I walked in, the men bent over the pool table dropped their cue sticks. Their jaws went slack.

"Good afternoon, gentlemen." I was astonished to see our Executive Officer, Sonny Barth, among the group and Will Fleming, too. I'd thought them better men than that. "I've come to be a part of this decision making process."

Henry Johnson was the first to find his voice. "Now, Hannah, don't you be jumpin' to conclusions. We jus' havin' a friendly drink before the meetin'."

"Well, order me a Jack and water and I'll join you as long as we are not discussing parish business. Have y'all forgotten the Sunshine Law? Do I recall the district attorney gave us those rules right in the beginning, the very first day?"

Their party shattered, they stood idly waiting for me to finish the drink Ben Hoaxley set before me. I was more than a thorn in their side. By their pained expressions, I was driving nails through the palms of their hands. I sipped very slowly.

"I must say, Sonny, I'm surprised to see you here." *After all, you son of a bitch, I got you this job, compromised my ethics to get you aboard and that stuck in my craw from day one, and here you are meeting with the traitors in a pool room,* "and a little disappointed."

Sonny, big, lumbering, lovable bear looked contrite. "Just a drink, Hannah, gotta know what's comin' down the pike."

"But there's no government discussion here, right?"

They mumbled incomprehensible responses.

"Red, how's your wife? Your cows?—"

"They're fine, everybody fine." He pushed his baseball cap back and ran a hand across his forehead. "I'm outta here."

"Oh, please stay, Red. It's still an hour before the official meeting, hardly enough time to go eat or anything. Have another beer."

"Don't want another beer." Sullen, aggravated.

Peewee stood. "I'm going witya."

"Don't rush out, guys. I came to warn you before you get us in so much trouble we'll never be able to bail."

"Warn us about what?" Henry had a wary look in his eye.

"About illegal, secret meetings—"

The men froze.

"You know you can't keep secrets in this parish. Everybody knows where you fellows are here Mondays, five o'clock. I was feeling quite left out. CAAd knows about these meetings. He is on his way." That bluff came from thin air and materialized without reason, like an unexpected comic strip balloon.

My words paralyzed the men. They stood rooted to the floor. The moment hung heavy, pulling everything sharply into focus. The metal lamps over the pool table flooded the green velvet surface. The juke box's neon glow bathed Peewee green, purple and yellow, giving his black skin a sickly glow. Red stood near the door. He spit tobacco juice. The disgusting trajectory made a slow arc and hit the brass spittoon next to Will Fleming's foot. The captain leaned against the wall, his perpetual amused look aggravating me beyond reason.

Red didn't bite. "CAAd won't come here."

From the door came the surprising answer. "CAAd is already here."

CHAPTER 29

August in the South and Dante's Inferno had a lot in common: blazing heat, pouring sweat, pitchfork tempers; urge to kill. August was, by all rational thinking, not a good month to gather numbers and wedge them into tight slots. However, the council persevered. We wrestled figures, fractions, decimals, percentages and couldn't make them work. Sonny Barth, expert comptroller who steered the biggest corporation in our parish, warped and twisted the numbers and flung the total to the mat. "It doesn't matter how you cut the pie, Hannah, there's not enough yen to go round."

The budget shortfall kept me awake nights. *No money* seeped through my bedroom walls. *No money* filled the darkness. *No money* hovered over my bed. Tossing under the covers, punching the pillow for more comfort, I counted sheep to induce sleep. At some subconscious level the white wooly creatures dissolved into *no money* one, *no money* two, *no money* three.

I whined to the CAAd. "If we could squeeze ten cents from every penny, there's not enough money. What should we do?"

"Withhold funds if the departments don't make a budget, no payment." A sympathetic look tempered his stern voice. "You have to," he said. "You have to hit them in the pocket book to make them pay attention. There's no other way."

The council treasury distributed the monies for each department. To withhold disbursement took real guts. Had I developed the necessary iron balls?

Producing a balanced budget for the parish took nine months, as long as it did to have a baby. In retrospect, birthing was a lot easier. At least in the delivery room no one argued and it was perfectly acceptable for the mother to shriek and scream. She didn't have to hold her breath for fear of offending somebody.

The special session to adopt the balanced budget drew an enormous crowd: the sheriff, his deputies, the justices of the peace, the marshal, clerk of court, registrar of voters, road workers, engineers, judges led by the Honorable Sam Blanchard and public defenders. Anyone connected to the parish by the money lifeline was there for one purpose only, to make sure that the council didn't tamper with their share or that their allotment didn't get cut by accident or design.

The regulars were there: ACLU Trench Coat, civic league and association reps, preachers of every denomination. Like the ancient Romans who filled the coliseum to watch lions attack gladiators, these people came to watch council dog fights.

The press was present: Shirley Smythe, the Daily Sun reporter was in her usual end seat, scribbling on a pad, looking bored. Ned Morales, WHHO, hadn't arrived. He normally missed the preliminaries and appeared after the break when he could stick his mike in everybody's face. The big TV stations in the nearby cities skipped because no sensationalism was expected at a dull budget meeting.

"Peewee," I asked, scanning the crowd, "what's your wife doing here?"

His eyes went blank as if he'd pulled down a shade over the pupils. "I dunno."

Will Fleming gave Peewee a disbelieving look. "Precious rode all the way to the courthouse in the car with you and you don't know why you brought her?"

"I didn't brung her. She come on her own."

Sheriff Branson had his pews crammed full. "Did the sheriff make all the clerks and deputies come?" I asked.

"You see 'em," Peewee replied.

"What's the catch?" There was always a catch.

Peewee couldn't look me in the eye. He was too nice a guy, too open, too kind, to play government poker. He walked away.

"They got to him," Will Fleming reflected, casually holding a protective hand over his mouth to thwart any visitor bent on lip reading. "That wife sitting there, she's a hostage. Peewee votes against the sheriff in any of these proceedings, she's fired. You have more to worry about. Take a look at that back pew."

Looking over the crowd, I spotted three Asians. They were neat, well dressed, quiet and diffident. "They're not in my district."

"But they heard you want to tax their water."

"What are you talking about?"

"The Japanese Sumiyama Corporation is negotiating to buy Kaplan Water."

"Does Red know? It's his district."

"The artesian well is inside the Kaplan corporate limits. The Kaplan mayor has jurisdiction."

"Does the mayor know?"

"That's not the question. The question is how involved is the mayor? How much is his cut?"

"Oh, God. That's why he raised hell with me this afternoon."

"Can't say I blame him. He makes a sweet deal with his water and you come along and propose to tax it. What'd you expect?"

"I expect we can't tax water. Sonny checked. The state treasurer thought the idea had merit, but severance taxes belong to the state, not the parish. If anybody taxes water it will be Louisiana, not Pohainake." Another dead end, another failure.

Henry Johnson cut short our whispered conversation. "Mrs. Kelly! Mr. Fleming! If you please!—"

In a stunted way the council meeting resembled a NASA rocket launch. Anticipation, danger, uncertainty and suspense hung over the room. The spectators sat on edge, observing the preliminaries, the council members walking around, whispering and conferring, Wendi setting down papers, Betty checking the recorder and a nervous Mel Green striving for nonchalance. The big wall clock hands steadily ticked a countdown: ten to six—nine—two—one! Henry Johnson's gavel hit the table and the council blasted forth to do our damage.

Henry quickly opened the meeting, hurrying the Boy Scouts through the Pledge of Allegiance. "This council is now in special session for the budget proposal only."

As if it were a lit dynamite stick, he immediately tossed the budget report to me. How happy he was that I was the treasurer! How elated that I got to read the incriminating report.

Wendi Walsh prominently set down a tape recorder. Knowing that the little machine captured every word uttered, the council members watched what they said and kept to the point.

Elbows propped, papers held low, steadying shaking hands, my eyes scanned the audience looking for a friendly face and saw only frowning, red-faced, tight-lipped men and women poised with the watchful intensity of cats stalking a bird, ready to pounce and rip the prey to bits.

Henry Johnson banged the gavel again. He was getting incredibly good at that move. He warned the crowd, "There will be no questions, exclamations or comments until the complete report has been read. Mrs. Kelly, please proceed."

"Ladies and gentlemen," my voice barely above a whisper— must do better than that. Captain Fleming slid a peppermint in my direction. I popped the candy in my mouth, ahem-ed once more and started anew, read the first page and no one jumped to attack me. Gaining confidence, the second page rang forth in a clearer, stronger voice.

The marshal's funeral wreaths bit the dust. His ammo was cut in half and a moratorium issued on buying any new guns or rifles. His charge account at Murt's Diner closed.

When Murt heard, she didn't grouse over losing good income. She nodded approvingly. "I wondered when someone would shut that faucet."

The sheriff had to park his traveling barbecue rig, a stainless steel job that went from fair to fair and from cook-out to cook-out, toted by champion cooks deputy chefs, Best Barbecue Cook, Best Jambalaya Cook, Best Gumbo Cook. The deputies had to park their cars in the courthouse lot at shift's end. No more driving to the grocery store after work or to the Gulf Coast for a Sunday outing. The sheriff could no longer buy drugs from his cousin's pharmacy. Drugs and medicine were to be purchased through the state hospital at half the price. Charging at grocery stores by road crews was stopped and on, and on, and on. One by one the loopholes were closed. CAAd advised the council not to touch the judges, he'd deal with them. The black-robed men intimidated us. They banged their gavels and equally meted justice and injustice.

At Barbara's Art Foundation fund-raising party a few weeks ago, I circled the pool looking at the silent auction items. Sam Blanchard grabbed my elbow and drew me aside. "The judicial branch regrets the parish's money woes, but that isn't our business. You can share that with the other council members."

I defended our stance. "It's everybody's business if we have no money."

"If the council tampers with *our* money, we'll order the clerk of court to attach *your* funds and pay the juries." The unpaid jurors was another noose around the council's neck, loose at present, but able to be tightened at any moment. "Those jurors don't sit *pro bono*, you know." At another time, in another venue, this contentious behavior would've been labeled blackmail. In Pohainake's bankrupt days, extortion was called expediency.

Barbara rescued me. "My God, Sam, this is a party. Leave her alone." No event was ever a party for me anymore. Every social session turned into a game of dodge ball.

"At some point," CAAd had informed the council, "the jurors must be paid, or the system of being judged by your peers will certainly tank." A few days later he reconsidered. "Let the judges go, let them ride temporarily. You've got enough to deal with at this time."

Once assured tonight that their money remained intact, the Honorable Untouchables, with a direct pipeline to the attorney general, rose in unison and noisily exited the chamber, shaking hands right and left, smug and superior. They left two empty pews immediately taken by others waiting in the hall.

The session lasted well past midnight. A few went home happy. Some nodded their heads and agreed the council was right. Something had to be done. Most went home mad as hell, threatening retaliation. The people stampeded down the stairs like mice after government cheese. Cork Kennison, the marshal, pointed a finger at me and yelled, "You haven't heard the last of this, Hannah."

CHAPTER 30

The budget sessions were terrifying. Every elected official whose department spending or personal perks were curtailed or cut, yelled, screamed, cursed, promised to sue or inflict bodily harm, threats that had to be taken seriously since everybody in the South owned guns. I'd return home shaken and tired, a real basket case. One evening a battered Ford station wagon blocked the driveway. I parked behind it and opened the kitchen door. "Whose car is that?" Suzy was eating a peanut butter and jelly sandwich. "Where's Gramma?"

"She went to play poker. There's someone in the living room waiting to see you."

"You let a stranger in the house? Suzy, you know better."

"Oh, it's okay. It's Jenny's grampa."

"Jenny Kennison?"

"Yep—"

Was there no end to this work day? Was Grampa Kennison planning to kill me, too? The marshal's father, looking tired and shriveled, sagged on my couch. "Hi, Mr. Kennison, how are you?"

He came right to the point. "Upset, Hannah, very upset."

"Aren't we all?" *Upset* was a new life dimension.

"But you're not starving."

"I beg your pardon?"

"You're starving my grandchildren."

"What are you talking about?"

"Cork hasn't been paid in three months."

"Oh, that."

"Yes, that. Think about your own daughter. How would you feel if Suzy didn't have three square meals a day?"

I had no idea if Suzy did or didn't have three squares a day. My children's lives seemed to be slipping through my fingers. There was always a meeting or a crisis that prevented me from getting home in time to cook for them. Mom nuked frozen Healthy Choice for her dinner. Suzy and Bobby ate enough Burger King whoppers to own a franchise.

"The court-appointed administrator has frozen all funds unless a budget is sent in. Marshal Cork has to give us some numbers, any number, something."

"That's not the custom." He stared at his black cowboy boots, hands dangling between his knees. "His wife is sick. His children need shoes."

"It might not be the custom, Mr. Kennison, but it's the law. It's beyond our control. We have the attorney general's man running the show. We have to do what he says." Pass the buck. Blame the situation on somebody else. Politicians were excellent at that.

The old man looked ready to cry.

The idea that I caused his grandchildren to lack food and have no shoes was daunting. How could I be held responsible for such dire straits? Wasn't Cork Kennison's lack of cooperation at fault? Shouldn't he partake in the guilt?

"I'll tell you what, Mr. Kennison, I'll go by there in the morning and talk to Cork, see if he can give me a budget, whatever number it takes to release his funds."

"Thank you, Hannah. My family has dedicated its life to public service and it's hard to believe this is the thanks we get." Mr. Kennison donned his battered cowboy hat. His knees popped when he rose and walked to the door.

"I know. It's awful, isn't it?" fully understanding. "I'll go by the marshal's first thing in the morning."

***

The marshal, whose starving children had no shoes, had left for Grand Isle in south Louisiana for a three-day Gulf of Mexico deep-sea fishing trip. His deputy, Illinois Central Dangerfield, guarded the fort. Illinois doubled as bartender at most private parties. We were old acquaintances. His familiar, gold-tooth smile greeted me.

"You got paid, Illinois?"

"No ma'am. Mr. Cork advanced me a few."

"You know the marshal needs to turn in a budget to the council."

"Heard that—"

"What's the problem, then?"

"Nobody's got an idea what anybody spends. Here, let me show you."

He led me to a closet-pantry and opened the door. Stacked floor to ceiling were overflowing boxes, bills and receipts. My non-reaction disappointed Illinois. This bookkeeping nightmare was nothing new to me. I'd already waded through a similar jungle.

"You need to pull out this stuff and go through it. Sort it into piles."

"Cork ain't gonna do that."

"Well, he has no choice."

"Supposin' I done it?"

"Can you?"

"Reckon good as he can."

"I'll help you."

Three days later, using CAAd's sorting, piling and anchoring the stack down with a brick, I had a handle on the expenditures. Most had to go. Funeral home wreaths for any and sundry deceased, rifle and shotgun bullets, gas, boats, four wheelers, safari vests and duck waders and tabs from Murt's Diner. Every three or four months, Cork paid his house mortgage from public funds. Just as often, he slipped himself two pay checks.

Wendi typed the findings and placed them before CAAd.

"What do we do?" I asked.

He studied the numbers then red-penciled unauthorized expenditures. I looked over his shoulder at another bloody ink bath.

"I'll take it from here," he said. "Good job."

When Cork returned from his fishing trip, he barged into the Habitat office. The sun had burnt his face crimson and bleached white his blond hair and eyebrows. His arms swung in windmill circles. His blue eyes were wild. He sputtered and stammered and didn't know where to start.

I offered him coffee. "Or would you rather a coke, water?"

"Not a thing, not one damn thing! You have no right!"

"Listen, Cork. Somebody had to do it. Your children are starving."

"Bullshit! I got money! I don't need this crummy job to feed my family!"

"Tell your father that."

"My old man better not meddle in this! He ain't the marshal anymore!"

So they had a family problem. Well, I'm no psychiatrist. In fact, the deeper into this job, the more convinced I was that I myself needed a good shrink.

"Listen, Cork," suddenly angry, angry at his yelling, angry at everybody dumping on me, angry at not spending more time with my children, angry at not having a husband who would share my woes, angry at the people who encouraged me to become a public servant. "Do whatever the hell you have to do. Just remember that mortgage payments from public funds and double paychecks can land you in jail."

His eyes spit fire. If looks could kill, I was dead. He slammed the door. The impact rattled my wall. The family pictures, certificates and Habitat Awards tilted askew.

CHAPTER 31

Several days later, I poked my head into the CAAd's corner and stopped short. Ken White had packed everything. Labeled boxes were stacked one atop another. His desk was cleared and his computer gone.

Had he already left? Was he coming back? He couldn't abandon us here at the mercy of these rebellious voters.

Ken White had been a comfort, our security blanket. As long as he sat in his makeshift cubicle, FBI or not FBI, he was an authority symbol, a presence from the attorney general's office. He was the umbrella under which we took shelter. And now CAAd was taking the umbrella with him, leaving us in the storm's eye to dodge flak, duck lawsuits, and sidestep blame.

Ken White was the single, strongest presence in the council, not physically because he was a slight man with a silly little mustache intended to make him look older. The horn-rimmed glasses gave him an intellectual, school boy look. The fedora, when everybody else wore a baseball cap, made him conspicuous. What was impressive were his methodical ways. How he unearthed a wrong-doing. How he followed the dirt to the source. How he unraveled knots, sorting efficiently through the maze. How he confronted the culprit in a serious, business-like way. How he worked late nights from the onset, digging through the unpaid bills, drinking coffee and humming a silly little tune. How he played Beethoven and Mozart because he found the music soothing. What would happen when CAAs left the premises, when the attorney general's guillotine man was no longer present? Ken White had been a constant presence at this council since day one. Every decision the council made, he had checked and double-checked and made sure every move was legal so we wouldn't run into added troubles. He would look at stuttering Mel Green and say, "Excuse me, I don't want to interfere, but you see this?' and he'd point to a word change here, a little tweak there. "Just a suggestion," he'd say, "Makes it clearer, more specific."

Would the parish slide back to the point it was before? Did the council have the strength, the character, to stick to its guns and not let things revert to their former status?

We were like high wire trapeze artists about to perform without a safety net.

Why didn't he give notice? Did anyone thank him? I wanted to thank him, to tell him how grateful we were, how much we appreciated what he'd done for the parish.

"Has he already left?" I asked Wendi.

"No. But he will soon. Tomorrow, I think."

"Could you ask him to call me before he goes?"

"You got it."

***

Ken met me for lunch at The Plantation, a converted antebellum house set in a camellia garden that bloomed spectacularly in January, but not in August. Nothing bloomed in August. Even caladiums, the most colorful tropical, wilted in the relentless heat. The wrought iron chairs leaned against the tables, the patio closed. Next to the steps, a heat-defying rose bloomed pink.

Inside the restaurant, the air conditioning was an arctic breeze. Ken was waiting at the bar having a drink. "Hello, Hannah. I've a table over there." He beckoned the waiter and we trailed into the dining room.

He'd picked a table in a nook, away from prying eyes. In this corner the guests wouldn't trip over our table, stop to interject their opinion or disturb our conversation. A private outing in a public place was impossible for an elected official, even non-celebrities such as the CAAd and me.

"I hate to see you go," sincerely meaning it.

"My job is done."

"Where do you go from here?"

"Wherever the AG sends me, there's work everywhere in Louisiana." He shrugged his shoulders. "A beautiful state mired in corruption."

"I want to thank you for all you did for us. We could never have done it without you."

"I did my job, what I'm paid to do. But you put your heart in the work, far and beyond the call of duty. All those nights until midnight! I really thought you'd give up at some point. When the gossip started—"

"You knew that?"

"Oh, yeah, knew the minute you heard it, too. You walked into our closet and I could tell by that stubborn lift of your chin things were not the same."

"I was appalled, embarrassed and concerned, a particularly difficult time. I worried about my reputation, what would happen if my children heard or if my ex-husband heard, very stressful. Your wife was spared, I hope."

"No wife, divorced."

"Sorry."

"No need. Best thing ever happened to me. Only snag is my two kids every other weekend. That hurts."

"I bet it does." How well I knew! I would die if I were in those shoes. "I talked with my friend Barbara, her husband Sam is the judge, and Barb said don't acknowledge, don't explain, don't justify, just ignore it."

"But you stuck to the end."

"I'm really worried what's going to happen when you leave."

"It'll be all right. You and Will Fleming stick together and keep the agenda from falling apart. You can rely on him. And as for you," he gave me a myopic look through the thick lenses, "here's my card. You run into any trouble, you call right away."

"Thank you."

"And if you don't run into trouble, keep in touch anyway. You should run for state office. Intelligent, dedicated people, men or women, are hard to find."

The unexpected compliment made me blush, the heat warming my cheeks and I mumbled a reply. "Ken, we don't know the half of what we're doing. We just muddle through."

"How do you think the state is run? The nation?—Everybody who's elected muddles through and hopes that it will all wash out okay in the end."

"That's scary."

"You bet it is. Someone can go to Harvard and learn to be a diplomat, but there's no school that teaches politics. It has to be learned in the trenches. You have to have a natural flair. The trading, swapping and the compromising, that's the government way. Nobody gets 100 percent."

"I wanted to do so much," regret in my voice, "It looked so easy from the outside looking in."

"Once you're in, it's a hornet's nest," Ken replied. "The aim is to get away with as few stings as possible. If you never forget why you're there, who put you there, and always work for the people's best interest, then you rise like cream to the top and get past being a politician and become a statesman."

"You think so?"

"I know so. Politicians come and go. Statesmen," he chuckled his funny little laugh, "or stateswomen, we remember forever. They are few and far between, like finding a pearl in an oyster."

His sincere words affected me deeply. A dull ache tightened my chest. "If I need you?—"

"You've got my number."

His goodness, his kindness, and all he meant to us, to the parish, combined with an excruciating exhaustion, brought tears to my eyes. "Is it okay for a councilwoman to cry?"

He reached for the white handkerchief in his breast pocket. "Perfectly, all right," he said, and leaning closer, dabbed my wet cheeks.

CHAPTER 32

Every year between Christmas and New Year, Silver Chicken, Inc. hosted an overnight gala in New Orleans for all public officials. The hand-delivered invitation was attached to a case labeled FROZEN CHICKEN BREASTS.

I laughed so long and hysterically Wendi came running to see if I'd finally become unhinged and gone over the edge.

I pointed, blubbering and spitting, to the crate. "I've received gold invitations, engraved invitations," choking with laughter, "mimeographed bingo invitations, pink and blue shower invitations, but never, never a chicken invitation."

Mr. Percival on his way to the judge's chambers, hearing my crazy laugh, detoured into the council office, took his Swiss army knife, cut the wires holding the top closed and looked inside. He moved the frozen breasts around, counting them. "Twenty-four, making sure you didn't get any more than I did."

"You got a chicken invitation?"

"Uh huh, I can keep mine, but you can't keep yours. You must give them back."

"Why?"

"The gift can be considered a bribe."

"I consider it hamburger substitute."

"Silver Chicken comes before the council with a special request, zoning variance, a special permit, you'd be chicken compromised."

"I bet the other councilmen keep theirs."

"It's up to you, then, but remember it's not the act itself, which may be innocent enough in its intent, it's how the public perceives it."

"And the public always perceives the worst."

"You're learning."

"Maybe I shouldn't go to this shindig at all."

"No, no, that's not a good idea. All politicians attend this function. You need to be there."

"You're not a politician."

He chuckled. "Well, I do own a few."

Wide-eyed, I asked, "Me?"

"Hardly, my dear, you're too stubborn and independent. Nobody can own you."

***

Suzy helped me buy a new dress, a black crepe number, flared skirt, a tight bodice and spaghetti straps. My credit card in her hand, her good taste knew no bounds.

"This isn't me, Suzy."

"You have to stop dressing so matronly, Mom. Gramma says you need to buy some spiffy clothes or you're never going to get another man."

"I don't need another man."

"Mom," Suzy asked a serious note in her voice, "Will you be forever mad at Dad?"

The question took me aback. "I'm not mad at your dad."

"Yes you are." She looked downcast. "You say things about him."

Me? Who tried my best to be open-minded and not resent the bimbo who stole my husband? Me? Who with pseudo-cheer packed the kids for the weekend swap? Me? Who cooked and washed and cleaned and slaved for my children's benefit? Me? Who worked two jobs to make ends meet? "I don't say anything about Joe."

"And he says things about you."

"What things?"

221

"Just stuff, you know what? Bobby and I just wish you guys would settle it once and for all. Lots of kids in school have divorced parents. Nobody cares. Everyone gets along."

I put my arms around her. "You are so right. I promise I'll try harder."

***

Pohainake Parish Council encouraged farmers to diversify as mandated by the Louisiana Department of Agriculture. The farmers planted fallow pastures in Christmas trees, a new industry struggling to survive in a sub-tropical climate. Shouldn't the council members be the first to support the budding endeavor?

"This used to be fun," Suzy grumbled as we trudged the narrow lanes between Leyland cypress. "These ugly things don't even look like Christmas trees," she griped. The trees were different sizes and different price tags. "Are we getting mistletoe?"

"Just a tree," I said, tight-lipped, tired.

Bobby agreed. "I liked it when we went in the woods."

"So did I, Bobby, but things change."

Such great days, those old days! We had no money for store-bought trinkets and decorations. The week before Christmas we'd ride in Joe's truck to his grandfather's farm, pick our way through the woods searching for the perfect pine tree, the weather cool, sometimes nippy, a slight frost covering the ground. Along the way Suzy filled a big basket with pine cones that we'd paint and glitter when we got home. I snapped holly limbs, the leaves shiny satin, red berries dripping from the stems. Joe taught Bobby how to brace the shotgun against his shoulder, aim at parasitic mistletoe clinging to a high branch, and bring it down. We gathered the green-leafed twigs, tied them together with a red bow and hung them over every door. Any excuse for a kiss.

Such great days! Those old days! Sunlight filtered through the branches and into our lives, bright splotches that assuaged schoolteacher poverty. As we walked through the woods, we tripped over blackberry brambles that pierced through our jeans and scratched the skin. Squirrels scurried as we invaded their territory. Birds flitted from one branch to another, twittering, sweet and clear. On one occasion we startled a deer that froze in place for a second or two then bounded away.

Such great days! Those old days! The kids ran here and there, finding woodland treasures. Often, Joe hoisted Suzy onto his shoulders so she could reach for a gray Spanish moss beard. Our daughter giggled and laughed. Her father turned and looked at me, happiness in his eyes, and we knew, deep in our hearts, life didn't get any better than this, paradise lost.

Christmas, Thanksgiving, Easter, holidays brought nostalgia for what was and would never be again, precious moments the mind touched, a weight on a bruised heart. These were the very same moments Gramma advised I let go. How could I possibly erase past happiness?

***

As the Silver Chicken gala drew near, I dreaded going solo to this big flashy party, odd woman, third wheel.

"Go with Mr. Will," Suzy said.

"I don't think so."

"Mom, please quit being mad at him. He really likes you."

The very idea! "You have a teenager's imagination. I will not go with Will Fleming."

Gramma put aside the crossword puzzle. "If you won't go with the nephew, try the uncle. Ask Charles Percival."

"Be serious."

"He's an old man. He'd be flattered to take a good-looking woman like you."

"It's you he likes."

"Because I'm a good poker player and can massage his back."

"Massage his back?"

"I'm a nurse, remember?"

Oh, hell, why not? All he could say was no. I screwed my courage, bounced into his office, took a deep breath and plunged ahead. "Mr. Percival would you be my date for the Chicken Banquet?"

He lifted his big head and the triple chins quivered, "An old man like me?"

"Well, you're the one said I should go, and I hate going by myself, how about it?" I'd never seen him go out with anybody except his old cronies and half expected him to say no. His thick, pursed lips and triple chins made him look so much like an old frog, that perhaps if I kissed him, he'd turn into a prince. I half-rose and kissed his cheek. "Aw, come on!"

He was so astonished, his head bobbed and I took that to mean yes.

Late afternoon Saturday, Gala Day, he sent his Rolls Royce to fetch me, his chauffeur in full costume.

"What you did to the old man?" he asked, tugging at his visor cap with a gloved hand. "I've been with him twenty years and this is the first time he's taken a date to this ball. When I was shavin' him this mornin', I swear I think I heard him hummin.'"

In our area, where the average worker earned minimum wage, where upscale coffee shops and yogurt bars didn't dot the hemisphere and limos were few and far between, arriving in a chauffeur-driven Rolls Royce drew attention. We had immediate red-carpet treatment the second we arrived at the New Orleans Convention Center. The place was lit like the Milky Way. Miniature yellow light strips outlined the marble steps. Cabs honked, jazz music filled the air. Diesel fumes and brick dust smells rose from the streets and sidewalks. The endless traffic noise followed us from the Rolls to the entry door. The women rustled in silk, shoulders bare, jewels circling necks and wrists. The tuxedos turned the men into handsome gentlemen. Amidst all the glitter my black dress looked ordinary to me and my pearls, dated. I gave myself a pep talk. Pearls were classic, never passé.

What a party! A way-out-of-my-league gala! After intense hard work without letup, being both mother and main provider to my children, learning to live single, everything from changing a flat tire to mowing the lawn, dragging the garbage to the curb, and lighting the barbecue pit, this gala was like entering Disney's Magic Kingdom.

Gathered in the humongous convention hall were Louisiana's elite. Every table had a silver candelabrum anchored to a white, stuffed chicken. When the door opened and a draft blew in, the flickering candle flames flared forth then diminished.

Behind us I heard a familiar voice, a sarcastic comment. "Let's hope they have fire extinguishers handy."

Will Fleming arrived, an exotic, foreign-looking brunette clinging to his side. Her dress was red satin, a V-neck down to her navel. For the last ten days he'd been abroad.

"Europe," Henry Johnson had said. Will had disappeared abroad twice since we'd been thrown together in this government business.

"Spain again?—" I asked.

Henry replied, "He didn't go to Spain this time, just Europe."

Will Fleming draped a friendly, familiar arm over his uncle's shoulder. "This is Andrea, Uncle Percy. Andrea, meet Hannah Kelly and Charles Percival, *amigos mios.*"

Andrea was not much older than Suzy. She looked through me as if I were glass, checking the meandering guests, the expression in her dark, liquid eyes saying boring, boring, boring. She looked at Will, a pout on her glossy lips, *"Podemos irnos pronto?"*

Amigos, pronto, I remembered from my high school Spanish. The rest was gibberish.

Will stroked Andrea's hand, the way one patted a dog to calm it down. "Not long," he said.

She stood on tiptoes and whispered something in his ear and he laughed. "Okay."

I could well imagine what she'd proposed, but then, it wasn't exactly my business.

"How did the trip go?" Mr. Percival asked.

"Went fine, got the order."

"Congratulations."

What did Mr. Percival know about Will's yacht business? Was Will's company legitimate or just some cover for chronic unemployment? Yacht, motorcycle, no wife, no kids, no responsibility, sailing and playing with beautiful girls young enough to be his daughters, every man's fantasy.

"Nieces," he said, startling me so that I jumped. He reached and touched my chin. "Do you know that when you disapprove of something you jut your chin and get this bulldog look?"

That was exactly what Mom said. "I do not!"

"Yes, you do. Disapproval is written all over your face. You're very judgmental."

"I am not!"

Andrea could barely understand English, much less Southernese. Her eyes had the baffled look of a deaf person trying to follow a conversation, catching only a word here and there.

"My two favorite people bickering," Mr. Percival noted. "Come, let's go find our table."

We followed a waiter wearing a white shirt, black bow tie and black pants. Everybody stopped Mr. Percival, wanting to get in their "howdys," shake his hand or touch his shoulder. The most important man here escorted me. He was more popular than the lieutenant-governor acting temporarily as governor because the real, elected governor was in prison writing his memoirs. The acting governor kissed my hand, looking over my shoulder to make sure he wasn't missing a greater opportunity. I met the insurance commissioner; the state treasurer who said, "Good job!" and the interim commissioner of elections, (the real one was in the cell next to the governor) who said, "Now, honey, don't let the dead ones vote. It'll get you in trouble every time. Keep hearing your name. You are quite respected in our circles."

His flattery got him somewhere. After so much constant, relentless criticism any little compliment pleased, the way throwing a starving dog a bone brought some satisfaction.

Mr. Percival bumped into a corpulent man in a wheel chair. He had a long, pock-marked face and hooded eyes. I'd seen that face someplace before, a vague recollection, not pleasant. His skin had a grayish color as if he lived underground and never saw the sun. His upper torso was as developed as a weight-lifter's. His legs hung limp, useless.

"Joe Buddy, here's someone you need to meet. Hannah, Joe Buddy's our attorney general."

The man who'd sent the CAAd to supervise bankrupt Pohainake! The man who had me so terrified I couldn't sleep at night.

The AG shook my hand. "Ah! Ken White has good things to say about you. You're doing some good work over in Pohainake." A knowing smile cut across his face revealing big, white crooked teeth. He reminded me of an alligator who could snap his jaw and swallow people whole.

These men who shook my hand, congratulated me, and told me "Good job!" or "Keep up the good work!" didn't know me, but they knew *of* me. My name was familiar to them. Suddenly I felt as if I belonged there, could hold my own in their midst, a heady sensation.

Pohainake Parish Council's table overlaid with a white cloth, had twined ivy running down the middle. The proximity to the head table was probably because Silver Chicken's only Louisiana processing plant was in Pohainake Parish. The company was vital to our economic welfare. It contracted local farmers to raise broilers, layers and pullets. The state and parish constantly turned cartwheels to keep Silver Chicken in Pohainake, battling Mississippi to the north, who yearly offered the company better incentives and tax breaks if they'd just move across the state line. I presumed if Mr. Percival had arrived solo, he'd be at the head table, but gentleman that he was, he sat by my side.

Pohainake council members were all accounted for. Red Harper, wearing a suit, looked red-faced, as if the tie round his neck strangled him. Ellen, who lived in blue-jeans and plaid shirt, dairy farmer's wife attire, looked uncomfortable wearing a long evening dress, shiny jewelry and heels. The Silver Chicken processing plant was in Henry Johnson's district and by his puffed chest and proprietary demeanor, one would've thought he owned the company. As far as Henry was concerned, he hosted our table, Mr. Percival aside. All he needed to be full mettle was his gavel.

The most at-ease person was Peewee's wife Precious. She worked with the sheriff's PR department, and this function, as far as she was concerned, was simply another rubber-chicken banquet. Peewee looked impressive in a tux, probably rented.

Charlene, Sonny Barth's wife, was already four sheets to the wind when she got there, giggling, laughing, loud, obnoxious, guzzling champagne straight from the bottle as if she were siphoning gas. She was years younger than Sonny who made no attempt to control her, opting instead to look the other way, periodically saying, "Now, Charlene!" and "Settle down, Charlie baby."

Will Fleming's Andrea's bored look didn't leave her eyes until the Olympia Brass Band clambered on stage and began blowing their horns, pre-banquet entertainment. A stout musician ran a white handkerchief over his sweaty face and pounded a big, bass drum, the signal for the band to launch into a rousing "When the Saints Come Marching In," considered by most natives the state anthem.

> "Oh when the Saints go marching in
> Oh, when the Saint go marching in
> Oh, Lord I want to be in that number
> When the Saints go marching in—"

The tempo more than the words, stirred the crowd and they sang along. The musicians raised their trumpets and trombones. The sound bounced on the ceiling. Before long the band left the stage and paraded through the aisles, heads bobbing in time to the drumming. The banquet guests left their seats, fell in behind the band and second-lined, one foot out, one foot in, waving white napkins. The party was on! If Silver Chicken intended for their political guests to forget their worries and "pass a good time," they had a good start. Bad roads didn't exist and drainage was a mirage. Budget worries were eider down feathers drifting in the music.

The hall, so huge a little while ago, shrank as people packed the room and it grew warm. Perfume, flower scents and burning candles filled the air. To be heard above the noise, people spoke louder, louder, the sound a rising tidal wave, cresting and spilling over.

"I can't hear a thing," Mr. Percival said, digging in his ears. "These ear gadgets do nothing but squeal."

The band returned to the stage and played a rousing "You Are My Sunshine," the song written by Jimmy Davis, the Louisiana governor who spent most of his term in Hollywood. The people loved and revered him because he sang and made movies instead stealing the state blind.

The brass band packed their instruments and left, replaced by three violinists, sweet music to calm the guests as waiters bearing silver trays held high over their heads entered the room. The banquet was a chicken feast, chicken cooked a hundred different ways: sweet, sour, fried, stewed, dumpling, shredded, breaded, broiled and boiled. The courses kept coming: soups, salads, vegetables. I barely had room for dessert.

We sipped after-dinner coffee and finished bread pudding topped with white chocolate and rum sauce. Henry, inflated as big as a toad in a small pond, sat to my left. "How was your invitation addressed?" I asked.

"Honorable Henry Johnson, why?—"

"Mine was addressed to Occupant," I whispered.

"Occupant?" he drew back. "What do you mean?"

"Silver Chicken invited the Honorable Occupant of the District 2 seat. This year it's me. Next time it may be somebody else."

Henry frowned. I had struck a chord he didn't want played. "You have a weird sense of humor, you know that?"

Across the table, Will Fleming laughed outright.

Silver Chicken had my total admiration. They gave a great party. Other than a short, welcoming speech by the company president (his name escapes me now) and an equally short acknowledgment by the acting governor lauding Silver Chicken's importance to our state's welfare and Pohainake Parish in particular, there were no speeches. To assemble politicians and not allow them podium time was as cruel as sending a condemned man to his death without his last meal. The restraint brought a tortured expression to many a face.

After dessert, we adjourned to the auditorium where a singer wearing a skimpy, shimmering outfit, commanded the stage as if she owned it. She grabbed a mike and went right into traditional bluegrass followed by country rock favorites. She strummed a guitar, blew a harmonica and played a fiddle. The tempo accelerated and the audience went wild.

My busy life didn't allow time for music. "Who is she?" I asked Mr. Percival, who shrugged indifferently. He couldn't hear.

"Tina Lobell. Country Music Singer of the Year," Will Fleming said. "She's starring in a Broadway hit musical. This is the opening act."

He'd probably stopped in New York on his way to Spain.

For the final extravaganza, Tina was joined by twelve singers and dancers, the men clad in tight blue pants and the girls in brief satin short-shorts. The dancers wore red and white striped coats, and blue top hats. They were Broadway perfect. They dazzled and electrified the audience. For the final song, they belted *God Bless America* with such vigor and enthusiasm, their energy exploded under the spot lights.

Mr. Percival's chins rested on his chest. His eyes were closed and his mouth hung open. His loud breathing would soon turn into a snore. Should I nudge him awake?

The musical over, a standing ovation later, those ready for bed edged toward the doorway and hailed cabs. My arm linked through Mr. Percival's, I said my good nights.

Mr. Percival gave me a fatherly pat. "I've had all I can take for one night. Dancing is not for me." The old man looked tired and rumpled.

"Oh, that's fine. I've had plenty myself." I certainly didn't want to sit and watch others dance.

Will Fleming overheard, "Stay with us, Hannah. We'll take you back to your hotel."

Incredible that he would think I'd hang with him and his new Barbie. "Thanks, but no thanks."

"How about you stay with me?"

I whirled towards the familiar voice and there was the CAAd! Ken White! Impulsively, I threw my arms around his neck, "Sooooo glad to see you! What are you doing here?"

"Got my chicken breasts so here I am—we have catching up to do. How are things going?"

I kissed Mr. Percival's cheek. "If it's all right with you, I'll say good night. Thanks for a wonderful time. I'll let Ken bring me in a little while."

Mr. Percival seemed relieved and pleased as he walked toward the entry. His old cronies, Messrs. Songe, Agee and Gendre joined him. Saying little, the foursome passed through the door and stood outside waiting for their rides. These old men were like the underpinnings of a Louisiana offshore oil platform. Unseen, they kept the rig afloat.

CHAPTER 33

Riding the Marriot Hotel elevator to the ninth floor, I couldn't believe that I'd danced the night away with Will Fleming, the man I thought I most despised. I first danced with the CAAd, then Red, awkward and rigid as his John Deere tractor. I could hardly keep pace with Peewee. He had all the moves. He and Precious were a floorshow to behold. They were in absolute sync, Peewee twirling Precious then reeling her back against his chest, their feet skimming over the floor as if they were on skates. Henry was a pretty good dancer, but his wife pouted when he asked another woman to dance.

Let me clarify something. I'm not a great dancer and not having danced for the past ten years or more (dragging Joe to a dance was like pulling a recalcitrant mule uphill) I was pretty rusty. Whenever we were invited to a ball, we always quarreled, Joe saying "Okay, we're leaving by ten o'clock, I've got class early in the morning," while I argued, "If we're just going to come and go, what's the use of going at all?"

Between dancing intervals, catching my breath, drinking another old-fashioned, chewing the orange slice and digging for the cherry at the bottom, I listened to Henry Johnson's wife, Gina, prattle. "Look at that dress, that one over there. Her boobs are hanging out. That top is probably glued on, otherwise it would be down to her waist," and never missing a beat, "Doesn't Precious look like a dream? I've never seen her in anything other than her gray uniform, but even in that, she's always elegant, almost like she's white."

Offended by her remark, I parried, "I've seen plenty inelegant, trashy white people," almost adding, "you included," but bit back the words. Since being thrust into the public eye, I developed a thick ridge across my tongue from holding in check truths best left unsaid.

Precious truly had a princess carriage: long, neck, slim shoulders thrown back, spine straight, and a regal lift to her pointed chin. Her skin was a creamy chocolate color. Under perfectly arched brows, her starry dark eyes sparkled.

Gina's eyes left the Reeses and turned elsewhere. "There's Sam and Barbara. He's screwing Wendi any chance he gets and everybody knows it but Barbara."

What was it Barbara had said not so long ago? "There's always a woman after Sam, but I don't care. They can have my husband, but they can't have my station in life."

Gina meowed and scratched at peoples' lives the same way a cat clawed upholstered furniture. If Henry Johnson planned to run for the senate, he'd better clamp her mouth. A few seats away, I heard Red, Sonny Barth and Will Fleming talking garbage. By comparison to the dirt Gina dished, garbage seemed a much cleaner subject. I couldn't help laughing.

"What's so funny?" Gina asked.

How could I explain? She'd never understand, "Nothing."

"That little bitch is after Henry, too, but if I ever catch him fuckin' her, they're both dead."

A young man returned Sonny's Charlene to the table, but she didn't sit down. She flipped her auburn hair and batted mascara lashes, pursed her red lips, made kiss-kiss sounds, and grabbed Will Fleming by the hand. Mid-sentence, he let himself be pulled onto the dance floor. She placed both arms around his neck and plastered her body against his. He tried to remove her arms, but she clung tighter. They took a few staggering steps and then went full swing. Even drunk, Charlene was an amazing dancer.

Gina Johnson leaned closer and shared information. "Danced in New York, a Rockette," she said, "owned a dance studio in New Orleans after that. That's where Sonny met her."

"She has a travel agency here."

"Sonny bought her that with his severance pay, so she'd have something glamorous to do and wouldn't go back to the big city."

Sonny previously had a devoted wife and four children. "How long have they been married?"

"Four maybe five years—He's crazy about her, you know how old men can't resist a young skirt. Men's brains are between their legs, just look at Will Fleming. He's not happy unless he's robbing a cradle, but that bombshell he brought is stalking Ken. He's probably talking Spanish."

"Ken speaks Spanish?"

"Honey, you didn't know? The man speaks four languages."

"What's he doing working for the AG then? He should be in the diplomatic corps."

Gina leaned closer. "Undercover. He's after big fish."

What pipeline did Gina have that supplied her endless inside information? The only thing the CAAd was looking for was malfeasance, misappropriation of public funds, embezzling, little foxes that ruined a vineyard.

"He's divorced, you know," a pregnant pause, "but I guess you *do* know."

I felt the heat rise and warm my cheeks. I had to escape. Gina's wicked tongue could ruin my perfect evening.

Captain Fleming returned Charlene to Sonny and drawing near whispered to me, "Do me a big favor." His hand on my bare shoulder felt warm. "Dance with me. Save me from Cleopatra."

"Charlene."

"She vamps like a Cleopatra." He held my arm and I preceded him to the dance area.

I didn't fit his preferred MO, young, beautiful and sexy. I was 39, average-looking, ordinary clothes. Nothing about me would stop the world. But I did fit comfortably in his arms, and before we'd taken too many steps my head rested on his shoulder. I fought against the heat rising and spreading through my body, making my skin tingle. Will had his priorities and I had mine.

"Where's Andrea?"

"Dancing with Ken—he speaks Spanish a lot better than I can."

"So Gina told me." I looked over his shoulder and spotted the couple. "You'd better rescue her." Not that Andrea was the damsel in distress. I was. My emotions were running away with my common sense and only Andrea could save me. "She looks bored."

Will's arm tightened around my waist. He bent his head and his cheek rested against mine. His breath against my ear warmed his words. "I can feel your heart beating."

I cut my eyes at him. "Good thing. Otherwise I'd be dead," and caught myself. Flirting with Will was not good form. I looked away.

"Ken and I have engineered a swap. He's taking Andrea to Bourbon Street."

"The CAAd on Bourbon?—" Amazing, after months locked every night in a broom closet, how little I knew about the man.

"That's right, Bourbon."

Music filling the seedy street spawned evil. Strip tease joints and bouncers, jazz notes and shady balconies, street musicians, the wanton laughter of women having a good time, tourists clutching beer cans and go-cups spilling colored drinks, the heavy air reeking liquor and depravity, wrapped in the steamy humidity rising from the Mississippi River.

"They're going to the Quarter and I'm escorting you to your hotel."

"Anybody bothered to ask me?"

"This wasn't a committee decision, carried by a majority vote. This agenda is mine." He squeezed me so close I could hardly breathe. "All mine."

Sometime after midnight, the CAAd and Andrea departed for the French Quarter. As the evening swirled into dawn, I wasn't worrying much about anything. I had cocktails before dinner, wine with dinner and more champagne than I'd ever imbibed in a lifetime. The world seemed very bright and glittery. The sound I heard was my own silly giggling. I don't silly giggle—ever—never— burp—excuse me.

We danced until the wee hours, electricity sparking between us, my head against his shoulder, his arms holding me tighter, tighter.

He didn't say anything and neither did I. Perfect moments didn't need words. In Will's arms I found a new home—a scary, complicated and impossible event.

Morning lightened the eastern sky when Will hailed a doorman to fetch his red Corvette. I arrived in a Rolls Royce and was leaving in a Corvette, Cinderella herself. Had I found Prince Charming? Or had I gone over the edge?

"You want to hit Bourbon?"

I shook my head negative. "I think I'm drunk. Am I drunk?"

"Pretty much so—you're fun when you're loose."

"You're a good dancer," I said.

"I can hold my own."

"Did I dance with Ken?"

"You danced with everybody. Coffee and beignets at Café du Monde?—"

Negative again. "I wanna go to bed—oops!" That remark could be taken the wrong way, an invitation of sorts.

At my hotel room door he said, "Your door card."

I dug through my purse.

"That's your credit card."

"Oh. Sorry. Try this—"

He laughed. "That's your driver's license. Here, hand me your purse."

He pawed through the shiny evening bag Suzy had bought and retrieved the room key card.

Love was a locked door. Somewhere, someplace, somebody had the key. When that special person inserted the key, turned the lock and found the treasure, life was rich.

We were an unlikely pair: a Romeo and a divorced mother of two; a man with not a care and a woman drowning under responsibilities. He didn't give a hoot about his reputation while I obsessed over mine. What if I went to bed with Will and the news like a toxic cloud spread over Pohainake? And it would, for sure. Gina would be the first to gossip. My children would hear. Joe would pounce and use any little infraction to take away my kids. My mind catalogued the negatives, but every heart beat pumping blood through my veins said this is right... right... right.

Will was kissing me tenderly, thoroughly. His warm lips drowned the debate in my mind, melted the arguments. His arms locked around me and we were backing toward the bed, reason set aside for sheer pleasure and I didn't care. Whatever happened—happened.

What happened was that Will abruptly stopped kissing me and said, "The message light, your phone is blinking."

A dozen panic scenarios ran through my mind: the kids had a wreck, Gramma had a heart attack; the house burned down. I pushed the message button. Suzy's scared voice alerted me to the only tragedy that never entered my mind. "Mama, please come home quick! Bobby is in jail."

***

After leaving a hasty message for Mr. Percival at the front desk, Will drove me from New Orleans to Harmony in record time. The Corvette speedometer never registered under 100 mph. I jumped from the car before it stopped completely, took the courthouse steps two at a time. My son locked up! Those nasty, stinking cells! That horrible jailer! I jammed the elevator button again, again. Where was the damn thing? I turned away, ready to climb the stairs. Will's hand on my arm restrained me.

"He's not there. He's a juvenile."

"What?"

"They'll be holding him in the sheriff's department. You go find him and I'll see what this is all about."

"Thank you." I needed to talk to Bobby alone. Maybe Will sensed that. "Please call Sam Blanchard." The Judge would help us. Judges knew about arrests, bail bonds and legal procedures.

At five in the morning, a skeleton crew manned the courthouse, the building empty except for the jail upstairs and the sheriff's station where law-breakers were booked and held. An eerie quiet prevailed. The hubbub and commotion constant during daylight hours when bodies packed the hallways, leaned against the walls, sat on the floor, gathered in anxious knots waiting for their case to be called, their verdict to be pronounced, their fate to be decided hadn't yet started.

Illinois Central Dangerfield, the marshal's deputy, doing courthouse double duty since the budget constraints, sat behind the booking desk. "Howdy, Miz Hannah," and seeing my ashen face, the panic in my eyes, he added quickly, "He's okay. Come with me."

What a relief to talk to someone I knew! Who knew me, knew Bobby. Illinois helped me sift through the marshal's boxes while Cork went fishing. Illinois tended bar at everybody's party. He was one of us.

Illinois led me down the long, deserted corridor, the marble floors echoing our footfalls. The walls closed in. The morning light struggling through the barred windows offered no hope.

The first room we looked into held two scared-looking girls and a nonchalant black boy who obviously had been there before. He knew the system.

"Coke machine down the hall," he said.

Bobby wasn't with the other juveniles and that made my knees go weak. Had some gun-crazy deputy shot my son? Were the deputies interrogating him in the room that had one-way glass and sensors that raised the temperature hot enough make a culprit feel he'd arrived in hell, or lowered it to a sub-Arctic freeze that made teeth chatter? The council had just paid a bill for repairing the system.

My son sat in a room by himself, handcuffed to a straight-back metal chair, disheveled, his face bruised, eyes defiant, blue-black baseball size shiner, a sulk on his fat, swollen lips, dried blood smeared his nose. His shirt was ripped, jeans torn, belt and one tennis shoe missing.

"Are you all right?" Mad and upset as I was, my first thought was his welfare. I knelt for a closer look at his battered face. He pulled away. "What happened?" my voice ten decibels above normal.

"Nothing—"

Shake this kid! Grab him by the shoulders and rattle his brain. "Don't you tell me *nothing*!—you've been arrested! You're handcuffed! It can't be *nothing*! What did you do?"

"It wasn't my fault."

Illinois shed light on the situation: "He threw Deputy Anzamore through the plate glass window at Hoaxley's." Illinois wasn't accusing or hostile, rather his tone implied Anzamore got his due, had it long coming. "For starters—"

"Oh, my God— Anzamore hurt?"

"Doc gave him a few stitches. He's okay. Mad as hell, though."

"He came at me," Bobby mumbled through a fat lip.

Though angry and upset, my motherly instinct was to comfort and protect my little boy. "Does Bobby have to be handcuffed?" Illinois pointed to the ceiling, but I didn't lift my head. My eyes were riveted to Bobby's face, as if the steely mother look could extract the truth. "What in Christ's name were you doing at Hoaxley's? You're under age. You have no business in a bar!"

"We went there after the dance at the gym. Everybody went."

The generic teenage excuse, it's all right because everybody else is doing it. I took a deep breath to calm myself, to get a grip then asked in a more civil manner, "Who got arrested beside you?"

"Nobody—"

"Nobody?—"

"They all ran off." His tone implied the rats abandoned ship.

Illinois said, "Football boys got into a big scrap in the back room."

"Is that right?" I asked Bobby.

He didn't look at me, didn't answer.

"I'm talking to you." Like talking to the wall—

Illinois explained, "Deputies went in there to break it up and Bobby resisted arrest. One tried to handcuff Bobby and they struggled. That was the beginning."

"The beginning, there is more?"

"It went on from there."

Bobby lifted his chin. "I didn't mean to throw him so hard, but he came at me and I just grabbed him and shoved."

Shoved him with the same angry strength he'd hurled the ball at the dunking booth and toppled me into the murky water.

"Were you drinking?"

"We had coupla beers." He tossed the reply as if he'd been drinking punch instead of an intoxicating beverage. A couple could mean a dozen. Hoaxley's had no business selling liquor to underage kids. The sheriff should padlock the place. Didn't the deputies and most council members spend their down time at Hoaxley's? Wasn't the pool room my son wrecked privy to every parish secret?

I wanted the whole truth. "Were you smoking pot?"

He looked away.

"Answer me!"

The tone in my voice reached him at some level. "We passed a joint around. No big deal."

Pot-smoking was a big deal to his mother who was getting straight F's in parenting, a big deal to the councilwoman exposed to public opinion. Would this be front page news tomorrow morning? *Don't think about that right now, think about getting Bobby released and safely home.*

Hurried footsteps—Will coming down the hall—he'd help me. He'd drive us home and we'd sit at the kitchen table, the three of us, and talk over this business and maybe Will Fleming could knock some sense into Bobby's head.

Will said. "They're releasing Bobby to your custody. The deputy is typing the paper work. You should probably call his father."

Joe! Joe hadn't entered my thoughts. "He's skiing in Aspen." What would happen when Joe heard? "I'd rather not let him know."

"This is Harmony. Better that he hears from you than somebody else, count on it. He'll hear."

"I'm calling Sam." The Judge and Barbara left the Silver Chicken banquet early, Sam complaining about his sinus and not feeling well. There probably wasn't any need to disturb the judge, but Sam knew these cases and could reassure me in his calm, earthy manner.

The phone rang several times. My throat tightened and a choking feeling overcame me. What if Sam wasn't home? Who should I call then? Mel Green, the council lawyer? No way, no way, no way.

Barbara finally answered. "Hello?"

I imagined her on the king-sized bed, propped on satin pillows, reaching for the white, gold-trimmed phone that matched everything else in the bedroom. Champagne and Caviar, her two white tea cup poodles curled at her feet. I heard their shrill yapping.

"Yes? Who is it?"

"Barbara, Hannah. Can you wake up Sam? I have a problem. It's Bobby."

"Sam's not here. What's the matter? Can I help you? Where are you?"

239

"The sheriff's office—"

"What happened?"

"Bobby got in an altercation and got arrested."

"Oh, dear, I'll find Sam."

Barbara knew where to look and I didn't care if she had to route her husband from his lover's bed. Neither Barbara nor Sam would talk. Would the little hussy blab?

Will had not left. He'd drawn a plastic chair next to Bobby's and they sat, knee-to-knee, talking in low voices which was more than Bobby had done with me. The idea riled me that my son was confiding in a stranger when it was me who gave him birth, raised him from a child, sat through every Little League game and tolerated his teenage hang-ups. This was the thanks I got! Ignoring me in favor of a man he hardly knew, a man whose girlfriend had seduced my son.

Illinois came through the door. "Paperwork ready, Miz Hannah. Come this way."

Will rose. "Bobby will be okay," he said, his voice confident, as if he were a pro at parenting. People with no children were always experts.

Bobby was my trust, my life. Nothing he could do would alienate us. I was his mother, for God's sake.

The deputy talked to me through a hole in the bullet-proof glass. "Sign here, Miz Hannah. Be sure he shows up in juvenile court January 10."

The date had a final ring to it, as if from that day forward life would never be the same.

CHAPTER 34

Beginnings were supposed to be clean slates, resolution time; fresh starts. January missed the mark.

January 6, first Monday Council meeting—elect new officers
January 7, parent-principal conference, Harmony High
January 10, Juvenile Court
January 15, Preliminary Employment Hearing, matter concerning Jeb Chance

I looked at the schedule and wanted to play mole, dig a deep hole and hide.

After Bobby was released to my custody, it took me a few days to sort through the facts. Precious, who had access to the sheriff's files, let me hear the arresting transcript and filled the gaps. "The Harmony High boys came to even the score with the Amelia High boys. You know that football rivalry."

Pohainake citizens were rabid football fans. Fridays, they supported their high schools as if a world war outcome depended on the scoreboard. Saturday, college fans drove to Baton Rouge for the LSU game and Sunday, beer and TV football, or New Orleans for a Saints game.

"Remember the playoff game Thanksgiving week?" Precious asked, "When Amelia Whirlwinds beat the Harmony Tigers and you south end folks said the referee made the wrong call?"

Last ten seconds, thirty yard line, Jim Langdon, the center, hiked the ball to Bobby who tossed the pigskin to Cork's boy, a last-ditch Hail Mary pass. Lil Cork caught the pass like a ballerina, a leap and a twist, and ran for the touchdown. An inch away from the end zone, referee said Lil Cork stepped out of bounds. Questionable! Amelia won 7-3. Every available sheriff's deputy and city cop, fearing the worst, ran down from the stands and ringed the field. That's how passionate football fans were.

Precious brought me back to the present. "At Hoaxley's the boys got to hitting each other over the head with the cue sticks, then began using them as fencing swords, slashing one another. They trashed the place, ripped a hole in the pool table, and y'know that pool table is bread-and-butter to Ben Hoaxley, expensive equipment."

"How expensive?—"

"I expect those tables cost a couple of thousand dollars or way more."

"He must have insurance." God, I hoped he had insurance.

Precious shrugged. "You best get ready for Hoaxley. He'll give you grief and for sure the tab for repairs to his place." She continued the harrowing tale. "Seems Bobby was beating the crap out of Jay Zettling—"

Bobby was tough and wiry, long arms and legs, sinewy and muscular. Jay was solid, tough and mean. High schools weren't allowed to openly recruit, but everyone knew that Amelia High's new head coach, who'd been assistant coach at nearby McComb, brought the boy across Mississippi state line. Jay Zettling didn't come to Amelia High for book-learning. Everyone knew Jay came to excel in football, get a scholarship to LSU, and be drafted by the National Football League.

"Ben Hoaxley tried to pull the boys apart and couldn't, big football boys that they are, so he grabbed the shotgun he keeps under the register and fired a shot over the boys' heads, spattering the wall with buckshot, but that only stopped them for a second, so he called the deputies to break it up. Had to be pretty bad, Hoaxley doesn't call the law for just any little thing. He doesn't want law men nosing around his place.

"Ben Anzamore was on duty, his cruiser closest to the scene. He came in, jerked the boys apart. Bobby swung and Anzamore exploded like dynamite. Sheriff's called down Anzamore for excess violence more than once. The story varies from there, but the end result is the same. Anzamore went through the plate glass window and landed on his ass on the sidewalk." She shrugged, her silence insinuating that the deputy was long overdue his comeuppance. "Whether Bobby threw him or Anzamore lost his balance and stumbled backward, nobody knows, glass everywhere and Anzamore bleeding like a stuck pig. By the time the backup deputy arrived the other boys had scattered, except Bobby who was standing there staring at Anzamore. The backup deputy sprayed Bobby with mace, subduing him long enough to handcuff him and take him into custody."

"I can't believe this." My son! Raised right in a good home, a good student, a stellar athlete, a boy who attended church every Sunday, under duress, but nevertheless, getting into this horrific trouble. It couldn't be! It couldn't be!

Precious continued, "This is where it gets dicey. Listen."

She started the tape. The machine made a whirring sound then I heard the deputy's voice. "State your name, please."

A blank space—no answer.

"Your address?—"

No answer.

"Let's have your driver's license, then. There's more than one way to skin a cat."

Shuffling noises—

"I know who you are."

"Do you know who my mother is?" Bobby asked.

"Yeah, I know who your mother is—the councilwoman."

"That's right and she runs this parish and she'll have you fired for sure—" Belligerent, cocky, not in the least repentant.

"And I also know that you're a minor and we're calling your mother right now to come and get you."

"I got my own truck. I can drive my own self home."

"The only way you're leaving this room is in the custody of your mother. Consider yourself lucky. You could be facing an aggravated battery charge for attacking a deputy—still might."

Silence again.—a big gap in the tape—scraping, shuffling sounds—

"What happened here?" I asked.

Precious said, "The deputy left to go phone you to come get Bobby. You were at the banquet. We were all there, so he talked to your daughter."

"What time was that?"

"Around midnight—"

Midnight and I was swooning in Will Fleming's arms while my son was wrecking a pool room and half-killing a deputy. While my panicked daughter tried to reach me. While their world turned upside down and their mother tripped the light fantastic.

Next on the tape, the deputy's deep, gravelly voice, "We're trying to find your mother. We've left word at your house and we've left word at the hotel. Wait here for now. If she doesn't come before 7 a.m., we'll transfer you to the juvenile detention hall."

Precious continued, "Davidson removed the handcuffs, locked the door and left. We're so understaffed everybody is doing double duty, and this was just a routine incident, a high school kid, no big deal, no need to keep the boy restrained. Seems Bobby paced for a while then lined the six plastic chairs in a row, making a makeshift bed. By this time it was 5 a.m. and you hadn't come. If you didn't appear pretty soon, he'd be transferred to the juvenile facility."

Precious restarted the tape. "Listen." The next recorded words were: "What the hell— Where you gone to, boy? – Goddamit, get down from there!"

"Bobby stacked the plastic chairs, put the metal waste basket on top, poked a hole through the ceiling tiles and climbed into the rafters. The deputy grabbed his legs and pulled him down."

I cringed.

"Anybody else, the deputy would've read him his rights, booked him and charged with resisting arrest, felony battery and criminal negligence for destroying public property and probably set a $50,000 bond."

The consequences were dire. My hands turned cold.

"But since it was you, Sam Blanchard talked to the sheriff—"

"I never did reach Sam."

"Barbara found him. She knows where to look."

Too agonized to face another ugly truth, I let the remark slide. "The sheriff knows?"

"Oh, yeah, he gave the okay."

Indebted to the sheriff! Sooner or later everyone was beholden to the big man.

Precious said softly, kindly. "Hannah, you have an angry boy on your hands. He needs help."

Yes, he did. I did. We all did. Should we go as a family to a psychiatrist? Should we muddle through on our own? Should we ignore everything and let the situation take its own course, pass by somehow? What life-long scars would these family traumas leave? Would Bobby and Suzy be forever warped because I was a terrible mother? I squeezed my head between my hands. What to do? What to do?

***

I had no other choice but to ground Bobby. He wasn't a little boy I could spank anymore. He was taller, bigger and stronger than I was. The last confrontation we had about letting his friends pile into his truck turned into a mother-son argument. I became so frustrated I slapped his forearm to get his attention. He bunched his biceps, and the iron bulk turned the side of my hand black and blue for a week.

School closed for Christmas-New Year holiday break and wouldn't resume for another eight days. That made the punishment much more severe because Bobby couldn't leave the house. He stayed in his room, the curtains drawn, the room dark, his bed rumpled, clothes strewn. He didn't let anybody enter. Sometimes he went in the back yard and spent hours dunking a basketball through the hoop.

I'd have to face the council. Depending on who was dishing the gossip, varied accounts concerning Bobby's escapade floated around town, everything from he almost killed Deputy Anzamore (with each telling, the injuries increased) to Bobby might get anything from probation to life.

Deputy Anzamore actually had nothing more than a slight cut on his right arm, the one he used to draw his gun, and a gash over his left eye. To my misfortune, the deputy was Bubba Egger's cousin, the man I'd defeated for the District 2 seat. No way would Bubba let the incident slide and disappear. He and Anzamore picked at the indiscretion as if it were an itchy scab. While the deputy's pride was injured more than his body, our family doctor found that Bobby had a broken nose and enough bruises and contusions that it would be three weeks before his face went back to normal. Either Anzamore or the fullback, Zettling, was responsible for the mauling, individually or collectively.

Bobby's friends, the same guys who had deserted him at the bar, were constantly phoning the hero of the day. I seriously considered taking away phone privileges, but feared the punishment would push Bobby over the edge and he'd run away from home. Then my juvenile delinquent would become a runaway teenager, creating even bigger problems.

Bobby ignored me, pretended I didn't exist. When I insisted he sit down and eat at the table, he said not a word. When asked to clean his pigsty bedroom, a blank look came in his eyes as if he were staring at me from a hundred miles away.

He talked to Suzy. She'd become his conduit to the world. She brought him messages from his friends, sneaked Zonic strawberry malts into his bedroom and sat cross-legged on his bed and commiserated. When did I become the villain? Was the punishment too severe for the crime? I didn't think so at all!

Sunday after the Saturday night brawl, Gramma knew what had happened. The well-meaning church ladies didn't want her to be uninformed. After 11 o'clock Mass they surrounded her, offering condolences, help, anything they could do. They advised her not to worry unduly, such a thing had happened to Terrence Adolph, and look at him now! Mayor of Harmony!

"I have to hear about my grandson in church!" My mother railed. "How do you think that makes me feel?" I felt like a pariah.

***

New Year's Day Suzy said, "Mom we're taking down that horrible tree today." The skeleton had shed half its needles and most of the ornaments.

"Aren't we keeping it up until Epiphany?" We normally took down the tree after the Three Kings arrived bearing gold, frankincense and myrrh.

"Pitch that sorry-ass tree," Bobby said, his first words in nearly a week.

I didn't care what he said. He could curse, yell, whatever, I was so happy to hear him say something, anything, I almost grabbed him and kissed him, but remembered in time that 16-year- old boys have a physical aversion to being kissed by their mothers, particularly a resentful teenager who liked to pretend he didn't have a mother.

"You're right," I said. "Pitch that sorry-ass tree."

Louisiana growing Christmas trees was as incongruous to me as the mother of two rebellious, hormone-driven teenagers sitting on the Pohainake Parish Council.

CHAPTER 35

The new council was no longer new. We had made progress, not at the speed we had promised the voters in that rosy campaign blitz where everything seemed possible, but at a slow, arduous pace, each step gained with arguments and battles, court orders and restraints.

Monday, the first meeting of our second year and final term, electing officers led the agenda. Speculation ran high. The air was charged. The council members were as skittish as race horses at the starting gate. Henry Johnson wanted the presidency again. He planned to run for state senator as soon as this council stint ended, and a two-year presidency would look good on his resume. Red Harper wanted his turn in the spotlight. Captain Fleming, amused and detached, observed the shenanigans and maneuvers. Peewee's sole interest was to eliminate Mrs. Brown, One year later, she still didn't have approval for her Camelot Subdivision. Every meeting she dragged to the council more architects, lawyers, engineers, environmentalists and soil conservationists who wasted our precious time with reports, charts, projections and photographs. Mrs. Brown drove Peewee crazy and made us all nuts. Underneath her polite demeanor was a bullheaded bitch who wouldn't take no for an answer.

After the Bahamas trip, after Bobby's escapade, my initial dedication and commitment to the public job, considering every challenge my own personal mountain to climb, the council slipped to second place. I had worked myself to a frazzle, day and night, neglected my family and abandoned them to their own devices. The thought brought a mental anguish I couldn't shake. Maybe after the January 10th juvenile court date, this feeling would dissipate and I'd return to normal. Once I knew whether Bobby had to serve detention time, do community service, pay a fine or receive a suspended sentence, maybe I could again care about Pohainake Parish's condition and welfare. As the situation stood now, I didn't give a rat's ass if Mrs. Brown's Camelot had eight-foot lanes or boulevards 100 feet wide, if the new prison had 135 cells or 550, if the garbage got buried or strewn. Burn-out with good reason. I felt betrayed by everyone. What had my diligent efforts brought me? More heartache than I'd ever experienced.

***

Henry Johnson banged the gavel. The tittering among the observers, visitors and regulars packing the pews dwindled, then stopped altogether. Boy Scout Troop #32, earning merit badges, led the Pledge of Allegiance.

First matter was the election of new officers.

"Do I hear nominations for president?" Henry Johnson asked.

An uncomfortable silence followed broken only by rustling paper and an occasional cough from the audience. Henry turned his head and gave Peewee a long, hard stare.

"Yeah," Peewee said. "I have a nomination."

"State your nomination."

Peewee said, "I nominate you."

Henry appeared nonchalant, though he had spent many hours and great energy insuring his name appeared on the slate. "Henry Johnson has been nominated for a second term as president. Any other nominations?—"

Red looked at me, at Will.

Henry Johnson didn't wait a blink. "If there are no further nominations—"

Red's already florid face turned beet purple. His chance was sliding by. He raised a big, beefy arm. "I have a nomination."

A surprised Henry Johnson kept his cool. "Mr. Harper has a nomination."

Red said loud enough that the people standing in the hallway heard. "I nominate myself."

Trench Coat, ACLU guard dog, hollered from his pew: "Can't do that! Not legal to nominate yourself!"

Red shouted angrily, "Who said so?"

"Robert Rules—"

"To hell with Robert's Rules—I am *so* nominating myself."

Henry Johnson settled the argument. "Okay, go ahead. Nominate yourself."

Our choices were bad or worse. We either voted for Red, an honest hothead who would drag us to where we were before, hiring family and cronies, charging at crossroad groceries, dumping garbage everywhere, or we voted for Henry, the inflated ego using the council as a stepping stone to a bigger station, his eye so far into the future that he was no help whatsoever in the present. In the end, politics amounted to just that, selecting the lesser of two evils.

How much work we had done! How hard we had toiled! Every advantage gained at great cost, personal, financial and emotional. We'd rescued the parish from bankruptcy. Granted, we had help. The AG's rep, Ken White, had overseen our every move and we'd accomplished the impossible. The landfill was halfway finished, jail construction started, bonds sold and roads being repaired. Could we let all this backslide by electing the wrong leader?

I swallowed my pride, buried past injuries, scribbled a note and passed it to Will. "Let me nominate you."

He shook his head negative and raised a hand. "I have a nomination."

Johnson acknowledged the District 1 councilman. "Mr. Fleming."

"I nominate Hannah Kelly for president."

What? Was Will serious or was this a perverse joke, warped humor? These guys wouldn't elect me president. They'd never let a woman run the show.

As much as I hated for the parish to retrogress, what I needed now was total dedication to my family. I would not sacrifice them at the altar of public service. Not anymore, not ever again, Bobby's escapade had been a wake-up call.

Will Fleming better give it a rest, leave me alone and quit aggravating me. Until I met him my life had been difficult, but uncomplicated. By touching my heart and stirring emotions long dormant, he had made me feel alive again, negating the comfort that existed in going through each day without the thrill of sensitivity or the misery of boredom. Running a life in neutral was safe, and I needed safe.

Henry Johnson had figured Red his competition, and that the two would settle it between them. My nomination snagged his scheme. "You're nominating Hannah Kelly?"

"That's what I said."

At the moment I opened my mouth to decline the nomination the preacher in the jail over our heads began sermonizing. His, loud, stentorian voice quoted a Psalm: *"Put no confidence in extortion, set no vain hopes on robbery; if riches increase, set not your heart on them."* He pounded his floor, our ceiling. Plaster flakes drifted— "Robbers! Thieves! Stealing the people blind! You'll burn in hell!"

Those familiar with the upstairs jail situation shrugged and laughed. The new visitors looked alarmed, searching the ceiling for the unseen voice. The deputy left to gag the preaching inmate and bumped into my family entering the council chambers.

Suzy and Gramma followed Bobby, each holding a square sign, bold black letters printed on poster paper: *Elect Hannah Kelly, Council President.* My surprise was monumental. My mouth dropped open like a fly trap. The spectator seats were full. There was no sitting room. My family wormed their way to the back and stood against the wall, holding high the signs.

My initial amazement was replaced by a profound pride. We were family. We stuck together and weathered the trials. They were my pearls, each precious bead strung in a necklace of love that encircled my life. My children and my mother never looked as beautiful to me as they did at that moment, standing against the wall, holding their signs high.

The audience sensed it, too. They looked at Bobby, Suzy and Gramma, the young and the old, the reckless and the staid and saw family. In the South there was nothing more important than family, present family, past family, root family. Good families clung to each other through trials and tribulations, happy times and mournful days. The solidarity and support those signs represented moved the audience.

As if on cue, a dozen spectators seated in the pews raised their arms. I gaped as I saw Precious and the DA's secretaries risking political retaliation, standing solid, holding signs. Murt from the diner! Who'd told her? Oh, my—the ACLU watchdog! What would he do? Wendi and Betty, sitting at the council table, sucked their cheeks, holding back big smiles.

Henry Johnson was beside himself. He ordered the deputy returning from upstairs.

"Tell them to put those signs down."

"What law they breaking?"

The audience tittered.

Henry Johnson was flustered. "I'm sure there's a law. Make them put those signs down."

I turned to Will. "You have anything to do with this?"

"Who, me?—I'm innocent." He put his big hand over mine. My fingers were trembling. "Why should I want the best council person for president?"

Henry Johnson had no recourse but to call for a vote. "Is it the council's pleasure that we vote by secret ballot?"

"Hell, no," replied Red. "Just call the roll, Wendi."

Wendi looked to Henry for confirmation. He nodded. She eyed the pews as if to make certain that the people, too, were in agreement. She checked the papers before her, poised her pencil dramatically mid-air, and started the roll call: "District 1, Will Fleming."

"Fleming for Hannah Kelly—"

"District 2, Hannah Kelly—"

I glanced at my children. What would this do to them? Would this drive them so far from me I could never reach them again? But they were here. They supported me. Bobby nodded his head emphatically. Suzy jiggled her sign and mouthed the words, "Go for it, Mom!"

Bolstered by my family's backing, I voted. "Kelly votes for Kelly."

"District 3, Henry Johnson," Wendi called in her sing-song Southern drawl.

"Henry Johnson votes for Henry Johnson."

"District 4, Peewee Reese."

"Vote for Hannah Kelly."

Wendi's pencil snapped in half.

Henry Johnson jumped to his feet. "Whadaya mean you vote for Hannah! You nominated me!"

In Peewee's school bus no student dared leave his seat. If Peewee looked in the mirror and saw a kid's bottom leave a cushion, he'd turn and give a frizzling stare that instantly sat the kid back down. Peewee gave Henry his best 'sit back down' look. "You asked me to nominate you and I did, but that's no sign I was gonna vote for you."

Wendi proceeded quickly. "District 5, Red Harper."

Red Harper sighed, a big, rumbling sound, humped forward, balled his hands into fists and hit the table. I had three of the five votes. He might as well join the winning side. "Hannah Kelly."

Wendi said tentatively, stunned by the results: "Four for Hannah Kelly? One for Henry Johnson?—"

Johnson swallowed the crabapple lodged in his throat and banged the gavel. "Hannah Kelly is now the new council president."

My unexpected supporters cheered. They waved their signs. Gramma gave me a V for Victory sign. Bobby's grin split his face, as if he'd personally conducted the winning campaign. Will Fleming, next to me, leaned over and gave me a bear hug.

Henry Johnson bolted from the room.

News traveled fast in Pohainake Parish. By morning everybody knew I was the new president and that late last night Henry Johnson knocked on Peewee's door waving a pistol. Precious called the sheriff and two deputies came and carted Henry away. The three stopped at Hoaxley's and got stinking drunk.

CHAPTER 36

After my election as council president, Will and I reached a friendly truce. I became more involved than ever with parish problems, not much time left for anything else.

Bobby completed six weeks community service picking up trash around Hoaxley's Tavern and several other locations. His dad, with little grace and less forgiveness, footed the damages.

"This has got to stop," he said tight-lipped.

"I completely agree. What do you suggest?'

As usual, he had more complaints than solutions.

"You want him to go live with you?" *I'd die if he said 'yes'.* "I can have him packed in ten minutes."

I knew Joe as well as I knew the palm of my hand, every line, curve and wrinkle. A man who didn't buy a car until he did a year's research, who lost it if his recliner was moved a foot and who didn't let Dixie come to his new place because the dog upset the Princess. He needed time and space to confer and discuss, evaluate and decide. I counted on that. The only snap decision Joe ever made was to leave me and maybe it wasn't as precipitous as I thought. He might have been planning it for months, maybe years.

"Yes, I want him to come live with me. I think it would really be for the best."

My heart dropped to my stomach. His love for Bobby (I had no doubt he loved his children) might prove stronger than his vacillations.

"But—"

Thank God! Here came *but*!

"But—"

Heaven's sake, he was sputtering like a kid, "But what—?"

Of all the excuses that crossed my mind, the one he uttered, self-conscious, half-abashed floored me.

"Elizabeth is pregnant. She's not feeling well, vomiting every morning. If we could delay this a month or two, how long does that last?"

"Depends," *Reprieve! Reprieve! Reprieve!* "Let's discuss this later when she's feeling better. A teenage boy is quite a handful."

Whew! That was close!

Because Elizabeth's first pregnancy (heard through the Harmony grapevine she demanded extreme care and attention) distracted Joe and confused our children, Will spent more time with Bobby going to baseball games and occasionally inviting him and the entire team, the Harmony Tigers, for an outing aboard the *Serenity.* I worried constantly that Joe would revert to his old form and throw a usual fit, but he seemed to be handling Will's presence in Bobby's and Suzy's life with equanimity. He was either mellowing or in shock.

***

This particular afternoon, as he usually did, Will Fleming stopped by the house and helped Gramma in the garden.

"You haven't changed your mind about running again?" I asked. He stood at the kitchen sink, drinking water.

"No." The finality in his voice made my heart skip a beat. "It's hot."

"What will you do?"

"Pull up anchor and sail."

I should've known. Will was free as the wind. No family, no responsibilities, skimpily clad girls aboard his yacht, the Hugh Hefner of Pohainake Parish. He had sailed south, no particular goal, moored his boat and temporarily joined our party.

"I suppose you've stayed docked here longer than anywhere else, and now we bore you."

"Not at all," Will's voice had a wistful tone. "What drew me South was that every Southerner I ever met anywhere in the world had an anchor, a dirt patch they called home, that was unequivocally theirs, a place to come back to, always. It didn't matter whether they lived in little town where nothing ever changed or in big cities, New Orleans or Atlanta. They missed the food. They missed the music. They missed their family. That struck me right here." He made a fist and tapped his heart. "Magnificent place, home. I had to come see for myself, pinpoint the attraction, find this core, this center they carried with them wherever they were."

"And did you?"

"Yes. There's a terrific sense of community here, of family," he snorted, a small depreciatory sound, "and of exclusion. If your mama and your papa and your great-greats haven't been planted in this soil, it's not your home. You're a visitor."

Will was right. When I married into the Kelly family and joined a tree that could be traced to the Civil War, to a family who fought to keep their way of life and lost, my acceptance became total. Divorced from Joe, that cloak didn't feel as warm.

"Well, you could find a home here, truly, Will. Leave that boat, buy a house and live the way other normal folks do. Why in the world did you run in the first place?"

"I never explained that satisfactorily, did I? It was a bet. The old guys were aboard the *Serenity* playing poker, lamenting the parish bankruptcy, the sorry politicians. We'd been drinking more than enough. One thing led to another Songe I think it was who said, "Let's put Will on that council." Uncle Percy, who'd enticed me to bring my boat from Lake Michigan down to Lake Pontchartrain, said, 'I bet we could do just that, anybody ready to bet?' Gendre said, 'Will Fleming couldn't be elected dog-catcher,' threw down the gauntlet, so to speak. I moved the boat to Cloy's Marina to be in the right parish. Uncle Percy showed me the ropes, how to win over the people."

"It's not easy."

"I'll say. You've got to get past the weather and the family and listen to their stories. Southerners are the best story tellers in the world. A person can't blurt his business. Sometimes I'd visit with somebody for an hour and never get the opportunity to solicit their vote."

"They knew."

"Sure they knew, but not because they heard it from me, then—voila!" Will snapped his fingers. "Much to my surprise, to everybody's surprise, really, there I was, councilman for District 1, not knowing a damned thing, sitting in the chair next to District 2, who knew a lot more than I did."

I laughed. "Big bluff, at that point I didn't know a blessed thing and right away I knew my fellow councilmen didn't know anything either. Does that make sense?"

"Perfect sense, as much as anything else—oh, well—it's been a very enlightening two years. I wouldn't trade it for any other experience I've had."

Will Fleming was leaving, going around the world. Nobody in Pohainake had ever gone around the world, except war veterans. Nobody in Pohainake ever wanted to leave God's country and go anywhere else. Once locals drove over the Shackman Pass Bridge and crossed the swamp, they considered themselves in foreign territory. For all he was charming and debonair, Will was a displaced person, a rich but homeless one. He had no tethers or connections, no string of pearls around his life, a loner and adventurer.

He had a faraway look in his eyes. "After my wife and little girl were killed by that drunk driver and I nearly lost my mind. I rejoined the navy, leaving behind the memories. After my hitch, I joined the merchant marines for a few more years. Then I captained a yacht for a millionaire Greek. The boat was such a tub, I suggested some changes, and one thing led to another and before I knew it, these fellows who had more money than sense were paying me big bucks to design their boats."

I thought about the parade, driving down Harmony's Main Street in Will's Corvette, Will and I barely speaking, Suzy in back, sponsored by a man whose girlfriend had seduced my son.

"International Yacht—"

"Don't poke your chin at me," Will said. "It's all water under the dam. I'm outta here. You'll surely run again. You're very good at it."

"I'm not sure what I'll do" My whole life was confused. "The last two years have been a challenge, that's for sure, but it feels as if I no longer have my own life. Do I want to do that for another two years? I don't know. But there's so much left to accomplish!"

"Didn't I tell you a while back? Time comes and you feel you must complete the job. Only governing is never done. One snake is trampled to death and another coils, ready to strike."

He was so right. One followed each happening, attentively, frightened, not knowing the end results, the situation changing minute by minute putting one foot first and then the other tentatively, cautiously, following the unknown path the way a blind person does. A simple event took an unexpected, meaningless, unreasonable twist without any valid reason, provocation or logic and escalated to traumatic. When the council reached the end of a particularly knotty situation and the result turned out okay, sometimes we felt as if we'd died and been born again.

"I really hope you change your mind."

CHAPTER 37

As Will Fleming predicted, I did file for re-election. Leaving everything half-done wasn't an option. Who knew what the next councilperson would do? Having toiled diligently to bring the parish this far, I felt duty-bound to stay and finish the work.

The second time wasn't as easy. Now I had a track record opponents could attack in the same ruthless manner I'd attacked my predecessor's performance. The reforms I voted for hadn't been popular. The year as treasurer made me formidable enemies. The sheriff, marshal, district attorney, the judges (for the first time in history they'd faced a challenge) recognized the council's power, our grip on their funding. Deep down, these government officials were seething to get even. The sheriff hadn't forgotten the escaped prisoner. The marshal no longer went hunting and fishing at tax payer's expense. A belligerent clerk of court relinquished his excess cash. The registrar of voters spent months purging the naked and the dead from the voters' roll, not the way it'd been done before. Public officials entrenched in the old ways resisted and resented change.

Henry Johnson, already campaigning hard for senate, cut me down every possible opportunity. The four votes that made me council president destroyed his ego and he intended to even the score. He gave me credit for every bad turn the council ever took.

Bubba Egger entered the race. He wanted his old job back. Hannah Kelly was incompetent and made people justifiably mad.

Her son had been arrested for drugs and alcohol, for wrecking Hoaxley's, destroying public property and attacking a deputy. And where did the escaped convict go? Strait to Hannah Kelly's shed. Didn't that tell you something? She voted for the garbage fee, for the 911 charge tacked onto the phone bill. Due to her, the people had less money in their pockets. And had anybody checked that country club jail she spearheaded?

Lies! Lies! Lies! No one person did anything. The council fought, struggled, compromised and hammered the best possible solution at the time. The result wasn't set in concrete. Another meeting, another agenda and everything could abruptly change. But when Bubba Egger twisted the words, his rhetoric made sense. He hadn't added any taxes. He hadn't lightened the people's pockets. He hadn't done anything except line his own.

Deputy Anzamore defied non-involvement laws and openly supported his cousin, Bubba Egger. Hear Anzamore tell it, he'd been torn from limb to limb by my son, a violent, uncontrollable teenager. Was someone who couldn't discipline a teenage boy fit to run a parish?

The mother of the three mentally challenged children (who lived across the rickety bridge the ambulance refused to cross) went door to door for Bubba, telling her pathetic story, even though the council managed to get her bridge fixed. The protesting howl coming from people who had their own dangerous bridges to cross almost brought the council walls tumbling down.

No good deed went unpunished. Fixing Maryjane Perkins's bridge took an unbelievable toll.

Mrs. Brown held parish-wide rallies on her proposed Camelot. If this council didn't approve her narrow, winding, cinder roads, by God she'd see to it that we were individually and collectively defeated and new elected officials take our place, men and women who were receptive to new ideas, not mired in the past, council persons who didn't have to be *paid* for their vote.

The only missing voice was Robert Standish, the garbage dump owner. He'd been indicted and quietly awaited his day in court.

The hot, grueling summer sped by, politicking and hard work filling the shimmering days. Knowing too well how difficult accomplishing anything was, the glow disappeared from my campaign rhetoric. I promised nothing spectacular, simply reminded the voters that they now had a sanitary landfill, a humane prison facility would soon be a reality, roads were paved, the parish budget balanced. Compared to Bubba Egger's histrionics my fact-filled speeches were dull. Truth, like bad medicine, was hard to swallow. The voters preferred the rainbow version better.

Not that I minded a fight. I'd morphed from a meek housewife into a public figure. And the work was fascinating, absorbing, an eddy pulling me down into its vortex. There was much left to do.

Bobby, contrite that his rash actions affected his mother's chance for re-election and determined to help, tapped his buddies and they stood on street corners, distributing cards and pamphlets.

"Relax, Sweetie. Bubba's blowing in the wind. That idiot has as much chance of regaining the District 2 seat as a snowball in hell."

Hadn't I defeated him once already? I could do it again! I wasn't shy and floundering any more. I had experience, knowledge. I wasn't terrified the way I was at the initial political forum when I first confronted Bubba face to face. The encounter had terrified me the way a hurricane ready to strike land did. The urge to flee had engulfed me. The only speeches I'd ever given were to PTA mothers concerning bake sales, manning concession stands, transporting students to athletic events and field trips. What could I say? How could I convince anyone to vote for me, when I knew nothing about government? This time around the circumstances were different. I had experience. I knew.

CHAPTER 38

Three lousy votes! Three! Bubba Egger had his old job back! The public smile on my stricken face didn't mask my disappointment as I shook his hand and congratulated the triumphant, grinning bastard. Like a turtle crawling into its shell, I retreated home, closed the door and shut out the world. These people didn't appreciate me. They had no respect. They didn't understand or care about all the sacrifices Hannah Kelly had made on their behalf—Judases who said straight-faced they voted for me and didn't.

Barbara suggested housekeeping as therapy. My neglected house definitely needed a good cleaning. Dust gathered in un-swept corners, campaign junk stacked everywhere and floors streaked and scuff-marked from recent non-stop traffic.

"Scrub the floors," Barbara said. "It'll make you feel better."

A zombie with a dust rag could do a better job.

Days following my crushing defeat were like falling from a star, hurtling through space and touching reality. Reality wasn't pretty. Reality was rejection, a slap in the face that took the breath away. Defeat was always a factor when campaigning, that's what gave the trip its edge, the fillip, like a bullfight where the bull might at any moment, turn and gore the matador. Well, I'd been gored, all right.

The phone rang and rang. Suzy, Bobby or Gramma answered, made excuses, covered for me.

"Thank you, Aunt Barbara, I'll tell Mom." Bobby's voice no longer slipped up and down the scale when he talked. The tones were deep and sonorous, a man's voice.

"Hi, Mr. Barth, no, she can't come to the phone right now, but thanks for calling." Suzy's tone was hushed as if she were acknowledging condolences at a wake. The energy that filled the house a few days ago, the coming and goings, phones constantly ringing, knocks on the door, cars blocking the driveway, the high that came with that last campaign thrust had dissipated, leaving in its wake a quiet stillness nobody dared break.

In the spirit of Southern tradition where food cured all ills, friends delivered casseroles and desserts, cold salads and California wines. They left their offerings with Gramma and assured my anxious mother I'd be okay. In a few days, I'd get over it, be my old self again.

Who was my old self? I no longer knew...no longer knew.

Peewee Reese, who was re-elected, left a key-lime pie, Precious's specialty. "Hannah will be fine, Miz Belle. She's solid as a brick shithouse."

Sitting at the kitchen table sipping hot chicken soup, I heard him leave. Mom wasn't Jewish, but she believed in chicken soup.

"Was that a compliment?" she asked.

"I'm debating, but I think so."

Assessing voters was a crap shoot. Red Harper retained his seat. By doing nothing, he did the least damage and offended the least people. His wife Ellen brought condolences and homemade peach ice cream, milk from their own cows. Henry Johnson voluntarily didn't re-run for council, opting instead to throw his hat in the upcoming senate race. By choice, Will Fleming didn't run. That left Red, Peewee and three new council persons to finish the work we started. My replacement was Bubba Egger. The humiliation! The horror!

Later that afternoon Suzy poked her head into the bedroom. "Mom, are you dead or are you still breathing? Mr. Percival wants to talk to you." I shook my head. "You can't say no. He's here."

"What? Here?" Astonished, I washed my face, ran a comb through my hair, shed the housecoat and slipped into jeans. Mr. Percival who never went anywhere sat on my couch, my mother hovering, bringing him iced tea. He was jovial, florid face beaming, as if he'd entered into a party house instead of a morgue.

"Hi. It's nice of you to come." That's what a bereaved spouse, swallowing the pain said to the mourners at a wake.

"Hannah," he asked, "who holds the world record for home runs?"

What did baseball have to do with my misery? I blurted the only name that came to mind. "Babe Ruth, I guess."

"Right—and do you know he struck out 1,330 times? And you know what he said?"

"Not really."

"Each strike brings me closer to the next homer."

After this profound statement what could I say? "Mr. Percival, I don't even want to play anymore."

"Sure you do. Buckle up."

Easy for him to say—he didn't have to face those who sacrificed and donated to my campaign, volunteered time to man phones, went door to door handing tracts that highlighted my glorious accomplishments. Defeat had no good explanation, only a litany of excuses.

"Government needs good people. You may not see it, but you must run again. You're as bull-headed as I am. I liked that."

Mr. Percival belonged to the generation that made easy fortunes, carved empires and controlled destiny. They made money, lived well, shared wealth. They built libraries, universities, parks, repaired bridges, bought bonds and nudged generals. No one could take their place. The proliferation of laws, rules and regulations bound the entrepreneurial spirit, a strait jacket that curtailed risk and creativity and stymied generosity.

Mr. Percival had embraced an ordinary woman, a divorcee, and helped transform her into an influential person. The scared girl who tiptoed into his office for an interview was no more. I was powerful and strong, defeated and desolate, and lonely, desperately lonely.

Not long after Mr. Percival's exit the phone rang again. Suzy answered. "Mom, Captain Will."

"No."

"Aw, c'mon, Mom—"

"No.

Gramma added her two cents' worth. "What if the person on the phone wants to tell you Bobby died in a car wreck?"

The terrifying thought bolted me upright. "Mother!—"

"See the difference? That's tragedy. Losing an election is bullshit. Put it in perspective, honey. Lose the "we" and become an "I" again."

When had Hannah Kelly lost her identity and become a generic, political 'we'? When she realized that getting elected was a team effort? When every move became a group endeavor and to say 'I' would be ego-centric and untrue? How long had it been since I had been an 'I'?

"Leave me alone!" Go away. Let me lick my wounds in peace.

CHAPTER 39

The Saturday after the November disaster, the Harmony Women's Auxiliary held a ball at the Holiday Inn to present the Man and Woman of the Year. Votes for the recipients had been cast by secret ballots. This stellar occasion was also their main fund raiser. Tickets were $100 a couple.

Previously, on a professor's salary, the price was too steep. Sam and Barbara often invited us as their guests, but Joe was too proud to ride anybody's coattails to a social outing he cared nothing about. As far as he was concerned, renting a tux to attend a ball was never high priority. Friends who went gave me second-hand accounts. They reported what the women wore, who danced with whom, who catered, how nice the decorations were. Through their tales, I lived a vicarious social life.

"Let's go to this ball Saturday?" Will asked, casual, no pressure, holding back, the way he did everything.

"Thanks, Will, but I don't think so." The last time I danced with Will, I lost track of time and place, of my responsibilities and Bobby got arrested.

"You should be there, you know. You're still council president."

"I'm a lame duck," I replied, for the first time realizing the stigma of the term, present, but ineffective, active without a voice, alive with as much authority as a corpse.

Suzy insisted I go. "Oh, yes, Mom! You've got to go. Will said he'd reserve a table and Gramma could come and me and Bobby and his girlfriend—"

"Girlfriend— What girlfriend?"

"He gave Marie Anne his senior ring, didn't you know? They're going steady, Mom! Isn't that terrific? We can go shopping and buy new dresses. Can I have a new dress, Mom? And you absolutely *must* get something positively gorgeous!

"I have the black one."

"Oh, no!—heaven's sake! You can't wear the same dress twice. All the same people will be there and they'll have seen it before! Call Will! Call him right this minute and tell him we're all going!"

My kids had become unduly attached to Will. He often stopped by the house and he and Bobby dunked a few baskets. He'd pile Suzy and her friends into his Corvette and take them for a spin down Main Street. They'd wave to the lesser minions and stop at Zonic for an ice-cream blast. He'd bought Gramma a big floppy straw hat she wore when working the flower beds. Gramma had the side yard looking like a park. Sometimes Will Fleming, on hands and knees, helped her weed. He yanked crabgrass and looked happy.

"Will may leave one day," I said, paving the road for their ultimate disappointment.

"Oh, no, no!—He loves you, Mom!" Suzy said.

"Excuse me. Where did you get that idea?"

"Gramma says so. She says you're so stuck in the past, so dense, you can't see it."

"Dense? She said *dense*?"

Gramma came into the kitchen, pulling off the big straw hat and setting down fresh, yellow roses from the garden. "Yes— dense. Wake up, Hannah." She extended a long-stemmed flower, pale petals and delicate scent. "Smell the roses. Don't let love pass you by."

"Mother, don't be putting notions in my children's heads."

"Hell, buy a new dress and go dancing with the man."

***

Life took strange twists. The whole family attended the HWA ball. The red taffeta dress cost a small fortune, had a tight bosom and a big glittery shoulder bow, nothing sedate or matronly, a dress in my opinion a high-class call girl would wear.

Suzy sparkled, youthful and gorgeous, her blue dress exactly matching her blue eyes. Bobby looked manly in his new suit we bought for graduation, Marie Anne at his side. They clung to each other through the night as if they'd drown if they let go. Gramma had a silver sheath, beaded jacket, very elegant. She, Suzy and I spent the day at a Touch of Paris, having manicures and pedicures, massages and facials, hair washed and coiffed, a fun day, a day without care or duties, a spoil me day like other women had, our first time ever pampering ourselves and we thoroughly enjoyed it. We left the spa much better friends than we were when we arrived.

Will Fleming rang the doorbell and Suzy let him in. A tremendous shyness came over me, as if he were a beau come to call on a first date. His presence filled the room, brought order to our chaos. My mother and my daughter said he loved me, but he'd never, never said that himself. I'd gotten the right feeling with him on more than one occasion, the feeling that in his arms I could find a home, but before long the sensation had been eclipsed by my children's problems, by the young women he harbored. And now, comfortable and at ease in my living room, he waited while Suzy waltzed around him, while he gave Bobby last minute instructions.

"You're letting him take your car?" I asked, enveloped in red splendor.

"We'll drive your Cadillac. Is that okay?" a wicked gleam in his eye, "You look terrific."

Never one to graciously accept a compliment, I asked, "What if he wrecks your Corvette?"

"It's insured."

And Bobby was on his way to get Marie Anne, happier than I'd ever seen him. What a splash he would make driving a Corvette! His peers would envy him. He'd be the hit of the party.

***

Believe me, I've never been the Belle of the Ball. In high school I was always the one twisting my fingers, crossing and uncrossing my legs, fiddling nervously with my hair and waiting. The handsome athletes danced with the cheerleaders and the prom queens. This wallflower was grateful when a nerd or a geek in their awkward, fumbling way led me to the dance floor.

A night and day difference existed between entering a room triumphant, fresh from winning a medal, a title, a council seat, riding a wave of success, soaring to stratified heights few attained, and entering a room defeated, a forced smile on my lips, chin held high by sheer mental force, eyes purposely glazed so that pain wouldn't show.

I couldn't have stepped into that huge ballroom without Will at my side, his reassuring hand guiding me. I took shelter in the energy he radiated, letting the aura created by his magnetic personality envelope me and sweep me forward.

The hall was decorated to the max, but I couldn't focus on scenery. My mind was a vacuum, a dark cave. I saw people moving, colorful puppets, music and laughter, confusing din. Only the warm touch of Will's hand on my arm felt real.

The worst was over! The first hurdle conquered! We'd entered the hall, made it through the crowd and found our table. The walk felt longer than a marathon. Will helped me to a chair and I sank into it gratefully.

Safely seated, feeling calmer, I checked the room. Bubba Egger and his wife shared a table with Mrs. Brown of Camelot, her architect, Deputy Ansamore and his wife. Across the room, Barbara and Sam Blanchard sat surrounded by their entourage, lawyers and clerks, doctors and bankers, country club people. Several tables away I spotted Joe and the Princess. She did suit him better than I did. He wore a tuxedo and was present, more than I was ever able to get him to do.

"There's Dad! I'm going over there!" Bobby reached for Marie Anne's hand and pulled her along with him, my admonitions left unsaid, maybe better that way.

"We're going to eat," Suzy said.

At the buffet table, a chef carved Virginia baked ham. His twin tackled roast beef. An assembly of plump shrimp, stuffed mushrooms, bacon wrapped chicken livers, cheese crackers arrived on large silver platters. Veggie trays, broccoli, cauliflower, cherry tomatoes, thin cucumber wheels, carrots, turnips cut to resemble red roses, splashed color across the table. Fruits turned into flowers, magnolias crafted from pears, hibiscus from red apple wedges, black-eyed daisies fashioned by yellow plums and raisin centers. Cheese: yellow, orange, white, squares, cubes, rectangles and crescents rose in golden mounds. Desserts occupied a different table, Mississippi Mud, rum cake, bourbon balls, pecan pie, and thin-layers of cream-filled Dobache. And the piece de resistance, an Italian cream cake shaped like Pohainake Parish, long and slender, bulging in the middle, red icing interstates crisscrossing blue state roads, a green Pohainake River flowing south.

"We won't go hungry here, tonight," Will Fleming plucked a cheese cube and plopped it in his mouth.

"May I fix you a plate?" That's what well brought-up Southern girls did, waited on their man.

He chuckled. "No need. I can manage this."

Maybe he didn't want me fawning over him. I had struggled so long to be equal, a different type equal, equal in intelligence, in business, in performance. When it came to man-woman, I wanted the old norm. Could I have it both ways? Maybe— Will didn't need a clinging vine to assert his masculinity.

Charlene tapped Will's shoulder. "I need this pleasure."

Will was too gentlemanly to send her packing. Turning to me, he said, "I'll return shortly."

Standing alone by the buffet table, feigning inordinate interest in the food, imagining every eye staring at the lame duck councilwoman, checking for cracks in my psyche, I chilled. Hands to feet I felt cold. I exchanged pleasantries with a white-haired man who filled his plate and made inconsequential cocktail conversation. It took me a second to recognize the ACLU watchdog, Edgar Evans, lawyer for the fired worker.

"Why, Mr. Evans! How handsome you look. You should shed your trench coat and wear your tux to the council meeting sometime."

"Whatever I wear, I'm keeping close tabs on that Bubba Egger. Shall we dance?" He led me to the dance floor. Mr. Evans's elbow pumped rhythm.

"Bubba Egger was the people's choice, if only by a few votes." Uttering the truth aloud, affirming the vote count, the statement cast off a weight, gave me unexpected relief.

"He'll reap the fruit of your labors. That's politics."

The thought brought little comfort. "Thank you."

We twirled past Will and Charlene. Will whirled and tapped Edgar's shoulder. "Let's swap, my friend."

I sighed, relieved.

"You should've seen your expression," Will Fleming said, putting his arm round my waist, "Steely endurance, y'know how you lift your chin when you've resolved to get through something."

"Oh, dear, did it show?" His hand on my hip, he held me close. I was happy.

At 10 p.m. the band took a break. The trumpet blew a blast that drew everyone's attention. Barbara Blanchard, HWA president, stood behind the mike. "Ladies and gentlemen, the time has come to announce our man and woman of the year!"

A hush came over the crowd. Will and I returned to our table. Others ringed the dance floor.

Speculation ran high all week. For the men's award, would it be Dr. Morrison, who worked so hard for the hospital accreditation? Jim Wilson, Kiwanis Club president who had an impressive list of civic work to his credit? Mr. Percival, the silent angel? He should definitely receive this honor. He'd quietly done so much for so many.

Barbara Blanchard's name headed the women's list. She single-handedly kept Pohainake's limited culture from dying. She arranged art shows, piano concerts, Little Theater performances. Mrs. Agee's name had been submitted. The old dowager swam in the Senior Olympics and brought home the gold. I'd heard my own name whispered, but the rumor lacked credibility. Nobody honored a loser.

"And our male award winner is," Barbara stopped for dramatic emphasis. "Mr. Charles Percival!"

Joy filled my heart. How well deserved! The crowd clapped furiously. The old gentleman walked to the stage and received his engraved Steuben bowl. He beckoned to Mom. She joined him. He handed her his award and—

"He kissed Gramma!" Suzy cried.

The crowd went wild, rose to their feet clapping and cheering. That act couldn't be topped.

When the commotion died, Barbara rapped the podium for attention. "We are honored to have a special guest today who will present the female award."

A rustle went through the crowd as necks craned to spot the special guest. Ken White, our very own court-appointed administrator, the CAAd, smiling resplendently, FBI-CIA-CPA masquerading in a tux, walked toward the stage.

I fought the expectant feeling that engulfed me the moment Ken stepped to the podium. No percentage existed in anticipating what wasn't going to happen. I'd had enough disappointments lately, no sense setting myself up for another pratfall.

Barbara and Ken exchanged pleasantries while Ken lowered the microphone. He braced his hands on the speaker's stand and looked over the crowd. "It gives me great pleasure to present this award to a hard-working woman," his eyes scanned the audience.

My heart beat in my throat. Under the table, Will reached and held my hand.

Ken's eyes stopped on me. "Hannah Kelly!"

Will was helping me to my feet. "Did you know?"

"I'm innocent."

"Did you know, Suzy?" The room swirled. I drowned in the swish of taffeta and my mother's joyful laugher.

Suzy smiled, blue eyes sparkling. Bobby walked across the dance floor, Marie Ann in tow, and let go his girlfriend long enough to give his mother a big hug.

Joe and his *prin*—Elizabeth— tagged behind Bobby.

"Congratulations," Elizabeth said, sounding genuinely glad.

"We're proud of you," Joe's unexpected compliment erased a million sins. Suzy was right, time to throw away the little black book and reconcile.

"Thank you." My red, sparkling slippers left the floor and I'm sure I levitated.

The standing crowd applauded.

I took a few steps away from my family, my security blanket, toward the podium. The walk to the stage seemed a mile, too long to travel alone. After these many, many turbulent months, I knew in my bones, a feeling that couldn't be denied. "Will, please?"

He rose, tall and handsome, caring and loving, always there for me, for the children. "You can do this yourself."

"I know I can," I extended my hand. Our fingertips touched. "But I don't want to."

EPILOGUE:

Bobby is a freshman at LSU. He comes home weekends, visits both his dad and me, and the truth be told, our relationship is much improved.

Suzy's school activities keep her busy. She passes through the house and yells, "Hi, Mom! I'll be back at ten!" and disappears.

Two weeks after the Harmony Auxiliary Ball, Mom married Mr. Percy. She moved into the big house. Will Fleming didn't sail away. Instead of yachts, he's into Louisiana off-shore oil rigs. I have no idea exactly what he does, but he's well respected and oil men the world over come to consult and seek advice. He plays poker Thursday evenings with the old men and Mom. He sleeps over at my place most nights, and Suzy has no objections. Will asked her permission! Joe said that since our divorce, I'd "blossomed." He and Elizabeth have a baby girl. He'll be 65-years old when little Betty starts college.

I'm no longer nursing a bruised ego and licking my wounds. The Pohainake Parish Council is part of my past, over but not forgotten. I took Mom's good advice and moved on.

My answering machine has several important and unanswered messages. Ken White called, the attorney general's secretary called and so did the lieutenant governor's. I'll return those later. Will is hollering for me to hurry. I'm searching all over the house. Where is the darn thing? I must find it! Can't go without it! "Suzy!—Suzy! Have you seen my helmet?" We're riding the captain's Honda motorcycle from Harmony to Fort Lauderdale, from Pohainake Parish to a new world. We're honeymooning in Mom's condo. Life is good.

The End

ABOUT THE AUTHOR

Katie Wainwright, a native of Cuba and a resident of Louisiana, owned a real estate agency for many years before retiring to write and travel. *Pohainake Parish*, her fourth novel set in Louisiana, is an account of Hannah Kelly's tenure on the council. It explores with satiric humor and deep insight the problems and politics of governing. Two previous novels, historical fiction, *Cuba on my Mind* and the sequel *Secuestro*, published by Livingston Press, highlighted life in Cuba before and during the Castro revolution. In her third novel, set in the picturesque town of St. Francisville, Wainwright returned to what she knew best—real estate. The sale of a haunted plantation involved many twists and turns. *Pohainake Parish*, fiction based on fact, is as absorbing and entertaining as the rest of her works.

Made in the USA
Lexington, KY
06 October 2015